TRUE KING

BOOK ONE

(PART ONE)

Q. Jones III

Lost Word Publishing

TRUE KING: Book One (Part One)

ISBN: 978-1-734-2202-1-6

Lost Word Publishing
P.O. Box 50004
Richmond, VA 23223

For upcoming books, events and more visit www.lostwordpublishing.com

Tele: (804) 220-0650
Any business inquiries address to: lostwordpublishing@gmail.com
Send Fanmail to: contactlostword@gmail.com

Like us on Facebook: www.facebook.com/lostwordllc
Keep up with our products on Instagram: www.instagram.com/lostwordpublishing
Or get cool and insightful info: www.instagram.com/lostword_woke
Subscribe to our blog: www.lostwordnation.com

"Do not believe in anything simply because you have heard it. Do not believe in anything simply because it is spoken and rumored by many. Do not believe in anything simply because it is found in your religious books. Do not believing in anything merely on the authority of your teachers and elders. Do not believe in traditions because they have been handed down for many generations. But after observation and analysis, when you find that anything agrees with reason and is conducive to the good and benefit of one and all, then accept it and live up to it."

-Buddha

Acknowledgements

There are so many people who have been involved in this project that I don't know where to start. First and foremost I have to thank M W. Sunday for making me believe that I could actually write a novel worth reading. I've come a long way since those cups of cold coffee in the city jail bro. Next up, would have to be my aunt Germaine for all of the research that she's sent me throughout the years. Those printouts allowed my mind to travel far beyond this cell. I can't thank you enough for that. Of course I have to thank all of the Gods who've helped me to grasp the science of everything in life: love, peace and happiness. More specifically I have to thank Lord Serious Hakim Allah for his immeasurable support and especially for being my first editor. You're a true brother. Kosmic Stellar Ether (Lord Sheshonq) thank you for teaching me the true meaning of Knowledge of Self. Love you big bro. Victory Cee Reality Allah thank you for first introducing me to the science of the 85%, 10% and 5%. You were the first to tell me "each one, teach one" and hopefully I've written one that can teach thousands. And to everyone else who has aided me in this journey: thank you. You are greatly appreciated. I haven't forgotten a single one of you.

TRUE KING

BOOK ONE

(PART ONE)

PROLOGUE

Time never was when man was not.

The cryptic line echoes over and over again in Dr. King's mind.

Time never was when man was not.

It just doesn't make any sense.

Time never was when man was not.

Dr. Jacqueline King examines the stone fragment in her hand. She's seen something like this before, from one of her father's excavations in Egypt—only she's nowhere near Egypt now. She's in the middle of the Iraqi desert, approximately a mile outside the ancient temple of Ur.

But why is a Sumerian fragment covered in Egyptian hieroglyphics?

A strong wind cuts across the land. Bits of sand fly through the air jeopardizing their hours of tedious work. Chaos ensues as her team scrambles to cover their areas. Holding a rag to her nose, Dr. King hurries to shield the spot where she found the fragment.

Geologists date the Earth at about 14,000,000 years old, she thinks, spreading out the tarp, *and man is only 4,000,000 years old.*

She looks at the fragment again. *It just doesn't make any sense. Time never was when man was not. Unless—*

The rapid report of machine-gun fire erupts in the distance. *U.S. troops letting off some steam,* she assumes, glancing to the soldiers guarding her site. She can see the amusement peaking from the corner of their eyes as they turn towards the sound. It's obvious they would rather be doing something more exciting than standing around "guarding" her dig and if it wasn't for her husband's insistence they could be.

She grins. *And after 30 years of marriage I'm still unable to resist that smile.*

More rounds sound off, further in the distance now. The soldiers smirk at the sound of gunfire.

The gust finally dies down and Dr. King uncovers her nose. "Okay!" She shouts. "It's over! Back to it!"

Her team rushes back to work and she smiles as she watches them. More and more she's been losing students to the technological fields. *A sign of the times,* she tells herself. *Kids today just don't really care much for the ancient mysteries or lost teachings of the ages.*

All video games and computers, she thinks, picturing her son sprawled out on his bed fixated on one of his game systems. She pushes the thought aside. There is no time to worry about him now. She must stay focused on the task at hand: finding an entrance to the subterranean kingdom of Shamballah.

She examines the fragment once more. *Could the two be related?*

"Doctor," a young female aide calls to her, "what's that you got over there? Found something good?"

Dr. King looks up at the bright young face and is reminded of her age. "I'm not sure yet." She shrugs. "That's what we have to find out."

As a field archaeologist, Dr. Jacqueline King has been all over the earth searching for an entrance to the fabled Hidden Kingdom. Every ancient nation has their version of the subterranean world. For Christians it is Hell; for the Jew it is Sheol; for the Akkadians it was Abzu. In Norse mythology, Odin is said to have

TRUE KING

attained his knowledge and powers of raising the dead, prophesy, shape-shifting and flying during a visit to the underworld. In the Sumerian tale, the goddess Inanna gathered the seven attributes of civilization and fashioned them into adornments to protect her as she descended into the Great Below to retrieve Tammuz. The Indians of North America, similar to the early Scandinavians, considered their subterranean world to be a dark abode of shadows and sub-mundane powers. In Greek lore it was Pluto who ruled Hades, or the underworld, where Persephone was held captive half the year.

Dr. King ponders all of this as she stares down at the fragment.

But the ancient Egyptians had their own hidden civilization tradition. The neter Ptah and his seven Ali are said to have tunneled through the Earth and built the underground paradise of Amenta. So why would this turn up here?

Despite her remarkable discoveries in the 'roadway of the Incans' tunnels, the majority of Dr. King's colleagues still dismiss her excavations as unrealistic wastes of time and money. These days her naysayers are generally divided into three camps: the modernists who feel as if the ancients could not have possessed the knowledge or abilities to have built underground cities; the more liberal-minded who feel that the myths are philosophical treatises concerning the inner-workings of the human mind; and the largest group who simply believe the tales to be religious stories and nothing more. Dr. King, on the other hand, holds firm to that Hermetic maxim: as above, so below. For every occurrence in heaven there exists its corresponding occurrence on earth, whether this heaven is the human mind or celestial realm.

"Dr. King. "The aide says again. "Did you hear me? You

zoned out on me for a second."

She snaps out of her reverie and grins to the aide. "Oh, uh, sorry." She looks to the fragment again. *Time never was when man was not.* "Just puzzled."

The aide smiles. "Yeah, I've definitely been stumped before, but c'mon, I can't believe that you— "

"Doktoor King!" A deep baritone laden voice cuts in. "Anti jaa lou samaht?!"

Dr. King smirks. All she can make out is her name and the word "please."

"Speak English, Abdullah! "She yells back. "You know I do not speak Arabic!"

Abdullah's throaty chuckle can be heard across the site. "Sorry, doctor." He says, switching to an English that is better than most Americans. "What I said was: could you come here please? I believe I have found something that you will want to see."

Curious as always, Dr. King leaves the aide to her work and makes her way across the site. The midday sun is bearing down on her neck as she joins Abdullah at the other end of their site.

"There." He says, pointing down at what appears to be some sort of door. A metal ring glints in the light, attached to a rectangular board buried beneath the sand. Excitement overtakes her.

"Abdullah!" She shrieks. "Do you know what this means?! This may be our entrance!"

"Ishallah, Dr. King. It was the wind that uncovered it."

Dr. King bends over and uses her hand to gently wipe away some of the sand. A young man pulls a brush from his back pocket and hands it to her. As she thanks him she takes notice of the crowd growing around them. Apparently news of Abdullah's door has spread. It looks like everyone at the site has come to view his

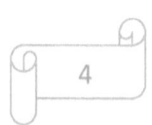

discovery.

"Give us room." She tells them. "I know you're all excited but, we all know, if this is a door then that means—"

"Tunnels." Someone blurts out.

"Exactly. We could be potentially standing on top of tunnels thousands of years old right now. We don't want them to cave in under our weight, do we?"

Reluctantly the crowd begins to spread out, allowing her and Abdullah plenty of room to work. With brush in hand, Dr. King squats down beside the door and begins to sweep away the thick layer of sand covering it. Every sweep reveals a new symbol: Egyptian hieroglyphs, Babylonian cuneiform, Hebrew and Greek script; the door is a veritable collage of ancient languages.

Abdullah is drawing a sketch of the door when Dr. King calls to him.

"Abdullah, come look at this." She says. "Have you ever seen this before?"

Abdullah steps closer and peers down at the board covered in ancient languages. There are so many markings he's not exactly sure which one she means.

"This one here." She says, pointing to a strange hieroglyph. "It looks like a scarab. You see?" She glances back at Abdullah— he's attempting to keep an odd amount of space between them—and chuckles. His Islamic mannerisms won't allow him to get too close to an uncovered woman. She steps to the side. "Come closer so you can see. It's amazing."

Abdullah hesitates. Although he's been working with Dr. King for over a month now, he has yet to grow accustomed to her Western ways. Her spaghetti-strap tank-tops and thigh-high shorts are discomforting enough without being asked to squat down beside her, so close to her bare flesh.

Just don't rub against her, he tells himself as he takes a knee.

Dr. King runs her fingers over the impression. It feels smooth, as if it's been recently sanded. "It's an Egyptian beetle right? A scarabeus?"

"Yes." Abdullah nods. He recognized the symbol as soon as she pointed it out. Although he was born in a time when the Islamic faith rules the Egyptian nation he has always been fascinated with the gloried civilization of old. After graduating from Cairo University with advanced degrees in anthropology, ancient history, and paleography, he went on to specialize in the Ancient Mesopotamian and Nile Valley civilizations, with a focus on Egypt and Sumer. Such extensive knowledge of this region makes him the perfect addition to Dr. King's current team and she looks to his expertise in times such as these.

"But that is odd." He says, pointing to a circle on the scarab's shell. "I have never seen it on a scarabeus before now."

"Neither have I." Dr. King replies, scanning her mind for a clue as to what this symbol may mean.

As daughter of the legendary Egyptologist Jonathan St. Clair, Dr. King has been digging in the dirt for as long as she can remember. She's explored the ruins of South America, the Aztec and Mayan sites in Mexico, and the ancient Dravidian city-states of the Indus Valley, relentlessly scouring the earth for the lost entrance to the Hidden Kingdom. Not only did her father transmit his enduring love for the mysteries to his daughter, his passion pushed her to pick up her own shovel. She is one of the few field archaeologists to hold advanced degrees in anthropology, ancient history, petrology, and paleography supplemented with extensive knowledge in ritual symbolism, comparative theology, and

mythological studies; if there is anyone qualified to find the entrance to the Hidden Kingdom it is Dr. King. Now, at 55 years old, with silver streaks highlighting her golden brown locks, she thanks the gods that she is not standing in front of a classroom, for she may be standing before the door she's spent her entire life waiting to open.

She looks to Abdullah with mischievous delight dancing in the corner of her eyes. "We should just do it, right? We should, shouldn't we?" Her eyes move to the anxious crowd surrounding them. "You know they want us to. Everyone's waiting for it."

Abdullah doesn't know what to say. She couldn't be suggesting what he thinks she is. He has often caught himself admiring her smooth almond- complexion and soft graceful features but that is what happens when a woman goes around uncovered. She belongs to another. He would never think to—

"You do it." She says, her eyes sparkling with excitement. "No, we'll do it together. Come on Abdullah." She takes hold of the ring. "On the count of three."

With an audible sigh of relief, Abdullah wraps his hand around the ring, careful not to touch her hand. "Al-Hamdulillah." He mutters.

Dr. King looks to him, grinning. "You ready? Be careful now. This wood is probably centuries old."

He nods.

"Okay then." She says. "Here we go."

With one last deep breath Dr. King begins her count down. The seconds seem to stretch on for eternity. Each one filled with decades of anticipation and a lifetime of excitement. At the sound of "three," she and Abdullah gently pull up on the ring and the door slides open with little resistance. She turns to him smiling from ear to ear.

"Abdullah, do you know what this means— the door, it just opened like, like--"

"Yes, Doctor, I know." He says, almost clinical. "The fluid motion of the door would suggest that it is either frequently used or tended to by someone rather regularly."

She nods. "Exactly. And I have always suspected that there are factions of the ancient priesthoods extant. It is likely to be them that have maintained the entrance or... or even utilized it themselves."

Standing now, she takes a step back to survey the door. The crowd begins to inch forward, spurred by their curiosity. This is more than any of them could ever hope for. Most of them are undergraduates looking for field experience and a good letter of recommendation. They all want to know what wonders may lay beneath their feet. Dr. King walks around the now vertical door and peers down into the portal they have just uncovered. The sun casts its light into the darkness.

"Sorry." She yells. "No tunnels. But there's a ladder. It looks like it goes down for a while. I can't see the bottom."

Dr. King forces herself to hide her disappointment. She can't risk dismaying her team now—not with such a find lying, literally, at their feet.

A doorway and an underground passage in the middle of the desert. A door covered with ancient languages and Egyptian hieroglyphs.

She has a thought. Something her father would always tell her. *The Egyptians were the best builders of the ancient world. They had a complex system of mathematical tunnels and passages built into the great pyramid. Could they have been brought in to help construct whatever lies beneath us? But then, that would mean—*

"I have to go down there." She turns to one of her aides. "Dante, go get me a harness and some rope."

"Yes, Doctor." He says and sprints off across the site.

"And a flashlight!" She yells after him.

Abdullah grabs hold of her arm. "No, Doktoor, I cannot allow you to do this. We don't know what's down there. It is too dangerous for an old woman like you."

She cuts her eyes at Abdullah's hand. "You can't *allow* it?" She glares at him and then shifts her eyes to his hand again. Abdullah reluctantly releases his hold. "I appreciate your concern for an old woman like myself," she retorts, "but 55 is the new 35. I'll be fine."

As if on cue, her aide runs up carrying the harness and rope. "Here you go, Doctor."

With his help she begins to attach the harness to herself. "Besides," she tells Abdullah, "I'll have you up here looking out for me. Here," she hands him the rope, "mark it off at five foot intervals."

Abdullah passes the rope off to the aide. "Well, I'm coming with you then, Doctor. I insist."

She smiles. "Sorry, honey."

With the harness now secure, she pulls her long dreadlocks up off of her neck and wraps them into a bun. "We don't know exactly how much weight this ladder can bear. And it's obvious who the lighter load is here."

She takes a red scarf from her back pocket and ties it around her hair. Abdullah shakes his head in frustration.

"Then we are back to my point. You shouldn't go down there. It is too dangerous. We should call in a team and have them

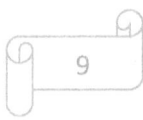

do some readings and maybe send down a drone first."

"Okay, Abdullah, you're right. You're exactly right. But," she glances around at the site, at the soldiers standing guard and all of the young faces watching her, "it's still *my money, my site*, and *my life*. If I die down there, at least I die for my beliefs."

"But, Doktoor--"

Dante's return interrupts Abdullah's protest. "Here you go Dr. King." He says, holding out the rope.

"Thank you." She says, taking it. Dr. King examines it and--satisfied with his work--has it attached to the back of her harness. "You guys make sure you're logging my descent." She tells the aides and then places the end of the rope in Abdullah's hands. "And you, Abdullah, you hold on to this. If anything happens I want you to yank me out of there, okay? Just because I am willing to die for my beliefs doesn't mean I want to."

Abdullah stares down at the rope. He wants to go down with her; he needs to go down with her. This is the moment he's been waiting for since he joined the team. It is the reason that he started working with her in the first place.

"Doktoor King are you certain that I cannot--"

She stops him. "Just do what I asked, please, Abdullah."

He stares at her and grins. This little old lady has the spirit of Allah coursing through her. It is not his duty to stand in her way. "Okay, Dr. King." He nods. "Allah knows best."

It feels as if the entire world is watching her as she moves toward the portal. Beads of nervous sweat prickle the skin beneath her scarf as she focuses on the descent. There is a slight give of the plank as she steps onto the ladder. She grips the rope tighter, feeling the dry rough fibers scratching into her hand and the rush of heat rising up through the hole. The coarse taste of sand licks at her tongue; it has a salty flavor, like the sweat now forming above her lip. It's like all her senses are working on overdrive. She has spent all of her adult life searching for the wisdom that has been lost throughout the ages and now she's closer than ever to accomplishing her goal.

"Flashlight!" She bellows. "Here," Dante says, "take mine."

She takes it and smiles. "Okay team, this is it. Let's make history."

She turns on the flashlight and aims it down into the darkness below.

- -

The ceiling is the first thing Dr. King notices. It is decorated to resemble the night sky.

And it's high. Whoever built this wanted plenty of room. It has to be at least thirty feet.

Her flashlight scans the ground. The ladder has dropped her off at a stone veranda about ten feet long. She looks around and notices a familiar Egyptian phrase amongst the myriad of symbols covering the walls.

Man know thyself, she reads. "And here you go again, my little friend."

The same scarabeus found on the fragment has been carved here beside the phrase. If she remembers correctly, the ancient Egyptians used the scarabeus as a symbol for their neter, or god, Khepera-Ptah, who was reborn as his own son, Iu- em-hetp. Typically, the scarabeus was used to denote the 'only begotten' or a father, at times the 'self- created.'

The close proximity of the scarab and the phrase suggests that the two are related but with the addition of the circle on the scarabeus' wings...well, it could mean anything really.

"I'm at the bottom." She yells up to the surface. "Mark off

my descent!"

Abdullah's deep voice comes bellowing back. "Approximately thirty-three feet, Doktoor!"

"Log it!" She shouts, shining the flashlight around. There's a doorway up ahead, down a small flight of stairs, and she moves towards it. "I see a room! I'm going forward!"

Her skin tingles as she steps inside the room and the hairs on her arm stand on end. *This is sacred ground, she thinks, taking a deep breath. Could it have been a burial chamber?*

The room is approximately 15x15 feet, not much bigger than a motel room. She looks up and the ceiling has disappeared into the darkness. There are four decorative torch holders by the entrance and she moves to examine them. Beautiful is the only word that comes to mind. Each one has been fashioned in the shape of a portly baboon and made to look as if they are grasping the end of the torches.

Further into the chamber her flashlight strikes a row of stone slabs jutting from the left wall. *Probably shelves*, she thinks, considering their height in relation to her body.

She moves closer, careful to watch every step. As an archaeologist, she will be the first to attest to the multitudes of treasures trampled on throughout the years. People seldom care about the ground they walk on until it becomes unstable.

She brushes a thin layer of dust from the shelf. "Why didn't I grab a camera?" She asks herself, examining the structure. A marvelous mixture of ancient markings is carved deep into the stone. The precision is uncanny. She hasn't seen workmanship like this since...since.....*never.*

"I'll definitely have to get some Egyptologists down here." She scans the room with her flashlight. "Maybe there's something in

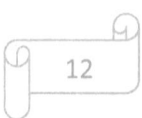

my father's notes."

Something catches her eye—an old table situated against a wall on the far side of the room.

She goes to inspect it and finds a blank scroll lying atop it. *Could it be a desk? A scribal desk?*

She rubs the scroll between her fingers. "Papyrus."

Dr. King continues to scan the area with her flashlight. The scarab appears again, this time on the wall behind the desk. "What are you trying to tell me?"

This particular scarab is the largest so far, about the size of a dinner plate, she guesses. But there is something else different about this one. She steps around the desk to get a better look. It's the circle on the scarab's wings. It protrudes from the wall. And there's something else.

She brushes away a layer of dust and shines the light on it.

"The diameter's wrong. It's horizontal instead of vertical like the others." She studies the glyph further. Not only does the disk protrude from the wall but it sits inside a deep ridge.

"What if..." She takes hold of the disk and turns it clockwise until the diameter is positioned vertically.

"Okay, Jackie." She says and takes a deep breath. "Here goes."

With the palm of her hand she presses the disk into the ridge until it is flush with the wall and waits.

And waits.

And waits.

The disk pops back out and she smirks. "Really, Jackie, what did you expect? You're not Indiana Jones. Be happy that you found this at all. It'll be another 25,000 years before—wait."

25,000 years! Of course!

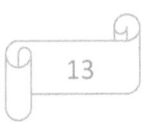

When she was a child her father would regale her with stories of ancient Egypt and their mysterious initiation rituals. According to him, the Great Pyramid of Giza is not just an ostentatious piece of architecture; it is a temple of initiation that holds a 25,000 year prophecy built into its sacred geometry. This 25,000 year period is very important. If she remembers correctly, the ancient Egyptians utilized a calendar based on what they called the 'Great Year,' a period of 25,920 years equal to the time that it takes the magnetic north pole to complete a full retrograde circle around the Earth's vertical north pole.

"If the Egyptians helped to construct this chamber then it would make sense that--" She turns the disk again, this time counter-clockwise, following the retrograde path of the magnetic north pole, until the diameter is upright.

"Okay." She says. "Let's try this again." With the palm of her hand she presses the disk in again and waits.

And waits.

The disk pops out again.

Shaking her head Dr. King takes a step back and shines the flashlight on the protruding disk. She refuses to give up, convinced the scarab is the key. *But what am I missing?*

25,000 years; the procession of the equinoxes; moves backward through the zodiac; 12 zodiac signs; takes 72 years to complete one degree of movement; 2,160 years to get through an age; 360 degrees in the zodiac.

She's overlooking something and she knows it. But what is it?

What is it I'm missing?

She stares at the scarab, searching her mind for the key to this puzzle.

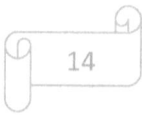

Khepera; a symbol of divinity; the Neteru; Paut Neteru; first nine born gods: Shu, Tefnut, Geb, Nut, Asar, Aset—

"Nine!" She exclaims." It's nine! Of course!"

She takes hold of the disk again and turns it counter-clockwise until the diameter is vertical. "That's one." She says and turns it again.

The Egyptians were too smart to make it that easy, anyway, she thinks. *It takes 72 years to move one degree through the zodiac and there are 72 complete cycles in a Great Year. 7+2=9. There are the first nine gods that came forth from the creator— the Paut Neteru—and there are nine cardinal numbers issuing forth from zero. A child spins nine months in its mother's womb, and the esoteric characteristics of nine are the characteristics of man.*

She continues to turn the disk. "That's six."

But could a people have been that advanced and integrative in their thinking over 4,000 years before our modern world even came about? She answers the question as quickly as she poses it. *Of course! And it is to these ancient minds that the modern world owes its greatest treasures.*

"That's eight." She takes a deep breath. "Last one."

She can feel the resistance building as she twists the dial. Just one last twist of her wrist and there it is. She hears a slight click, like a key fitting into a lock, as the disk snaps into place. Grinning, she watches as the scarab descends into the wall.

A faint grinding of stones can be heard from the darkness above. Loose sediment, dust and debris fall from the ceiling. The grinding grows louder and the ground begins to tremble beneath her feet. With a puff of air, the wall shifts and a gust of air slams into her face.

"I knew it." She says, peering through the doorway now in

front of her. *The number nine indicates a portal, like a womb, and therefore a doorway into another realm.*

Dr. King aims the flashlight into the darkness and scans the chamber. The room is at least triple that of the previous chamber. She glances back.

"You were a decoy room, weren't you? In case any uninvited guests managed to get this far they would assume that there was no further to go and turn back." She looks at the desk. "Those scrolls, the papyrus, they're all decoys. Whoever built this was probably working for a group of scribes. Priestly scribes."

She checks her harness and steps forward into the darkness, swinging the flashlight in front of her as she goes. "This would explain why there are so many blank scrolls hidden so far underground. There must have been a temple built above here. That door was probably hidden in someone's room. A secret passageway to a scribe's sanctuary."

She glances around the room and notices shelves similar to those in the decoy chamber. She walks by them, passing seven baboon-shaped torched holders.

"But why would a scribe need a hidden chamber? What could he have been writing that--" She comes to a large round table surrounded by twelve wooden chairs. The same scarabeus is engraved in the center of the table, encircled by a collage of ancient symbols.

She shines the flashlight on the chairs. The first chair she examines is crafted in the shape of a bull. The one beside it is adorned with the symbols of a ram and the chair next to it is decorated with fish of all kinds. "Zodiacal symbols," she says.

She has ventured deep into the interior of the chamber and the darkness surrounds her like an ocean of night. Even the flashlight's beam must succumb to the massive weight of the abyss that envelopes it. Its glow does not extend more than a few feet in front of her and she makes it makes her business to be careful of every step she takes.

"The people of Sumer were great astrologers. If they were working with the Egyptians then that would explain--"

Suddenly, the ground beneath her feet begins to tremble violently. The chairs crash to the floor, reducing the old wood to a pile of splinters. Something smashes into the ground behind her. Frightened, she spins toward the sound but the flashlight's beam cannot penetrate the darkness. Stones shoot from the ceiling like meteors crashing into Earth. A jagged rock smacks her arm and cuts her deeply, knocking the flashlight loose.

"Shit!" She shrieks, grasping the wound as she watches the blue stream roll away. She gets down on her hands and knees and starts to crawl towards the light, cautiously. A boulder falls from the ceiling and smashes into the center of the table. Shrapnel explodes into the air scratching trails of blood into her face. The entire chamber is collapsing around her now. She speeds up her crawl, praying she isn't struck by an errant boulder. The flashlight is right in front her. She reaches out for it and a thick chunk of the ceiling smacks her hand.

"Aaah!" She yelps. The time for exploration is over. Fighting back the pain in her hand and arm, she grips the flashlight and rises to her feet. If she doesn't get out of here soon she'll be trapped until a team can get to her. *And with all this rubble piling up--*

"Yeah, it's time to go." Holding the flashlight in one hand, she takes hold of the rope and begins to follow it back towards the entrance. Everything in her is screaming, "Run!" but with all of the stones lying around it'd be like sprinting blindfolded through a mine field. All she can do is keep following the rope and pray that the universe spares her one more time.

"Doktoor King!" Abdullah's voice tears through the darkness. "Doktoor King, can you hear me?!"

A wave of relief washes over Dr. King's face. She's been following the rope for the longest three minutes of her life. "Abdullah, my God. Yes, Abdullah, I am here. Be careful! The ceiling is collapsing!"

As she says this, a large chunk of the ceiling crashes into the ground a few feet in front of her. She jumps back, dropping the rope in the process. Steeling herself, she takes a deep breath, picks the rope back up and starts to follow it but as she pulls, it draws taut in her hands.

"Abdullah, I think a stone has landed on the rope. Can you see my flashlight?"

"No, I cannot, and I raced down here without bringing my own. When the ground began to tremble, I did not think. I only--"

"It is okay, Abdullah. Just follow the rope as far as you can and we should meet."

"Al-Hamdulillah."

Abdullah grabs the rope from beside his foot and begins to follow its trail into the darkness. He has never been so worried. He joined the Doctor's team with a mission in mind and if he lets her die down here then he has failed. He cannot fail.

Repeating a slow melodic prayer he moves further into the chamber, faithful that Allah will protect him. Pieces of the ceiling crash down around him. Small shards cut into his skin but he is undeterred.

"Doktoor, where are you?" he calls out.

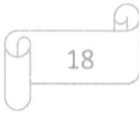

"Just keep moving until you see the light, okay. Just keep moving."

Hearing her voice calms him. It is only through the blessings of Allah that she has survived this long, he thinks. He cannot allow her to die down here. "Okay, Doktoor King. I am coming."

Abdullah quickens his pace as the ceiling rains down faster.

Dr. King has come to the end of her line. A large boulder sits in front of her, lying on the rope. She doesn't have time to wait for Abdullah. Moving around it she finds the other half of the rope on the ground and continues to follow it.

"Keep talking, Abdullah," she yells, "keep singing." She moves towards Abdullah's deep hums. Another boulder crashes down behind her. "Keep coming. Hurry."

There is no more time to be cautious. The room is imploding on itself. Loud cracking can be heard as the ceiling fractures. The air is filled with the staccato of falling stones. It is like a thousand shotguns being shot in rapid succession.

"Doktoor!" Abdullah yells, "I can see your light! I'm coming!"

The roar of the room grows louder. Dr. King races towards Abdullah's voice. She can see him, a faint outline in the shadowy distance.

She speeds up. "Abdul—" A large lock strikes the back of her head and she falls forward, knocked unconscious.

Abdullah hears her shriek and watches in horror as the flashlight's beam shoots up then falls to the ground. "Doktoor, are you alright?! Dr. King, say something, please!"

There is no response. He moves quickly, dropping the rope and racing towards the light. Blocks of stone slam the ground inches from his feet. He doesn't care. He keeps going, reciting the same prayer over and over.

He finally reaches the flashlight, picks it up and scans the area. Dr. King is laying unconscious on the ground with blood trickling down her forehead.

"Doktoor, get up." He says, lifting her to her feet. "Get up, Doktoor King. We must leave here now!"

The room quakes violently. Large pieces of the ceiling continue to crash down around them. Dr. King rubs her forehead, dazed but otherwise okay. "What happened?" She mumbles. "Abdullah! I've got to get to Abdullah!"

"I am here, Doktoor. We have to go. Now!"

She smiles in the darkness. Abdullah said he would keep her safe. She always could tell he was a good man.

"Give me your hand, Doktoor."

Dr. King leads the way and Abdullah follows closely behind. They stay close to the rope until they can see the outline of the doorway in the distance.

"Hurry, Doktoor King. We are almost there."

A large chunk of the ceiling crashes behind them. Another piece falls. A chain reaction sounds off, like a string of landmines being detonated in rapid succession.

"The walls are giving out. The ceiling is falling all at once. There is nothing left to support it." Dr. King snatches the flashlight from Abdullah's hand. "Come on!"

Abdullah sprints behind her and the ceiling races to catch up. He looks over his shoulder. It's coming down too fast. They're not going to make it.

In one daring motion, Abdullah sweeps Dr. King up into her arms and dives forward. They soar through the air and his shoulder crashes into the floor just as a wall of boulders seals the entrance shut behind him.

"Al-Hamdulillah."

"Al-Hamdulillah." Dr. King repeats. "All praises due."

The two of them lay there for a moment appreciating the silence. Abdullah stares at the ceiling thanking Allah for his mercy while Dr. King smiles, thinking about her son, daughter, and husband— and how she can't wait to tell them this story.

Well, maybe not Derrick. He'll never let me leave the house again.

An aftershock rattles the chamber and shakes them from their reverie. The desk tips over and stacks of scrolls spill out onto the ground. Abdullah stands and almost steps on one.

"Wait!" Dr. King shouts. Abdullah pauses with his foot in mid-air and then carefully sets it down beside the scroll. She grabs the flashlight, picks up the scroll and begins to examine it. "That's odd." She says. "It's blank."

She grabs another and turns to Abdullah. "Watch your step, okay? This is still an unmarked site." She glances around the small room and imagines the mysteries it could contain. Who knows what may have occurred here.

She sets the scroll down--*another blank*—and goes to examine another. "Do you think that those tremors could have come from this wall shifting? Maybe it's been so long since someone accessed it."

Abdullah brushes the dust from his clothes. "Let's just get out of here before they begin again." He glances around the dark cavern. "It is not wise to tempt Allah."

Dr. King smirks. "Or maybe it is Allah's will that we are now here." She picks up another one of the scrolls. "See if you can find anything in here with writing on it. Maybe whoever worked here left something that can help us find Shamballah?"

Abdullah shakes his head in amazement, but concedes. He digs in to the stack beside Dr. King and examines a scroll. "They're all blank." He tells her. "We should go now."

Ignoring him, she unrolls another scroll. "Abdullah, look at this. Come here. Do you recognize any of these symbols?"

"No." He lies. "There is nothing here. It is time for us to go. We will have a team come down and catalogue everything tomorrow." He reaches for her hand. "Let's go."

She pulls her hand away. "Wait, there's something over there. By the desk." She points the flashlight at a corner of the desk that's been busted open. "You see that? That thing sticking out of the corner?"

Without waiting for his response, Dr. King makes her way to the desk and slowly slides the item out of the wreckage. It is a book; a thick, tightly bound, and very old book by the look of it.

"It was hidden in the desk." She says, turning to face Abdullah. "Now why would you hide— Abdullah." Her voice cracks as she takes in his grimace. "Abdullah, wha- what's wrong? Why are you looking at me like that?"

"Just hand me the book, Dr. King." Gone is the sweet baritone of the nice young man that has been working with her for the past six months replaced by an intimidating bravado as frightening as his sudden transformation. She watches him reach around to the small of his back and unsheathe his hunting knife—a knife she had given him as a gift for all his hard work.

"Don't make me use this. You are a—uhh!" She slams her foot into his crotch and makes a run for it. Abdullah reaches out for her leg and trips her. She falls, dropping the flashlight but still clutching onto the book. She can't see anything now but the

22

flashlight's blue beam and the ground in front of it. She reaches for the flashlight but Abdullah grabs her leg and yanks her back. She kicks at him as he fights to flip her over. He finally gets the doctor on her back and pins her arms down with his knees.

The book is still is clutched against Dr. King's chest as she stares up into Abdullah's menacing snarl. "Okay." She says, panting. "I'll give you the book." She takes a deep breath. "Here! Take it!" With all of the force she can muster she rams the book upward, smashing it into Abdullah's nose.

"Bitch!" He shouts, clutching his bleeding nose. "No, you'll give me more than the book now." He smacks her with the back of his hand and grabs her by the wrists. With one hand he pins her arms above her head and forces her legs apart with the other.

"I've had to watch you strut around uncovered for months, knowing I could not have you." He tries to keep her legs open with his knees but she fights him. He smacks her again. "But you're mines now."

He fight to spread her legs apart but she struggles against him. "Stop fighting!" He smacks her again and blood leaks from the corner of her mouth. "I'm going to give you what you want."

She feels a vibration run up her spin and her eyes widen. "Wait!" She shouts. "Wait! Do you feel that? The ground, it's moving again. We have to get out of here or we'll die."

"No, Doktoor, the ground is not yet moving, but it will soon." He slashes open her harness with his knife and then cuts through her shirt, exposing her bra. Another quick slash slices her belt in half and he presses the knife against her throat.

"Take off your shorts." He orders and gives her a soft kiss on the cheek. "If you try *anything* I'll slit your throat and bury you in the rubble."

She stares at him, refusing to move, and he slides the blade across her neck. A thin line of blood follows its path. "Take. Off. Your. Shorts!"

Abdullah stands and unbuckles his pants, oblivious to the debris falling from the ceiling. The flashlight is still behind him, illuminating the ground beneath his feet as he stares down at Dr. King.

"What are you waiting for? Take off your pants now or I'll—"

A chunk of stone crashes into Abdullah's skull and he crumbles to the ground. Dr. King watches his head twitch in the light as the floor fills with his blood.

"Al-Hamdulillah." She mumbles. She pulls herself to her feet quickly. The tremors are growing stronger now. She has to get out of here and fast. Snatching the flashlight from the floor, she grabs the scroll and book, and glances down to Abdullah's lifeless body one last time. There is a tattoo on the nape of his neck: an image of a serpent eating its own tail.

Ouroborous, she thinks.

Large chunks of the ceiling continue to rain down around her. She heads towards the exit, hoping the ladder is still in place. There is nothing but death, darkness and decay left down here but as she takes her first steps forward she thinks of the light ahead. Who knows what these new discoveries may hold?

They could be the key to finding Shamballah.

Clutching the book and scroll tightly against her chest Dr. King ascends the steps and heads towards the light.

CHAPTER ONE

A dismal silence blankets the night. The crickets have grown still; the birds have ceased their chirp; and the wind refuses to blow. It is as if Mother Nature herself can sense death's approach.

A van door slams and its grisly echo disrupts the calm. Scattered rocks crumble under the weight of a thick-soled leather boot. The driver leans across the cabin and the van's old suspension sighs.

"Make this quick." A deep voice orders. His accent is Russian; his tone ex-military. "You have your orders. None of your handiwork tonight, Victor."

Victor runs the edge of his blade against his finger. "No need to worry, Commander. How hard could it be to take a book from monkeys?" He sucks the blood from his finger and grins. "Monkeys cannot read."

The driver is not amused. "Franz," he says, "keep him in line. I'll return--"

"In an hour." Franz interrupts. He pulls a black ski-mask down over his face. "We have been working together for too long, commander. Just stick to protocol. We've been in worse situations than this."

"But we have never worked for men such as this." The commander responds, shifting the van into drive. "Do you two have all you need?"

"Yes sir," Franz says, giving his six-foot frame a quick once over. He cocks the slide of his 9mm Sig Sauer and adjusts the straps of his backpack. "I have everything."

"And you Victor?"

Victor slides his hands into a pair of black leather gloves and smirks. "Yes, Commander." He gives himself a quick inspection. The black suit he's wearing fits snugly against his tall muscular frame. He takes his pistol out of its holster, checks the clip, and readies a round. "I have everything that I'll need."

"Just remember your orders, Victor." The commander lifts his foot off of the brake and the van begins to creep forward. "These men will not tolerate error."

Franz is at the beginning of the driveway, studying the security gate, when Victor joins him.

"He worries too much." Victor says. He looks at the large iron gate then back to Franz. His impatience is discernible. "So, comrade, what are you waiting for? Do your gizmo thing and open this gate already."

Franz doesn't have time to feed in to Victor's games right now. They have work to do—serious work. He goes into his backpack and removes a small plastic box he likes to think of as his master key. Next comes a thin cord about five inches long. He connects one end of the cord to the box and the other to the gate's access pad. The box's screen lights up he pushes a button to start its brute force attack on the gate's pass code.

While his master key goes to work Franz examines the supposedly secure gate. This ten foot high mechanical barrier is intended to keep out any unwanted guests, he presumes, guests like us.

But if this is your only defense, he muses, *you cannot have true enemies.*

The gate clicks and Franz removes the device.

Victor starts through it eagerly. "Come. Hurry." He skulks up the driveway with Franz close behind. They cut across the lawn like two black cats, moving from a Rolls Royce to a marble fountain, from the decorative bushes to an antique Jaguar, before they finally arrive at the side of the house.

Crouched beneath a second story balcony Franz looks to Victor. "Do you remember the layout of the home?"

Victor nods. "Do you think that I'd spend a week cutting and trimming these nigger's bushes only to forget my reconnaissance, comrade?"

"You'd think with all of that money they would be able to afford better security than that gate." Franz says, still amazed by their lack of security.

"Or maybe they just believe that their chef is enough." Victor replies.

Franz can hear the delight in Victor's voice. "You know the plan, Victor. First we immobilize the cook. Then we enter there." He nods in the direction of the balcony.

"Do not treat me like a child." Victor stands and a start to walk off but Franz grabs his arm.

"Where the hell are you going?" Franz asks. Victor snatches his arm away from Franz. "To stick to the plan like you said, comrade." He grins beneath the mask. "If I happen to have some fun immobilizing the chef then so be it."

"No, Victor. First we must locate the-" "Look there, comrade," Victor points to the guesthouse up ahead. "The light is on. I am going to check it out. You locate the husband and wife. You can handle that on your own, can't you?"

Franz ignores the jab. "We'll meet back here then."

Victor checks his watch. "I shouldn't need more than five minutes."

Franz nods and watches Victor stalk off toward the guesthouse. Once Victor is out of sight, Franz begins his work. Staying crouched, he moves around the mansion's perimeter with his gun at ready. He locates the wife and husband quickly. Usually around this time the wife is preparing dinner while the husband sits in his study reading and nursing a drink—tequila is his favorite. The only unpredictable variable is the chef. At times he is helping them with in the kitchen, other times he is in the study playing video games with the husband, and sometimes he is off on his own.

As expected, the wife is in the kitchen and the husband is in the study—he does not find the chef. Franz grins. "Maybe he's somewhere giving Victor what he wants. He needs a good beating."

He starts to head for the guesthouse but decides to let Victor enjoy himself. *The man's sick*, he admits, heading to the rendezvous point, *but he is good at what he does.*

"So is he out?" Franz asks Victor as he approaches.

"Yes," Victor says, kneeling beside him, "but I did nothing. He was sleeping with the light in. A deep sleep. I could not wake him."

"You tried to wake him?"

"I told you I wanted to have some fun, comrade."

"You did not kill him?"

"Were our orders to kill him, Franz?"

"Okay." Franz says. They need to get on with it. They can't

be here all night. He relays the location of the two targets. "Go on." He nods at the decorative ladder built onto the side of the house. "You first."

Victor shakes his head as he moves to the ladder. "Dumb niggers. So lazy they have a ladder built on their house. What if they need to move it?"

"It is there so that someone can access the roof." Franz tells him, hoisting himself up behind Victor. "In order to clean the gutters."

Victor chuckles. "I didn't know monkeys needed ladders to climb."

For people so rich, the lock on the balcony doors is rather cheap and Victor picks it easily. He steps inside and his flashlight scans the room. Old comics, a stack of dog-eared novels, an economic textbook, and a few travel magazines litter a hand-crafted mahogany desk. Pictures of luxury sports cars and sexy pin-ups cover the walls. A snowboard leans against a king size bed complete with ruffled sheets and a strewn about blanket.

"Spoiled brat." Franz mutters, stepping over a pair of old sneakers. "No pride of ownership."

Victor picks up a Spider-Man comic and flips through it. "What did you expect, Franz?" He tosses the comic book back onto the desk. "You are in a monkey's cage."

Franz glances around the room. "You get the husband. I'll take care of the wife. Do not kill him until--"

"I know my orders, comrade." Victor deliberately bumps Franz shoulder as he walks out of the room. "You just get that bitch to talk."

The husband would have fought back, Victor thinks. If he had heard Victor's footsteps approaching behind him he would have resisted. *I know it.*

Maybe it was the comfort of his favorite chair; maybe he was too focused on the research paper he was reviewing; maybe it was the effects of the tequila he was drinking—maybe it was all three.

Whatever the reason, the husband was oblivious to the man creeping up behind him until his head was being held against his chair and a chloroform-rag pressed to his face.

Yeah, he would've fought back, Victor muses. He can tell by how hard the old man resisted. Their fight would not have lasted long but it would have been fun for Victor.

I should've broken a lamp.

In the kitchen the wife is breaking plenty. Held up behind the island counter she hurls another plate at Franz's head. He ducks it quickly and the plate shatters against the wall.

"Stay back!" She yells, welding a massive butcher knife in her left hand while slinging another plate with her right. "Derrick! Derrick! Saka!"

"Your husband isn't coming." Franz taunts, moving around the counter. Another dish flies at his face and he weaves it easily. "Maybe if you calm down we can do this without anyone getting hurt."

The two of them continue to circle the counter, their eyes locked on each other, both waiting for the perfect moment to steal the upper hand—like the last round in a deadly game of musical chairs.

"Do what?" She asks, still moving, still wielding the knife. "Why are you in my home? And where is my husband? Derrick!"

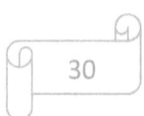

She calls out to her husband but there is no response. "Saka!" She yells.

Franz is getting tired of this. "I told you he is not coming. All I want is the book, okay? Give me the book and I'll leave."

"A book? What book? Where is my husband? What--"

Franz stops circling the counter and pulls his 9mm from its holster. "Don't play dumb with me, lady. I was sent to retrieve the book and you know what book that is. I'm not leaving here without it." He aims the gun at her chest. "So tell me where it is or I will just kill you and find it myself."

"Okay, please. Wait." She sits the knife down on the counter and raises her hands in submission. "You're right, I know what you want and I'll take you to it. Just don't hurt my husband."

She walks from behind the counter, right up to Franz and stares straight into his dark eyes. Somewhere in the back of her mind she has been expecting a moment like this. Ever since the moment she realized what she had found. His presence here now only confirms her suspicions.

People have died for less, she thinks. *There are some things that are just never meant to be found.*

Franz looks down at his watch. "Come on." He says, shoving her out of the kitchen. "I don't have all night."

With a speed that startles him, the wife spends around and smacks Franz across the face before he can think to react.

"You bitch!" He shrieks. Infuriated, he snatches her by her hair and digs the barrel of his pistol into her temple. "Oh, you'll pay for that."

"Kill him!" Franz orders, shoving the wife into the study. "The old bitch won't cooperate. She thinks he is going to save her.

Remove that option."

Victor is leaning against the husband's desk, enjoying one of his cigars, when Franz storms in and throws the woman to the ground. He watches her fall to the floor and land by his feet and is tempted to kick her teeth out. He glares down at her instead, his mask hiding a sadistic smile.

"Had some trouble, comrade?" He asks.

"Don't patronize me." Franz barks. "I gave you an order."

He nods. "My pleasure, sir" and slowly unholsters his Sig Sauer.

"No. Please." The wife crawls to Victor and grabs hold of his pant leg. "Don't kill him, please. Please. I'm begging."

Victor kicks her away like the annoying dog she is and takes aim.

"No, wait," she pleads, "I'll give you the book. Just, please, don't hurt him."

Victor turns to Franz. "Sir?"

Franz raises his hand. "Wait. I think she may have changed her mind."

Snatching her by the collar, Franz yanks the wife to her feet. He leans in close and whispers into her ear. "Tell me where the book is now, or you will spend the last hours of our life watching your husband die. And then," he looks to Victor, "I will let my friend make you wish you were dead."

Franz tosses the wife back to the floor and takes the cigar from Victor. He enjoys a few puffs while she considers his proposal and then grounds it into the ashtray. "Now, for the last time, where is the book?"

Silent tears roll down the wife's almond cheeks. She looks to her husband, sitting unconscious in his favorite chair; the chair that she brought him for their 10th anniversary.

Why us, she muses. *Why now? What could I have done to deserve this? We're good people. We—*

"Where?!" Franz shouts.

"Here," she says, "It's in here."

Makes sense, he thinks. The study is filled with books. It is the husband's personal library. Every wall is lined with rows and rows of volumes; some new, some old. Franz glances at the shelves, wondering if he can spot the one they're here to retrieve. Their Intel did not include any photographs or descriptions of the book. All they were told is that they'll know it when they see it.

Franz checks his watch. "Thirty-six minutes."

"Go!" Victor orders, aiming his gun at her head, "Now! Get the book!"

It feels like there's a kettle bell attached to the wife's legs as she drags herself across the room to a set of bookshelves. Slowly, she selects three books, each on a different row, and tilts them forward. On the opposite side of the study a painting swings forward from the wall, revealing a digital safe.

Franz goes to it. "Combination?"

The wife hesitates. It's not intentional—it's just the thought of those numbers and the gravity of what they mean. "My son's birthday." She mumbles.

Victor smacks her with the butt of his gun. "That's not what he asked you."

The numbers fall from her lips like dead leaves falling from a barren branch. Blood leaks from the gash on her forehead but she doesn't notice it. There is a part of her still in this room, watching Franz remove the book and load it into his backpack, but that part is no longer is important. The important part-- the part that still loves to play Donkey Kong and watch old movies-- that part is somewhere on a beach with her husband and son, discussing their lives and goals.

"Now that that's finished," Franz says, turning his attention towards her, "it's time for you to pay for that little outburst you had in the kitchen." He rubs the side of his face. "You're like a stick of dynamite."

With a nod to Victor, Franz takes a noise suppressor from his bag and screws it on the end of his pistol. Victor does the same.

The wife turns toward them. Fear is absent from her face and so is worry—replaced by the confident gaze of righteous acceptance. "I always said that when I died there were three things that I wanted." She smirks slightly. "I wanted to die for my beliefs, die doing what I loved, and die in the arms of my wonderful husband."

She crosses the room and takes a seat in her husband's lap. Running her fingers through his soft gray curls she studies the gentle beauty of his face and kisses him softly. "But now I have another wish." She looks up at the intruders. "If I am to go to my heaven tonight, grant me the honor of knowing who is sending me there."

Victor can't hold back his laughter. "What?!" He blurts between chortles. "Our names? You want to know our names. What does it matter anyway? You're dead. These fucking niggers!"

Franz shakes his head and raises his pistol. The wife snuggles up closer to her husband, kisses him one last time and then lays her head on his chest.

"I love you, my king." She whispers the words against the slow beat of his heart.

The pistol's muffled report barely pierces the air.

With phase one complete, Victor checks his watch. "Let's get to work then. We don't have long to finish up."

Franz moves towards the departed couple. "Help me with the old man's body."

"You just get her." Victor tells him, hoisting the husband's corpse over his shoulder. "I can handle him."

Franz bends over to get the wife. *What the hell,* he thinks; *if someone had me murdered I'd want to know who ordered the hit.*

"The Elite." He tells her but it's only the walls that can hear him now.

CHAPTER TWO

W hy can't death ever be this late?"
Natalie mumbles, once again checking the time on
her cellphone. "Maybe then I'd catch a break.

It's been, what—an hour now. Her eyes scan the room. *Well,
I guess if you're going to be stood up, this is where you'd want it to
happen.*

Café de la Rogue is New York City's newest premier
nightspot. Since its inception, the cozy lounge has fast become a
launching pad for the world's next big thing. Singers, poets, painters,
photographers, and MCs; artists of every ilk have come to announce
themselves before the Café's eclectic crowd.

Natalie has wanted to catch one of the club's famous Open
Mic Nights for years now. Not only does Café de la Rogue bring
in the biggest underground stars, its Open Mic Nights have also
been known to attract premier acts to the stage. These exclusive
performances are the club's crowning jewel. Watching the entrance
now, she wonders if any celebrities will drop by tonight.

A waitress in loose jeans and a red tank-top
strolls by. Natalie stops her. "Excuse me. I'm waiting on Devin King.
I'm Natalie Washington. Me and--"

"Yeah, I thought I recognized you." The waitress cuts in.
"You used to work for...umm..."

Natalie smiles. "Do you think you could bring me a bottle of
wine? Riesling if you have it. Anything white if you don't."

"Oh, okay." The young woman pulls a pad from her pocket

and scribbles down Natalie's order. "Anything else?"

"You know what? How about a Sunset Sprits?"

"Alright."

"And this is all going to be covered by Mr. King, right?"

The waitress nods. "I'll be right back with that Sunset."

A poet takes the stage—a curvy sun-kissed woman with bangles on her wrist and a scarf tied around her hair—and Natalie admires the woman's natural grace. Her own hair is too straight to stay in those tight kinky spirals. Beneath the rosy lights of the stage the muse begins to speak over the jazzy vibe of a bass guitar and alto sax. Natalie listens to her tale of love and lost, missed opportunities, finding one's self and living with regrets.

Story of my life, she thinks, drumming her pen to the rhythm of the drums.

The waitress returns with the Sunset and Natalie slips her a five dollar tip. She remembers being in college trying to make ends meet like distant relatives at a family reunion. She smirks—*at least; I hope she's in school.*

Applause follows the poet off the stage and a young rugged man with a guitar and a glare takes her place. Natalie checks the time again.

He has ten more minutes.

She takes a sip of her drink (*too much grapefruit juice*) and bites into the orange slice. On stage the guitarist begins to strum his song.

"Well, at least twenty minutes." She says. "It's not like I have somewhere better to be tonight."

Thirty-seven minutes later—according to her cell-phone—the object of Natalie's irritation comes strolling through the doors and she cannot believe what he's wearing.

"Shorts and a t-shirt. He can't be serious."

True, Café de la Rogue is a quaint and casual environment but it isn't the YMCA. At any moment some big name A-lister could drop in, bringing a hundred cameras and even more paparazzi—patrons tend to dress to impress. The black backless gown that Natalie dons tonight still has the price tag on it and her heels set her back a month's rent. *And after everything I had to put up with to get a seat in Camilla's chair.*

"Does he really think he's *that special?*"

She watches him as he struts pass the concierge's desk without so much as a nod, waves to a couple celebrities, and then stops to chat with some rising stars. Every movement he makes exudes confidence, from the tilt of his head to his dazzling white smile.

"Guess I'd be that confident too if I owned the place."

She continues to watch as he flashes a smile to a buxom young woman and then shakes hands with the rugged guitarist. *A handshake that might've just changed his life,* she thinks.

"But, still, when you're Devin King, the most eligible bachelor of the year, top ten Forbes' 30 under 30, and almost an hour late for an interview, you don't show up in shorts and a t-shirt."

Devin spots Natalie sitting at a secluded corner table. He makes his way toward her, shaking hands and stopping to chat along the way. *She looks out of place,* he thinks, *too bourgeois for this crowd; especially in that dress.* But as he draws nearer to her table he smirks. The heels of her feet are hanging over the back of her pumps just like his mother's would when she was forced to attend some fancy function on his father's arm.

Most of the people here tonight are likely to be familiar with Natalie Washington, even if only vaguely. She had a short broadcasting stint on Good Morning America before heading to CNN for a chance at some weightier reporting. Now she's covering celebrity profiles for HLN. Watching her on TV, Devin always gets the feeling that she's one of those people that take life way too seriously; but, seeing her here now, with her heels hanging out the back of her shoes like that, *and that tag still on her dress—*

Maybe I need to reassess, he figures. *If she's not used to spending hours in heels there might be more to Ms. Washington than I thought.*

"Hello." He says, taking a seat. "You look beautiful tonight."

Her eyes roll like bowling balls. "Yeah, thanks. Glad you finally decided to show. You know, I almost called Bellevue."

Devin chuckles. "No, you didn't." He says, picking up a menu. "You almost called my publicist."

"Yeah, well--"

"We do have time to eat, don't we?" He asks, scanning over the menu. "I'm starving."

Natalie glances down at her phone. "Well, we *had* time to eat. But I guess as long as you can talk between bites."

"Can do." Devin flags down a waitress and instantly the young lady stops what she's doing and hurries to their table. She looks to Natalie and smiles apologetically.

"Oh, I'm sorry ma'am. I forgot to bring your wine, didn't I? Riesling, right?"

"That's right." Natalie replies, resenting the *ma'am* in her apology.

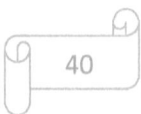

Devin lifts his eyes from the menu. "Riesling, huh? Good choice."

"Yeah. Normally I can't afford it, but," she grins, "hey, I figure, if I'm going to be stuck waiting on you for over an hour I might as well take the chance to enjoy the finer things. Always take the opportunities presented, right?"

"My sentiments exactly."

Devin gazes into Natalie's intense brown eyes. There is a perceptive focus there, a sharp penetrating keenness, and he wonders if it is this ability that has made her a good journalist or if journalism is what brought it forth. The life in her eyes only adds to her classical beauty. She's stunning actually, with her high cheek bones, full lips, and long black hair flowing over her shoulders.

Natalie isn't the only one being studied and as she takes in Devin she realizes that his pictures don't do him justice. His presence is as much a part of his allure as his tall, dark, and handsome build. Not to mention, she's always had a thing for dreadlocks and judging from that coy smile on their waitress' face, Natalie assumes his employee's like them too.

"Give me the chicken breast and saffron rice," Devin orders, "but tell Waldé to add that Moroccan marinade to the chicken for me, alright?"

"Yes sir. And you, ma'am?"

"Huh?" Natalie sputters. She had gotten lost in the performer's set. "No, I'm fine. Well, maybe another Sunset. Light grapefruit juice, please."

The waitress scribbles down their orders.

Devin looks across at Natalie. "You're not one of those 'salad only' girls are you?"

She smirks. "You're not one of those guys that care, are you?"

The waitress chuckles. "Is that all?" They both nod. "Okay then. Be right back."

She scribbles something down and heads to the kitchen. Natalie watches her hips sway as she crosses the room. "She told me she'd be right back too and I still haven't gotten that bottle of wine."

She turns back to face Devin and finds him smiling for no apparent reason. It's surprisingly irritating. "So," she says, hoping to knock that smirk off his face, "do you make a habit of showing up to your engagements over an hour late or should I feel special?"

"Well, I apologize for keeping you waiting so--"

"So what happened?" She interrupts. "Did a bus full of Knicks' cheerleaders get stranded on the road and you felt it was your duty as a gentleman to help them?"

Devin feigns insult. "You know, Ms. Washington, I agreed to do this interview to prove that, contrary to public opinion, I do have some degree of class. And frankly, as a fan of your work I can't believe that you, as an objective reporter, would ever assume something like that. You should know better than others that things are rarely what they appear to be."

Regretting her words, Natalie takes a sip of her drink. "I'm... I'm sorry, you know. You're right. I shouldn't have judged you so--"

He smirks. "Right. They were Lakers girls!"

"Oh, right." She lets out a brief chuckle. It's a half-hearted mix of amusement and disappointment given for his ego's sake. "Yeah, you got me. Very funny."

"But, no, seriously." He says. "I was at my apartment, preparing for this new stunt I'm planning. I have this custom winged suit. You know, the ones that make you look like a flying squirrel. I wanted to take off from the Statue of Liberty on the Fourth of July but the suit wasn't done in time. Now I'm thinking of flying over the pyramids of Giza. But anyway, so, I was doing some planning when I got caught up in a web conference I couldn't cut short. I mean, I tried to get here on time but--"

"Stop. Just stop right there." She says, unable to let this farce go on any longer. "I mean come on. You want me to believe that you, Devin King, multi- millionaire, globe-trotting, playboy businessman, couldn't get out of a Skype chat? Who, short of the President, has that kind of clout? Maybe that's who I need to be interviewing."

Devin grins. "Well, my mother is as interesting as she is demanding." He says. "She insisted that we talk before she started dinner. She just got back from Iraq a few months ago and has been trying to get me to come visit ever since. I've just been so busy, you know."

"Oh, well." She's finds herself at a loss for words, once again regretting her prejudgment. Natalie was sure that Devin was standing her up for some woman but she never thought that woman would be his mother. Fortunately their waitress returns just in time to spare her any further embarrassment.

Smiling, the waitress hands Devin a small piece of paper. "This is from that table over there." She nods in the direction of a table across the room where two young women are waving at Devin. "The one in the green dress. She asked me to give that to you."

"Thank you." Devin says and nods to the young ladies. Grinning, he turns back to Natalie. "Sorry about that. Some--"

"No need to apologize." Natalie tells him, smirking as she watches Devin tuck the note into his pocket. She allows her eyes to follow the slender waitress across the room for a while before turning back to Devin. "So, friends or fans?"

"Never seen them before."

"Oh." She takes a sip of her drink and does her best to steal a peek at the young ladies. *They are attractive,* she thinks*, especially the one in the green dress. And it's hugging her body just right.*

"So should I open the wine?" Devin asks.

Natalie declines. "I think I may have had too much already." She checks the time while Devin pours them each a glass. "How about we just start this interview? It's getting late and you had another engagement, right?"

"I hope you don't mind." He says, handing her a glass. "I mean... you have to take the opportunities presented, right?" He takes a sip. "But, yeah, we can start."

A sultry soul singer steps onto the stage. Natalie fishes her tape recorder from her purse, along with her notepad, and Minnie— her good-luck pen.

"Ready?" She asks.

Devin grins at her set-up. "You got a little retro thing going on here, huh?"

She chuckles. "Yeah, guess so. Let's get going."

"Okay." He nods. "You ready?"

The singer continues to serenade the crowd. Natalie turns on her tape recorder and captures a bit of the woman's song.

"Yeah, I'm ready. I was ready an hour ago."

Their interview is over before Devin can finish his dinner.

"Wish I could stay," he says, dipping a piece of chicken into the marinade, "and give you that in- depth piece you were looking for."

Natalie shrugs. "What could be more in- depth than your

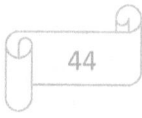

full name and birthday? You know what I could do with that?"

"Yeah." He grins. "Get me a cake."

She laughs a little harder than she intended to. "Yeah, and that's about it."

"So, look." Devin says, pulling his dreadlocks back into a ponytail. "I have an idea. There's this food and wine festival in St. Croix I hit every year. It's actually where I'm heading now. Why don't you just come with me and we can finish this interview there?"

Natalie gives the appearance of considering his offer but only for his ego's sake. A free trip to St. Croix sounds great, but being another notch on one of Devin King's designer belts—

Just might be fun, the Sunsets chime in.

"Sorry, but I don't think that that'll be very professional on my part. Imagine what people will say. The two of us are seen lying around the beach together and then I publish a story about you with information you've never told anyone. My credibility would be shot. It'd look like I sleep with men for exclusives."

Devin's face is a mask of disappointment and amusement. He starts to protest but Natalie stops him. "I have an idea, though, and it could help both of us. How about I call your publicist and you grant me the exclusive, no-stone-unturned interview that this was supposed to be? And then we both pray that your mother doesn't decide to call."

He smirks. "Counteroffer: I give you your no-restrictions piece and you give me a weekend in St. Croix? Relationships are all about compromise, you know?"

"This isn't a relationship, Mr. King."

"Not yet, Ms. Washington."

Devin's smile is as intoxicating as the two Sunsets and glass of wine coursing through Natalie's bloodstream. Mixing his charms with such strong spirits is not the best idea she's had tonight. Here she is, on the verge of getting the biggest scoop of her career to date (Devin King never talks about his family in interviews) and all she has to do is to entertain a rich, handsome, and charismatic young man who obviously wants to give her multiple orgasms on a beach in St. Croix.

Do it stupid, this time it's the Riesling shouting at her. *Do it before it's too late.*

"I can't." She tells them—Devin and the Riesling. "I'll be in touch with your publicist though."

Devin just watches her for a moment. It's not often that he's turned down by a woman.

"Well okay." He says, rising from his chair. "If you're sure then."

"I'm sure." She says, also beginning to rise.

Watching her, all Devin can think is *Wow.* Her dress is like a second skin, accenting every twist and turn of her perfect frame as she stands. She tugs on the bottom, straightening out the fabric, and Devin does everything in his power to keep his jaw from smacking the floor.

"Umm... uhh..." He stammers, still staring. "Are you sure you're sure? I'd really love to take you out. I feel something between us."

She smiles at that. "Yeah, me too. Soft music, white wine, and too much gin."

"Well, can I at least get a good-bye hug?"

She glances around the lounge. The last thing she needs is to be on the front-page of some tabloid. She can see the headline now: D. KING GETS SCOOP OF SEXY REPORTER. Fortunately,

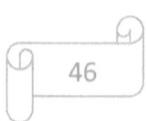

46

no one seems to be paying the two of them much attention. Well, except those two women that sent over that note.

"Yeah, sure. I guess. Why not?"

The two of them step out from behind their table and share a sensual embrace. Natalie holds on a little longer, and squeezes Devin a little tighter, than she intended to but his warm hands feel too good on the skin for her to pull away. She feels his hands sliding upward, from the small of her back to the nape of her neck, and closes her eyes. She can't be sure if it is the alcohol or the—

"Hey!" She shouts, jerking away from him. "What're you--"

She stops and stares at Devin. He's standing in front of her with the stupidest, most childish, grin that she's ever seen on a grown man.

"What?" He asks, holding the tag of her dress up for inspection. "This thing has been annoying me all night. Guess you forgot to take it off, right?"

"Uhh...yeah." She lies. "Yeah. I forgot. Thank you."

He looks at her quizzically then glances down at the price on the tag. *$1,700, huh.*

"Yeah, you're welcome." He says, slightly dismayed. "I guess this is goodnight then. I mean, if you're sure you're sure you're sure."

He takes out his wallet and lays two thousand dollars on the table. Natalie isn't sure if the money is for the bill or her dress and she's too embarrassed to ask. She can only imagine how much a bottle of vintage Riesling costs.

Devin turns to leave but Natalie stops him. "Wait." She says. "We have a few more minutes left, don't we? Tell me more about Stacey and that tattoo on your arm."

Persistence, he thinks. *I like that.* "Okay." Devin smirks. "I'll tell you this: Stacey was my best friend and this tattoo," he glances down at the Sanskrit symbols carved into his arm, "this was Stacey's idea. He was a great dude and if he was here," he flashes that intoxicating grin of his, "Stacey would want you to come to St. Croix with me."

Smiling, she shakes her head. "Then Stacey would be a disappointed man tonight."

"He wouldn't be the only one."

"Goodbye, Mr. King."

"Good evening, Ms. Washington."

Devin walks off and Natalie retakes her seat. She flags down a waitress, orders another Sunset, and slips her feet out of her heels.

"Hey." She calls to the waitress. "How much is the bill tonight?" She scoops up the stack of hundreds. "Mr. King left this to pay, I think."

The waitress appears confused. "No, ma'am. Mr. King keeps a tab here. I mean, he owns the place. He never pays in cash. Just leaves a tip."

"Oh." Natalie says, suppressing a smile. "That was my mistake." She peels a bill from the stack, sets it on the table, and looks around for Devin. Her eyes find him standing by the door entertaining a few customers.

"Will that be all, ma'am?" The waitress asks.

"Uh-huh." She nods, wondering why in the world this young woman keeps calling her ma'am. Natalie's not even thirty years old.

The waitress scoops up the hundred dollar bill, takes the check, scribbles something down and walks off.

Natalie still has her eyes on Devin and the longer she watches him the more she's tempted to take him up on his offer.

Just leave already. She tries to will him through the doors but it's to no avail. That rugged young guitarist walks up, followed by a young lady in a very short, very tight, green dress. Green-Dress Girl steps in front of the guitarist and starts shamelessly flirting with Devin, running her hands over his chest and arms while whispering softly into his ear.

"You liked that, huh?" Natalie says, watching Devin smile and nod in response.

The waitress returns. "Here's your Sunset, ma'am."

Natalie takes the drink without even looking up. She's too focused on Devin and this girl in green.

He's probably going to take her to St. Croix with him and I bet she'll show her appreciation all weekend long. Fuck that!

In one swift motion, Natalie throws back her drink and slides her chair away from the table. In the years that pass, when she tells this story she'll say that she doesn't remember standing up or crossing the room. She'll swear that it isn't until she's standing in front of Devin that she becomes aware of what's happening. But, as she'll say, by then it was too late. The sun had set on her chance to resist. And now she, Devin and the young lady are heading out of Cafe de la Rogue's stained glass doors and towards the backseat of his limousine.

The young woman gets a free trip to St. Croix and, she hopes, a new wardrobe.

Natalie gets her exclusive interview and, she prays, nothing else.

And Devin, well, Devin gets Natalie and Amber. Or was it Angel? He can't remember Green- Dress Girl's name.

CHAPTER THREE

P alm trees, live bands, exotic women and delicious food; the St. Croix Food & Wine Festival is Devin King's type of fun.

Last night he, Natalie and Angel partied beneath Christenad's red sky until they could no longer stand. It is a miracle that he is up this morning, yet along jogging down the beach.

The Caribbean, with its beautiful landscape and rich history, has captivated Devin's heart ever since he was a child. While at boarding school, he and Stacey would spend hours surfing the web, engrossed by the glorious tales of Henri Christophe and Toussaint L' Overture. They would stay up all night immersed in the Caribbean's electric blue waters, cloudless skies, and dense rainforests. They would imagine themselves as outlaws on horseback, living off the land, surviving on the banana and mango trees, sunflowers and pineapples; sleeping beside the bright yellow Ginger Thomas' and bougainvillea bushes; seeking the shade of papaya and dragon-fruit trees to escape the sweltering mid- day sun.

Now, many years later, Devin has fulfilled all these dreams and more—not as an outlaw—but as a wealthy businessman driven by the loss of his best friend. This is what really brings him back to Christenad every year. And, though he's never said this aloud, it is the real reason for his early morning jogs down the beach, why so many of his stunts have been performed in the Caribbean, and the reason that he rarely visits his parents: being in the area brings Stacey back to life.

He quickens his pace as the last leg of his jog approaches.

This is where it counts. Breaking into a sprint he wills himself to run faster and dig harder. With each long stride the warm sand splatters the bottom of his old shorts. He digs harder still, forcing himself to be better than he was before. A fire spreads through his lungs as his chest stretches to its limit. His legs are like dead logs being drug down the beach but he won't stop. He can't stop. He has to be better. He *must* be better.

The chime of his watch gives him permission to slow down. He checks the time: two miles in six minutes and forty-eight seconds.

Could be better.

Gazing out at the teal waters of the Caribbean Sea, Devin drinks in the cool morning air. It is a beautiful day. The faint squawk of birds floats on the breeze. He takes a deep breath and the smell of sea and salt fills his nose. The sea and sky melt into the horizon, creating a crystal blue canopy that stretches as far as the eyes can see and, like a masterful painter, the sun's rise splashes its golden streaks of orange and pinks onto this aqua-colored canvas.

His thoughts drift to lost times; to another era when he and Stacey would spend summers hiking through the Peninsula's dense hills, climbing the tall *cigua blanca* trees, and swimming at the bottom of their secret waterfall.

He sits down and crosses his legs. How long has it been since he's meditated—weeks, maybe months? He chuckles at his self-delusion. It's been ten years since he has actually tried to meditate, to still his mind and transcend the bounds of his external consciousness, and he knows it. It has been ten years since his mind was the sanctum that he worked so hard to make it.

Ever since Stacey was murdered.

He closes his eyes and takes a deep breath. A bittersweet

slideshow starts to play before his mind's eye: Stacey, tall and lanky in his old school uniform; Stacey dressed up like Harry Potter at a Halloween party sophomore year; Stacey's lifeless eyes staring blankly out of his driver-side window; Stacey's sun- tanned face slumped against the steering column; Stacey's auburn hair caked with blood.

Devin's eyes shoot open. *Another failed attempt.*

He checks his watch again. It's been about an hour since he left the suite. The girls should be awake by now.

Grinning, he rises to his feet and stretches. *Well,* he thinks, picturing the naked bodies of the two women he left lying in his bed, *guess it isn't so bad. Right bro?*

He stares up at the sky and shouts to the heavens. "Bro! If you can hear me man! You missed out on one helluva night, Stace! Another one for the history books!"

Humpback whale watching on the coast of the Dominican Republic (Brittany); the Famous Pink Sand Beach on Harbor Island (April); hiking through the jungle hills of Tobago (Heather); scaling Mount Catherine in Grenada (Angie); skinny-dipping at the bottom of El Salto de Limon (Jasmine and Ashley); hang-gliding from the top of La Citadelle Laferriére (couldn't find a woman who wasn't chicken)—

"So many good times, bro. And you would've loved them all."

He stares out at the calm clear waters and wonders what stirs below the surface. Nothing is ever what it appears to be and Devin knows this more than most. He bends down to adjust his shoe and with the rhythmic crash of the waves setting his pace, memories marking the distance, and childhood dreams laying the course, Devin takes off on another jog down memory lane.

The penthouse floor of Christenad's seven- story Waldorf Hotel is a paradise unto itself. For six- figures a month the owner receives a fully furnished three bedroom suite, private gym, access to the hotel's helipad, and all the luxuries of a five-star hotel service, including a very discreet housekeeping staff. Devin makes sure to tip his maids well. He can only imagine the things they have had to clean up after his wild parties and, with the hot tub so close to the master bedroom, there have been many mop-filled mornings. And now, as a naked woman roams about the master bedroom, dumping drawers and flinging clothes through the air, she is guaranteeing that Devin's three women team of housekeepers finally gets to take that trip to Vegas they've been planning all year.

"I can't find any towels!" Angel yells, ransacking Devin's dresser. A tornado of t-shirts, shorts, and underwear fly through the air. Wet and frustrated, she abandons the dresser and wanders around aimlessly.

All this money and no towels, she thinks. "This shit is stupid. You know what?" She turns toward the bathroom. "Fuck it!"

"What?" Natalie calls out. She can barely hear Angel over the shower's spray but she sounds mad. Grinning, Natalie's turns off the water and steps out of the shower.

"What'd you say? Find any towels yet?"

"Nope!" Angel yells back. "I'm just going to use the sheet!"

The bedsheet. Natalie can't believe it. *Is she really that dumb?* Shaking her head, she leaves the bathroom to stop Angel but it's too late. By the time she gets to the bedroom Angel already has the bed sheet wrapped around her and is posing in front of the mirror like— *What, Devin's bride?*

All Natalie can do is laugh.

"What?" Angel asks, looking back over her shoulder. "Don't I look beautiful?"

Natalie does her best to compose herself but she can't stop chuckling. "Umm... honey, did you forget what we just did on top of those sheets? Not to mention last night. That is so disgusting." She shakes her head again. "In more ways than one."

Angel's skin starts to crawl and she drops the sheet as fast as her cheating boyfriend. "Yuck! Yuck! Yuck!" She shrieks, swiping at her skin in an irrational fit of cleansing.

Natalie continues to chuckle as she watches Angel. When she's finally had enough Natalie points out that Angel can always just take another shower. Angel's eyes dance with delight.

"With you?" She asks.

Natalie smirks, taking in Angel's amber colored flesh and soft curves. Lust fills her mind. Wearing nothing but a coy smile, she takes Angel's hand and guides her to Devin's king-sized bed. Last night she blamed her actions on the intoxicating aura Devin had created and the copious amounts of wine she had ingested but today she doesn't have that luxury. The simple truth is that she wants this and she has for a while. All of her long suppressed desires, now unbridled and allowed to run wild, are not going to be so easily tamed again.

With Angel lying on her back Natalie places teasing kisses on the inside of her thighs. Her every movement is an attempt to mimic her first female lover and the things she would do to bring her to euphoria. That was back in college; almost ten years ago now. Natalie hadn't been with another woman until now. Her career wouldn't allow it.

The bedroom door opens and Devin steps in. He grins at the sight before him. "Am I interrupting something?"

Both women turn their attention to Devin and his heaving chest. Natalie can't help but stare at the tall muscular frame glistening with beads of sweat and specks of sand. He's like a brown Adonis, she thinks, and she wants to be his Venus. Eyeing him lustfully, she climbs out of the bed and approaches him slowly.

"We were about to take a shower." She says, unbuttoning his shorts. "Looks like you need one too."

He looks from Natalie to Angel and then to the bed sheet lying in front of the mirror. "What'd I miss?"

Angel smirks playfully. "Oh, that. Yeah, I couldn't find any towels."

Devin looks around at the mess that his suite has become and shrugs. "Yeah, guess that makes sense."

Natalie unzips his shorts and pulls them down to his ankles. He's raised a monument in their honor and as Devin steps out of the shorts her eyes stay focused on the tribute.

"Come on." She says, taking his hand. "I need you to get my back."

"Hold on." Angel says, following behind them. "What about the towels? Where are they?"

Devin smirks. "There aren't any. This is a no towel area. That's what the balcony's for. Air-dry only."

A ringing telephone demands attention. It doesn't matter whose phone it is or what is going on when the ringer sounds. It is only a matter of time before someone asks, *'You going to get that?'*

So, try as he may, Devin can no longer ignore the ringing coming from his bedroom. Despite Natalie and Angel's begging him to stay, his mind just won't stop asking that infamous question. He has business to handle, it seems. *Whoever it is and whatever they want, it must be important for them to have called the hotel.* He can count on one hand the number of people that know he's here.

"Be right back." He says, forcing himself to leave the steamy scene. "Feel free to continue without me. Just don't finish."

Bypassing his bathrobe, he jogs across the room and snatches the phone from the receiver.

"Yo, it's Devin. Make it quick. I'm kind of in the middle of something right now." He grins. "Actually two somethings."

The man on the other end is a detective for the Peninsula Police Department.

Devin's grin suddenly turns sullen. An unscheduled call from the police is never good and his euphoria fades as fast as his erection. There aren't many people turning in wallets or bags of money these days. He listens intently. When the detective finally stops speaking "What?" is all he can manage to say.

"Sir," the detective starts, hating this part of the job, "it's your parents. They've been murdered."

"What?! No, you're wrong. I just talked to my mom last night. How can she be dead? You must've made a mistake."

The detective assures Devin that the two bodies that they have found belong to Doctors Derrick and Jacqueline King. He offers a few consoling words but they fall on deaf ears. Devin has stopped listening. All he can hear is his heart pounding in his chest.

"Who is this!?" He erupts. "You're no cop! What?! This some fuckin' joke?! Huh!? You think this shit is funny?! I'll fuckin' kill you, you hear me!? I'll fuckin' kill you!"

Devin's shouting draws Natalie and Angel from the shower. Naked, they peek from behind the bathroom door, watching him scream into the phone. Natalie steps out cautiously and studies the scene. Devin is pacing back and forth with his jaw clenched tightly as he listens. She can't really piece together what is happening but she's sure that someone is dead. *By the way he's reacting it must be someone close,* she thinks. Stacey comes to mind and she wonders if he is somehow connected to this.

Devin walks to the balcony doors and stares out at the ocean. Tears roll like waves down his face. "Dead." He mumbles. "They can't be. I just talked to them yesterday." He stops, listening. "Okay." He says. "Yeah. Okay. I'm on my way now. Yeah. Alright. See you then."

Natalie continues to watch him. He's as still as a statue and staring blankly ahead. *What's he thinking,* she wonders. *Something in her says to go and comfort him but they just met last night. Do I really want to get that intimate?*

"Fuck!" Devin erupts. "Fuck! Fuck! Fuck!" He throws the phone across the room and it crashes into the wall, smashing into pieces. He grabs his hair and collapses, just as broken as the phone.

Natalie inches forward. "Come on." She looks back to Angel. "He's crying. I think his parent's died or something."

Angel backs away. "Uh-uh. You see him just snap like that? Maybe he just needs to be alone right now."

Natalie can't believe her. "Really? You're just going to hide in here while he sits out there crying? Seriously?"

Angel shrugs and Natalie shakes her head, disgusted. "Fine." She says. "You do that."

A soft hand touches Devin's shoulder. He looks up and sees Natalie standing beside him, grinning uncomfortably.

"Everything okay?" She asks.

Devin forces a grin. "This off the record?"

Natalie returns the smile and takes a seat beside him. "Honey, after the last 12 hours, everything's off the record."

"Hey." Angel cuts in and the two of them look toward her. She is wearing her bra and panties now and cradling a bunch of clothes. "This just really doesn't feel like a naked moment, you know." She smirks playfully. "Here."

While the three of them get dressed, Devin explains that he has some things to deal with back home and has to cut their weekend short.

"The police say they tried to call me earlier." He continues, bent over to tie his shoes. "Guess I had left my phone here when I went running. My sister's on the way to the house now. I'm meeting her there."

Fixing her hair in the bathroom mirror, Natalie raises a brow. "Didn't know you had a sister. Older or younger?"

Devin ignores her. He is definitely not in the mood for an interview. He goes and takes a seat on the bed and waits for the girls to finish up. Sitting there, he thinks about some of his happiest moments with his parents: the day he received his black belt, high school graduation, getting his M.A. in Business—his parents were always there, cheering him on from the front row. He thinks of all the holiday dinners, birthday parties, and family vacations they had when he was little.

And now Mom you'll never get to meet my wife and Dad you'll never get to meet your grandchildren. Wonder if—

"I'm ready." Angel announces, stepping out of the bathroom in a tight skirt and revealing top.

Natalie follows behind her, rolling her eyes. "Are you ready, Devin?" She reaches out her hand and helps him up. He doesn't respond and the three of them head to the door in silence.

"Hold on." He says, stopping at the threshold. "Well, Angel, you can go on ahead. I have a car waiting downstairs." He turns to

Natalie. "I need to talk to you."

Angel gives Devin a soft kiss and walks out the doors. Just as soon as she is out of eyesight, Natalie starts. "Okay, look. I didn't want to say anything in front of Miss Apathy and all but you don't have to have me sign anything. Maybe her, but I understand. It's all off the record. You don't have to worry about me posting anything on social media and none of this will be part of the interview. I know we were—"

Devin smiles. "Stop. Stop. There's no need for pretenses, okay. Look, you can come with me. I mean, as long as you don't feel too...uhh...*compromised.* I guess, I mean, everybody's going to tell a story of what happened and who my parents were, you know? It'll probably be all over the news tonight. But, you, well you're good at capturing the truth of a person, you know. So, I'm inviting you. If you want the '*official*' story, it's yours. I mean, if you want it."

This was the last thing Natalie had expected. She was sure that he was going to pull out a non- disclosure agreement, a pen, and a notary stamp. She places a soft kiss on his lips. "Thank you." She says, fighting back her smile. Despite the sudden pressure that she feels she does her best not to dwell on the future, her career and what this story can do for them both. She can't. Not now. It just feels too selfish.

"I promise I'll do my best."

Devin nods and she kisses him again. "Come on." He says. "Let's go. The car's waiting."

Devin takes Natalie's hand and, like Adam taking the fruit from Eve, is lead into a world of deception, pain, and mystery.

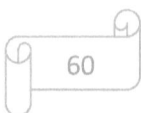

CHAPTER FOUR

At the northernmost tip of the Dominican Republic rests the Samaná Peninsula, a tiny strip of land ten miles wide from shore to shore.

It is here, between lush-filled rainforests and coconut- lined beaches that Devin's childhood home sits. Known as "The King's Castle," their two-story mansion sits high above its neighbors on a mirador- like plateau bordered by the ocean on two sides. It is the crowning jewel of the Peninsula.

Devin takes a deep breath as he steers the car into the driveway. This driveway, having once doubled as a basketball court and roller hockey rink, now greets him with squad cars, flashing lights, and crime scene vans. The doors of the Lamborghini swing up and Devin takes another deep breath.

How long has it been, he thinks, stepping out of the comfort of the car and into the madness that has now become his life. *Could it really be five years?*

Standing beside him, Natalie slides her arm around his waist and pulls in closer. Devin glances at her, wondering who that squeeze was meant to comfort—him or her. Two uniformed patrol officers are working crowd control at the entrance to the grounds.

"Who are all these people?" Natalie asks.

Devin looks around at the faces in the crowd. He doesn't expect to recognize as many as he does but the Peninsula is not a place with a high turnover rate. "Well, my parents were very active here. They did a lot of stuff for the Peninsula and the Caribbean in general. These people, they're humble, respectable folk. They're probably just here to show their love and pay their respects."

"Oh." Natalie has never seen such an outpouring for people who weren't celebrities. There are even a few small shrines and memorials erected along the gate. One of the patrol officers approaches them and asks for identification. Natalie is reaching for her wallet when his partner recognizes Devin.

"It's okay." The officer tells her and then turns to Devin. "You are supposed to meet with Detective Clarkson. He's waiting inside."

Devin nods and continues up the driveway. Natalie walks beside him as they pass the crime scene technicians and all their curious glances. She can't stop looking back at the crowd.

"Your parents were really loved here, huh?"

Devin stops abruptly. "Look at all this. There's never been this many people at the house before."

Squad cars and lab vans are packed on the lawn; police officers are running in and out of the house; and people are coming and going everywhere he turns.

"Mom would kirk if she saw all this. All these people running around, scuffing up her floors." He grins, picturing him and Samantha racing through the house with Saka yelling warnings about scuffing Jackie's floors.

"Floors?" Natalie asks. *His parent's just died and he's worried about the floors.*

"Yeah. My mom redid them herself. The whole house. Back when we first moved in. I remember there was this big fire."

"A fire. Oh my God, was anyone hurt?"

Devin smirks. "No, no. Mom started the fire. She burned all

the old floorboards in this big bonfire."

"Really? Why? Why not just throw them out? Or recycle? She sounds like the type to recycle."

His smirk grows into a chuckle. "You know you ask a lot of questions."

"Oh. Uhh...sorry. You know, reporter. I just...I guess, well you probably don't feel like talking right now. I'm sorry. I didn't mean to--"

"It's okay." He glances around the yard and a fresh wave of memories crash the shore of his mind. "It's probably good to remember, right? I mean, I was little when we moved here so I don't remember much about all of it, 'cept the fire. It was so big. But when I got older Mom told me the story. Said she'd burned all of the old floors because of the people who originally owned the place."

"Who were they? What did they do?"

"Well, this used to be a plantation back in the 1600s. Part of the Triangular Trade, where the African slaves would get traded for sugar and molasses. But Mom told me that the Caribbean was also where the real tough and unruly slaves would get sent to be indoctrinated and broken. She said there were slave masters and owners who specialized in breaking free strong-willed people and turning them into good slaves. Supposedly, one of them lived here."

Natalie cringes at the thought of what it would take to turn a person into a suitable slave— *whatever that is.*

"Yeah, so Mom said she bought the house because she wanted to own the land where our people had shed their blood. You know, my dad's Haitian. Guess, being an archaeologist, Mom was always big on culture. She used to tell me that I was going to be the perfect fruit of those slaves' labor: a strong, intelligent and free black man. But she said she refused to walk in the slave owner's footsteps and neither would her family. So her, Dad and Saka pulled up all the floors and burned them all in this huge ritual fire thing."

"Wow." Natalie says, wondering if the actual Dr. King was as intimidating as her memory. She takes Devin's hand, regretting the fact that she'll never get to meet her. "Your mother sounds like an amazing woman and wonderful mother. I'm sure she was so proud of the man you've become."

Devin pulls his hand away. "Yeah. I guess."

Elegant cocoteros line the mansion's well- manicured lawns and cast their shade on the driveway below. An especially tall one catches Devin's eye and he walks toward it, leaving Natalie standing alone in the driveway. He runs his hand over the coarse bark and gazes up toward the sweet fruit. Groups of arrow holes pocket the old tree like a scatter chart of times passed.

Mines were deeper, he thinks recalling his and Samantha's archery lessons, *but she was always more accurate.* For extra practice the two of them would hold contests to see who could shoot down the most coconuts and then—after they were done— they would sit in the shade of the trees sharing their spoils. The winner would get the satisfaction of watching the loser climb the tree to retrieve the arrows.

Devin can imagine himself then, tall and skinny, standing barefoot on the lawn, with Samantha beside him, ready to receive the day's lesson. Every lesson would always begin the same: with Saka setting up targets and calling them outside.

"Samantha-child! Devin-sun!" He'd yell and the two of them would come bolting down the stairs and out of the house, with his mother fussing about her floors the entire way.

"You stand there," he would say, always starting with Samantha, "and you, here, Devin-sun."

The two young pupils would obediently take their spots, ready their bows and take aim. Standing before the tree now Devin smiles, remembering one day in particular.

"Now, remember," Saka had said, "the Tao never does anything, but through the Tao all things are done. Do you understand?"

"Yes, sensei!" They shouted in unison.

"Man may join spokes together in a wheel but it is the center hole that makes the wagon move. We may shape clay into a pot, but it is the emptiness inside that holds what we want. A builder may hammer wood for a house but it is the space inside that we live in. We work with being, but non-being is what we use. Do you understand?"

"Yes, Sensei!"

With his hands clasped behind his back and a knowing grin on his face, Saka then moved around his pupils as graceful as a swan on the water. "Devin- sun, tell me, what is being?"

"Yes, sensei." Devin said, his words clipping out with military precision. "Being is the illusion. Non-being is the reality."

"Good, Devin-sun. Now, Samantha-child, what is the reality?"

"Sensei, the reality is the Tao. The no-thing from which all things arise." Samantha quickly responded.

"Hmm." Saka hummed. "Very well then. You two say you know these things to be true?"

"Yes, Sensei!"

"Well." He grinned, and then with a nod of his head and clap of his hands, he stepped out of their way. "Let the Tao be your guide. Take your shots when you are ready."

Devin nodded, drew his bow back as far as he could and took aim. Beside him, Samantha too loaded her bow and locked eyes on the bulls-eye. They took deep breaths and as they emptied their lungs, the bowstrings slipped from their fingers. Their arrows sliced though the air like two ancient missiles.

Devin's arrow slammed into the target just inches outside of the bulls-eye. "Ahh!" He shrieked as a bucket of the coldest water he had ever felt poured down on him from the branch above his head. Samantha looked at him—face balled up and dripping from head to toe—and couldn't stop herself from laughing.

"You forgot the Way." Saka explained, passing Devin the towel tucked into his waist. "All you know is power, Devin-sun. But for every force there is a counter-force. Violence, even well-intentioned, always rebounds on itself. This is why you are wet, Devin-sun."

"So I should not seek power, Sensei?"

"The ordinary man keeps seeking power and so he never has enough. The Master does not try to be powerful and so he is. Mastering things outside of you is only a show of strength, Devin-sun. Mastering yourself is true power."

Humbled, Devin bowed to his teacher's wisdom. "Thank you, Sensei."

Saka then turned to Samantha. "And you, child, why are you laughing? Did you hit your mark?"

"Yes, Sensei." She said, poking her chest out proudly. "I hit the bulls-eye."

"So you did." Saka remarked, walking to her target. Her arrow sticks out of the center of the bulls- eye like the stem of a sunflower; an almost perfect shot. He turned to her and she could

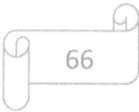

see the disappointment on his face. "But you had the wrong target, child."

"I don't understand, Sensei. I hit the bull's-eye."

"Samantha-child, had you taken the time to see the all, you would have noticed that I had connected your target to this chord." He then pointed to the ground where two strings could be easily seen running from their targets, through the grass and up the tree where two buckets rested on a branch above their head.

"Devin's misuse of power snapped his chord and he received his justice. Had you struck the target on any place besides the center you would have received this." In a stunningly swift motion, Saka unsheathed a knife from his waist and sent it flying at Samantha's target. Striking just outside of the center circle, it released the tension in the chord and tipped over the second bucket; a waterfall of candy rained down on Samantha's head.

"Samantha-child," Saka said, picking up a piece of the candy and popping it into his mouth, "you must remember, success can be just as dangerous as failure. Whether you go up or down the ladder, unless your feet are on the ground, how can you stand firm? Have but do not possess. Act but do not expect."

"But...but," she stammered, "the goal is to hit the bull's-eye and that's what I did."

"Says who, child? The Master has no preconceptions. She allows things to happen and she shapes events as they come. She shapes events because she, herself, is shapeless. Like water she nourishes all."

Samantha bowed to her teacher's wisdom. "Both of you must remember, fixation is death, fluidity is the way to life. We are all born soft and flexible, and when we die we are stiff and hard. The hard and stiff is easily broken, while the soft and flexible lasts through many twists and turns. Be as water, for nothing is as soft and as yielding as water, yet nothing is better at dissolving the hard and stiff."

Saka paused then, knowing that although his young pupils could not truly grasp the depth of his words now they would need them in the years to come. "Observation and perception are two different things." He continued. "Observing is better than perceiving, and had you both observed your surroundings you would have prevailed. It is essential to see both sides without moving the eyes. Today you have forgotten the Tao, therefore you have forgotten the Way, but in the archer there is a sign for the wise. When the archer misses the mark he turns and seeks the reason for failure within himself."

Natalie touches Devin's arm and the warmth of her hand brings him back to the present moment.

"So, is there a story behind this tree, too?" She asks. "You've been staring at it for a while now."

"Naw." He says. "I was just thinking about the good ole days, you know. Come on. Let's go inside."

Devin takes her hand and they continue on up the driveway. An antique '65 Jaguar Roadster glistens in the sunlight. He runs his hand along its silver-bullet finish.

Dad must've had just took her out, he thinks, shocked that his father's baby is uncovered in the sun like this. *He and Saka loved this old convertible.*

Natalie follows Devin up the small flight of stairs and onto the mansion's wide veranda. He looks to her, grinning. "I remember me and Sam would be home from boarding school, and we'd steal some of Dad's socas and sit out here on the steps trading stories from the school year."

"Oh, you and your sister didn't go to school together?"

"Yes and no. It was a joint campus but all the classes and dormitories were girls- or boys-only. The only time we'd really mingle was for dances, school festivals, and sports. Oh, and outside lunch."

All Natalie can say is "Oh." She went to a poorly funded inner-city public school and can't even begin to imagine what boarding school was like. Scenes from *Richie Rich* and *Cruel Intentions* keep coming to mind. "Did you like it?"

His eyes drift off towards the sky. "It was okay, I guess. I was popular, you know. That's what was always funny to me, Sam would say that all I ever talked about was girls and stuff, but, really, all she ever wanted to talk about was books she'd read and projects she'd done. And I think Dad knew we were stealing his socas too."

Natalie isn't sure what to say and so she just smiles. It is obvious that Devin is grieving. She read about the process. There is an order to the stages, she remembers, and denial is one of the early ones. *That is where Devin is now,* she thinks, in denial, continually reliving moments from a past that no longer exists. They have been standing in front of the door for about a minute now and he hasn't even reached for the knob yet. *At least he's stopped talking. That has to be good,* she thinks. *But now he's just staring at the door handle.* He reaches for it and his hand hovers above the knob.

What is he waiting for, she wonders.

As the first and only child of Doctors Derrick and Jacqueline King, Devin was born with a pair of silver shoes to fill. Not only was his mother a descendant of the affluent St. Clairs and a world renowned archaeologist in her own right, Devin's father was the epitome of rags to riches.

Born to an impoverished single mother in a war torn Haiti, Derrick King grew up in circumstances direr than anything his son has yet to face. When, at six years old, a young Derrick lost his mother to an unknown illness he was left alone in the streets with only his ambitions to guide him. After months of stealing and begging he was soon arrested and placed in the custody of a local orphanage. By the age of ten he had managed to get himself smuggled to America. He arrived in Florida with nothing but a small collection of family heirlooms— his mother's most prized possessions—that he had fought hard to keep over the years. In America, now, history repeated itself and he was soon arrested for petty crimes and sent to a rundown Miami orphanage. Despite never being adopted, the gritty Derrick King excelled in his studies and graduated high school in the top of his class. With no money for college he decided to enlist in the army where he became an accomplished scientist. Resisting the temptation to spend his newfound wealth on women, cars and clothes like many of the other poor blacks he knew, he instead invested in the bourgeoning internet industry and other developing technologies. By the time he retired from the service he had laid the foundation for what would become *The King's Gold*, a multi-million dollar venture capital firm with shares in the world's most innovating technological companies.

And what have I done, Devin asks himself. *What have I added to my family's legacy?*

These questions have haunted Devin like a specter of discontent since graduating college. He was supposed to sit on the board of the family business and use their wealth to usher the world into a new era of prosperity. Instead, he's opened a few clubs and became a celebrity thrill-seeker. Staring at the door now, he realizes that he's stalling and he knows why.

Because there's nothing good on the other side of this door; nothing but questions—the police's questions, Saka's questions, Sam's questions.

Where have you been? Why weren't you here? What was so important? What have you been doing?

What are you looking for?

What are you so afraid of?

That's the real question. That's the question that he's been running from since Stacey's death. Maybe before.

No more running, he thinks to himself—a silent vow to face whatever is on the other side of this door. Yet and still, as Devin places his hand on the knob, he cannot stop himself from feeling like he's let everyone down.

And now it's too late.

He grips the doorknob and with a twist of his wrist the handle turns.

He takes a deep breath.

If only it was this easy to turn back time.

CHAPTER FIVE

The atmosphere inside the King's mansion is overwhelming and as Natalie steps through the large bay doors she imagines herself entering the Vatican's private vault.

"Wow." She exclaims, glancing around the spacious foyer. "It's like, a personal museum."

Devin forces a smile. "Yeah, Mom would bring home a story from every dig."

As he looks around at all of the artifacts filling the foyer a fresh wave of nostalgia washes over him. This is his mother's life's work and she had a special connection with every piece here. He can picture him and Sam sitting by the fireplace listening to her tell the amazing legend of whatever and how the world is going to be so much better now that whatever has been recovered. He misses her more with each thought.

Up ahead, across the rotunda, a staircase leads to the second floor. Those are the same steps that he and Sam would race down every day and the same rail that he would slide down when she'd cut in front of him. He can almost hear Saka yelling for them to slow down and his mother screaming about her floors. He looks around at all the crime scene technicians busy at work, taking pictures and bagging things that will probably be of little importance later.

Where the hell are Sam and Saka?

Natalie is still awed by the sheer size of Mrs. King's collection. The foyer's ceilings must be at least twenty feet high, she assumes, and yet, handcrafted shelves cover virtually every inch of the frescoed walls; each shelf holding a plethora of artifacts. The constant cacophony only enhances the mansion's museum-like aura.

It is like opening day for a new exhibit, she thinks, recalling the one and only time she visited the Met. It was one of the worst dates of her life. Well, there was one good thing about it: she got to attend the opening of a new Basquiat showcase. Looking around, she watches the lab techs and police officers scurry about like tourists at the Louvre and hopes to God that they're careful. Natalie can't begin to imagine the value of all of this and she clings tighter to Devin as they move further into the house, afraid to damage something that she can't afford to replace.

They come to the end of the hall and it opens into a large rotunda. The King family crest— two serpents entwined around the letter 'K', accented with a glowing golden crown, and enclosed by a vesica piscis—is emblazoned upon the floor. A marble podium, carved with signs and symbols long forgotten, sits atop the crest like a sacred altar.

Is that a crown? She asks herself, staring at the glass case sitting atop the podium. *How rich is he?* Inside the case, resting on a vermillion pillow sits a sparkling golden crown. Dazzling jewels illuminate the diadem like tiny suns in a morning sky. She thinks to ask Devin about it but stops herself. It might not be good for him to keep dredging up old memories like this.

She gazes at the crown again. The colorful stones glimmer in the light.

Well, she thinks, *he did say...*

"Hey, Devin," she says, pulling his attention from some guy in a white coat, "who's the royalty?" She motions toward the podium. "Is that one of your mother's finds too or is Devin King really some sort of prince?"

"Naw." He says, walking over to the podium.

"It's my Dad's, well, it was my Dad's. When I was a kid he told me it was my grandfather's but I never believed him. My dad grew up poor in Haiti, you know, and never knew his dad." He runs his hands along the glass case. "I never asked him about it after that, you know, to umm... get the truth." *And I guess I'll never know now.* "It might not even be real."

Natalie looks at the glistening jewels in the crown again and is pretty sure that those are real. If they're not they're some damn good forgeries.

She looks back to Devin. "You and your dad didn't talk much?"

Devin shrugs. "He always said that you learn more by listening."

"Yeah." She grins. "God gave us two ears and one mouth, right? At least that's what my mother would tell me whenever I started asking too many questions."

Natalie squeezes Devin's hand and presses her body against his, tempted to rest her head on his shoulder as she thinks of her own parents—alive but still lost to her.

But not for forever, she reminds herself. *I could still go and see them if I wanted. I probably won't but I could. Guess that's what matters.*

"Devin, are you sure that you're alright? I mean, it's one thing to try to be strong and smile through the pain, but you've—"

"Mr. King." A deep accented voice interrupts Natalie. She turns towards its source— a tall sweaty man that reeks of cheap cologne. The man extends his hand to Devin. "Detective James Clarkson. You were looking for me?"

Devin shakes the Detective's meaty hand, taking notice of

the beads of sweat prickling up around the remainder of his fading hairline. *It's probably that hot-ass polyester he's wearing. Looks like something out of an old '70s cop movie.* "You're the one I talked to on the phone?"

Clarkson combs his fingers through his hair and lowers his head a bit, a gesture of condolence that he's all but mastered by now. "Yeah, kid. You know, no matter how many times I see this stuff, it's always sad. Just one of those things you never really get used to, you know?"

Devin shrugs and looks pass Clarkson. The last thing that he needs right now is some grease-ball detective's platitudes or spurious show of sorrow. Devin hasn't trusted a cop since Stacey's murder was ruled a suicide. He looks around at the chaos that has become his parent's home with only one thought coursing through his mind.

Where the hell is Saka?

While Devin scans the room, Detective Clarkson's eyes fixate on the young lady accompanying the kid. He hasn't survived over thirty years on the job by being naïve. It's obvious that the girl on the kid's arm is some sort of journalist. The signs are all there: the way that her inquisitive eyes keep scanning the surroundings, far too alert for a grieving girlfriend; her fingers' incessant strumming against her thigh, as if she is eager to jot something down but can't right now; not to mention the small notepad sticking out of the back pocket of her jeans. Clarkson can't decide what upsets him more: the kid's audacity or her lack of discretion.

Who's this guy think he is, he wonders, still staring at Natalie. *Thinks he can use some no name reporter to intimidate me. Since his parents are high- profile vics and they've got some big money lawyers working for them, guess the whole force's supposed to go above and beyond, huh? And, what, she's going to break the story if we don't?*

His lips curl into a slight grin. *I've seen much worse than this, kid. It'll take a lot more than some nosey reporter to scare ole James. A lot more.*

But we can play the game if you want, he thinks, smiling to Natalie. "And how are you doing, sweetheart? You're a reporter, right? Yeah, I know." He looks from Natalie to Devin and back again. "You here on business or uhh....personal?" He grins again. "Or maybe both. How long you two known each other?"

Whoa, Natalie thinks, *where the hell did that come from?* She recognizes that judgmental tone and she doesn't appreciate it. To insinuate that she would sleep with Devin for this story is disrespectful at the least and sexist at best. *He doesn't know anything about me. This is exactly why I didn't want to come with Devin to St. Croix in the first place.*

She glares at Clarkson, about to tell him in very descriptive terms what he can do and who he can do it with, but Devin intercedes.

"She's with me, Detective. That's all you need to know."

Clarkson gives Natalie a once over and she stares back defiantly. "Yeah, okay, Mr. King." He says. "Then follow me. Both of you."

He leads the two of them across the rotunda and up the stairs, relaying the facts of the case along the way. "The killers—there were two of them, judging by the boot prints we found—looks like they came through an open balcony window. Then they snatched some jewelry, a few paintings, maybe some other stuff, we don't know yet. Then, well...they killed your folks and escaped through the front door. The chef, he says he was out cold on some cough medicine."

The three of them arrive at the top of the stairs and begin to make their way down a congested hallway. Old pictures of family vacations adorn the walls. Devin gazes at them as Clarkson continues.

"Seems like the killers didn't expect your folks to be home. Your parents, they probably heard some noise and came to investigate. Then, well..."

The master bedroom is about fifteen feet up ahead. Clarkson stops in front of two corpse outlines on the floor.

"That's where the chef found the bodies. Right there." He pauses, allowing the kid to soak it in. "You know, you'll have to come and identify them later. Just a technicality, really. You know what, skip it. " He looks to Natalie. "But uhh...that's about it. Story's over."

The outlines of Devin's parent's bodies are screaming so loud that he can hardly hear what Clarkson is saying. He pictures their contorted bodies lying in their blood, dying without him. He doesn't even realize that he's squeezing Natalie's hand.

Natalie watches Devin stare fixedly at the corpse outlines, unsure of what to do or if she should even do anything. She decides that the best thing for her to do right now is just to pay attention to what this detective is saying, since it's obvious that Devin's mind is elsewhere. She squeezes his hand back and looks to Clarkson. "So what do you have?"

Clarkson shoots her a grin and intentionally directs his words towards Devin. "So, yeah, kid. It's pretty open and shut. Just gotta find these guys. They'll be looking to sell this stuff soon so we just wait until they do and that's when we get them. I have my people putting some pressure on well- known fences. Rare stuff like this doesn't go by unnoticed. You know kid, your folks were really liked around here. I remember they were at this charity dinner for the Force. They donated a nice chunk too, kid. We'll keep our best people on top of..."

The Detective's words once again fade from Devin's awareness. He's gazing at a picture of him, Sam, and his mom straddling a young humpback whale. It was taken during their summer volunteering with The Center for the Conservation of Samaná. He'd spent that summer leading whale-watching tour boats with his mother while Sam had helped his father teach tourists about the importance of water-life conservation. In December they had all taken a boat out into the bay to watch the young humpbacks perform their tricks when Devin jumped in and began to swim with them. Samantha soon followed and before long they had befriended a young calf. It was Mrs. King who suggested that they try to get the picture and so she dove in while Dad and Saka stayed on the boat to work the camera.

"...just keep in mind," Clarkson drones on, "that without any real witnesses, well... you know."

Devin looks to Clarkson and nods, not really sure what the hell he's talking about. "Yeah." He says. "I'm sure that you guys will do all you can. Just let me know if there's anything I can do to help."

What? She can't believe that Devin is buying this crap. There is no way that he could have been listening to the Detective. *Witnesses? Wait for the goods to show up? Is he serious? I mean, I know this isn't New York but come on, really?*

Natalie can't hold her tongue any longer. "Detective, this is the King family mansion. Everyone on this peninsula has to know that. So I'm just wondering, why would someone break into this house, with all of these artifacts everywhere-- I mean, they're laid out like knick-knacks--and then only take some jewelry and paintings?

Some of this stuff is worth hundreds of thousands, maybe millions. The motive just doesn't add up. You had to have noticed that too."

Clarkson grits his teeth, wishing that he could just tell her to just shut the hell up and let them do their job but he can't, not with the kid here playing her knight in shining Armor-All tires. He glares at Natalie and his eyebrows forrow together into a bushy V.

Natalie likes the irritation that she sees on Clarkson's face. He should have just told the truth— whatever it is—but since he didn't, now she'll have to find it herself. Grinning smugly, she continues on.

"Not to mention, Detective, this place isn't readily accessible. I mean, this is way too secluded to just be some random home invasion. This job was planned. And, like you said, the people here love this family. You see that crowd outside? Why would a local do this? It would have to be personal. And, if not, then it was obviously a planned job, likely to remove something specific, done by professionals, or at least foreigners. What about the tire tracks or fingerprints? Did your--"

Clarkson's had enough. "Listen lady, our techs are working every angle, okay. They've been checking for any clues that they can find. You think all these people are just here for fun? And you're not a detective. Let us big boys do our jobs. I've seen this type of thing before and until we get some solid evidence there just isn't any reason to be getting your boyfriend's hopes up."

Natalie waits for Devin to respond to this new brand line of BS. Whoever, this Detective Clarkson guy is, Natalie definitely doesn't trust him. Maybe it's his beady eyes and pointy ears; he looks too much like a rat and rats are dirty, sneaky, and filthy vermin.

Trust your gut girl. There's something going on here.

She glares into Clarkson's beady little eyes, daring him to lie again. Clarkson stares right back and a silent standoff ensues. Natalie is the first one to break and she reaches out for Devin's hand, eager to get him to some place away from all of these distracting memories and most importantly away from James Clarkson. That is the only way that she can get Devin to understand that there is more to his parent's murder than what he's being shown and that Clarkson— maybe the entire Force, could be trying to cover it up.

Her hand catches nothing but air and she turns around just in time to see Devin being spirited away by a short man in khakis and a t-shirt. Natalie watches as the two of them stop at the top of the steps and the man whispers something into Devin's ear. Devin nods then they are gone, down the stairs and out of sight.

That's strange, she thinks, and turns back to Clarkson but he too has started off down the hall.

"Hey Detective!" She calls out, jogging to catch up to him. "Wait! I have some more questions for you!"

For twenty-four of Devin's twenty-eight years, Mr. Sukamaya Matsumi has looked after his young master with an affection that far exceeds his duties as family chef. Truth be told, Mr. Matsumi has never simply been the King's chef—the fact that he knows his way around the kitchen was just a pleasant surprise.

Six months from now it will be twenty eight years to the day that Sukamaya's wife would die giving birth to their little Samantha. Heartbroken and distraught, the young warrior forced himself to forge on. *The Master has no possessions,* he would tell himself. *The Tao is all there is and all there is is the Tao.* Being a single father was like facing a new enemy on unfamiliar terrain and for four years he waged his lone war, working as a cook and part-time bouncer in some of Tokyo's seedier nightclubs. Despite the many admirers that approached him, Sukamaya was determined to remain a widower. For him there was no other choice. His duty was to his daughter and his heart was with Rachel. His only solace was the Tao; that, and the brightness of Samantha's smile. All would work out as it must, he knew, though not even Sukamaya would have imagined what was to come.

It was one of those beautifully rare days when he was off of work and Samantha was out of school. She had awoken before him, shaking him with demands that he make one of his special breakfasts. He happily obliged, thinking of Rachel and how much like her mother she was. While they ate Samantha gave Sukamaya a lesson on elephants and other animals that she had learned about in class. She then begged him to take her to the zoo but ended up settling for a trip to the park. At the park Sukamaya watched her play and slide and swing, reveling in her precious innocence. Children hold the key to the Tao, he had thought, watching as she reveled in a world of her own creation. She approached every game, every swing set, and every moment with the same vigor that she gave her lesson on elephants. Her energy seemed boundless. All Sukamaya could do was watch and learn.

After the park they headed back home and, contrary to his earlier beliefs, his daughter did have a limit to her energy. Before he could finish preparing lunch she was asleep on the floor with her thumb in her mouth. Standing there, watching Samantha dream, brought thoughts of Rachel to mind. She looked so much like her mother. Her sun-kissed complexion, the way that her long wavy hair fell gently over her face, the shape of her eyes, and even the two small dimples that pocketed her cheeks every time she smiled— Samantha was certainly her mother's daughter. It seemed all she inherited from his side of the gene pool was a pair of green eyes and a small button nose.

And though Sukamaya would have loved to spend eternity watching Samantha sleep, a deep yawn reminded him that after fifteen straight days at Qi Ching Palace, he too was in need of rest. After drawing the balcony's curtains closed, he dimmed the lights and lit an incense. Sitting cross-legged, with the soothing fragrance of lavender filling the air, Sukamaya began to take slow deep breaths, the exact way that his father had taught him as a boy. He pictured the serene stream that ran through his small childhood village and watched a bird soar higher and higher into a cloudless sky. His shoulders dropped, his body grew relaxed and his mind began to still. Before he knew it Sukamaya had begun to enter the depths of his consciousness.

He continued on this way, slowly losing himself as he journeyed toward the Infinite. He was in the midst of a trance now—beyond the realm of time and space—riding the wind, letting it take him where it willed. Suddenly, an image exploded in his mind: a little boy, no older than Samantha, was strolling down a busy street. Where were his parents, Sukamaya wondered. He intuited the answer just as soon as he thought the question: the boy had snuck off and his parents were searching for him now. But that wasn't all. There was something special about the boy; he was glowing. There was an incandescent light surrounding him, radiating from him; from within him. Sukamaya was viewing this child's Qi, his spirit, his life-force.

Sukamaya continued to watch the scene through his mind's eye. The boy, smiling and carefree, strolled along the sidewalk, slipping in between the towering legs of unconcerned adults. Then, as if someone had suddenly changed the channel, the vision switched to a police car chasing a white pick-up truck. With his sirens blaring, the cop sped behind the truck as it maneuvered through the congested road. There was a jam in traffic up ahead and Sukamaya could not see how the truck would get around it.

But then he did see it. The pick-up wouldn't try to go through the traffic; it would jump the curb and speed down a busy sidewalk, daring the cop car to follow him down a sidewalk full of innocent pedestrians. The same sidewalk where a little glowing boy stood, staring up at the tall buildings.

No! The thought echoed in Sukamaya's mind. Not that little boy with so much light inside him, so much power. He wouldn't allow it happen. But he was as unable to stop it as he was to stop from watching it.

The pick-up jumped the curb and raced down the sidewalk. The little boy turned away from the buildings and stared straight at Sukamaya. The truck sped towards him and—

"No!" Sukamaya's scream shook him from his trance. He sat quietly, breathing deeply, working to bring back the vision but, try as he may, it would not return.

Visibly disturbed, he rose to his feet and pulled open the curtains. The warm light poured in through the large balcony doors.

Why did I see these things, he questioned himself, *and the boy, who was—*

"Saka." Samantha cooed, tugging at her father's pants leg. "Saka, why did you scream?"

Sukamaya smiled then, thinking of his father and how he would react to Samantha calling him Saka. He'd be appalled by her 'disrespectful' Western ways and although Sukamaya was raised 'traditionally,' Rachel had softened his views long ago. Being married to a strong African-American woman, Sukamaya quickly learned the art of compromise, especially in matters as trivial as this. He used to joke that Sun Tzu had to have been dating a woman like Rachel when he wrote the Art of War. Rachel didn't think it was funny.

Samantha reached out to her father, yearning to be lifted up by his strong arms, but as Sukamaya bent down, something on the street caught his attention. Outside, walking down the busy street below—

Could it really be?

"The boy!" He yelled, startling his daughter. "Wait here, child."

Confused, Samantha nodded, and watched her father race out of the door in a hurry. She could hear his steps as he bounded down the stairs. Curious, she walked over to the balcony doors, opened them and stood out on the patio, looking down at all the people as she waited to see her father.

Racing down the steps Sukamaya kicked himself for his lack of awareness. *I should have known,* he thought, taking the stairs three and four at a time. *Why didn't I recognize the street?*

He bursted through the building's door and out onto the sidewalk, looking left and then right as he scanned for the sea of bodies for the boy. *Where are you child?*

There! He finally spotted the child, hidden between the legs of bustling businessmen and scurrying shoppers. The pick-up was nowhere in sight.

His father's admonition echoed in his mind: *Your surroundings, Sukamaya. Heed your surroundings.*

With a deep breath, Sukamaya calmed himself and became aware of all of his senses: the cool breeze pressing gently against his skin; the bitter taste of car exhaust in the air, the pungent mix of gas fumes and the local restaurant's kitchen, and a shrieking sound in the distance, approaching fast-- like an alarm warning of impending danger.

The police siren, he thought. *The truck will be here soon.*

He looked toward the child, knowing he had to do something and quick. Others had also begun to notice the oncoming danger and the crowd was on the verge of quickly becoming a panicked mob. The boy would be trampled, he thought, as people shouted and shoved their way to safety. Sukamaya maintained his focus on the boy as he twisted and turned his way through the chaos. His ears picked up a grumbling sound in the distance, drawing closer, like the guttural growl of a hungry predator anxious to strike. It was the roar of an engine—a truck's engine.

Sukamaya was now within a few feet of the child. He was surprised to see the boy standing calmly, staring at something above him. Sukamaya could not help but follow the boy's eyes and when he did he couldn't believe what he saw. It was Samantha, standing on their balcony, waving down to the little boy.

"Hey Saka!" She said, waving to her father. Just then the boy turned and stared straight into Sukamaya's eyes. It was a look of recognition so startling that it froze Sukamaya for a second. The sound of the truck grew nearer, snapping Sukamaya out of his daze and he and dived forward, scooping the boy into his arms as he rolled to the side. The pick-up came careening by, missing them by inches.

Sukamaya hadn't known his eyes were closed until he opened them and saw the crowd that had formed around him. He was lying on his back with the boy clutched firmly against his chest. A frantic woman was shouting and shoving her way towards him. He rose to his feet, still cradling the child in his arms. The woman finally arrived at the center of the crowd. She was a petite young lady with the same complexion as Rachel. A tall dark-skinned man was with her. Her husband, he thought. Tears were pouring down the young woman's face. Sukamaya knew instinctively that these were the boy's parents. He passed the child to his mother carefully.

"Oh, thank you!" The woman cried out, hugging her son as only a mother could. "Thank you so much for saving my baby!"

Sukamaya nodded humbly and turned to walk off but the couple quickly stopped him; surely there was something that they could do to repay him.

There was nothing, he told them. "I was only doing what I must."

"Well, at least tell us your name?" The woman asked.

Before Sukamaya could respond the little boy looked up at his savior and smiled.

"Saka."

Back inside the King's mansion, Sukamaya ushers Devin through the kitchen and out onto the patio. He needs to speak to Devin in private and there are too many strange ears hovering around the house.

"Desires wither the heart, Devin-sun. You must empty your mind and let your heart be in peace." Sukamaya studies his godson's sullen countenance. "Remember, there is harmony, even in great pain. Trust the Tao, Devin-sun. All is as it should be. I know it hurts to lose them, and I will also miss them very much, but they have completed their work here and so they must step back from it and move on."

Devin walks to the patio railing and gazes out at the vast estate before him, the same estate that he and Samantha would explore as children. Hiking in the serene hills, climbing up the jagged cliffs, racing down the beach and swimming in the distant ocean— every inch of this dazzling demesne was their playground. Sukamaya would tag along at times, turning their adventures into impromptu lessons in the science of martial arts.

"Hey, Saka." Devin says, turning to face his mentor. "You remember when me, you and Sam would go hiking?" He turns back to the railing and gazes out at the dense jungle hills in the distance. "Remember we'd try to get Mom and Dad to come but they'd always be busy working. I used to get so mad at them, you know. It's like they were always too busy. Then you'd come and tell me how it didn't matter if they came because the All is One and the One is All. You'd say that they were with me no matter where I was." He pauses, staring ahead but looking at nothing.

And now they're gone, he thinks. "Now all that anger just seems like wasted time."

"The truth never changes, Devin-sun. They are still with you now."

Devin continues to stare out at the expanse. Sukamaya comes and stands beside him, admiring the beauty of the landscape.

"You know what I remember, Devin-sun. I remember when you and Samantha wanted to go fishing in the creek. You were so anxious to leave that the three of us left without our fishing poles. You remember?"

"Yeah. You wound up sharpening the ends of some branches and we spear-fished. I caught that big sturgeon."

Sukamaya smiles. "Yes, but, before we had caught any fish, do you remember what you said?"

Devin tries to think back to that day but his memory fails him. "I don't." He says, shaking his head. "What did I say?"

Sukamaya grins again. "You said that we could not catch any fish in the small stream. You said that all of the big fish were in the rivers and the oceans, and that our little creek was stupid. You wanted to go further up, into the deeper waters."

Devin remembers now. "Yeah, that part of the creek was so shallow I thought we should go further upstream, Sam did too."

"Or maybe she was just following your lead." He counters. "But, anyway, I did what you two wanted and took you to where the water was above your waist, remember, and we all fished and had a good time. After, I asked you two to cross the stream without swimming, and then we could go home. Neither of you could do it because the water was too high. Because you could not see any good in the low water, I showed it to you. There are times in life that are like that day, Devin-sun."

"I don't understand what you mean, Saka. Times like what?"

"Devin-sun, on the sea of life there are high and low tides, storms and many waves. One must know all they can if they are to navigate this sea well. On that day, Devin-sun, you learned the location of a ford that you could use to cross the stream. The Tao is now your ford. Knowing the location of the fords will make getting across this point in your life much easier, Devin-sun. You must cross at the ford. Peace and harmony, Devin-sun. The natural way for all things. This is the Tao. It is not about fighting or hurting people," Sukamaya grins, "or doing your amazing stunts. That is not the way that I taught you. The Tao is about balance, allowing you to be yourself, to act without acting, to become one with the One. Death is a part of life. Just as the water in the stream filled the creek where it was shallow as well as where it was deep, so must the Tao fill your being, no matter the terrain."

Devin knows that Sukamaya is right. He looks into his

teacher's eyes, longing to set free all that he's trapped inside of himself for so long. There is so much to say; too much to say. The thoughts form faster than his words. He opens his mouth but no sound escapes. He tries again and stutters unintelligibly. The frustration condenses into tears and they rain slowly down his cheeks like drops on a glass window.

Sukamaya places his hand on Devin's shoulder. "There can be times when the weight of one's destiny feels too heavy to bear, Devin-sun. When a man would rather trade in the shoes he was born to fill for a pair of comfortable sandals."

Sukamaya chuckles at his own wit, hoping to coax a laugh or grin from his young friend. "They loved you, Devin-sun." He says, squeezing Devin's shoulder. "No matter what path you chose to walk, as long as you were happy, they were proud. You did not let them down. All they ever wanted was for you to be happy."

Such a simple truth only deepens the guilt that Devin feels. *How could I neglect the only people that truly loved me,* he wonders. *And for what—girls, beaches, hotel rooms? These things don't even really matter.*

These are the questions that he has been running from for too long now. Since Stacey's death Devin has been different and everyone close to him knows it. To most he has appeared more focused and more disciplined but his family knows the truth. Devin became obsessed with Stacey's case. He still believes that his friend was murdered and that he would never have committed suicide as the police claim. Devin wasn't focused; he was haunted. He wasn't disciplined; he simply lost interest in everything other than Stacey's case. When his parent's confronted him about his behavior, Devin felt betrayed, attacked and cornered. He left home then and hasn't set foot back in the house until today.

"Devin-sun, do not allow a few clouds to block your light." Sukamaya grins. "You are too bright."

My light? Devin can't believe what he's hearing. Sukamaya has been calling him Devin-sun since their first time watching The Karate Kid on VHS. Not only was it funny, Sukamaya had said, it was a good reminder of Devin's inner strength, that light that he's always seen within him. That light that is within is as bright as the Sun, he would say, and when that light shines forth it has the power to give life.

"Maybe when I was younger, Saka. But I'm far from being the center of anything now."

Sukamaya continues to smile. "You loved them and they loved you." He grabs Devin by his shoulders and holds him out as if inspecting him for something. "There was never any doubt, okay?" He says, staring Devin square in the eyes. Devin tries to look away and Sukamaya shakes him forcefully. "Okay?" He repeats, shaking him again. "No doubt."

Devin relents. "Okay, Saka, but—"

"No buts!" Before Devin knows what is happening, Sukamaya is lifting his 6'2 205 lbs. frame high into the air and spinning him in circles. Devin can't fight his smile. By the time his feet are back on the ground his mood is as light as Sukamaya just made him look.

"Now!" Sukamaya exclaims, clapping his hands together. "Welcome home, Devin-sun. I have missed you."

Devin smiles. "I have missed you two, Saka."

"No." Sukamaya grins. "You have missed my cooking. Like another young one I know."

Sam, Devin thinks, suddenly realizing that she still hasn't shown her face. *Where the hell is she? She should've been here by now. What's taking so long?*

As if testifying to the harmony of the Tao, Samantha slides open the glass doors and steps out onto the patio. It's been almost ten years since they've last seen each other, since the summer after their high school graduation. He had always found it odd that she would decide attend college in Europe, so far away from everything and everyone she had known, but back then he was too engrossed in his old issues to give it any deep thought.

She hasn't changed much, he thinks, looking at her jeans, t-shirt and ponytail ensemble. Samantha never really fit into any groups back when they were in school. With her pretty face, long legs and modelisque figure, she was never accepted by the nerdy girls; they were always jealous of the attention she received from the popular guys—attention that she never liked. She would rather have her inquisitive green eyes in a book than some boy's face and this fact, coupled with her lack of fashion sense, keep the pretty-girl clique far from her locker.

And now, almost a decade a later, she's still donning her signature look: loose-fitting jeans, t-shirt, and hooded jacket. Her beautiful sorrel complexion is still au natural and her long wavy black hair is pulled up into the same sloppy ponytail she's always worn.

Devin smirks. *Still gorgeous and still a nerd.*

"Devin!" Samantha shrieks, throwing her arms around him in the tightest hug he's felt in years. "Oh my God!"

It feels so good to have Devin in her arms again. All these years and the only times that she's seen him has been on his adrenaline junkie videos. For a brief moment she forgets the horrible circumstances that have brought them back together and loses herself in his strong embrace but when she gazes into his eyes the moment quickly fades.

"I'm so sorry." She whispers in his ear. "You know they were my parents too."

Ever since her and Sukamaya befriended the Kings, Samantha has said that she has three parents: Mr. King is Dad; her father is always, and has always been, her Saka; and Mrs. King is the only mother that she has ever known.

She lets go of Devin and looks to her father.

"Saka, what are we going to do? I mean...now that they're gone. I just sat in the car for twenty minutes, staring at the house, in shock. It's just... I can't believe it. It feels so unreal."

Soft tears fall slowly from her eyes. "Who would want to kill them? It just... they were such good people."

Sukamaya's heart breaks watching his daughter cry but as she rests her head on Devin's shoulder, he knows that she will be alright. Samantha has always been a dynamic soul; the opposing force that Devin needs to achieve his balance, just as he is for her. For all of Devin's bravado, Samantha is humble; for all of her brains, he has brawn. The two of them are like yin and yang, fire and air, earth and water. And if Sukamaya is correct, they will need each other more than ever in the days to come.

Stern and cautious he looks to the only family he has left. "I'll tell you what we are going to do, child. We are going to wait until all of these people leave the house and then we are going to Derrick's study."

"The study?" Samantha asks. "Why? What's in there?"

"Jackie." Sukamaya says, and turns to Devin. "Your mother left us a message."

CHAPTER SIX

Somewhere in the mountains of west Asia there lies a cave.

Inside this cave there lies a beast. Within this beast their lies our future.

This cave was not formed by the weathering of sediment. This is a man-made cavity cut deep into the recess of a mountain, engineered by a group of men who understand the importance of privacy. This is a towering edifice of offices—offices that are only used when secrecy is more valuable than the lives they contain. This is a veritable tree of knowledge, a modern center of research and development, guarded by the flaming swords of science and technology. Complex multi-layered algorithms form an impenetrable firewall, holding at bay all those who would undeservingly eat of its fruit. Such extensive measures protect not only the membership but the safety of all those ignorant to the effects of power.

The beast that dwells in this cave is not barbaric. It is not an ignorant animal driven by passion and desire. This beast stands upright, walks on two legs, and has a brain capable of reason. This beast is not only capable of learning, it can imagine, invent, wonder, and speculate. This beast is the most dangerous of all beasts. This beast has free-will. This beast can *think*.

And think it does, more so than its fellow creatures would ever fathom. It is doing so now. While other members of its specie wander about aimlessly through life, the beast is thinking. While others are going through their day to day motions, driven by feelings and desires they do not understand, easily manipulated and readily coerced, the beast is thinking. Thinking not of his own thoughts, but those passed down by the greatest intellectuals in man's history; men who have held conclaves similar to the one that he has called tonight.

Leaning back against the soft leather of his desk chair, Gustuv Barchulé sits alone in his penthouse office, watching the wall of monitors before him. An all black helicopter approaches the landing pad. It touches down and a group of men in black suits exit.

And now that they are all here.

Gustuv swivels in his chair around and scans his desk. Handcrafted centuries ago, this 6x6 foot work of art is a testament to the power of his station. His eyes focus on the bright red switch attached to the corner of the desk and a chaotic fit of laughter overtakes him.

"Is this how it feels to be Lord of Lords, King of Kings?"His hand moves to the switch. "Is this how it feels to be God?"

Toying with the idea of flipping the switch and triggering a string of explosions powerful enough to level a city, he thinks of the men entering the building now and how easy it would be to rid the world of their foolishness.

"Life or death." He says, taking hold of the switch. "To live or to die?"

A sadistic smirk creases the corners of his mouth. He takes a deep breath and closes his eyes, imagining all the lines of possibility that could extend out from something as simple as flipping a switch: the people that would mourn; the economies that would collapse; and the governments that would fall.

He moves his hand away from the switch and laughs. "The games of children."

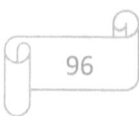

Gustuv rises from his chair, switches off the monitors and then heads for the elevator across the room.

And as a man I have put away childish things.

The doors of the elevator open and he steps inside. Above him a red light glows dimly and as the doors close the elevator is filled with a bloody hue. He stares forward, studying his reflection in the metal's dull shine. What was once a thick rich head of brown locks is now salted with sliver streaks of sagacity. His aging face— once smooth and tan—now looks back at him pale and sun-worn. His decades of hard work and sacrifice have carved deep trenches around the corners of his eyes like riverbeds running from his ocean blue irises. But those eyes, those bright blue portals to his soul, have yet to dim. They stare on with the same intensity they did all those years ago, only now buttressed with an understanding few others can comprehend.

For what I have seen, I have not seen with thine eyes.

The elevator ends its descent and the doors slide open. Before him, at a large rectangular table, sit his twelve compatriots, impatiently awaiting his arrival. He exits the elevator and lifts a hooded black cloak from the rack. Sliding the ceremonial garb around his shoulders he moves to take his seat.

Antique candleholders line the walls of this hidden chamber. Each candle is especially made— employing a formula that only a select few know— and as the flames dance on their wicks unearthly shadows are cast across the faces of all those seated. Gustuv surveys their expressionless mugs.

As the 13th member of their group, Gustuv Barchulé holds the highest rank amongst them. As master and leader he not only sits at the head of their table but at the head of their entire organization and though six hooded men sit on each side of him, none shall ever sit opposite. His position is one earned through decades of experience, study, and devotion to the path.

Though many of you do not agree, do you, he thinks, looking around the table at his so-called brothers. *Jesus had his Judas and I will have mine. Which one of you fools will have the courage to betray me?*

A diamond-edged knife and golden chalice sit on a silver tray in front of him. Beside his chair, a coiled snake stirs at the bottom of a wicker basket. Gustuv reaches inside the basket.

"Brothers!" He calls, his deep voice amplified in the acoustics of the vast chamber. He lifts his arm from the basket and a thick serpent is coiled around his forearm. A thin smile, barely noticeable to most, spreads his lips. With his free hand he takes the knife from the tray and lifts both knife and snake over his head.

"A conclave has been called, brothers, but before we begin, let us come together to commune in the name of our Lord, the one and true living God of this world. Blessed be the blade that maketh one into many."

In one swift motion, Gustuv slashes the blade across the serpent's belly and holds its dripping carcass over the chalice. The warmth of the blood arouses him. He doesn't blink as he watches the serpent's blood flow over his fingers like a dark crimson paint and drip slowly into the chalice. Its acrid odor waters his mouth.

With the chalice now full, he lays the dead serpent on the tray and slices away thin strips of its flesh. His brothers watch him silently; a mercurial mix of envy and awe coursing through their chilled veins.

"Let us now partake of the Father's knowledge and drink of His wisdom." He says and raises the chalice high into the air. "Cherish the cup that turns many to One." He sits the chalice down and passes the tray of flesh to his left, closely studying each of his compatriots as they take their portion. Not one of them is as delighted as he.

With the tray back in front of him, Gustuv takes the remaining strip of flesh in hand and clears his throat.

"Take," he says, speaking in the ritual Greek of their forbearers, "eat, this is the body of Me, for you being given; this do for My remembrance."

The melodic Greek rebounds off the chamber's walls. Gustuv raises his piece of flesh into the air and his brothers follow.

"In remembrance!" They chorus.

Each man sets the strip of flesh on their tongue and silently thank Him for the divine gift of knowledge. Gustuv savors the flesh's soft texture before finally swallowing. He takes the chalice and raises it before the group.

"Take, drink, this is the blood of Me, that of the New Covenant for you being given; this do for My remembrance."

"In remembrance!"

Gustuv takes a sip from the chalice and allows the sour blood to linger on his palate. Relishing in its bitterness he sips again, thanking his Lord for the gift of wisdom, then passes the chalice to the left. Each of his brothers take a sip as the chalice passes before them; all of them— ambassadors, statesmen, billionaires, and the like— thanking the Lord for the precious grace given them.

With the chalice now back in hand, Gustuv smiles. "Gentlemen," he says, using his finger to clean the last drops of blood from the chalice, "I have great news."

While his brothers await his revelation, Gustuv licks the last of the blood from his finger as delighted as a boy cleaning his grandmother's cake spoon. The rest of them look on in amused disgust.

His smile widens. "We have the Book! Our time is drawing near!"

CHAPTER SEVEN

Devin roams the shelves of his father's study, lost in his thoughts.

The sun has finally set, taking with it the mass of mourners, police officers, and forensic workers that had filled the grounds. Natalie had intended on staying and interviewing Samantha and Sukamaya but Devin insisted that she leave. He needed to be with his family, he explained, and after promising that she would still get her story, the two parted with a quick kiss. Now, in the study with Samantha and Sukamaya, Devin absent-mindedly scans his father's shelves. His finger glides along the books' bindings, tracing the words etched into the worn leather—titles and authors as unfamiliar to him as the man that owned them.

"You remember Dad would say: people are just like books?" He asks, speaking to no one in particular. "I remember, one day, I had asked him why he sat in here reading all the time, and that's what he told me. He said, people are just like books, son. They can tell you everything you need to know if you just read their stories."

He drifts from shelf to shelf, looking for nothing but finding everything. All of the old feelings he had stomached as a child are forcing their way up now, spewing forth memories he had tried hard to forget. Samantha and Saka listen as his thoughts flow.

"But how can you read someone if they'll never open up to you? I tried so hard to be just like him. I used to come in here and sit beside him, you know, with one of his books. Imitating him, remember? And he'd just keep on reading. Maybe he'd smile at me once or twice, but that's it. He'd just keep on reading."

Devin takes a book from the bottom shelf and grins. "This is the one I using that day. I remember, Sam, you were somewhere with Mom— probably digging in the dirt or something. Saka, you'd gone off to meditate by the waterfall. It was just me and Dad left in the house."

Leaning against his father's desk he leafs through the book. Underlined sections, scribbled notes, and yellow highlights mark every page.

He lifts his head and looks to the plush reading chair that was like his father's second home. "Dad was sitting there in his chair. Mom had just got it for him then. And he was smoking one of those strong cigars she hated, working on something that looked real important. He was chewing his tongue, you know, so I knew he was concentrating. Anyway, you know, I didn't want to disturb him, just I was so bored. Everybody else was gone. So, I went and pulled this book out, got a highlighter, and sat right there in front of the desk, mimicking him."

He flips the book over in his hands and reads the title. "I was like ten," he chuckles, "taking notes from Signs and Symbols of Primordial Man. Dad just looked at me and grinned. Like he always did, you know, and then went back to working. So that's when I asked him, Dad why are you always reading? I can still remember his words to this day."

As Devin gazes ahead, he sees an image of his father materialize before him. He's sitting in his chair, wearing his favorite navy blue cardigan, smoking one of his cigars, and holding a book open in his lap. He looks just as he did all those years ago. Even the gray streaks in his fuzzy beard are the same. When he takes a pull of the cigar and looks up at his son, Devin can smell the pungent aroma fill the room.

"Son," the specter says, "reading is the most important thing that a man can learn to do. In the past, our ancestors read everything—the sun, the moon, the stars, the Earth. They read all of the signs around them, from the animals to the movements of the clouds. They read each other and they read themselves. And then, son, after all of that reading, they gathered their knowledge together and inscribed it within books. This way the next generation would not have to waste time trying to explain what was already understood, you see? Sadly, though, son, many of these books have been lost or destroyed throughout history. Now, your mother is working very hard to find them but, until she does, we must learn to read like our ancestors did. We must read all of the information around us. So even when I do not have a book, son, I am reading. I read people, I read the signs of the times, and—most importantly, son—I read myself."

Devin can see his father sitting there in his chair as clearly as he can see Samantha and Sukamaya watching him now. He is tempted to go to him, to touch him and hug him one last time, but he knows that the image isn't real. He knows that it was his own voice speaking those words. Grinning, he turns to Samantha.

"And then Dad said something that he had to have stolen from a book or something. It was just too...poetic, for Dad, you know. It was too smooth."

Sukamaya smiles. "Devin-sun, your father loved to read poetry. He would even write poems for your mother. They were very beautiful." He chuckles. "Very *smooth*."

A part of Devin resents the fact that Sukamaya knew his father better than he did but there is another part—a more convincing part—that knows that it is Devin's own fault.

"Yeah, well, maybe he did make it up. I don't know. But this is what he told me. I'll never forget it."

He looks back at the chair, back at his father and those soft brown eyes. Deep crinkles crease their corners as he smiles at his son.

"People are just like books, son. They can tell you everything you need to know if you just read their stories. See, every person is born with a blank page. Now, some people's pages may be decorated, some might be glossy, some might even be recycled, but what matters is that they are all blank in the beginning. And then, as we live, each experience is like a letter. There are only so many different letters but they can be arranged to create any word you can think up. And when those words come together, you get a sentence. Depending on what words are used and their particular arrangement, this sentence can reflect a multitude of experiences or sensations, which create a moment. As we string these individual moments together an overall message starts to appear, a reason for all of these experiences, a meaning for it all. We find ourselves engrossed in the story, anxious to go ahead, believing that we have finally figured something out, but this is only a paragraph. There are many paragraphs inside a chapter and many chapters in each person's story. This is why I tell you to listen more than you talk, son. All reading is not done with your eyes. If you can learn to read your story while it is being written, you can create any ending that you like."

Devin picks up a partially smoked cigar from the ashtray on his father's desk and rolls it between his fingers—back and forth, back and forth—just like he watched his father do a million times before.

Samantha watches him and wonders if Devin will ever realize just how similar to his father he actually is. He is certainly not one to open up and this is probably the most that she has ever heard him talk about his feelings. Even when the two of them speak on the phone, Devin tends to just listen while she rattles on and on about whatever. Despite his fame, he rarely will sit down for an interview and when he does, he always comes off as mysterious and guarded. His power of silence is infamous.

He turns to Samantha. "You know, I've been trying to do that since Stacey died."

"Do what?" She asks.

"Write my own ending, you know. That's why I do all those crazy stunts. When Stace died, that's when I first really like thought about what Dad said, you know. It was like Stace had started trying to write his own story too, just, he started in the middle without any regard for how it could all end. Since then I've made sure to never forget what Dad said."

She nods. "Yeah. Guess we've both been busy writing our own stories, huh? How long's it been since we've seen each other, like this, for more than a passing moment or on Facetime? Like 10 years?" *Ten long years*, she thinks. "And it went by so fast."

Sukamaya gazes at the empty chair and pictures his best friend sitting there, smiling his wide smile as they trade tales from a time before they were husbands and fathers.

"Samantha-child, those are the paragraphs that Derrick spoke of. You two became so caught up in the manifestations and failed to see the mystery. The only way to write your ending is to be perfectly fulfilled, child. And it is only when you have emptied yourself that you are perfectly fulfilled. Detach yourself from things so that you can be one with them."

I've been detached, she thinks, her eyes still fixed on Devin. *I tried that for ten years. I've kept my feelings hidden away for so long. Maybe—*

She looks to her father and then back to Devin. "Umm... Devin..." She hesitates, not sure if this is a line she should cross, especially now. "Umm...I need to talk to you."

"Huh?" Devin blinks, broken from his reverie. Thoughts of Stacey had once again filled his mind. He looks to Samantha. She's fidgeting with her hair, staring down at the ground.

She's nervous, he thinks. "What's up, Sam? What's wrong?"

"No, nothing's...*wrong*, I guess. It's just, umm..."

He smirks. "What? It's Natalie, right? I could tell you didn't like her. But I like her, Sam. Well, at least I think I like her. So, whatever it is that you think you--"

"What?!" She erupts, not sure what upsets her more: the fact that Devin is too blind to see what is right in front of him, that he's so self-centered that he just assumes that she wants to talk about his love life, or that he is so quick to dismiss her feelings (whatever they are) about Natalie.

"You're a jerk, Devin. You know that? And by the way, I do like her. Well, I don't *not* like her. So stop assuming you can just figure me out, okay! You're not that good at reading people yet."

Samantha storms off to the opposite side of the study and feigns interest in a collection of books about the DNA molecule. Sukamaya watches the exchange, amused by it all.

"Samantha-child, remember, fixation leads to folly. You must simply be yourself," he gives her a knowing grin, "and then you will have all that you need." His glance darts to Devin and then back to her and he smiles again.

"But enough talk of things that were and what is to come.

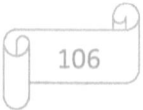

Devin-sun, I must show you the message your mother left behind."

Devin nods, still watching Samantha but she has her face buried in the shelves, refusing to look his way. *She'll be okay,* he thinks. *Sam's hated every girlfriend I've ever had. Every time we talk it's her lecturing me about something. It'd be weird if she didn't find something wrong with Natalie.*

He turns to Sukamaya. "Okay, so, what is it? What does it say?"

Samantha suddenly loses interest in the books and rejoins them by Mr. King's desk. Devin throws a smug grin her way and she rolls her eyes.

"I cannot tell you." Sukamaya says. "I have to show you, Devin-sun."

"What?" Devin doesn't understand. "Why can't you just tell me, Saka? What's going on?"

Sukamaya doesn't respond. Instead, he takes a seat behind Mr. King's desk, reaches under the bottom left drawer, and knocks twice. He looks up at them grinning as if he knows something they don't.

"Saka, what are you doing?" Samantha asks, wondering why her father is behaving so strangely all of a sudden. Could this be some ancient Taoist mourning ritual she hasn't heard of? "Is everything alright?"

"Just wait, child."

The three of them wait quietly but nothing happens. Samantha and Devin exchange confused glances. Neither of them wants to ask Sukamaya if he's lost his mind but they're both thinking it.

"Uhh, Saka," Devin begins, "I thought you were going to give me the message from Mom."

Sukamaya's grin fades. He doesn't understand what's wrong. When he knocked on the bottom of the drawer it was supposed to—

"Ahh!" He says, his grin quickly returning. "I tapped the wrong side." He thumps himself on the right side of his head and looks to his audience. "Sit tight and watch this."

Sukamaya reaches under the desk again and raps twice on the bottom *right* drawer. The three of them sit and wait but nothing happens. Devin and Samantha share another skeptical glance.

"Saka, are you sure--"

The low hum of a motor interrupts Samantha. It's coming from the curtain rod running along the window behind Sukamaya. A slit in the curtain rod opens up and a projection screen descends from it, covering the entire window and darkening the room.

Sukamaya bounces up from the desk chair and struts to the bookshelf running along the right wall. He selects two books from the middle shelf and tilts them forward. A panel in the ceiling slides open and a mini-projector angles down toward the screen.

"Derrick had this installed during one of Jackie's remodeling moments," he explains, "but he never told her about it."

With Devin and Samantha staring and speechless, Sukamaya crosses the study to complete the last part of the process. At the light switch now, he removes the plastic dial from the light dimmer, takes out his keys, and uses one to rotate the metal rod counter-clockwise. After two revolutions there is a slight *click*! and the projector whirs to life. The screen lights up displaying, what looks to be, some sort of surveillance command center.

"Whoa," is all Devin can say. "I knew Dad was into that high-tech stuff but this is crazy. Any more tricks in the house I don't know about. Are there sharks swimming under the kitchen floor or something?"

Sukamaya smirks. "Well, Devin-sun, you know your mother did not like big security systems and she genuinely did not feel that she needed to live afraid. But as a man your father wanted to make sure he kept his family safe. He wanted to use his military contacts to get armed surveillance but that would have only angered, and probably scared, your mother. This was his compromise. There is a silent alarm on the gate that's temporarily deactivated once someone is let in or enters the gate's code. And there is this here. And maybe a few other things we'll discuss later."

Samantha chuckles. "Compromise? Yeah, right. He got a Bat-cave built right under Mom's nose and didn't tell her about it. That's not a compromise." She scoffs. "Dad watched too many Bond movies."

"And that's coming from the engineer." Devin jokes. "You and Dad're both nerds."

She rolls her eyes. "Anyway, Saka. So how does all of this work?"

"Well, there are cameras hidden all around the grounds," he explains, "and they all relay their signal to a central feed that can be accessed and monitored with this screen. Derrick had the cameras set to record only when they detect movement, but they stay on all day, so there is always a live feed."

Sukamaya looks into Devin's eyes and nods toward the screen. "You touch the screen to control it, Devin-sun."

Devin's hesitant. His eyes move from Saka to the control panel but his legs stay planted.

"Go ahead, Devin-sun. Select last night, there, and the camera for this room."

Samantha also notices Devin's tentativeness and urges him on. "Come on, Devin. Don't you want to know what Mom left?"

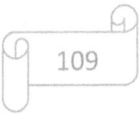

Devin looks to her. *This is too much,* he thinks. *Why can't Saka just tell me what the message says? Why do we have to go through this long drawn out process?*

He looks to the screen again and a wave of apprehension crashes down on him. *He can't tell me what it says because that's not what important.*

Finally understanding what this is all about, Devin looks to Sukamaya one more time and then drags his feet towards the screen. He doesn't feel the texture of the screen as he selects the date, the time, the room.

An image fills the monitor. It's his father, wearing a brown tweed jacket, sitting in his chair with an open folder in his lap and a highlighter in hand. A glass of Scotch sits on the cart beside him next to a box of cigars.

A large arrow appears on the center of the screen.

Devin takes a deep breath and taps the arrow.

It's not what the message says that's important, he knows.

There's a heavy weight in his chest now and it pushes him back towards his father's desk. He leans against it, bracing himself for what's to come.

It's what the message shows.

A thick silence blankets the room as Devin, Samantha, and Sukamaya stare at the screen. A masked man stalks up behind Mr. King and presses a rag over his face until he's out cold. Then, as if bored, the intruder begins roaming about the room, sifting through Mr. King's shelves, books, and drawers. Eventually his curiosity leads him behind Mr. King's desk and Devin grimaces as the man takes a seat and kicks up his feet.

A murderous rage snakes its way up Devin's spine and

enters his heart as he watches the footage. The intruder not only finishes his father's Scotch, he lights a cigar—one of the Cubans that Devin had shipped to him for Father's Day. As Devin watches the flame dance at the end of the lighter his rage turns to venom, poisoning his thoughts with each biting frame.

As painful as they are to watch, each one of the intruder's pompous puffs holds them like prisoners, unable to escape the perversity on screen. They stare on, watching the masked man look pass Mr. King as if he isn't there while he enjoys a smoke. Once he's done with the cigar, he rises from his seat and goes to have some fun. Devin imagines him smiling as he toys with the unconscious King, offering him a drink, blowing smoke in his face and slapping him around. Devin is furious.

This taunting continues until Devin's mother is thrown to the floor by the intruder's partner. Devin's eyes well with tears as he watches his mother being abused, threatened, and manipulated. Furious, he glares down at the carpet, at the very floor his mother crawled across.

I should've been here, he thinks, cursing himself for his neglect.

On screen a book is taken from the safe. The intruders attach silencers to their guns. Mrs. King goes to sit in her husband's lap and kisses him one last time. Samantha takes Devin's hand and lays her head on his shoulder. She's crying now and when the muffled report of two bullets being fired pierces Devin's soul, he squeezes her hand tighter as cold tears rain down his cheeks.

The cigar-smoking assassin carries Mr. King's body off screen. The other killer goes to lift Mrs. King but then he pauses and shrugs his shoulders as if to say 'what the hell'.

"The Elite." The killer says and then hoists Mrs. King's body up over his shoulder. He walks off screen and few seconds of the lifeless study lingers on like the last reel of an old film. The screen eventually goes black and switches back to the command center.

"Motion activated." Devin mumbles. He wipes away his tears and looks down at Samantha, searching for something in her eyes to quell the rage he feels inside him but all she has to offer is her grief.

He turns to Sukamaya. "Clarkson did he...uh, did he..." There is a lump of emotion lodged in Devin's throat, formed by a pain that hurts too much to swallow. He pushes his words out over it.

"Did Clarkson see this?"

Sukamaya shakes his head. "No, Devin-sun. He did not."

Samantha looks at her father, confused. "But he's a police officer. He's trying to find those two guys. He needs to see this, right?"

Sukamaya turns away from his daughter and her naïveté. She cannot understand the way that he feels, for she does not know what he knows.

"Right, Saka?" She asks again. "He is a cop, right?"

The look in Sukamaya's eyes is not very reassuring and he moves towards the screens with his head down. "Did either of you notice the ring he had on today?"

Samantha shakes her head quickly but Devin doesn't isn't so fast to respond. He starts to replay the day in his mind; tracing his thoughts back to before Sukamaya had found him. He was with Natalie, right in front of the stairs when Clarkson arrived.

Sukamaya touches the screen. He selects the front gate cameras just before nine o'clock and presses play.

"Look closely." He says. "Watch the man pulling his mask on."

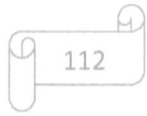

The three of them study the footage carefully, never taking their eyes off the man in black.

"There!" Sukamaya says and pauses the recording. The screen freezes on a man running his finger along the edge of his knife. There is a ring on the finger. He zooms in on it.

"It is just like the one the detective was wearing today. Devin-sun, I called you as soon as I realized. I called twice. I wanted you to know not to trust these men, Devin-sun."

"He put his hands in his pockets." Devin recalls. "Right when he realized Natalie was a reporter, he put his hands in his pockets. And he was acting weird about her being here too."

Samantha can't believe what they're implying. "But how we do we know that ring even means something? You can't really believe--"

"Yeah, I do, Sam." Devin cuts her off. "Clarkson's working with the people that killed Mom and Dad. He's a part of this Elite thing. I could tell Natalie didn't trust him either."

Sukamaya nods. "I think so, too, Devin-sun. And I think Jackie knew about these cameras. She wanted us to know who was responsible for her death."

"Do you think she knew about the police?" Devin asks, trying to piece this all together.

Sukamaya isn't sure. He's been asking himself similar questions all day. There is so much here that doesn't make any sense.

Like why, Samantha thinks. *Why would anybody want to murder the Kings? They could have never had enemies. They were the two most caring, loving and generous people in the world. There is nothing you could want that they wouldn't—*

It hits her like a bag of bricks.

"The book." She blurts. "Those assassins took that book, remember? All they kept talking about was that book. Maybe Mom wanted us to know who has it. It must be important. I mean, if someone would kill for it."

Devin has a thought, more so a memory, a recollection of something his mother would always say. "An archaeologist has a duty to make sure that their discoveries are used in the betterment of mankind. You remember Mom's oath, right, Sam?"

"Yeah, I remember." Samantha nods. "Mom would go on and on about the Catholic Church. How they burned the Gnostic Gospels and kept the Dead Sea Scrolls captive for 50 years."

Sukamaya walks over to the light switch and, with a clockwise turn of the rod, the projector rises back into the ceiling and the panel closes behind it. The screens move next, ascending into the curtain rod as if moving backwards though time. Soft blue moonlight fills the room.

"Your mother always believed that an archaeologist had to be careful who they released their finds to, Devin-sun. That is why she always funded her own excavations. So she could negotiate the rights to the finds."

"So what do we do now?" Samantha asks. "These Elite people have the book—whatever it is. We can't go to the police. What, do they just win?"

Devin isn't the least bit surprised that the police cannot be trusted. This isn't the first time he has had to deal with a crooked police force.

"No, they don't win, Sam." That coiled rage begins to slither up his spine again. "Not this time. Not again."

Sukamaya recognizes the fiery glare ablaze in his young friend's eyes. "Infection exists in all things, Devin-sun. Do not let

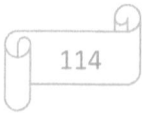

your emotions consume you. Let your mud settle so that your mind will be clear."

He lays a comforting hand on Devin's shoulder but Devin shrugs it off. He's had enough of this peace talk. "I just watched my parent's get killed! In *this* room! Enough thinking, alright! My parents spent their whole lives thinking. Look at them now! It's time to *do* something."

He pushes pass Sukamaya as cold tears spill from his eyes. Samantha watches him storm out of the room and starts after him but Sukamaya stops her.

"Let him be, child. He must find his ford. Tomorrow we have to meet with Dennis. After that, we will figure out what to do."

Samantha isn't listening. Sukamaya's words are being drowned out by Devin's grief. She can hear his heart crying out to her, pulling on her like a magnet seeking its opposite. She has to go and help him.

Just as Sukamaya could see the fire in Devin's glare he can now see the longing in his daughter's gaze. It's futile to try to stop what must be. "Go to him, child. Just remember, if you look to others for fulfillment, you will never be fulfilled. Be content with what you have and rejoice in the way things are. Understand, there is harmony even in great pain."

Samantha looks to him, as anxious as a dog pawing at the door, and nods quickly.

Sukamaya smiles. "Now go. Tell Devin-sun what tomorrow holds and be the friend that he needs."

She starts for the door before the last word leaves his mouth.

"Samantha." He calls to her. "You must remember The Way, child. He will need your strength and wisdom in the days to come."

She stops at the door and looks back over her shoulder. "I know, Saka. And I'll need his."

The two of them share a warm smile and Samantha disappears down the hall. Left alone with his memories, Sukamaya smirks; so many laughs, so many good times, and they all have come to an end.

But true perfection seems imperfect, he reminds himself, *and true straightness seems crooked.* "The Tao accepts all and so must I."

Sukamaya rubs his hand across the soft leather of his friend's chair and smirks. *With Donkey Kong's throne's empty, who will I play with now? What is Diddy without Donkey and Daisy?*

"Donkey Kong" is Derrick King's nickname—an easy play on his initials—given to him by Sukamaya the first time they played the old videogame together. Mr. King retorted by calling Sukamaya "Diddy" which by extension made Mrs. King "Daisy". In those beautiful moments when the kids would be off at school and Mrs. King would be in-between digs the three of them would empty all of the pantries and sit in front of the TV, pigging out while they took turns on the game. The Kings were like the siblings that Sukamaya never had. How he'll miss those times.

But when Jackie was gone we'd really have fun, he thinks, remembering some of the crazy "when I was in the Army" stories that Mr. King would tell.

Sukamaya takes his hand off of the chair and gazes around the lifeless room. He's spent his entire day working to console others and now, at the end of it all, there is only his knowledge of the Tao to comfort him. The feelings that he's worked so hard to detach himself from begin to form together, like a fine mist condensing into a cloud, until the weight of the loss becomes too much to bear and all the anguish that he's drawn up begins to rain down his cheeks.

He doesn't bother to wipe the tears away. It is natural to cry when you lose two good friends.

And there is nothing more natural than nature. When the wind blows there is only the wind; when it rains, there is only rain.

Sukamaya smiles. "And when the clouds pass, the Sun shines through."

CHAPTER EIGHT

Devin awakens to a nightmare; a twisted reality where both of his parents have been murdered and the police are trying to cover it up.

He pulls the covers up over his face, seeking to block out the light and live forever in his dreams. But as the illusion gradually fades, consciousness brings with it a world impregnated by the sins of man. This morning his mother won't be bursting into his room, bouncing on the edge of his bed and shouting for him to "come enjoy this beautiful day while you still can!" This morning there is only a shower, a change of clothes, and a lot to think about.

Exiting his bedroom, a sweet and sultry aroma fills his nose. He enters the kitchen and finds Sukamaya standing at the stove, singing over a skillet of sizzling shrimp.

"Good morning Saka." He says, slipping around Sukamaya. He goes into the cupboard and grabs a granola bar. "Smells good."

Before Sukamaya can manage a response Devin has slipped back around him and out the kitchen.

"No worries." Sukamaya sings, sliding the sautéed shrimp from the skillet and onto a saucer. He drops another batch into the pan and resumes his song.

- -

Upstairs, Samantha stirs. Her father's smooth song has drawn her from bed and she follows her nose to the kitchen.

"Good morning, Saka. Is that what I think it is?"

Sukamaya smiles. Seeing his daughter standing in the doorway, still in her slippers and pajamas, takes his mind back to a time long ago.

"Yes, child. Your favorite. I thought it would be good way to begin our day. It was one of Jackie's favorites too."

Samantha remembers. She and Mrs. King had so much in common. *She was the only mother I ever had. And now, I'll never—*

She turns away from the thought and heads upstairs. "I'll be back after I'm dressed." She yells back over her shoulder. "Want me to wake Devin?"

"No, child. Devin-sun has already begun his day his way." Sukamaya slides the batch of shrimp onto the platter and goes to slice the fruit. "You hurry, child, or it will be cold."

It doesn't take Samantha long to return. Dressed in shorts and a tank-top, she sits down with her father and enjoys a sliced mango, papaya juice, and generous servings of *camarones chinole*—with Sukamaya's special twist. As they eat, he runs through their day's schedule.

"We have to go by the coroner's office," he tells her, "and the police would like us to visit the station to--"

"What's the point, Saka? What do they want anyway?"

Sukamaya shrugs. "I am not sure. We do not *have* to go, child. It was merely a request. If you do not--"

"Yeah," she cuts in, "let's just skip that. I don't want to look into that detective's beady little eyes again if I don't have to."

Sukamaya takes a piece of mango from the bowl of fruit and pops it into his mouth.

"And then we have to meet with Dennis." He says, suckling the tips of his fingers.

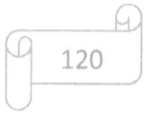

Samantha picks at a piece of fruit on her plate. "It just makes it seem so final. And rushed. Like, they haven't even been de... dea..." She can't bring herself to say it. "They haven't been gone for two days yet and we're already dividing up their stuff."

Sukamaya tosses back a shrimp and shrugs. "Life goes on."

Life goes on, Samantha thinks. She can't believe he would say something so cold. She knows that he loved them. They were his best friends. *He has to want to find out the truth as much as I do.*

"The Master gives himself to whatever the moment brings forth." Sukamaya continues. "He surely knows that he will one day die and he has nothing left to cling to: no illusions in his mind, no resistance in his body."

He picks up another one of the delectable shrimp. His mood is light and carefree, with every bite of the shrimp bringing more joy to his face.

"The Master doesn't think about his actions; they pour out from the very core of his being. He holds not a thing back from life, so he is ready for death just as a man is ready for sleep after a good day of work."

"You and Devin-sun, you are both building shelter from the indefensible. Devin-sun is caught up in his desire for vengeance. I recognized that look I saw in his eyes this morning, the one he tried to hide behind his smile. I haven't seen that look in twelve years and I'd hope to never see it again."

"Twelve years?" Samantha thinks back. Twelve years ago she and Devin were in high school. "Stacey? You're talking about what happened with Stacey?"

"Yes, child. Devin-sun obsessed over the circumstances involving Stacey's death and now he is sick again. To be obsessed with anything is a sickness, child. There is no harmony in obsession and harmony is the way of all things. His sickness clouds his vision. Caught in desire Devin-sun can only see the manifestations and not the mystery."

Her eyes light up. "You mean, what's really going on here? Like, why did those people have Mom and Dad killed for that book? What's so important about it? And who are The Elite?"

Sukamaya's head droops with disappointment. "Samantha-child, your shelter is the mystery. Your sickness is not an obsession for vengeance. It's a desire for answers. Obsession. Desire. It is all sickness. Free from desire you realize the mystery. Caught up in desire you can only see the manifestation."

He picks up a piece of fruit and studies it closely—its moist texture; the glisten of the sunlight on each individual fiber; its sweet sugary scent.

"But mystery and manifestation come from a common source, child. Realizing the mystery is not enough. You must realize the source. If you cannot, you will continue to stumble in sorrow and confusion."

He slides the piece of mango into his mouth and chews slowly, reveling in its juicy sweetness. "Hold on to the center, child. Surrender completely to the Tao and be like the Great Mother— empty yet able to give birth to many worlds."

"But Saka," she begins, "there has to be—" He raises his hand. "Those who know don't talk. You must ask yourself why you feel you must always speak."

Sukamaya continues to eat, watching his daughter all the while. Though she does not call him father very often it in no way lessens the fact that he is her father. Sukamaya understands Samantha better than she understands herself. She is just like her mother. *Both of you, on a never-ending quest for answers.*

When Samantha decided to major in physics, Sukamaya was hardly surprised. Since she was a little girl she has been searching for something that would make her mother's death fit into a grand scheme, a universal order. Religion has always been too personal for her, too subjective. Science offers answers she can prove.

"You must seek within yourself." He tells her. "If you want to find what you are searching for, child, you must begin inside. And then you will understand why I scheduled our meeting with Dennis so soon, and why I say life goes on." He takes a sip of his juice. "Do you remember their wishes, Samantha?"

Samantha looks dazed, as if she's just been awoken from a dream. *Their wishes,* the phrase echoes in her mind. "Yeah, I remember. It was weird how much they talked about dying."

"They knew that death is just a part of our existence on this plane. We're born, we live, and we die. Every being in the Universe returns to the Source. Returning to the Source is peace. To bring forth peace you must understand balance. Watch the turmoil of all things, but contemplate their return to the Source."

Samantha stares out into space, musing over the meaning of her father's words. The tender warmth of his hand takes hold of her fingers. She looks up at him and begins to cry.

"I know it is hard, child. But if we do not continue to live on, how can we honor those we love?" He wipes a tear from her eye. "Do you think Mrs. King would want to see you wasting your days?"

"No." She smiles, thinking back to all the times that Mrs. King would run in her room screaming to wake her up. "She'd tell me that I better get up, get out and enjoy this beautiful day while while I still can?"

"Yes, child. That is exactly what she would say. So live on child. But live on with their memory in your heart. Do this for them, and, when I move on, do this for me."

"Saka, please." She gazes into her father's gentle green eyes. "Please don't talk like that. Even if it is just the circle of life, just...not now. Please."

Smiling, he takes her face in his hands and places a tender kiss between her brows. "With your mind's eye, child. See them there and they will live forever."

Samantha nods and Sukamaya's smile widens.

"Now!" He exclaims, bouncing out of his seat. "Let us go and find Devin-sun. Today will be busy enough without us moving about like snails."

Samantha shakes her head, grabs a slice of mango and slides her chair back from the table. "Snails!" She laughs. "You're far from a snail, old man."

"Old! Aww!" Sukamaya clutches his stomach in feigned agony. "Your words cut deep, child!"

Laughing, Samantha follows her father out of the kitchen and into the rotunda. They are about to head up the stairs when Devin comes crashing into Samantha.

"Uhh, my bad." He says. "I was just coming to get you. You guys ready?" He turns toward the front door. "I'm thinking we should take the Masserati. Three of us won't fit in the Lambo. Plus, we won't lose much speed either."

His words clip along at an astonishing rate as he grabs the doorknob and looks back over his shoulder. "C'mon. What're you waiting for? Let's go."

Samantha and Sukamaya exchange knowing glances as they follow him out of the door.

He is sick, Sukamaya thinks, *and only he can save himself.*

The Masserati was a gift from Devin's father—a graduation

present for Devin receiving a MBA from Harvard.

Cruising down the beach side road, Devin reflects on all of the heated debates they would have. The two of them would argue over everything from the role of aerodynamics in acceleration to the importance of bodyweight in handling sharp turns.

The engine's hypnotic hum reminds him of his father—*peaceful yet powerful,* he thinks. Smooth yet strong.

He dips in and out of traffic, weaving back and forth like a slithering serpent.

"Devin, watch out!" Samantha shrieks, bracing herself against the door. Frowning, she punches him in the arm. "You almost hit that car, you idiot!"

"What?" Devin checks the mirror. A young man in an old Honda is furiously flicking him off. Devin smirks. "I wasn't even close to that guy. Just relax, Sam."

Samantha looks out of the window and thanks God for the open road she sees up ahead. She exhales and then turns to Devin. "What's the hurry anyway? Doesn't it already feel so...rushed?'"

Devin gazes out at the long road ahead. "I just want to get it over with, you know. So I can start looking for those two guys. Maybe I can pull some footage off the cameras with their faces. That one guy was pulling on his mask, remember?"

She nods. "Yeah, we need to find out who The Elite are as soon as possible. They're the ones that sent those guys. And they have Mom's book. Mom would definitely want us to get that book back."

"I don't care about that book, Sam. All I want to do is get my hands on those two guys that—"

"Enough!" Sukamaya erupts. He has been sitting in the backseat trying to enjoy the beautiful scenery outside the window but their constant obsessing won't allow it. "You two can never enjoy the majesty of the forest if you continue to focus on one single tree." He resumes his gazing. "You will never find the Way until you let go of those desires."

That doesn't make any sense to Devin. "Saka I owe it to my parents to find their killers. Mom wanted me to. You saw the recording. Why else would she leave that message? For the first time, Saka, I am going to make my parents proud."

Sukamaya looks away from the window again and scoots closer to Devin. He lays his hand on his young friend's shoulder and the two of them lock eyes through the rearview mirror. "Devin-sun, you do not understand a parent's pride. A parent is most proud when their child has overcome the obstacles that prevent them from maximizing their potential. When they can put aside all of the bad memories and feelings they use to define themselves, to limit themselves, and just be themselves; that is what makes a parent proud. When you are no longer this or that, only the true Self, you will always choose the right action for the moment, and you will honor your father and mother with your wisdom. Remember the Way, Devin-sun."

"But Saka, if—"

"No, Devin-sun. No more ifs, buts, and ors. Follow the light, the truth that is so strong inside you. You must go within for your answers, Devin-sun. The Way is always with you."

Sukamaya sits back and smiles. "Now stop talking. Both of you. Let your minds for once be at peace."

Devin and Samantha heed his admonishment and do not speak for the remainder of the ride. While the two of them wade through the murky waters of their souls, Sukamaya dives deep into the depths of thought.

With the Kings gone his future has now become uncertain and although he is able to accept the twists and turns of life, Sukamaya cannot deny how much he would miss the Peninsula. He does not doubt that Devin will allow him to remain in the family's mansion. His problem is different.

Do I truly want to wake there, everyday, with no one to keep me company? And if I do leave, where do I go?

Having never ventured outside of Japan, Sukamaya Matsumi was surprised by how quickly he fell in love with the Caribbean. While working in Tokyo he had longed for the simple mountain-side village he lived in as a child—for him and the young Samantha. He never thought that he would find that working for the King's but to his surprise Camino Cosón offered all that and more.

It wasn't the mountain or dense demesne that captured his heart. It was the days that he would spend alone, meditating beside the glistening waterfall, at one with the Tao, that would become his infatuation. Some of Sukamaya's most powerful experiences have occurred beneath that waterfall. The land is connected to his very being.

He thinks back to his last vision. It came to him the day before the King's death. A slight cold had started to come over him but he had felt the land calling out to his spirit. Despite his weariness, Sukamaya had decided to trust in the Tao and at his first glimpse of the fall, he felt the energy of the land pouring into him like earth magic renewing his body. Stripped down to his shorts, he chose a spot close enough that he could fell the fall's mist and assumed the lotus pose.

The trance came quickly. Like electricity in his spine, his *qi* rose through his chakras until it exploded in his forehead and he saw himself on a city street. It was raining out and bullet holes pocketed the bodies of nearby vehicles. A man lay on the ground bleeding. Samantha was there and Devin was too but they were adults now. Devin's light was brighter than ever. A man pulled a gun and took aim at Devin but Devin couldn't see it. Sukamaya sprinted, raced towards Devin and lunged forward just as he had done all those years ago. His body slammed into Devin and they both crashed into the pavement. Sukamaya smiled. He had saved the little boy with the light again. He had done his job. His work was finished.

In the backseat of the Masserati, Sukamaya continues to gaze out at the land he's come to love. In the distance he spots a lone coconut bobbing up and down on the surface of the water. He imagines it finding its way ashore, laying down roots and blossoming into an elegant palm.

We all have a journey, he thinks.

Devin makes a turn off of the dirt road and onto a narrow street. Once a row of fishing huts, this renovated tourist strip now includes a sports bar, a couple pizzerias, and an assortment of expensive restaurants.

With the Masserati parked, the three of them head for Bambú—a quaint little *colmadon* that Sukamaya and Mr. King would frequent on their way in from Samaná. They spot Dennis quickly, sitting at a small table outside the café.

"Long time no see." He says, rising to greet them. He shakes the men's hands and hugs Samantha.

"What's it been now?" He asks her, "Six or seven years? Since I set up that trust fund." He looks her over and smiles. "You haven't changed a bit."

Samantha blushes. "Yeah, and I guess lawyers aren't immune to the Caribbean's influence, huh?"

"Guess not." Dennis says, giving himself an once-over. He has to admit that if it wasn't for the briefcase and stack of documents on the table no one would believe that he's a lawyer. His clothes don't help his case much either. Dressed in denim shorts and snug tanktop, with long honey-brown dreadlocks swinging freely down his back, Dennis looks more like a surfer or dockworker than a partner in a legal practice.

He takes a seat at the table and they all follow suit. "I just wish something else would have brought us together, you know. It's really hard to believe someone would break-in and kill them like that. They were such generous people." He looks to Devin. "And your father, man. Derrick was a rare breed. Really one of a kind."

"Yeah." Devin nods. "I've been thinking about him all morning. Him and Mom."

"I see you drove the Q. You know, I was with him when he picked it out for you. Saka, you were there. Remember? Then we came here for drinks." He gaze drifts to the bar and lingers on the corner closest to the jukebox—Derrick's favorite spot—where the three of them would lounge and laugh over chilled spirits. "Man, I really miss the big guy."

Sukamaya smiles. He knows how Dennis feels. Dennis and Mr. King are old military buddies and had a bond that was unrivaled. Despite all of the people that he had met in life, Derrick King only had two true friends: Sukamaya and Dennis. The three of them were like the beginning of a bad joke—a mystic, a scientist and a lawyer walk into a bar—but they had a lot of fun together over the years.

Dennis takes a sip of his juice. "You know, it was because of your Dad's advice that I invested in those internet start-ups way back. I started my practice with that money. Your parents were my

first clients—my *only* clients—for a long time. I owe them everything
I have."

He glances at the stack of documents on the table. "At first
I was going to send someone, you know. It just hurt too badly.
Imagining myself reading their last words, I mean. But then I
thought...they would have wanted me to do it. To be the one,
you know. This should be done by friends and family. Not some
stranger in a suit."

He shuffles the stack of documents and glances around the
table. "Anybody want to say anything before I begin?"

"Yes." Sukamaya says. "I just want to say that this is only
legality. We already have everything that Derrick and Jacqueline left
for us. We have their love in our hearts and their memories in our
thoughts. These material things only hold the importance that we
give them."

Dennis nods. "Very well said. Sukamaya, you've always been
a wise man. I want us to keep in touch, you know, even now with
Derrick gone."

"Why wouldn't we?" Sukamaya grins. "You are good man,
Dennis, and a loyal friend. And besides, who else do I know on this
side of the Earth?"

"Yeah. Well..." Dennis takes a deep breath. "I guess I'll
begin then."

He pulls his cellphone, sets it to record, and runs though all
of the formalities. Once all the parties involved in the proceeding
have stated their name for the record, Dennis takes one more glance
around the table.

"Okay." He says, taking a document from the stack of
papers. "This is from Jackie:

Devin, Samantha, Sukamaya, if you are reading these words

then it has come time for us to step back from our work, as Saka would say, and move on to the next life. If there is any doubt that we loved you with every fiber of our being then you have never had faith in our love, for doubt and faith cannot co-exist.

During our many miles here on Earth, we were both blessed enough to have found success doing what we loved to do. Though our work has provided us with a level of comfort that many are never fortunate enough to find, our wealth does not lie in these objects. Objects are but illusions; here today and gone tomorrow. It is the good times that we have shared with each of you, and the times that were not so good; it was the love we gave and more importantly, that we received; it was the friends we made; the lessons we learned; and the peace we found; this is where our wealth lies. Before we bequeath anything else, let it be the wish that you too find wealth.

The world around you may judge the gifts that we are about to bestow as more than they are, but understand, this is merely a sign of what the thoughtless think. It is but the noise that that people make, and only shallow people judge merit by noise.

If we have left you anything, let it be an example for how one should live, how to bless others with your blessings, and how to truly love people. We are far from perfect but we have sought to be the best we could and to want for others what we wanted for ourselves. Always judge people by what they are and not what they appear to be, and what they are is but a part of you.

Love yourself and you will love All. To love yourself you must love All. We leave you peace, blessings and the courage to Live! Until we meet again, look in the mirror and there we are.

Dennis pauses there. He needs a moment. "Derrick and

Jackie, they were very special people." A lone tear rolls down his cheek and lands on the letter. He glances up at Devin and Samantha and their somber faces. *They're strong,* he thinks, *and they have each other.* "The world would be a better place if there were more people like them."

Smiling, Sukamaya nods. "They had learned the secret of all truth, Dennis. They had learned that we are all One. All of us, everything, it is all just a reflection of the One, the All, the Source, the Tao. They had found the Way and spent their lives walking the path to reunion. Now they are one step closer. I am so happy for them I cannot stop smiling."

Sitting beside him, Devin doesn't know what to feel right now, but he certainly doesn't feel like smiling.

If there is any doubt that we loved you then you never had faith in our love; the words twist around in his mind like a serrated knife; slicing through his misconceptions; slashing away at his insecurities.

Beside him, Samantha's tears have started to roll softly down her cheeks. They keep coming, another one for every word spoke, for each memory she has of the only mother she's ever known and the man she grew up calling Dad. She dabs at her eyes with her shirt but it's useless. The tears flow like a river draining a sea of grief.

"Mom and Dad, they were..." She sobs, doing her best to push through. "They were the best people I ever..." The words are like rocks in her throat. She can't go on. "I'm sorry." She sniffles. "I just miss them so much. I can't believe I stayed away so long."

Devin shares in her sorrow. It hurts to admit it but he knows it's true. *I could've stopped them. I should've been there. This is all my fault.*

Dennis gathers himself and continues on with the

proceeding. The actual allocation of their assets is next, he tells them. "Derrick and Jackie each wrote sections for all of you. Sukamaya you're first."

"What more could they give me than they already have?" Sukamaya replies. "I do not know where I would be right now if not for their love and kindness."

Dennis nods. "I understand buddy. You know I do. But these are the last words they wanted you to hear."

"You are wrong, Dennis." Sukamaya taps his chest. "I hear them here." He touches his head next. "And here."

Smirking, Dennis pinches Sukamaya's ear. "Well then hear them here too."

He picks up the next page and begins to read.

To Mr. Sukamaya Matsumi—our brother, friend, confidant, teacher and savior. If it was not for your beautiful spirit we do not know where we would have ended up. You not only saved the life of our only son, you allowed us to share in the joy of raising a daughter and brought us a true understanding of life. Your light shines as bright as the Sun and we are thankful to have experienced the blessing that is being caught in your pull. You always taught us to follow the Way and not merely with words but with the path clearly cut by your own feet.

Since you are well aware of the love that we have for you, sweet Saka, there is no more need for words. (You know Derrick; he thought that was too much.) You always said: those who know don't talk and those who talk don't know. We will be waiting for you with a bucket of candy and a joystick. If we see Rachel we'll send her your love.

Until then, sweet Saka, please enjoy owning all of our properties in Japan and our interests in any food-related businesses.

We have donated $500,000 to the Caribbean Conservation Program and another $500,000 to the Peninsula Preservation Project, both in your name. We also bequeath to you $10,000,000 to do with as you wish.

We know that Devin would allow you to live on in the mansion but for legality's sake, we bequeath to you, Sukamaya Matsumi, the title to our property on Camino Cason, under the conditions that you cannot sell it and upon your death it is to be transferred to our son, Devin King.

Farewell sweet warrior.

An indefinable gratitude washes over Sukamaya but it is neither the money nor properties that touch his heart, it is the care that they represent.

They did not know if I would want to remain in the house or move back to Japan, and so they gave me the ability to do whichever I pleased.

A single tear escapes his eye.

"You deserve it." Devin says, putting him on the back. "That and more."

Sukamaya can only nod. Such a powerful show of concern has him struck speechless.

Dennis picks up the next page from the stack. "The next person named in the will is you, Samantha. Jackie wrote a letter for you." He tries to hand it to her but Samantha refuses.

"No, Dennis. I'd rather you read it."

"You sure?"

Wiping a single tear from the corner of her eye, Samantha nods. "Yeah, go ahead. I'd rather you do it."

Dennis gazes down at the letter. "Okay then," and begins to read.

To my darling Samantha Matsumi, my wish come true—a beautiful and intelligent daughter without labor pains—and my best friend. Sammy, you mean more to me than you can possibly know. If you think that I have done anything spectacular Sammy, then you are wrong. All I have done is settle my debt to you.

For as long as I could remember I was always 'Daddy's Little Girl.' My father would take me out to the movies and for ice cream and to the museum. We went on so many daddy-daughter dates, and they were the highlight of my childhood. So when my mother filed for divorce and we moved from our big glorious home in France to Cairo, where my mother's from, I was devastated. I hated her, Sammy. I blamed her for making my dad leave and ruining my life. The only good thing that came from it was that after the divorce I was able to travel around the world with my father every summer, visiting his sites and even helping out sometimes. Those days, watching him work; those are what led me to the field.

The older I got, the more I looked forward to spending my summers away from my mother. She wouldn't let me do anything. I couldn't wear the cute American fashions or style my hair how I wanted, or give my phone number out to any boys. I thought she was so mean and uncompromising. As soon as I got the chance to leave home I took it. I picked a college as far away from Cairo as I could and after I graduated I tried my best not to take jobs with any Egyptologists. I wanted to stay as far away from my mother as possible.

When my father died I hated her even more. I started thinking about all of those daddy-daughter dates that I'd missed out on and all of the time I could've spent with my dad but wasn't able to because she had pushed him away. And he had still loved her.

He had always said that my mother was his other half and his soul-mate and he never knew why she left him. She never even told him why. My hate for her grew to a level that I can't adequately describe. If Derrick had not come along when he did I may have grown into a very dark and mean person. But my love's timing was perfect and he was just what I needed to keep my mind off of her. You know, Sammy, I didn't even invite my mother to our wedding, and she didn't meet Devin until after you and Saka came along. Looking back on all of it now I cannot believe I could be so cruel.

Oh, Sammy, dear, I owe you so much. It wasn't until I met you—this adorable little girl with the brightest green eyes in the world—that I began to forgive my mother. Saka had told us how you had lost your mom and when he decided to come live with us I made a promise to myself that I would never be anything like my mother. I swore to myself that I would be better than she was. But then I found myself doing all of the things that I swore I wouldn't.

You remember how I wouldn't let you watch certain TV shows or wear certain clothes or eat all of the junk food that you begged for? It wasn't because I was being mean. It was because I love you and want the best for you. Do you remember how I would read to you every night while you took a bath? You would always get two stories because then Saka would sit by your bed and read you to sleep. Devin hated it but I insisted on reading to you by the tub because I remembered how much I loved when my Mom read to me by the tub. I cooked with you and taught you how to skip rope; all of the same things that my mother did with me. Once I had a daughter of my own I could see that everything that my mother did, whether I agreed with it or not, she did it out of love. It was because of you that I was able to let go of my anger, Samantha. So thank you.

That is the gift you gave me, Sammy. You gave me back my mom.

And you were also my best friend. If you haven't noticed there are not a lot of women interested in digging in the dirt and reading about ancient civilizations. The few girlfriends I had were usually just social relationships that I'd struck up at one of Derrick's business dinners or lunches or something like that. Those women would bore me to death complaining about their bratty kids, how they thought their maids were stealing silverware, or the new secretaries that their husbands were sleeping with. Sammy, darling, you were my saving grace.

Whenever I came home from a dig I couldn't wait to give you the dirt (pun intended) on whatever I'd discovered. Some of my fondest memories are with you, sitting by the fireplace with a big bowl of popcorn, searching through books for clues to some lost treasure. Derrick and Devin were their own type of nerds, with their comics, cars and kung-fu movies. They could never really get into my work, but you, Sammy, you always made me feel important and understood. And after digging in the ground for weeks on end and then coming home to three men, it was always nice having another girl to talk to. I would have gone crazy in that house without you. So once again Sammy, thank you for being everything I needed. I love you darling.

Dennis stops there and picks up another sheet from the stack. "This is where they outlined your gifts, Samantha."

She nods and he continues.

To Samantha Matsumi, we leave $250,000,000 to be added to your trust fund and bequeath to you all of Jacqueline King's collections, artifacts, and relics. Cherish them as we have cherished you.

And as your Mom, Sammy, I leave you with this piece of advice: men are dumb. They will spend their entire lives searching for something they have always had. But women are dumb too because we'll watch them search and never think to tell them that they already have it. You are far too smart to be dumb, darling.

Sammy, I know that you never got to know your biological mother and I know you've had a lot of questions that I have not been able to answer, but I've done my best to fill in for her. I hope that when we meet up, she is as proud of you as I am, Samantha. We love you darling. Farewell.

A pile of wet napkins sits on the table in front of Samantha. Their waiter was nice enough to sit a stack in the center of their table—the closest thing they have to tissues, he reasoned. Samantha blows her nose and adds another wad to the mound.

"I'm going to miss her so much." She says, reaching for another napkin. "You know she called me last week. She wanted to talk about something she had discovered but I told her I was busy. I wasn't busy. I had just gotten home from work and was tired." She covers her mouth with the tissue. "The last thing I said to her was a lie. I'm such a horrible person!"

Sukamaya takes the tissue from his daughter and dries her eyes. "You are not horrible, child. Didn't you hear how much she loved you? How much you meant to her? You were closer to her than any of us, Samantha. Do not dwell on the last words you spoke to her. The truth lies in the depths of love that you two shared."

Devin hands Samantha another tissue. He is the only one who has yet to cry. He cannot-- not until something melts away the cold block of vengeance frozen to his heart. The same words that have Samantha's face wet with tears only fan the flames of his fury.

"And Devin," Dennis continues, picking up the next page,

"you're next."

Devin nods, not sure what he should he expect. *What do you say to a child who has turned out to be nothing but a disappointment?*

Dennis takes a sip of his juice and begins to read.

To our dearest son, the light of our days and our shining star at night. Watching you grow into a strong fearless young man has been a joy all of its own and knowing that we played a part in that growth has been an achievement worth bragging about. Since you were a little boy your father and I knew that you were destined for greatness. You were only two years old when you first showed us just how special you are.

Your father had run to the store and I had fallen asleep watching you play with our toys. I awoke to the sound of your father coming through the door, yelling your name. When we found you, you were in the kitchen holding on to the handles of two knives that you had somehow stuck into the walls, hanging at least five feet in the air. And you were laughing your little butt off like you were just having the time of your life. I didn't see anything funny. I was terrified, watching my baby hang so high off the ground. Your Dad, though, he was laughing right along with you. He was amazed that you had managed to sneak away from me, somehow climb onto the countertop on your own, pull two knives out of the block without hurting yourself, and then stab them into the wall as if using them to climb. To this day your father believes that you were trying to reach your favorite cookies that we kept on top of the refrigerator. All I know is that that was only the beginning of your amazing feats. Do you remember when you were six, with me at a site in Australia, and you fell into that snake pit? Everyone was frantic and panicking, trying to figure a way to get you out, while you just sat there calmly petting the snake. *You got out without one scratch. And, now, as an adult you have managed to perform your spectacular stunts while running several businesses and multiple investments. Son, we are astounded. Whenever you have put your mind to something there has been nothing on Earth that could stop you from achieving your goal. That is something that your father and I have always admired in you, sweetheart, and you have inspired us to face challenges that we may have otherwise shirked away from. Your willingness to accept the truth when it confronts you and your open-mind has also brought us great pride. You have always been a good friend, a great brother, and the best son any parents could ever ask for.*

Our only wish is that we could have spent more time with you. We sent you to boarding school because we wanted you to have the best education possible, but we had always had hoped that the times we missed in your childhood we'd make up for when you were an adult. That's why I'm always trying to get you home for dinners and visits. But if you stay away from us now, darling, it is only ourselves to blame for making it so easy. For this, we apologize. Please know that we were only doing what we thought was best for you and as much as we would love to get those days back, we wouldn't change a thing if it would change the wonderful man that you have become. We love you, honey. You are the key to our treasures.

Dennis takes the next page from the stack. "This section here is from your father."

Confused, Devin dabs at the tear forming in the corner of eye. How could two people who dedicated their lives to uplifting humanity be proud of him? Strong? Fearless? *Could this really be how they felt all along?*

It's like falling; when everything that you have built your life upon, every idea that you once used to define yourself, everything that has fueled your movements, shatters beneath your feet and you are left with nothing to stand on—the feeling can be only describes as falling.

Falling like tears from the eyes of a shaken soul. Devin doesn't bother to wipe them away. *What's the point? It's not over.*

He takes a deep breath and looks around the table. They too are crying; spewing forth emotion like wells drawing from the same pool of pain and as the tears fall from their face they darken the ground with despair.

"Go ahead, Dennis."

Dennis nods, takes a tissue from the stack, dabs his eyes and continues.

Son, I know I don't talk much, and it's largely because I have always sought to show my love rather than speak it. I hope that I completed my mission, son. But just in case there is any doubt—I love you, Devin. You have made me a very proud man. I never had the chance to know my father and so I did the best I could. I attempted to be the father that I always dreamed of having when I was a child. You are the delight of my life and I can look back at all these gray hairs and smile, knowing that each one has aided you in some way. When we first moved to the Peninsula I remember our mother telling you that you would be the fruit of your ancestor's labor: a strong and intelligent black man. Your mother has always been better than me with words—which is why she helps write all my books—but I just want you to know, Son, you've become all that and more. Remember the spirit that flows through your veins, son. You are a King always. I am glad to have had the honor of being your father. I love you, Devin.

Dennis stops. "And this last part here is the actual bequeathing of property and assets. It reads: *To you, Devin King, our only son, we leave to you your birthright: everything that belongs to us, not otherwise allocated, with the hopes that you will use these resources to keep manifesting your destiny. You were born to lead, Devin, but every leader must have the courage to follow their heart. Remember this in times of adversity. We love you, Devin. Farewell.*"

Dennis pauses, allowing Devin time to comment but Devin remains silent—lost in his own world of thoughts and emotion.

Dennis picks up the last sheet from the stack of documents. "There is something else here. It's strange. I don't recall them adding this but it seems that they amended their will again. They did it so much. I always thought it was weird how nonchalant they were about death."

He scans the bottom of the page. "Everything looks to be in order. Their signatures are here and someone—J.R. Boughton—signed as a witness." He shows them the signatures. "He's from my firm."

Samantha nods. "So what does it say, Dennis? Read it."

"Okay." He reads the first line to himself and smirks. "It's for me. They added me to their will. It says, '*And to our friend Dennis Gull, Derrick King bequeaths his 1965 Jaguar Roadster that you have secretly coveted for years and Jacqueline King leaves the recommendation that your firm continue to handle the family estate.*'"

Sukamaya smiles. "So, you get the Jaguar. It is a beautiful machine. We'll have to go for a ride sometime."

"Anytime buddy." Dennis jogs the stack of documents together and returns them to his briefcase. He glances around the table, stalling. It feels wrong to just leave. "So, uhh... I guess that's it. I mean, I don't know. Unless anyone has any questions?"

"Naw, not me." Devin lies. He has a million questions; just none that he thinks Dennis can answer.

Samantha shakes her head, lying as well. All she has ever had were questions running through that pretty head of hers and, after today, she has just added a thousand more.

"Well," Sukamaya says, smiling at Dennis, "do you have any plans after this? If not, you should stay for lunch. It would feel wrong to just leave now, don't you think? Lunch would be better."

"Exactly what I was thinking." Dennis nods. They flag down a waitress, place their orders and over four bowls of Samaná Seafood Soup the quartet reminisce on all their good times with the Kings. After an hour they are smiling and laughing like the old friends they are.

"Okay guys, I have to get back to the office." Dennis says, standing. "Oh yeah, I almost forgot." He reaches into his pocket and pulls out a small key.

"This is yours." He hands the key to Devin. "Your mother mailed it to me about six weeks ago. All she told me was to put it in a safe place for her. I think it goes to a safety deposit box."

Looks electronic, Devin thinks, turning the key over in his hand. He has seen keys like this before. There is a digital chip hidden within the grooves of the key that allows issuers to provide modern security measures while keeping the old look and feel of a key that wealthier clients enjoy.

"Okay then," Dennis says, picking up his briefcase, "if you need anything, and I mean *anything*, don't hesitate to call, okay. Saka, we'll go for that drive whenever you're ready."

Sukamaya smiles. "Just come by the house anytime. Maybe

we can play Donkey Kong."

"Yeah, okay buddy. I'll do that." Dennis shakes Devin's and Sukamaya's hands, gives Samantha a parting hug, and turns to leave.

"Hold up!" Devin calls out. "You didn't say what bank it goes to."

Dennis turns around and shrugs. "She didn't say. I thought you'd know."

That doesn't make any sense to Samantha. "Why would Mom mail you a key for her to hide?" She looks to Devin and Sukamaya. "Especially when she knew about Dad's security system."

Another one of Mom's riddles, Devin thinks, turning the key over in his hand. "And you're sure she didn't say anything else or send something to go with this?"

Dennis shakes his head. "No, Devin. I'm sorry. Six weeks ago I got that key in the mail with a note from your mother telling me to put it in a safe place. When I called to confirm, she only said it again."

"It is okay, Dennis." Sukamaya intercedes. "We'll figure this out. You just make sure to stop by so we can go on that drive. Maybe then we can take a hike to the waterfall?"

Dennis smiles. "Sure buddy. Maybe in a few weeks." He turns to Devin. "Sorry I can't help you with that key. But anything else you ever need, call me. Your parents were always good friends to me. Your father got me through some rough times, you know." He smiles again. "Just consider me Uncle Dennis."

Now Devin is the one smiling. "Yeah, alright, *Uncle* Dennis."

Samantha laughs. "Nice to have a lawyer in the family."

"Alright," Dennis says, "let's not wait so long to see each other again, okay."

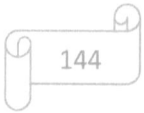

"Goodbye Dennis." Sukamaya waves. "Hope to see you soon."

The three of them watch as Dennis disappears into a crowd of tourists. Once he's gone they turn and head for the car.

"Another mystery." Samantha says, taking the key from Devin.

Sukamaya stops in the middle of the road and turns to Devin and Samantha. His buoyant smile is replaced with a look of sternness they haven't seen since they were children. They exchange worried glances.

"No, Samantha-child." He says. "There is no mystery. I know what bank the key is from."

CHAPTER NINE

You sure?" Devin asks, unlocking the Masserati's doors.

Sukamaya glances around the now bustling tourist strip and nods. "Yes, Devin-sun. Not long after she returned from Iraq, your mother took something there. I went with her."

Okay then, Devin thinks, *the First Bank in Santo Domingo.* The three of them enter the car and he punches the destination into the navigation system.

"It's about 3 hours from here." He says, reading the monitor. A slight grin stretches across his face as he starts the car. Samantha does not like what it implies.

"Devin, don't!" She says, fastening her seatbelt as he pulls away from the curb. "I know that look. Devin, don't even think about it."

He turns to her with a look of feigned ignorance concealing his intentions. "What?" He smirks. "You know I can cut it in two."

Samantha shakes her head. "Devin, please." She sighs. "Please, don't be stupid. For once. How are we supposed to figure out what this keys for if we're locked up for speeding?" She glances up at the speedometer, frightened by the numbers she sees. "Or dead in a car crash?"

Ignoring her, he switches lanes and looks up into the rearview mirror. "So Saka," he calls, "you know what Mom dropped off there?"

Sukamaya looks at Devin through the mirror's reflection. "It was a long black tube, Devin- sun. When I asked her what it was she only said, 'it could be nothing or it could be everything.' You know your mother. I thought it may have been a rare painting, because of the tube. Now I am not so sure."

Right, Devin thinks. *What can any of them be sure of now?* This time yesterday, Devin was taking a sensual shower with two beautiful women eager to please him. Less than 48 hours later, his parents have been murdered, his mother's book stolen, the police can't be trusted, The Elite have appeared, and now he's been given a key to only God-knows-what.

Merging into highway traffic, he maneuvers the Masserati to the left lane and opens her up. Samantha clutches the door as the car climbs to uncomfortable speeds. Holding her breath she watches the needle of the speedometer, *160 180 190 180 195 200—*

"Devin." She says through clenched teeth. "Slow. Down." Her heart stops as Devin dips the Masserati around a less anxious driver. "What if we get pulled over, huh? You ever think of that?"

Devin grins. It is for that exact reason that he's had a police scanner installed in all of his cars. "You're right." He tells her, flipping on the scanner. "I'll see them before they see me. Thanks."

Samantha slugs him in the shoulder. "You're stupid. You know that?"

"Hey Sam." He says, still sporting that obnoxious grin. "You know, if you're worried about me crashing, it's probably not a good idea to be punching me in my driving arm." He shifts gears and the car accelerates faster. With the limiter disabled his Masserati can do every bit of the 260 mph on the dash and maybe more. The modification is highly illegal but well worth a few tickets for an adrenaline junkie like Devin.

"Okay Sam." He says. " You know the deal— just admit that you're scared and I'll slow down. Okay? You know how it goes."

Sukamaya grins to himself. He hasn't seen (or is it heard) this particular game being played in years. Devin has been teasing Samantha with his driving since he first got his license but to Sukamaya's knowledge it has yet to work. Samantha has never given Devin the satisfaction of hearing her say—

"I'm scared, Devin." She spits the words out reluctantly. "There. You happy? You won. Now just slow down, please."

Devin's face droops with disappointment and he eases up off the accelerator.

"What?" Samantha asks, noticing his change in expression. "Look, Devin, eventually we have to grow up. It's like Mom said, I'm too smart to be dumb."

Sukamaya leans forward in his seat, smirking curiously. "So is that what she meant child? I was wondering about that myself."

Samantha shoots her father an admonishing glare. "So then why don't I believe you, Saka? I think you know exactly what Mom meant, don't you?

"I think there may be only one person on this island who does not," he says sitting back in the seat, "but you are too smart not to see that, right child?"

First Bank of Santo Domingo.

The cool breeze is the first thing that Samantha notices as she steps through the doors; that and the faint sound of a Spanish guitar being played through speakers. Devin and Sukamaya stand beside her as she glances around the bank, taking it all in. Above them a crystal chandelier hangs like a sparkling disco-ball, scattering the sun's rays out across the room. There is a section of cubicles straight ahead. She watches as a smiling young couple is led to one of them and seated at a desk. A buxom attendant quickly comes to their aide and the young woman glances at her boyfriend suspiciously. Samantha looks to her right, to an elderly woman sitting behind a receptionist desk eyeing them curiously. Samantha smiles at the old woman and smirks when she guiltily goes back to work. There is a hallway behind the receptionist's desk but Samantha can't see down it—*probably the break room*, she thinks. Opposite this hall, to her left, is a small carpeted area, somewhat quaint in its simplicity. Two L-shaped couches and a few soft backed chairs sit around a large glass coffee table full of magazines and pamphlets. She watches as two laughing women head to a glistening cappuccino maker and fill their cups. The smell of French vanilla catches her nose.

"I thought banks were busy on the weekend." Devin says, glancing around. He takes notice of the three uniformed guards positioned strategically around the lobby and thinks of the men— *trained* men—that killed his parents. For all he knows The Elite could be following them now. His mom didn't hide this key with Dennis for nothing.

He continues to survey the room and smirks at the obvious fourth guard, sitting in the waiting area. Devin has seen enough of his father's friends to know undercover military when he sees it. Not to mention the bulge beneath the guy's shirt, coincidentally located just where a hip holster would be. *Sloppy*, he thinks.

"Well, I don't know." He continues, looking at Samantha now. "I do my business electronically. I don't know how busy a bank is supposed to be."

Samantha rolls her eyes in disbelief. "See that guy over there?" She motions toward a tall slender man in a tailored blue suit. "He looks like he works here, right? I'm going to see if he can help us."

She heads towards the man and Devin and Sukamaya follow close behind. The man, dressed in a well tailored navy blue suit, spots them coming his way and moves to greet them.

"Hello." He says, smiling as he extends a manicured hand to Samantha. "Welcome to the First Bank of Santo Domingo. My name is William Barrea. I am the manager of this establishment here. How can I help you this afternoon?"

Devin steps forward and removes the key from his pocket. "Well, Mr. Barrea, my mom left me this key in her will. I think it goes to a safety deposit box here."

Barrea takes the key from Devin and looks it over. "Yes this is certainly one of ours. If you would please come with me sir. I assume that you would like to retrieve the contents."

Mr. Barrea leads the group across the lobby and into a small office. Taking a seat at the desk, he turns on the computer and motions to the two chairs across from him. "Feel free to have a seat." He offers.

"We are fine." Sukamaya says, eyeing Barrea closely. He doesn't trust him. There is something about the man's energy—it feels dark, restricted, and violent almost.

Barrea shrugs—a slight raising of the shoulders—and smiles. "Okay, sir." He says, turning his attention back to Devin. "The first thing I need is your mother's name. We have to make sure she was actually a customer here."

"Yeah." Devin nods. "Jacqueline King. Doctor Jacqueline King."

"A doctor?" Barrea says. His eyebrows raise as he types. "What field, if I may ask?"

"Yeah, sure, she was an archaeologist."

Barrea nods as he types. "Sounds interesting. Did she ever

find anything exciting?"

"Uhh..." Devin glances to Samantha and Sukamaya, wondering if they find that question peculiar as he does. Samantha seems to share his concern.

"She was actually famous for some of her finds," she says, "in Peru especially."

Barrea nods again and stops typing. The computer monitor now shows Mrs. King's smirking face beside a list of her account information. "Okay sir. It says here that your mother does have a box with us. She opened it very recently and has only made one deposit, no withdrawals."

"Alright." Devin says. "I would like to retrieve whatever is in that box, then."

"Yes, you can do that, but first I need to have some identification, sir. Your driver's license will suffice."

Devin removes his license from his wallet and hands it to Mr. Barrea. Barrea gives it a quick review and passes it back.

"That's fortunate." He says. "You are listed on the account as a joint holder, Mr. King. That saves us a lot of time. If you had not been listed, I would have needed verification that your mother had died and bequeathed you the ownership of the box. Never mind that now, though I will still need that information if you decide to close out the account or have it transferred to you."

Barrea shuts down the computer and rises to his feet. "If you would come with me, sir, I will show you to our high-security vault." He looks to Samantha and Sukamaya. "You two can wait here until we return or there is the waiting area in the lobby. We've recently installed a cappuccino maker."

"Hold on." Devin says. "This is my sister and godfather. They're family. I, uhh... I want them there for sentimental reasons, you know. Like emotional support."

"Well, sir, it is really just a matter of security." Barrea explains, hoping that Devin will just accept this and he won't have to go into all of the procedures that must be followed when it concerns a high-security box or the reasons why. A thought occurs to him. "Mr. King, did you say that this is your sister?"

Devin nods and Mr. Barrea goes back behind the desk and logs into the computer. "Do you have your ID, miss?" He asks Samantha. He looks to Sukamaya. "And you too, sir. You are his Godfather, correct? Can I see your ID as well?"

Mr. Barrea takes the two IDs and pulls up Mrs. King's account profile. It is just as he suspected: both Sukamaya and Samantha Matsumi are also listed as joint holders. He hands them back their driver's licenses, smiling the smile of a man impressed by his own wit.

"There are four names listed on the account besides your mother," he explains, "and I had noticed that one of them was a girl with an, uhh...," he hesitates, not wanting to offend anymore, "Asian last name, and a man also. When you said that she was your sister..." He studies their faces briefly, searching for some sign of resemblance. "Granted, you two do not look alike, but, I just assumed that she—"

Devin cuts him off. "You said there are four names? Is the other one Derrick King? Doctor Derrick King?"

Barrea's glance shifts down at the floor. It is a quick gesture but one that Devin catches. "I'm sorry, sir, but I cannot divulge that information until the account has been transferred or—"

"It's okay." Devin stops him. "He's dead too."

A somber silence settles on the room and Mr. Barrea adjusts his tie, not sure what he's supposed to say. With every second that passes he grows more uncomfortable. Fortunately for him, Sukamaya also senses the uneasiness in the air.

"Mr. Barrea." He says. "If it is okay with you, I think we would like to see the box now."

"Certainly, sir. You all follow me."

Mr. Barrea leads them out of the office, down a narrow hall and to a large metal door. The solid black door strikes an imposing contrast against the hall's white walls. A palm reader sits to the right of the door handle beneath a numeric keypad. Mr. Barrea punches in a four-digit code, lays his hand on the reader and waits as it registers his unique biological signature. The faint sound of locks being disengaged is heard a few seconds later.

"Welcome to our high-security vault." He says, stepping inside the brightly lit room. "This is the safest place for your most valuable possessions in Santo Domingo."

That is not true, Sukamaya thinks to himself. He steps inside the room behind Devin and Samantha and looks around. It isn't very impressive. Three monochromatic walls of stainless steel have been divided into six hundred and sixty-six rectangular slots, each containing a steel box. The bright fluorescent lights cast a dull shine that is instantly drab and sterile. *It is like a cloudy day inside a new factory*, Sukamaya thinks.

Mr. Barrea motions to the chairs surrounding a large rectangular table in the center of the room. "You can have a seat if you like. It will be a few minutes while I disarm your box." There is a podium to their right. He goes to it, slides back the cover and begins to tap on the touch-sensitive screen.

Devin's eyes move from the corner of the ceiling—where he's spotted two security cameras disguised to look like speakers—to Mr. Barrea. "Yeah, okay." He says and then leans in close to Samantha and whispers. "So what was up with that question about Mom's findings? You think?"

Samantha looks at him skeptically. "What? You think... seriously?"

He shrugs. "I don't know. It was just an odd question, especially with, you know, the book and all."

"I mean, it's just a coincidence right? You're just being paranoid." She looks over at Mr. Barrea. He's typing something into the screen. "It has to be, right?"

Mr. Barrea looks up from the podium and smiles proudly. "Okay, Mr. King. Now all I need is the pass code and I can deactivate the box. Once that is done then you just slide in the key and retrieve the contents."

A pass code? Devin doesn't know anything about a pass code. He looks to Sukamaya and Samantha and they stare back just as dumbfounded as he.

"Uhh..." He stammers. "Well, umm..."

Barrea's smile grows even wider. It is once again the smile of a man that knows better than to pat himself on the back in public but secretly yearns to. "You do not have the pass code, do you sir? That is okay. You'd be amazed at the number of people who leave boxes behind in their wills without leaving the access codes to go with it."

He swipes the touch screen monitor. "Fortunately we have a system in place for such occurrences. Actually, I designed this back-up measure myself." The smile returns again. "It is very simple, you see. In case of something like this our customers, like your mother, are asked to submit a list of questions and answers—5 actually—that only herself and those, well, you all, would know. Each answer has a portion of the code hidden within it. If all of your answers are correct then the box will be unarmed and I will print you out a copy of the code for future references. If you like, once the account has been transferred to you, you can submit your own questions and answers."

Devin looks to Samantha and Sukamaya again. There is no limit to the questions that his mother may have asked; she was a published author, doctoral recipient and real life Lara Croft. His only comfort is that the questions are supposed to be ones that they would be able to answer. *Sukamaya had shared a home with her for over two decades and Samantha was her best friend; between the two of them they should be able to figure this out.*

That thought, that Samantha and Sukamaya knew his mother better than he did, hurts him deeply but he pushes the pain aside for now; just one more reason for him to find her killers and make them pay.

"Okay." He says. "Shoot."

"Alright." Barrea ques up the first question. "Number one: what is the key to life and death?"

Just as he thought; Devin is stumped. He doesn't even know where to begin answering that. He vaguely remembers something about Egyptian philosophy but it isn't enough to give him the confidence to speak.

Fortunately, Samantha doesn't have that problem. "It's man." She says. "Remember? It's from the Sphinx riddle."

Barrea begins to type in the answer but Devin stops him. "Wait." He says and turns to Samantha. "Hold on. You sure about this?" He looks back to Barrea. "How many misses do we have?"

"You can make two errors, sir. After that the box cannot be accessed until it is placed under your ownership."

"I'm sure Devin." Samantha assures him. "Don't you

remember the riddle? Mom used to ask it every time we came home from school."

Devin thinks back to the days when Saka and his father would pick him and Samantha up from the airstrip and the two of them would ride in the back of the Jaguar, eating ice cream and trading stories. When they got home, he and Samantha would jump out of the car and race for the door, to be greeted by a smiling Mrs. King. She would be standing behind a four foot high bronze statue of a sphinx.

"What animal goes on four feet in the morning," he says, "two feet at noon, and three in the evening? That was the riddle right? The Sphinx had told some guy that if he got it right then he'd live but if he got it wrong then it was lights out. Oh, okay, so knowing the answer is the key between living and dying?"

Samantha chuckles. "Yeah, and remember I told you the answer? It's man, humans; we crawl as babies, walk as adults and use a cane in old age."

"That seems like the answer to me." Sukamaya chimes in. "Go ahead, Mr. Barrea."

With a nod, Mr. Barrea types the word 'man' into the blank space then taps 'enter', and waits. A few seconds later a green light radiates from the screen. "That's correct." He says. "Now, question number two: What is the key to all of my treasures?"

Sukamaya looks to Devin. "Devin-sun, your birthday. Remember the video."

Devin nods. "I remember. Mr. Barrea, the answer is July 11, 1988. Seven-eleven-one-nine-eight- eight."

Barrea enters the sequence of numbers and waits. The screen glows green. "Correct." He says. "Third question: What is the difference between a loss and a lesson?"

Devin doesn't need any help this time. "I remember when I lost my first martial arts match. I was so mad I wanted to quit. But then mom pulled me aside and said I only lost if I lost the lesson. She said I had just learned what I needed to work on. She said it was all on my perception. He smirks. "The answer's perception."

Barrea types the word 'perception' into the screen and a few seconds later the screen turns green. He nods approvingly. "Only two more questions. Number four: Each year the universe comes into alignment on what day?"

Baffled, Devin looks to Samantha. "I didn't even know that was possible." He says. "As a matter of fact, it's not possible. You know, you're a physicist."

Samantha smirks. "*Applied* physics, dummy. I'm an engineer. But anyway, Mom wasn't talking about the physical universe. More of an abstract concept that—"

"So you know what she meant?" He cuts her off.

"Yeah, well, I think so. See, Mom had told me about the Hebrew science of gemetria. She was telling me about the kabbalah, you know, their oral teachings. Well, she said that there were schools of thought other than the Hebrews that used gemetria. The Freemasons use a system where the numbers 1, 2, and 3 were represented by the sun, moon and stars, in that order. So when Mom says the universe, think of it as the sun, moon and stars. I mean, really, that's basically what it is. Even planets could be, in a sense, described as the sun's moons and each sun is just a star."

"Okay." Devin says, wishing she would skip all the commentary and just give Mr. Barrea the answer. "So..."

"So the answer is 1, 2, 3, stupid. January 23rd." She rolls her eyes and shakes her head in disbelief. "How do you have a Master's degree?"

Devin ignores her and watches as Barrea types the date into the system. Once again the screen turns green.

"Now last question." Barrea says. "It seems simple enough. She asks: if I had a pet, what would I name it?"

Samantha bursts into laughter. "Oh, that's so easy. Almost too easy. The answer's Agarthi. No doubt about it."

Barrea begins to type. He stops at the second 'a', realizing that he has no clue how the word is spelt. Samantha is about to tell him when Devin stops her.

"Sam, are you sure? I mean, I didn't even know mom was into animals. We never had any pets."

"Mom loved animals, actually. She just knew that she couldn't get a pet because all the work would've fallen on Saka."

"I would not have minded looking after a dog. "Sukamaya says. "She should have asked me."

Samantha laughs again. "A dog. Yeah right, Saka. Mom didn't want a dog. Mom wanted a mole."

"A mole!" Now Devin is the one laughing. "Come on, Sam, who has a mole for a pet?"

"Exactly right. Mom used to joke that if she ever did get a pet she'd get a giant mole, and she'd train it to search underground for ancient tunnels. She said she'd name it Agarthi, one of the names of the hidden civilization she was looking for. Trust me, the answer's Agarthi. A-G-A-R-T-H-I."

"Alright," Devin yields, "if you say so, Sam. You've been right so far."

"The answer you are going with is Agarthi then?" Barrea confirms. The three of them nod and Mr. Barrea types the word into the system. He waits. A red light flashes.

"I'm sorry." He tells them. "That is incorrect. You have one more attempt."

Samantha's confused. It has to be Agarthi. There is no other choice. "This doesn't make any sense. Mom always said she'd get a mole and name it Agarthi. I almost bought her one once for her birthday." She turns to Devin and Sukamaya. "I don't know what else it could be. I was sure it was Agarthi. It's what Mom always said."

Sukamaya lays a comforting hand on her arm. "It's okay, child. Just take a deep breath and let your mind be at ease. The answer will come to you." He looks to Devin. "You too, Devin-sun. We must recall any time she may have—"

"There's no point." Samantha cuts in. "It's Agarthi. I know it." She looks to Mr. Barrea. "A-G- A-R-T-H-I."

Barrea glances down at the screen and then back to Samantha. His face is apologetic. "I'm sorry miss but did you say, 'I'? It seems that I misheard you. I was sure that you said 'Y'." He corrects the entry and the screen flashes a comforting green. "I apologize for the mistake. It'll just be a minute now."

While the four of them wait, Mr. Barrea watches as the five rows of boxes containing the answers to Mrs. King's questions fade away until only ten characters remain. These remaining characters then scramble on screen until the pass code has been generated. The entire process takes but a few seconds to complete.

"It is finished." Barrea says, tapping the screen. "Just another second while I print out your copy."

A small slip of paper slides from the printer hidden inside the podium and—with that same self- satisfied smirk on his face—Mr. Barrea hands it to Devin and directs him to box number 421. "Just insert your key." He tells him. "The electronic signature will disarm the last of the security measures and then you just have to unlock the box." He looks to the group. "I'll leave you to your business then. Sorry for your loss."

Mr. Barrea exits the room and closes the door behind him. Devin walks over to the wall, opens the slot and removes the long rectangular box from its port. Sukamaya and Samantha crowd in as he sits the box on the table. The cling of metal against metal reminds Devin of the old sword fights that he, Saka and his father would watch. It is a random thought and as he enters the key into the lock a more poignant one enters his mind. *Why did Mom hide the book at the house but leave this thing here? Whatever it is.*

"Come on." Samantha says, growing impatient. "What are you waiting for? Open it already."

Devin looks from her to Sukamaya. He knows that they have questions of their own; questions that they deserve to have answered. It seems like since he's been home that's all there have been: questions, questions and more questions.

"Alright." He says, inserting the key into the lock. "Here goes."

Slowly, he turns the key, lifts the metal lid and peers inside, hoping he can finally get some answers.

CHAPTER TEN

I t looks like one of those satchels that you see painters or architects with."

Devin says, lifting the slender cylinder from the box. It's about three feet long, he guesses, all black and made out of a thick plastic. "It even has the strap." Samantha looks from Devin and the container to her father. "Is this the same case that Mom had that day?" She asks.

Sukamaya nods. "Yes, child. It is the same one."

Hearing that, she turns her eyes once again to Devin. He's staring at the container fixedly and Samantha can practically read his thoughts—mostly because they are her own. *Could Mom have left some clue to the killers' location? Could she have left them some answers; some explanation for what is happening? Did she really know that all of this would occur?*

"Go on, Devin-sun." Sukamaya says, interrupting their reverie. Devin looks at him and nods. With butterflies in his stomach, he unscrews the lid and peers inside the tube. There's something there but he can't be certain what it is. He turns the satchel over and the contents begin to slide out. Shocked, Samantha lurches forward and cups her hand over the bottom of the container before any of the contents can spill out onto the table.

"What the hell, Devin!" She exclaims, snatching the satchel out of his hands. "Think stupid! Whatever this is, it could be thousands of years old. You can't jump dump it out like Pick-Up-Stix."

Very carefully, Samantha slides the contents into her hand

and out onto the table. It appears to be some sort of ancient paper-like material made of interlaced and cross-weaved strips of thick fibers. "I've seen something like this before." She says, gently taking hold of the rolled up document. The material is old and stiff and she takes extra care as she unrolls it before them. "It's a papyri scroll. Mom showed me a few of these once but they were just fragments. She always said it was rare to find a whole scroll."

She looks up at them, grinning. "What if this is like a lost book of the Bible or something? Or like some proof that Jesus really lived? Or that he didn't? Something paradigm-shifting."

"You think we're living the *Da Vinci Code* or something?" Devin teases although he doesn't completely dismiss her thoughts. *What if she's right and this thing is potentially world changing?* He grins to himself. *When your mother is the black Lara Croft anything's possible.*

And, he muses, *if she did think that this scroll was something that the Vatican would conceal from the public or try to exploit, she would have done everything she could to prevent them from having it.*

What if The Elite are like that albino guy from the movie, he wonders.

"But, seriously." He says. "Do you think those men could've been working for Rome? Like some modern day Crusaders or something? Killing for the cloth."

"Stay in the moment." Sukamaya says. He glances up at the speaker-cameras in the ceiling. "We must find out what this is before we do anything else."

Samantha has finished unrolling the scroll. It is about a foot to a foot and a half wide and close to double that in length. The light brown fibers are covered with a collage of ancient signs and symbols.

Other than some stuff that looks like hieroglyphics, Devin doesn't have a clue what any of it is.

He turns to Samantha. "You recognize any of this stuff from your dates with Mom?" He asks, regretting his words the second he hears them.

Samantha ignores the snide remark and points to a cluster of wedge-shaped markings in the center of the scroll. "This looks like it could be cuneiform," she says, "but I'm not sure. These here." She touches the set of pictograms filling the scroll's upper portion. "These are definitely Egyptian hieroglyphics. The rest of this; I have no idea."

Devin continues to look on. Pyramids, crosses, hands, trees—not one of these images mean anything to him. *Why couldn't she just have left a note or an address, even a picture; something simple? What the hell are we supposed to do with this now?*

A figure catches his eye. Something on the bottom right corner of the scroll beneath an odd looking hand holding up three fingers. He runs his fingers across it. It feels as if he's seen this before, maybe a very long time ago, maybe in a dream. He isn't sure. He tries to think back but his memory banks are empty.

"Know anything about this?" He asks Samantha, still touching the figure. "I feel like I've seen it before."

She nods. "Yeah. It's a scarab. An Egyptian beetle. Mom had a necklace with one on it. Those beetles were sacred to the Egyptians. It was something that had to do with the movement of the Sun. I don't remember seeing one with that circle on its wings like that though. But, I mean..." She pauses, disheartened. For of all the time that she spent with Mrs. King Samantha feels like she should know a lot more about this stuff but it's been so long that she's forgotten much of what she was taught. "It's been a while since I've seen any of this stuff."

"What about you, Saka?" Devin asks. "You know anything about this stuff?"

"No, Devin-sun." Sukamaya's response comes quick. He has yet to even take more than a momentary glance at the scroll. Since Samantha laid it out on the table his focus has been on those two fake speakers in the ceiling. If Mrs. King went to the trouble of hiding this scroll away then he assumes that she wouldn't want video footage of it floating around either. The entire time that Devin and Samantha have been talking Sukamaya has been attempting to use his body to block the cameras' view but he can't be sure that it's working. Then there is also the matter of audio recording. For all he knows, every word that they say is being recorded. There is an uneasiness stirring within him; a disturbance in the *Tao*.

Solemn-faced, he turns to Devin. "That is enough, Devin-sun. Samantha-child, roll the scroll back up please and place it into the case. It is time for us to leave this place."

Neither of them question Sukamaya's judgment. Samantha carefully rolls the scroll back up and slides it inside the satchel. Devin takes the satchel from her and slides the strap down over his chest. He turns his gaze to Sukamaya.

"Okay Saka. What's up?" He asks, puzzled but always trusting in Sukamaya's instincts.

"It is time to leave here, Devin-sun.Something is wrong." Sukamaya goes to open the door but it won't budge. He tries it again. Nothing. They are locked in.

Samantha tries the door and gets the same result. She turns to Devin. "Why would Mr. Barrea lock us in here? You don't think he's—"

Her sentence is interrupted by the sound of disengaging

locks. She steps back instinctively and shifts her weight to the balls of her feet. Her hands clench into tight fists and her breathing slows. Devin and Sukamaya are standing beside her, staring at the door, waiting but ready.

The door swings open slowly and in strolls Mr. Barrea. "Is it okay if I—" He stops and takes a step back. Devin, Samantha and Sukamaya are all glaring at him, ready to attack. He's frightened and concerned all at once. Forcing a smile, he looks to Devin and asks, "Is everything okay, sir?"

Devin glances to Sukamaya, seeking guidance. There is a slight shifting of Sukamaya's brows that only he and Samantha see. He turns back to Barrea. "I think we're done here." He says, moving towards the door. "Is there anything else I need to do?"

"Well sir..." Mr. Barrea moves around Devin and heads to the table. He picks up the box and returns it to its port. "In order to close out the account or either transfer it to your name, I will need the death certificate and legal evidence that it was bequeathed to you."

"Yeah. I'll have my lawyer contact you about all that."

Mr. Barrea smiles. "Yes, that will be fine, sir. Though I do hope that it is the latter you choose." He follows the group out into the hall. "Come with me then and I'll show you three out."

As the three of them follow Mr. Barrea down the narrow hall Devin wonders what it is that has Sukamaya so spooked? He knows better than to question the old man's hunches; they've saved his life more than once. *Whatever it is I'll be ready for it. There is nothing that's going to stop me from finding these guys.*

They arrive at the end of the hall and Mr. Barrea bids them farewell. "And I do hope that you will continue your family's business here." He adds, extending his hand to Devin. Devin takes his hand and, as they shake, Mr. Barrea looks him straight in the eyes. "The Elite deserve elite service. Don't you agree?"

Devin drops Mr. Barrera's hand and steps back, not sure if he heard correctly. "What'd you just say? What about The Elite?"

Barrea grins. "I was simply saying that here at First Bank we pride ourselves on offering the best services to the region's best people."

Devin nods, unconvinced. He looks to Samantha and Sukamaya "Let's go. Mr. Barrea, my lawyers will be contacting you."

With that Devin, Samantha, and Sukamaya walk off across the lobby.

"Hey!" Mr. Barrea calls out. The group stops and turns toward him. "You all be safe. The world is not as secure as our vaults."

Crossing the lobby, Samantha turns to Devin. "You know we have to find out what this means, right? That's the only way we'll be able to find out why Mom hid it?"

"Yeah," he nods, "and maybe it'll help us find the killers."

Turning his head, Devin spots a burly man approaching them quickly.

"Hey!" The man yells. "Hey! You! Stop!"

Devin stops and turns. Samantha and Sukamaya do the same. Devin recognizes the man— he's that undercover security guard who was in the waiting area—and as the guard jogs toward him, Devin's eyes instantly shift to the gun on his waist.

"You're Devin King, right?" The man asks, standing before the group now. His hand starts to move toward his waist.

Before the man can get to his gun, Devin rams his knee into the man's stomach and he lurches over in agony. Devin sidesteps quickly, repositioning himself, and flips him over his shoulder.

Standing over him now, he jams his foot into the man's neck. "Who do you work for?! Who are The Elite?!" He shouts the words with all the fury that is inside him. The man tries to speak but Devin's foot is choking him. He reaches out for Devin's leg and Sukamaya steps on his arm.

"Devin you're choking him!" Samantha shouts. Devin eases up the pressure, never removing his glare. "Talk!" He shouts. "Now!" Bug-eyed with fright, the man tries to speak but can only gasp for air. Devin eases up some more.

"What the hell man?" The guy says. "I just wanted an autograph, man. I'm a fan, dude. I just saw that hang-glide you did off that castle in Haiti. That was max dude!" He tries to move his arm but Sukamaya is still standing on it. He looks to Devin. "Tell grandpa to let up. I just want to get my pen dude."

Devin nods to Sukamaya and he lifts his leg from the man's arm. The man goes in his pocket and pulls out a pen and piece of paper. "See, I only do this security stuff part time. It's just until I land me a Red-Bull endorsement, maybe a Mountain Dew contract or something."

Devin lifts his foot off of the man's neck and helps him to his feet. "Sorry 'bout that man. Things have been crazy lately." He takes the pen and paper and scribbles down his name and number. "Call my girl, Carol. If your stuff's good, I'll sign you myself." He hands the guy the paper and apologizes again. "I mean it man."

Smiling from ear to ear, the man nods. "Yeah. Don't worry about it, dude. It's okay. I can't wait to tell my friends I got slammed by D.K. The D.K! They'll never believe it." He looks at the paper again. "Thanks, man. Soon as I get my tape together, I'll call."

Devin shakes the guy's hand and he walks off. "Hey!" Devin

calls. "What's your name?"

"Sean, Sean Turner!" He yells back.

Devin nods, wondering if the guy has the talent his team needs. He's built his extreme stunt career performing heart-pounding tricks in illegal locations all over the world. It would be nice if he could find a few more performers because until he finds these killers, he may have to give up—

Samantha slugs him in the arm. "Sean Turner." She says, breaking his reverie. "Yeah, that'll be the name on the lawsuit he sends you. What were you thinking?"

Devin tries to explain as the three of them continue to make their way across the lobby. "I just saw the gun, you know. With everything that's been going on. Did you hear that shit that guy Barrea said? Be careful and all that. What was that supposed to mean? Then before that, he said something about The Elite. Saka, you felt it too, didn't you? That's why you told us to leave?"

Sukamaya stops at the doors and gives his young friend a somber stare. "Have no expectations, Devin-sun. The Master remains empty and is thereby always fulfilled." He smiles. "But that was a good throw. Just next time, use more hip."

He pats the side of his thigh and Samantha can only shake her head. "What am I going to with you two?"

- -

Mr. Barrea turns and walks back down the hall, passes the high security vaults and enters a small room where a wall of monitors greets him. These screens, accessible to only one other, show Mr. Barrea the happenings of every inch of the bank-- vaults included. At the current moment there is no sound accompanying these images but if Barrea were to touch any one of the monitors the image would enlarge, dividing itself amongst the entire wall of monitors, and every word would be broadcast throughout the room. But right now the monitors are not important. He has already seen all he's needed to see. What matters now is the phone hanging on the wall and the number he dials.

"Speak." A raspy voice commands.

"Let the Beast know that they have left the bank. He was right. The daughter had the scroll. It is with them now."

TRUE KING

CHAPTER ELEVEN

As Devin follows Samantha and Sukamaya down the stairs he gazes up at the dark gray clouds rolling in.

Behind him a digital billboard flashes: FIRST BANK OF SANTO DOMINGO 1:15PM 68°F.

He glances down at his watch.

1:20pm, he reads. *Mom did always say I moved to fast.*

A thunderous boom explodes in the distance. Devin turns to Samantha and Sukamaya.

"Let's hurry up and get on the highway before it starts raining." He takes a step down onto the sidewalk but Sukamaya yanks him back. A tingling sensation shoots through Devin's torso, moving up through his arm, to his shoulder and across his chest. He turns toward Sukamaya and the two of them stand face to face, completely still.

"Did you sense Mr. Barrera's aura, Devin-sun?" Sukamaya motions up at the storm growing overhead." It was like this—dark and heavy clouds. Could you feel it, Devin-sun?"

"I don't know Saka, but I definitely felt yours."

"I wanted you to, Devin-sun. I directed my ki to you." He looks to Samantha. "And you child, could you sense his aura? The darkness within him?"

Samantha shakes her head, ashamed by her lack of perception. "I was focused on the scroll Saka."

Sukamaya looks at them both and shakes his head. "Sickness," is all he can say. They have moved so far from the center that they have lost their way in the world; yet Sukamaya smiles, amused at the play of it all. He looks to them again. "Come. Let us go."

He steps into the sea of bodies and Devin and Samantha follow behind like two scolded children.

Samantha moves closer to Devin and whispers, "Do you still meditate?"

Devin shakes his head. "Well I try sometimes, but..." He pictures the gruesome images of Stacey that always flood his mind. "I just can't focus, I guess. You?"

"Nope." She says. "I haven't even tried in years. I guess since I left for college."

Devin smiles and nods. "Yeah, our last summer together. Hey, why'd you leave so quickly anyway?"

Samantha stares at him in disbelief. There is no way that he doesn't know why she left early. Could he really be that self-centered? "You can't be serious." She says. "You don't know why I left early that summer, Devin? Seriously?"

"I don't know," he says, scanning his memory, "graduation, prom, uhh..."

Sukamaya has stopped in the middle of the sidewalk and Devin—caught up in his conversation with Samantha—is about to crash into him until Sukamaya turns and grabs him. "Do you feel that?" He asks, scanning the crowd. "It's coming from that direction. It's violent; enslaved; determined." He turns and looks in the opposite direction. "There, too. Don't you sense it? Still yourself and be one with the Tao."

Devin nods and in the middle of the sidewalk, amidst a swarming sea of bodies, he stands perfectly still, takes a deep breath, and closes his eyes.

Sukamaya looks to Samantha. "You too, child."

Standing beside Devin, Samantha shuts her eyes and attempts to quiet her mind. She tries to focus on her breath, flowing in and out, in and out, but she cannot concentrate. People are bumping into her, and there is just too much noise. Devin, on the other hand, senses the danger instantly. It is moving towards them, approaching from opposite directions. He opens his eyes and shifts his gaze over Sukamaya's left shoulder. Sukamaya stares out over Devin's right.

Who, Devin thinks, scanning the crowd.

Behind him a woman shrieks. He turns his head just as someone yells, "He's got a gun!" Everyone moves at once, scattering, tripping, and falling atop each other as they flee for cover. In the midst of this chaos Devin, Samantha and Sukamaya stand calm, scanning the crowd for the would-be gunmen.

Two shots ring out and the bullets smash into the concrete, inches from Devin's feet.

"Move!" Sukamaya shouts. Everyone ducks and crouches, seeking cover wherever they can find it. He shoves Samantha towards a parked car and the three of them sprint for it as the two gunmen spray the sidewalk with a flurry of bullets. Shards of cement and glass fly through the air.

A biting pain cuts into Samantha's leg and she cries out. Devin grabs her arm and yanks her behind the car just as another fusillade pockets the trunk. "Shit!" She shouts, sitting against the car and clutching her bleeding leg. "Why are they shooting at us? At me!"

Sukamaya leans in and examines Samantha's wound. "You have not been shot." He says, pulling a thick chunk of the car's window from her leg. "It is only glass."

The shooters begin to move in, taunting their prey with short spurts of gunfire. "Just give us the scroll", a man's voice calls out, "or we can come and get it ourselves!" He squeezes the trigger and a bullet pierces the trunk of the car. "I don't think you want that, do you?"

The scroll, Devin thinks. *How could they know that we have the scroll? Better yet, why do they want it?* It must be related to his mother's book and if it is, these may be the men that killed his parents. He looks from Sukamaya to Samantha—neither of them like the look they see in his eyes.

"Okay!" He yells back. "I'm coming out with the scroll! Just...don't shoot!" He begins to stand but Samantha pulls him back down.

"Are you crazy Devin? You can't just give it to them. What are you thinking?"

A sinister grin spreads across Devin's face and he glares at her with a frightening resolution. "I'm thinking that I'm going to take that gun from him and shoot him with it. One time in the head, just the way they did Mom and Dad."

"No, Devin. What—"Samantha stops. She knows that arguing with him is futile. He's made up his mind and there is no changing it now. Sukamaya sets his hand on her thigh and grins.

"Sit here and do not move." He tells her. "I am going to go with Devin-sun. Two against two."

Resigned, Samantha shakes her head and slumps back against the car. Both of you are crazy, she thinks. She just hopes they don't get themselves killed. She couldn't handle another loss; not right now.

With their hands raised above their heads, Devin and Sukamaya step out from behind the truck and approach the gunmen.

"What do you want this scroll for anyway?" Devin asks, stepping forward and letting his hands fall to his side.

"Put your hands back up!" The heavier of the two gunmen order. Still walking, Devin looks the man over. He's all muscle; too stiff to have any speed. His voice sounds scratchy too, like he smokes too much. Grinning, Devin raises his hands back above his head and continues to move forward.

"Okay! That's far enough!" The taller one shouts. "Now just toss over the scroll. Nice and slowly."

Devin glances at Sukamaya, hoping the old man still can move like he used to.

"Look, man," he says, staring at the gunmen, "if you know what this is, then you know that this thing is too old, delicate, you know. I can't just throw it over. You have to come and get it."

"Just do what the hell he said, man." The heavy one yells. "Throw us the fucking container. Slowly."

Sukamaya takes advantage of the shooters' focus on Devin and sneaks a few steps forward. He watches them, observing their movements and studying their rhythms. If Devin's plan is what he thinks it is, knowing their rhythms could be the difference between life and death.

A flash of lighting shoots across the sky and thick drops of rain smack the pavement below. Sukamaya looks to Devin. "Hear the sound of wind of water, Devin-sun. Remember the Way."

Devin nods, moving closer to the gunmen. Thunder booms in the distance. "This is very fragile, man. Whoever sent you, they wouldn't want it damaged."

The heavy one has had enough. "Look, man, it's raining now and I'm not in the mood for this bullshit." He releases the clip from his gun and takes another from his jacket pocket. "Either give me the scroll," he says, sliding the clip in, "or I swear to God that you'll feel every bullet in this gun. Understand?"

"Yeah, I understand. Just calm down, man." Devin lifts the satchel's strap over his head and steps forward. "You won't come and get it so I'll just bring it to you."

He holds the end of the satchel like a club and stretches it forward. "Don't shoot, okay."

Sukamaya begins to move and the gunmen draw down on him. "What're you doing?" The tall one yells. "Stop! Stop moving!"

"He's okay." Devin says, diverting their attention back to him. "He's an old man. What's he going to do?"

Frustrated, the tall one turns back to Devin. "Just give us the scroll already, man!"

"Okay." Devin sticks the satchel out further, holding it just outside the heavy one's reach. "Here. Take it."

Devin takes another steps forward and just as the gunman's fingers graze the tip of the satchel, he lets go. Instinctively, the shooter lurches forward to catch it. Devin makes his move, kickimg the satchel upwards and sending it smashing into the gunman's face. Dazed, he stumbles backwards, clutching his bleeding nose.

In the split second that it takes for the taller one to turn his head towards Devin, Sukamaya closes the space between them and strikes the man's wrist, knocking the gun out of his and. Before the gun can hit the ground, he grabs the man's arm and snaps the bone in two. The gunman bends over, reeling from pain, and Sukamaya sends a spinning elbow to his face, knocking him unconscious. He crumples to the ground like a bag of potatoes.

The short one is still clutching his nose when Devin sends a hard chop to his throat, crushing his larynx. A front heel kick to the

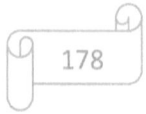

knee shatters the bone and the man drops down. His gun is lying at Devin's feet. Devin picks it up and stands over the would-be killer.

"I can tell you didn't kill my parents." He says, aiming the pistol at the man's head. "Those guys were professionals. Still, you probably know who did, don't you? So, tell me. Tell me who it was and I'll let you live. You have my word."

The gunman glances around the street. There are people watching them from a distance, some hiding behind cars, and others looking out of store windows.

"There are too many witnesses." He says. "You won't kill me here."

Devin pulls the hammer back and presses the barrel against the man's temple. "Good lawyers." He says. "Now tell me, who are The Elite? And where can I find them?"

The gunman's eyes grow wide when he hears that name. It's obvious he's afraid. "Kill me." He says. "I don't know who you're talking about."

Samantha has come out of hiding and is now limping towards the scene. "Devin, don't." She begs, afraid that his thirst for vengeance will get the best of him. She almost tells him to call the police but then she remembers Detective Clarkson. Who knows how far the corruption runs?

"Devin, wait—"

"I got this, Sam. Just get the scroll."

"Devin, please." She pleads. "Don't do anything. Please, Devin."

"Child." Sukamaya calls to his daughter. "Do as he says." The satchel has rolled out into the street and he motions for her to go retrieve it. She nods and Sukamaya turns his attention back to Devin.

"Put the gun down, Devin-sun. The police will be here soon. They can take over."

"The police, Saka?" Devin can't believe that Sukamaya would even suggest that. "How do we know the police in Santo Domingo are any different than the Peninsula? And how will they help us find The Elite?" He glares down at the man kneeling before him. "No. I'll handle this myself."

Sukamaya has to think of something. His duty is to protect Devin from all threats, even if that threat is himself. All of the years that he spent training Devin in the way of the warrior, the way of the Tao; it was only to aid in the unfolding of his potential. Devin is destined to do great things. Sukamaya knows this like he knows his own name.

"Devin-sun," he begins, "you must—" Samantha's shriek steals his attention and his head snaps in her direction.

"Noooo!" She shouts. "Devin! Devin, watch out!"

The other gunman has awoken and made his way to the discarded gun. Barely conscious, he doesn't stand or aim; just points and pulls the trigger.

Sukamaya doesn't see the man behind him pointing the gun but he doesn't have to. The moment Samantha yells Devin's name he springs into action. He lunges forward and tackles Devin to the ground, shielding him with his body as the gun explodes. By the time that Devin can get out from under Sukamaya the two gunmen are sprinting down the street in opposite directions.

Hell no, Devin thinks, grabbing the gun off the sidewalk. His attacker is hobbling down the street, attempting to escape responsibility for what he's done. *You won't get away with it.*

Whoever killed Stacey got away with it and the men that killed his parents got away with it. At least for now. He aims the gun, fires at the man's back and watches as the man splashes face first into a muddy puddle of water.

Consumed with rage, Devin heads towards the man to make sure the job is finished but an agonizing cry stops him in his tracks.

Sam, he thinks. There is something frightening familiar to her wails: pain, fear, disbelief, and something else.

"Please. No." She cries, cradling her father's head in her arms. "No more. Please. No more."

Devin watches her rock back and forth, holding Sukamaya like a mother would a newborn child. He watches the tears fall from her eyes, down her cheeks and onto Sukamaya's brow. He glances down at his shirt. The bottom half is stained crimson, covered in blood.

And then it hits him; the other thing he heard in Samantha's cry.

Blame.

"Somebody call an ambulance!" He yells, pulling out his phone as he sprints to Samantha's side. "Sam, is he breathing? Tell me he's breathing."

Samantha just continues to rock—back and forth and back and forth—as the thick raindrops smack the ground around them. It is as if the heavens themselves are mourning the moment.

The faint sound of sirens grows louder in the distance. Devin looks at the gun still in his hand and tosses it as far away from him as possible. It bounces off the curb and slides into a sewer drain. Kneeling beside Samantha he's starts to say sorry, to say something, but everything just feels too shallow. There is nothing for him to do but wrap her up in his arms and rock back and forth to the sound of the sirens.

CHAPTER TWELVE

I t is becoming harder and harder for Gustuv to control his temper at these gatherings and it's because of insolent, ungrateful and disrespectful men like Romano Hapsburg.

Men with sagging cheeks, creased foreheads and midsections spilling out over their waistlines; men that Gustuv could kill without breaking a sweat; men who owe their seat at this council to no work of their own. These men, these so-called Black Nobility—Europe's most rich and powerful.

Humph, Gustuv is not impressed.

"Mr. Romano, William, Felix." This loathsome trio has been the irritating itch on Gustuv's back for too long now. He glares at all of them. "Do you not trust in your leader? Do you not believe that our Lord has granted me wisdom, discernment, and understanding?"

"Do not dare question our faith in the Lord!" Romano erupts, pounding the table with his well manicured hand. "It is you who needs to show faith, brother!"

Romano's outburst elicits no response from the table. If his brothers did not outright expect it they are at the least accustomed to his fits. Romano Hapsburg is the head of the Black Nobility, a position that is granted to the family that can claim direct descent from the last Roman emperor. Through his father, Romano can trace his lineage back to Emperor Zeno who ruled Rome as the sole emperor for 11 years and through his mother he is a descendant of

Sigismund, the last sole emperor of the Holy Roman Empire. With so much noble blood coursing through his veins, Romano feels that it is he, and not Gustuv, who should be seated at the head of their table.

"Gustuv, brother." This time it is Felix who speaks. As the World Head of the Knights of Malta and a direct descendant of the House of Bourbon, Felix Marcellus is the most significant spawn to spew forth from the Black Nobility's unholy union with the Vatican. "I believe what our brother Romano is saying is that we all deserve to know the location of the book." He pauses, scanning the table for looks of support. "*If* the book is what you claim."

If it is what I claim, the accusation echoes in Gustuv's mind. *Such big words from such a small man,* he thinks. *But the French have always been known to use more rash than reason.*

"Now you doubt me too, Felix?" Gustuv replies, feigning hurt. "Was it not I that had the daughter watched? Was it not I that had our people placed throughout the island? Was it not I that had the foresight to plan for such a discovery? So is it not I that you owe your respect and praise? How often must our Lord work through me before you believe?"

He looks around the table, peering into the soul of each in attendance, daring someone to speak out against him and deny such facts as these. But Gustuv knows they will not; not his brethren who worship knowledge, science and technology as gifts from their Lord. They would never dare to challenge the facts—

And it is because of their rules that I will always triumph.

You self-proclaimed wise men, still bound by the laws of your religion. Call it what you must, but confused and power-hungry is all you are. No better than the very priests you claim to loathe.

"Listen brothers." He continues. "I have recently received

184

news from Santo Domingo. It seems that the daughter had also retrieved a scroll." Waves of murmurs roll through the room. In their utterances Gustuv can hear their excitement, surprise and wonder.

"The grandson still has it." He says.

The murmurs continue and Gustuv can sense another element in the room now, coursing beneath the surface like the quintessence of all they feel—the strongest and most influential of them all; it is fear.

Fear of the unknown: that human condition that none can escape. Which of us wants to feel abandoned and alone? Who doesn't fear the feeling of helplessness? Who but me?

Who but I am is worthy to lead these sheep? Even my brothers do not share a like mind, a mature mind. Who else has my knowledge of the universe? Who knows the Truth?

"And gentlemen." Gustuv smirks, ever aware of the irony in calling these men gentle. If by gentlemen it is implied one who adheres to the social customs of society, these men are gentlemen in the same manner that a pack of starving hyenas ravaging a rotting carcass are gentlemen.

And even creatures such as these need their rules to live by, he muses. *I would hate to see how they would behave without their religion to restrain them.*

"I have already alerted my people that the scroll is to be retrieved immediately." He continues. "I suggest that you excuse yourself for as long as you require to do the same."

Gustuv watches with slight amusement as his brothers retire to their offices like dutiful little soldiers going to relay his commands to their respective organizations. There is a small button on the underside of the table. He waits until all his brothers have left and then presses it. In the antechamber below him a red light flashes. Within minutes a young brown-skinned woman enters the room, wearing a mask fashioned in the look of a horse's head, and nothing more.

"Yes my Lord." She says, standing before Gustuv. "How may I serve you?"

"Has our special guest arrived?"

"Yes my Lord. The helicopter is landing now."

"Please, bring him to me as soon as possible."

"Yes, my Lord. Is there anything else I can do to serve you, my Lord?"

Gustuv nods. "You are excused."

He grins, watching as the young lady goes to rejoin her sisters, knowing that each of them is anxiously awaiting their chance to be summoned forth. If only everyone was so obedient, he thinks, but in due time. *All things in due time.*

His brothers begin to return, pouring out of the elevator in clusters of small groups; a reflection of the state of their brotherhood, he muses, and humanity in general. History has proven time and again that it is those closest to you that inflict the most damage.

How many of the world's greatest geniuses have been destroyed by the exploitation of an interior turmoil? Caesar and Brutus. Jesus Christ and Judas Iscariot. I will not have my name added to the list.

Gustuv rises from his seat and opens his arms to all before him. 'Brothers," he says, "welcome back. I have a surprise for you. Come. Sit."

"So you have come to see the light then brother?" Romano inquires, taking his seat beside Gustuv. "You have decided to tell us the location of the book?"

"No, Romano. I have not come to that conclusion."

Felix takes his seat beside Romano. "So you have the book here," he says, "and now you will show it to us?"

Gustuv switches his gaze to Felix. "No, brother. I will not do that either."

William takes his seat. "So then, you must—"

"Silence!" Gustuv shouts with a power that forces William's words back down his throat. "Enough of these games, brothers. A wise man asks and answers his questions to the point. Since you three would obviously like to know what I have for you, I will just tell you."

A door opens across the room and another young woman, naked except for a similar mask, escorts a nervous and battered man into the chamber.

"Better now brothers, I will show you."

Gustuv stands to greet the young man and the rest of his brothers watch as the frightened boy is lead to the head of their table.

Romano glances at William. It is a subtle gesture, a discreet way of asking if the young man belongs to any Masonic lodge. William returns the gaze. The corner of his mouth lifts and purses, as if saying, I do not know. There are many ways for William to identify a fellow Mason and having attained to the 33°, he knows them all. But this young man has been beaten, maybe stripped of any properly thst he had, and they are in no position to exchange grips and passwords. Unless he gives the sign of distress, William cannot know for sure.

He glances at Romano again but Romano does not notice. It is good, for the look William wears now is not one of comradely.

It was the nobles and the Church—in their thirst for power—that persecuted his order, murdering many of his family and their friends in times long passed. Father Time's scythe will never remove the suspicion from William's mind.

But in due time, he thinks, *all things in due time.*

The young lady stands before Gustuv now with the stranger waiting at her side. The men look on as she speaks.

"Here he is, my Lord, just as you requested." Gustuv nods. "Thank you, darling."

"Is there anything else I can do to serve you, my Lord?"

"Yes." A slight grin spreads his lips. "Our guest here looks famished. Please, bring him his food and a bag to discard the waste."

"Yes, my Lord. Is there anything else I can do to serve you, my Lord?"

"You are excused."

"Thank you, my Lord. I live to serve you."

Gustuv turns his attention to the young man. "Excuse my bad manners." He says. "There seems to be no more room at this table. Would you like my seat?"

"Uhh..." The young man glances around nervously. He is not sure what he should do or if he should do anything at all. The last thing that he can remember is calling the guy that gave him and Alejandro the job.

And now Alejandro's shot, he thinks, *and I'm in some sex cult's cellar.*

"No, son, you don't want this seat. Trust me." Gustuv gazes out at his brother and their deceitful schemes. "Always remember, heavy is the head that wears the crown, son."

"Uhh...yeah, sir, but I was umm... I was wonderin' like, where am I? What's goin' on? I was at my house, taking a nap, I think, and I uhh...I don't remember anything after but wakin' up on 'uh helicopter."

"Do not worry son. You are safe from the world here."

Across the room the doors open again and another naked woman emerges, also wearing a horse mask—only this time, her mask is white. She has a cart with her and she wheels it to the head of the table. Stopping beside their guest, the young lady removes the steel cover off of a platter and a tray of fresh fruits sits before them. Gustuv picks up a blood red apple and offers it to his guest.

"Eat." He says. "It will not kill you, I promise."

The young man takes the apple and looks it over as cautiously as he can in the shadowy chamber. This whole scene feels too Snow White-ish for him but he is hungry as hell. He looks at Gustuv and then back to the tray of fruit.

"Uhh...I think I'd rather have something else, if you don't mind, sir." As much as his intuition is screaming for him to not eat any of this food he is just too hungry to listen. If he was paying attention he would notice that he actually feels too hungry, having just ate before taking his nap. A juicy orange slice catches his eye and he takes it, practically swallowing the slice whole. He takes another.

"Thanks." He says, wiping the juice from his mouth. "Man, I'm starving."

"These are the fruits of your labor, Jorge." Gustuv says, stepping around the young man. "You were given a job today, to retrieve a scroll. You were told not to harm the man that had the scroll, correct?"

Jorge stops chewing. "How do you know about that? H-How do you know my name?"

"It does not matter. We both know that I am correct and we

both know that you attempted to shoot the man carrying the scroll, don't we?"

Could these be the people that Alejandro had told him about, Jorge wonders. They got the job from Alejandro's uncle, a Mason, and supposedly it was for some powerful organization. They were given one rule to follow–do not harm the young black guy with the dreadlocks. The only way this old man could know that—

Jorge's throat begins to itch. He feels it tighten. Constrict. He clutches his neck, unable to talk.

Gustuv calmly removes a clear plastic bag from the tray and stands in front of his panicking guest. "What you are feeling now is your trachea expanding." He explains, staring in Jorge's bulging eyes. "If you do not ingest the antidote for the poison that you have just consumed you will suffocate. The antidote lies within one of these fruits."

Jorge's eyes dart to the tray. He begins to reach for a banana.

"Wait." Gustuv stops him. "It is not as simple as you might think. All of the fruit there is poisoned as well, all except one. If you continue to inject yourself with poison you will only quicken your death. As of now you have approximately three minutes until your trachea expands to the point of suffocation." He pauses, looking towards his brother's anxious faces. "But that is far too much time."

In the blink of eye Gustuv yanks the plastic down over Jorge's head, snatches a zip tie from the tray, and fastens the bag around Jorge's neck. Jorge's starts to panic, clawing at the tie frantically.

"Now normally there is between twenty and thirty seconds of air in those bags." Gustuv says, watching as Jorge reaches around his head, trying to find the zip tie, his bulging eyes gawking at his captors' sadistic smirks.

"But with your trachea swelling like that, I would figure you have—"

Jorge drops to the floor, still grasping at the tie, using his last breaths to try and remove the bag from over his head.

Gustuv's brothers watch him, amused as Jorge's body convulses and spasms in front of them. Gustuv takes his seat and gazes around their table.

Romano looks away from the now dead Jorge and shakes his head. "Why would he not simply tear a hole in the bag? This is a perfect example of their mentality. Common sense is the most uncommon of all the senses man possesses."

"Fools will always panic and let their emotions outweigh their rational faculties, brother." Felix adds. "This is a perfect example of the situation the world is in—why they need us to guide them— because they cannot think for themselves."

William rolls his eyes and cuts a glance towards Gustuv. Gustuv nods and takes a hefty bite out of the apple Jorge refused.

Just like you fools need me, he thinks.

He calls to the young lady in the white mask. "Would you please dispose of our guest, here? We have things to discuss. Thank you."

"Yes, my Lord. Is there anything else I can do to serve you?"

"No, dear."

"Thank you, my Lord. I live to serve you."

Repugnance fills Gustuv as he observes the lustful glares emanating from the very ones proclaiming to be mankind's saviors. Their eyes grow wide as the young mare bends over to take hold of Jorge's stiff leg.

Just like you fools need me, he thinks and takes another bite of the apple. *For who shall guard the guards?*

CHAPTER THIRTEEN

The young man is asleep when Detective Clarkson enters his room.

It has been a long time since Clarkson has paid a visit to St. Jude's Intensive Care Unit. The majority of his cases keep him local, relegated to the bounds of the Peninsula like some forgotten castaway. But this evening the job has brought him here, to the bedside of a badly wounded young man.

A broken nose, an arm in a cast, and a bullet lodged in his back; a younger Clarkson may have grimaced at the sight before him. But the dejected soul standing beside the bed now can only gaze blindly on, apathetic to anything beyond his sufferings.

The young man stirs for the first time in seven hours. His eyes flutter beneath the bright lights.

"Alejandro, right?" Clarkson asks, well aware of the young man's name. He read Alejandro Ruiz's entire file the first hour or so he was waiting and then again just to pass some time. "You were involved in that shooting outside of First Bank today, right? Been wondering if you were ever going to get up."

Somewhere in the deep recesses of Alejandro's consciousness, through a haze of pain relievers and post-operative anesthesia, the word *COP* is formed. His criminal mind hears this and yells for his body to move, to run, to do something but the searing pain slicing through his side will not allow it.

"You might want to stay still, kid." Clarkson advises. "You're pretty beat up."

Alejandro lifts his head forward and looks down at himself.

Faint memories begin to the resurface: *the fight over the scroll, the old man breaking his arm, slamming him to the ground, him waking up, shooting, running away and... and...uhh...now this.*

"Why am I in cuffs?"

Clarkson laughs; a loud obnoxious raucous that is at once disrespectful and demeaning. "C'mon kid. There were probably hundreds of people out there. You were in the middle of downtown at midday. Why do you think you're in cuffs?"

"So, I'm goin' to jail?"

Clarkson stares at the kid—he can't be over twenty-one—and wonders how a petty criminal like Alejandro Ruiz ever got himself involved in robbery for hire. The track marks on his arms provide an answer. Some addicts will do anything for a fix.

Self-preservation, he thinks. *You and I both, kid.*

Clarkson goes over to Alejandro's IV and removes a syringe from his pocket. He taps the vial of clear fluid and watches a bubble float to the surface.

"Wha...what're you doing, man?" Alejandro asks, his eyes wide with fright.

"You don't wanna go to jail do you, kid?"

"No... but...what're you—"

"No buts, kid. This is it."

Alejandro continues to plead but Clarkson is no longer listening. Quickly, he unhooks the IV drip, *plungers* the syringe into the line and dispenses the clear fluid into the thin tubing. He was told that the serum would be untraceable but that doesn't really matter. No one will ever be scouring over the death of a poor junkie robber shot while fleeing the scene.

"You shouldn't have took that job, kid." He says, reattaching the fluid line to the IV bag. "Too bad we can't go back in time, huh?"

Panicking, Alejandro tries to scream for help and Clarkson throws a hard right cross that knocks him out cold. The tenderness in his knuckles shocks him. *It hasn't been that long since I hit a guy, has it?* He rubs his knuckles and looks down at the slumbering kid. *I'm getting old.*

Well, he thinks, *nothing left to do now. The kid will be dead in a few minutes. Let me get out of here before he flat lines and the—*

"Hey, did you hear something?" A head full of long brown locks peeks inside the door. "Sounded like I heard someone shouting on my way to the vending machine. The one downstairs is broken. You hear it?"

"Naw, kid." Clarkson lies, walking towards the door. "The guy's still out cold. The old man really did a number on him, huh?"

"Yeah." The man says, stepping aside to let Clarkson pass. He steps into the doorway and looks around. Their suspect is still snoozing.

"I'm not crazy. I know I heard someone shout."

"C'mon, kid." Clarkson calls to him. "Let's go grab a soda or something. He's not getting up anytime soon."

There is a sense of foreboding in the air of room 213, settled in like a thick fog clouding Devin and Samantha's thoughts. It has been four long hours since the surgery on Sukamaya's clavicle was completed, as if the three hours he spent under the knife wasn't dreadful enough without this sadistic waiting game.

"What if he never wakes up?" Samantha's asks.

She had not intended to say the words aloud but the thought has been replicating itself for so long now she isn't surprised that the question slipped out. Sitting beside Sukamaya's bed, she takes hold of his strong hands, interlaces her fingers with his and closes her eyes. "You have to wake up, Saka. You just have to."

"He will." Devin says, as much for her as for himself. He cannot lose Sukamaya now. He's already lost his mother, father and best friend. Sitting in a chair on the other side of Sukamaya's bed, he lets his head fall into his lap and fights back tears.

No, he thinks. *I didn't lose them. They were taken from me.*

The door squeaks open and Devin doesn't bother to look up. It's probably another nurse. They had been coming in and out of the room like ants in a hill until about ten minutes ago when something happened upstairs.

"Mr. King." Someone calls. The voice is deep and coarse, coated with a roughness that can only come from a lifetime of smoking. It certainly doesn't belong to any of the nurses that he's met so far. "Are you Devin King, sir?"

Devin lifts his head and finds two men standing before him. One of them he recognizes immediately—the cop with that ring on (*and he's wearing it now*); the other, he has never seen before. The guy is definitely a cop, though. His cheap black suit, even cheaper shoes, and the holster hugging his hip are dead giveaways. Not to mention the shiny badge fastened to his belt.

"Detective Clarkson." Devin says, looking into the face of the last man he wants to see right now. "What are you doing here? Shouldn't you be out searching for my parents' killers?"

Clarkson shrugs. "Something came up. But hey, don't be rude, didn't my pal here just ask you a question?"

Devin smirks, picturing himself slamming Clarkson against the wall and snapping his neck before the other guy can even realize what's happening. No, he wouldn't snap his neck. That would be too fast. He'd break his arm first—

"Mr. King." Clarkson's pal extends his hand and smiles. "I am Detective Max Worthy. I work Homicide for Santo Domingo. First Precinct."

Devin ignores the Detective's hand. "What do you want, Max? We've already given statements to some other cops."

"Uhh...well..." Worthy hesitates. He is obviously uncomfortable and his eyes dart to Samantha and then back to Devin. "I think it's best that we do this in private."

Devin takes a deep calming breath but it doesn't work. "Look, Max. It's been a long ass day, okay. So, say what you got to say. Whatever it is, you can say it in front of Sam, alright. Just get on with it."

Detective Worthy hesitates again. Clarkson shakes his head, ashamed for the guy. This is exactly why he hates working with these wet-behind-the-ear rookies. They are too damn nice.

"Just say it, damnit!" Clarkson snatches a set of cuffs from his belt and grabs Devin's arm. "Like this. Devin King, you are under the arrest for murder." He looks to Worthy. "See. It's that easy."

Devin yanks his arm away from Clarkson and rises to his feet. The two men stand threateningly close, glaring each other down, until a furious Samantha pushes her way between them.

"Hold on." She says, holding Devin back as she looks to Detective Worthy. "Explain this. Devin didn't murder anyone."

"Well, actually miss, that man that Devin shot in—"

"You don't have to explain anything to her, kid." Clarkson cuts in. "C'mon, Devin. Don't make this hard." He reaches for Devin's arm again. "You know, it's like you're some kind'uh reaper or somethin'. Only time I see you, somebody's dead."

Samantha snaps, slamming Clarkson's back against the wall with more force than he would have thought was possible, and stares him down. "Don't you dare come in here and disrespect my father or any of my family. Who the hell do you think you are?"

Clarkson stares back and then raises his hands in a mock surrender and grins. "Okay, okay, lady. Calm down. You're a little firecracker, huh?" He looks to Devin. "Maybe we *should* just step outside for a minute. We definitely don't want to disrespect anyone, right Max?"

Detective Worthy cannot believe this guy. He apologizes to Devin and Samantha on behalf of the First Precinct then glares to Clarkson. "I don't know how you guys do it on the Peninsula but that type of behavior was unprofessional and we don't tolerate that mess down here. I *will* be reporting your actions."

He turns to Samantha, apologizes again and heads for the door. He stops at the doorway and looks back. "I'll be waiting for you in the hall, Mr. King. Do not be too long."

Clarkson follows behind Worthy, twirling his handcuffs on his finger like he's about to perform a musical. He looks back at Devin. "Don't try anything stupid, kid."

In the hall, Detective Worthy lights a cigarette and takes a long pull. "Clarkson, man, what the hell was that?"

"I was about to ask you the same thing, kid. A high profile bust like this doesn't come around every day, and you're pussy-footing like you don't want to arrest this guy. You haven't been a detective for five years, I bet. Shit, you're lucky. At this rate, you'll make Captain before I retire."

Worthy takes another pull and feels the warm nicotine-filled smoke in his lungs. "There's nothing lucky about having to arrest a

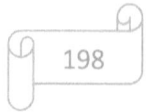

guy whose parents have just been killed, what, two days ago, because some bullshit robber died after surgery. Everybody around here knows that Alejandro and the guy that got away, they initiated all of this, and so Devin fights back and now he's the murderer. That's bullshit, man. That's bullshit and you know it."

"No, kid. That's the law. And the law is the law."

Samantha sits beside Sukamaya's bed watching Devin sulk. The last time she remembers seeing him like this, slumped over in his seat, shut off from the world, was right after Stacey's funeral. He sat like that for hours; his head buried in his lap, blaming himself for it all.

It's the best way that he knows how to nurse his wounds, she supposes, and now with his parents' murder he is forced to deal with another agonizing gash, even deeper than the first. Sukamaya's injuries and Clarkson's words are like salt in his sores.

"That guy's an ass." Samantha says, replaying the Detective's stinging comments. "A real fucking prick."

Devin can't help but chuckle. "You curse like a nun." He grins. "But you're right though, Sam. Clarkson's a dick."

And then it's gone. Just as quickly as his grin had appeared it vanishes, washed away as another wave of blames swells up. "But you know what, Sam? He's right. First Stace. Then Mom and Dad. And now Saka."

Devin lifts his head just slightly and his eyes wander over to Sukamaya; the rise and fall of his mentor's chest another jarring reminder that all of his highs have been followed by lows, and all of his own creation. "I need to leave Sam; to get away from here. What if you're next?"

It pains Samantha deeply to see him like this, so defeated,

seated beside her father—himself laying unconscious on a hospital bed; the two strongest men in her life now devoid of their power.

I have to be strong now, she tells herself. *For them and for me.*

As if pulled by an invisible cord, Samantha finds herself walking over and sitting on Devin's lap. She rests her head on his shoulder and looks up into those dark brown eyes she loves. "You can't think like that, Devin. Remember the—"

"Hold on." He says. "My phone. Hop up."

Samantha gets up, sits in the seat beside him and watches Devin take out his phone. He looks at the caller id and his face brightens.

"Natalie!" He says. "I was just saying how I need some good R&R time with you."

Samantha rolls her eyes. *Unbelievable,* she thinks, *not even five minutes ago he was borderline suicidal. Natalie calls and...Uhh! Look at him! He looks like a schoolgirl.*

Devin is now sitting up in his chair, leaning against the armrest just like he would do when they were kids and he was on the phone with some girl. Samantha can't stand to watch. With a final roll of her eyes she walks over to the window and gazes out at the full moon. She read something in college about the full moon and romantic lovers; something about it driving them crazy. She glances back at Devin, still crooning like a courting schoolboy.

Maybe it had to do with the word 'lunatic,' she muses, *because I must be crazy to love this idiot.*

But what's this, she wonders, grinning as she watches his smile dissipate.

"Oh." She hears him say, obviously disappointed. "Yeah. No. I understand."

Her grin widens.

"Umm-hum." He nods. "That's good... No, go ahead... I trust you... Yeah. Okay."

As Samantha continues to eavesdrop, she fills in the blanks between Devin's responses. *I have some new toys,* she imagines Natalie saying. *That's good,* Devin replies.

But I don't want to start without you... No. Go ahead.

Would you let me blindfold you...? I trust you.

I love you, Devin... Yeah. Okay.

She chuckles at that last one. Samantha can't imagine Devin ever telling one of these girls that he loves them. He never keeps them around long enough to really get to know them.

When will he realize that none of these girls will ever really care about him? It is a question that she has asked herself each time that they've spoken on the phone; each time that she sees him in a magazine with some model; and each time that she wakes up in a lonely bed. *They don't even know him,* she thinks, *all they know is what he shows them. Then there will be another one.*

It's just like prom. I'm the one—

She watches Devin's expression grow somber and he leans forward in the chair, listening intently to whatever it is Natalie's saying. *Now what? What's she got to say that's so important?* Whatever it is, Devin ends the call without so much as a goodbye. She wants to be happy but his mood is too sullen for her to bask in Natalie's dismissal.. An uncomfortable silence settles in the spaces between them, broken only by the steady beep of the heart rate monitor.

"So..." She finally says. "Who was that?"

Devin ignores her. They both know that he was talking to Natalie just like they both know that Samantha doesn't like Natalie;

she doesn't like any girl that he dates. Whatever. Devin's not in the mood for one of her lectures. Not today. Not now.

"Devin, did you hear me? Who was that? It looked serious."

He shrugs. "Naw. It was just Natalie."

Hoping that she'll just leave it alone Devin goes back to contemplating the consequence of Natalie's last revelation. At least he tries to but Samantha just won't let him think. Like a crowbar, she continues to pry and pry until he's forced to open up.

"You're sure you want to know this, Sam?" He asks, sure that she doesn't.

"Yes. I'm sure, Devin. Now, come on. Tell me."

"Alright." Devin relents. "You're sure."

By the time that Devin has finished his first sentence Samantha is already regretting her incessant prodding. She half-listens as he relives his evening in St. Croix, wondering just how many girls he has actually bedded. She figures if he slept with an average of five women a year during his high school period, then allowing for that rate to increase by one per semester of college, doubling after launching his clubs... *Whoa*, she thinks, impressed and disgusted all at once. She is trying to recall how old he was when he lost his virginity when he finally says something important.

"Hold on. She said she doesn't think you should trust *any* of the police officers here?" A look of incredulity fills her face. "Did you ever stop to wonder how she even knows that Clarkson's crooked? She never saw the tape. How could she—"

Devin cuts her off. "A hunch; she said she had a hunch. Some journalistic reporter's intuition type thing. Something about Clarkson looking like a rat."

"And you really went for that?" Her eyes roll like dice. "Whoa. She must've really showed you a good time." She shakes

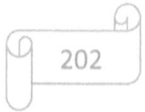

her head in disgust. "Typical. Typical Devin."

Devin shakes his head, frustrated with this whole mess. Not only are two detectives waiting in the hall to take him to jail but Sukamaya is lying next to him in a hospital bed and it's his fault. Both of his parents are dead and he should have been there to stop it.

It's all my fault, he thinks, the guilt crashing down like a waterfall of old tears. *It's always my fault.*

Memories of Stacey rise up like balloons at a pity party. *I should've set him straight. I should've done more to help him. He was just trying to be like me and all I did was sit back and watch. I watched him destroy himself.*

What am I doing? He glances to the satchel, leaning against an empty chair—*I lost years chasing ghosts and I still don't know what really happened. Now I'm...what? Searching for my parent's killers?*

He can't believe that he had actually considered tracking down The Elite—whoever or whatever they are. How selfish was he to ask that Samantha and Sukamaya just drop everything and join in some quest for vengeance; for a book?

I don't even know the first place to start looking. Soon as Saka gets better, I'm gone. I have to get back to my life. Now the police are looking to arrest me, too. People are trying to kill me. I didn't sign up for this.

Devin lifts his head and looks to Samantha. She's still fuming, digging under her nails, probably blaming him for everything, he thinks. He knows she would never say it *but maybe she should. Maybe I need to hear it.*

Samantha gazes in Devin's direction and for a second they lock eyes. The anguish that fills his stare forces her to turn away. She hates that. She wants to be angry with him right now. She deserves to be. He never listens. She just told him about Natalie and he brushed her off. Sukamaya is here now because of his stubbornness. She told him not to go out there. Look at what his bullheadedness has brought.

Her eyes find him again. He's buried his head in his lap, torturing himself, she knows. He's been like this since they were kids. If he missed a free-throw and his team ended up losing, Devin would be in tears blaming himself for it. She can't add to the guilt she knows he's feeling.

You've always thought everything was dependant on you. It's your gift and your curse. Carrying all that weight has made you strong but I can't imagine all the pressure that you must feel.

She calls to him. "Devin. What are you going to do? I mean... you know, Mom's book. The scroll. But... now with Saka..."

"Yeah, I know Sam." He lifts his head and smirks. "I was hoping you had some answers."

Answers? All Samantha has is questions. *What if Saka doesn't pull through? What about my job? These feeling for Devin? Do I really want to live so far from them now, after all this?*

Still, despite the mystery that is tomorrow, she knows that they cannot give up. That would not be honoring the Kings. They would have died for nothing. Sukamaya would be lying in this bed for nothing.

"I think the first thing for you to do is go and ort out this mess with Clarkson and what's the other guy's name?"

"Worthy. Detective Max Worthy."

"Yeah. You need to find out what's going on there, and then we can figure out our next step."

Devin takes a deep breath and rises from the chair. "Okay,

Sam, but look, if I'm not back in ten minutes come and see what's going on. You remember what Natalie said. This guy Worthy might be in on this too."

Samantha rolls her eyes but agrees and Devin heads for the hall.

"Aye Sam." He stops at the doorway. "Don't let anything happen to Mom's scroll. I mean... you know."

She glances over at the tube—that simple black tube that has changed so much so fast—and nods her head. "I won't." She assures him. "Don't worry."

He nods back and steps out into the hall. Samantha watches the door close and looks to her father. Thank the Tao that he is still sleeping soundly. Taking his hand she closes her eyes and beseeches that Tao that he loves so much.

"Don't take him from me." She pleads. "I still need him. His work is not finished."

Detectives James Clarkson and Maximus Worthy spot Devin coming their way and rise to their feet but not because it is the polite thing to do. As he watches him approach Worthy hopes that Devin doesn't resist or Clarkson says something stupid to set the guy off because, if the witness reports are true, Devin King is a dangerous man, especially in close quarters. If either of them happens, it will take everything that they learned in combat training to subdue him but, honestly, with his lungs and Clarkson's spare tire that still might not be enough.

"Thought you might've found a window to jump out of." Clarkson says as Devin takes his seat. "I bet Worthy here that you'd be a runner. Now I have to buy him a shot because of you."

With Devin now seated the Detectives take their seats—

one on each side of him. A soda can sits beside Worthy's chair, overflowing with smoldering cigarette butts and a half-empty bottle of soda sits beside Clarkson, who reeks of liquor. He pulls a flask from his jacket's inner pocket.

"So, Devin," he says, topping off the soda with what smells like rum, "guess you're one of those books with the misleading covers huh? That's alright." He pauses to take a swig from the flask before tucking it away. "Rich guy like you; you can cover my losses right?"

He laughs at his own wit and Detective Worthy looks on, finding none of this banter the least bit amusing. He hasn't even worked with Clarkson for a full day yet and he's already grown tired of this perpetual bad-cop routine he seems intent on working. But it's not just that. Everything about the guy just disturbs something deep inside him.

He's a walking museum exhibit, Worthy thinks, watching Clarkson take an exaggerated swig of his rum and coke. *Like he's modeled after every bad American cop-movie stereotype. The old cowboy boots, tight jeans, grungy t-shirt and leather jacket, and then there's that comb-over.*

He shakes his head in disgust. "Mr. King, once again I apologize for the Detective's behavior. Understand, sir, we do not conduct ourselves like that here in Santo Domingo sir. If you would like to file a report, I would—"

"Stop, Max. You don't have to worry about any of that. I'm not the file-a-report type of guy, you know." Devin glances to Clarkson. "I fight my own battles."

Clarkson smirks and looks to Worthy. *Coward,* he thinks. "File a report? What kind of bitch pussy shit is that?"

Worthy ignores him and lights up another cigarette. "Well,

then, how about we just skip all the formalities and I tell you what I know, okay?"

Devin has seen way too many police dramas to not recognize the good-cop/bad-cop routine that they're working. He nods to Detective Worthy and makes a show of listening to his spiel as he patiently awaits its end. Nothing that Worthy is saying right now means two shits to Devin. He learned a long time ago that no matter what a detective says you only reply with three simple words: CALL MY LAWYER.

"So, Mr. King," Worthy continues, "you understand my predicament here, right? We have witnesses saying that you shot Mr. Alejandro Ruiz in the back after he attacked you. All I need you to tell me is what you did with the gun, sir, and we can proceed with all of this. So..."

Devin is puzzled. "So...what, Max?"

"So, what do you have to say for yourself, Mr. King? Are you going to tell me what you did with the weapon?"

"Uhh..." Devin looks to Clarkson then back to Worthy and smirks. "This is what I'll tell you Max: Call. My. Lawyer. Got it?"

Clarkson erupts. "Ding! Ding! Ding! He's said the magic words, Max. Tell'em what he's won!"

Worthy shakes his head. His voice is somber. "Mr. King, if you want us to contact your attorney then I'll have to place you under arrest. Right now, we are just—"

"Cut it out, kid." Smiling, Clarkson bounces up out of his seat and takes out his handcuffs. "Devin King, you are under arrest for the murder of Alejandro Ruiz."

For a moment Devin considers shattering Clarkson's knee with a well-placed front kick, maybe snapping Worthy's wrist before he can get to that gun on his waist, but that may lead to shooting, he thinks, and that's the last thing he wants to happen in a hospital.

Smirking, he stands and sticks out his arms. "Okay then, coppers. Take me downtown."

Clarkson locks the cold steel around Devin's wrists, much tighter than necessary. "You've been watching too many movies, kid. This is real life here and you're *really* fucked."

He and Worthy each take hold of one of Devin's arms and proceed to escort him down the hall. They arrive at the elevator and Worthy presses the call button.

"Hey! Wait!" A woman's voice yells out.

Devin looks back over his shoulder and sees Samantha running down the hall. *Finally*, he thinks. He almost thought she wouldn't make it.

"Hold on! Wait a minute!" She yells, standing at the elevator now. She looks at Devin, standing there in cuffs, and can't believe her eyes. "Where are you taking him?" She asks.

"Look Sam," Devin says, "I need you to call Dennis and tell him that I'm being arrested for murder, okay?"

"Murder?" She shrieks. "You didn't murder anyone, Devin. What's going on? Somebody explain this."

The elevator doors slide open.

"There's no time to explain, Sam. Just call Dennis and uhh... take care of our baby." He winks at her. "You got it? I don't know how long I'll be gone so it's on you, right now. Okay?"

"Yeah." she nods. "Our baby. I got it. The baby's safe with me. And I'm going to go call Dennis right now, okay?"

Clarkson tugs at Devin's arm. "Alright kid, c'mon. You've said enough. Rich guy like you, you'll be out in the morning."

"This is serious, Sam." Devin continues, ignoring Clarkson and his shoves. "I need you."

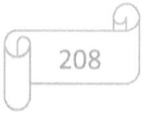

Those are the last words that Samantha hears before Devin is forced into the elevator and the doors close. She stares for a moment, debating whether or not she should go after him. But then what? Does she leave Sukamaya alone to wake up with no one by his bedside? There is no real point in following them, she decides and so she takes out her phone and heads back to Sukamaya's room.

With the satchel cradled in her lap she sits by her father's bedside and waits on Dennis to answer.

"You would always say the Great Way is within us." She says, looking at her father. "Hidden maybe but always present."

A voice comes through the phone. Samantha takes a deep breath.

I hope it's a way out of this mess.

CHAPTER FOURTEEN

Hey, Worthy! We saw you on TV!"

"Yeah, that bust was max, Max!" Detective Worthy ignores his co-worker's constant stream of cracks and heads to the Captain's office. Their taunts are like crude lyrics set to the First Precinct's chaotic clamor.

"Guess DK stands for Dumbass-killer, huh, Max?"

"Or Deadly King!" Someone adds.

"Okay. Okay." Worthy says, lighting a cigarette. "That's enough, you guys. His family was just murdered. Show some type of respect."

A brief silence blankets the office and Worthy puffs on proudly. *See, they're not that bad*, he thinks, until Daniela's nasally voice pierces the air.

"Okay, Maxy. There you go. You have it. Una muestra de respeto." She grins to her fellow officers "Everyone, por favor, hold your comments until he's in the Captain's office. You know Maxy, él está por encima de esas cosas. He's not like the rest of us. Right, Maxy?"

"Esta es la verdad!" Someone shouts, and the entire precinct breaks out in raucous laughter. All he can do is grin and bear it.

None of us are as worth as Worthy, that was the first one they came up with, after he refused a $250,000 bribe from the local drug lord and then risked death by agreeing to take the stand. That was also when he first started smoking.

We should all be above those things, he starts to tell Daniela but right now it would only add fuel to the fire. *And Daniela's not the one I'm worried about anyway.*

A young freckle-faced officer runs up. He reminds Worthy a bit of himself when he had first graduated from the academy: tall, slim, bright-eyed and eager to fight crime.

Except the freckles. Morenos don't get freckles.

"Detective." The young officer says. "Captain Velasquez said for you to stop pussy-footing and get in his office now." He grins. "His words not mine, Detective."

Worthy looks back over his shoulder; all eyes are on him.

"Get back to work!" He yells. "Hay mucho que hacer."

Before anyone has a chance to reply, Worthy slips his cigarette between his lips and heads for the Captain's office, pulling on the stick like it's the first day of trial.

"Detective Worthy." The Captain calls, his stout stomach bouncing with every syllable. "I'm so glad you could join us."

Us, Worthy thinks, stepping further into the room.

"Yeah, Captain." Detective James Clarkson says, pushing the office door close. "He comes strolling in here late, then almost smashes the door in my face."

"Umm..., sorry about that, Detective." Confusion contorts Worthy's brow. "I didn't..., uhh, know you were back there. *Why* were you back there? I mean, here?" He looks to the Captain. "Why is he *here?*"

"Judge Moralez." The Captain begins. "She's granting the guy a bond, but he'll have very limited travel abilities. Since his residence is on the Peninsula, Detective Clarkson has volunteered to keep an eye on him while he's in their jurisdiction."

An apologetic, yet ardent, smile appears on the Captain's face. "I want you to work with him, Max. Help him keep an eye on the guy for us."

Worthy is even more confused. "I don't understand. Are you assigning me a solo gig or is he supposed to be, like, my partner?"

Captain Velasquez's ardent smile appears again. Every officer in La Dominica has heard the rumors of corruption that plague the Peninsula, and every story has James Clarkson appearing in a starring role. And they all know Detective Worthy's obstinate stance on the issue.

"C'mon, Captain." Worthy can't believe this is actually happening. "You know I don't like working with people, Cap. And I just met this guy two days ago."

"I'm not asking, Max. This is—"

"Hey, Whiz Kid," Clarkson cuts in, "I didn't want to work with you either, okay. But this thing is bigger than you and me, so, pull up your panties, tuck in your skirt and stop acting like a puta. Do the job, okay, Maxy. It's what you do."

"What'd you call me?" Worthy moves toward Clarkson with clenched fists. "Watch your mouth you fucking relic! I've heard all about—"

"Max!" The Captain slams his meaty fist onto the desk. "I know you were not about to assault a fellow officer, in my office! I'll take your badge right fucking now, Max!" He turns his anger to Clarkson now. "And you, I'll make sure the Peninsula prematurely retires your ass too! Now, both of you stand there and shut the hell up!"

Detective Worthy glares at Clarkson and Clarkson looks back, still sporting his smug smirk.

"I really can't believe they're pursuing this case." The Captain says, flipping through the file in front of him. "Technically they have a case but this going to be a PR nightmare. His family was just murdered and now his god-father's been shot. Pray to God that this thing doesn't go viral. If people hear that their hero is being crucified for incidentally killing someone that tried to kill him first..."

The Captain runs his hand over his balding head, imagining all of the chaos that will ensue if any major media gets hold of this case. "That's why I need you on this, Max. I can't risk any shoddy or dirty police work adding fuel to this inferno. And the reporters..." He rubs his head again. "Dios mios, un montón de preguntas. Max, I need your trustworthiness on this one. We need to keep this quiet and contained."

Trustworthy Worthy; that'll probably be the next one. "Okay, Cap, I'll do this. For you. But tell Daniela that I get her parking spot."

The Captain rolls with laughter. "With that truck of yours, Max, you'd be better off taking the bus."

Clarkson snorts. "Uhh...sorry to interrupt your little joke session here, Cap, but do I really need to be here for this? I have things to do, you know?"

"Watch it, Clarkson." He retorts. "If I get any negative reports from Worthy—even one—I'll make sure Captain Sanchez retires you early and without pension. Understand me?"

Clarkson is not the type of man to take a threat lightly. "I'm not your little golden-boy Worthy." He says, staring at the Captain. "Don't think you can talk to me anyway you want, *Julio.* We all have our weaknesses. Do you understand *me?*'"

Captain Velazquez jumps to his feet, moves from behind his desk and walks over to Clarkson. The two men stand nose to nose, staring into each other's eyes like boxers searching for a glimpse of weakness. Neither man blinks.

Velazquez has had enough of this. "Get the hell out of my office!" He erupts. "Now!"

Clarkson smirks. "Thought you'd never ask." And with an arrogant bop he turns around and struts out of the office. Detective Worthy looks to the Captain and shakes his head.

"Keep your eyes open, Max." The Captain tells him. "That guy's trouble. Be careful."

Worthy nods, *but you still stuck me with him, didn't you, Cap? You're no better than everyone else. All out for self.*

He takes out his cigarettes but finds the pack empty. *First Clarkson and now this.* He releases a sigh of exasperation. *It's a sign. That's what it is. A sign of what's to come.*

What the hell have I gotten myself into?

Detective Worthy is riding shotgun as Clarkson's snow-white Cadillac cruises down the recently renovated Las Terrenas strip and pulls up to his local *colmadon*, a quaint seaside café named Bambú.

"My father used to work on the fishing boats around here." Worthy says as he steps out of the Cadillac. "When he died, that's when my Mom moved us to the capital."

Clarkson shrugs, uninterested. "New husband? Some guy with a load of money, right? Got her while she was still young and tight."

"What?" Worthy can't believe the guy. *I mean, who says that?* But for the sake of the greater good he ignores the comment. *You have to give him a chance, Max.*

"Actually," he says, walking beside Clarkson as they push open Bambú's double wooden doors and enter the dimly lit restaurant, "my Mom never remarried. She moved us to Santo

Domingo to be close to family. I miss the Peninsula, though."

"Yeah." Clarkson mumbles, wondering what in the hell you would miss about this small ass piece of nowhere. *I'll need a few drinks in my system if I'm going to be forced to listen to the kid's family history,* he thinks, flagging down a waitress.

"Hey senorita, get me a rum and coke, alright. And uhh..." He glances over at Worthy, "Get this guy a backbone if you got it. I'm guessing sangria, if you don't."

Worthy rolls his eyes. "Bacardi." He says. "151 if you have it. Any rum if you don't."

The waitress scribbles down the order and walks off. Detective Worthy glances around the shadowy restaurant. There aren't many people here tonight. Most of the tables are empty and there are open seats at the bar. He wonders if this is normal or if it's just a slow night. He has the feeling that it's normal, though. It would be the perfect backdrop for the lonely bad-guy cop persona Clarkson is working. Worthy continues to look around and smiles at a woman dancing with a guy—*boyfriend maybe?*—by the jukebox and she smiles back. Just then the song changes to an old reggae tune he knows. He hums the melody as he follows Clarkson to a secluded corner booth.

"So, James," he says as he takes his seat (*in a corner booth, are you serious*), "what's with that backbone comment? We might as well get it all out now. We're going to have to work together."

Clarkson looks around for their waitress. He's going to need that drink... like now. The kid seems hell bent on expressing his feelings. *It's worse than talking to my wife,* he thinks, *at least that can end in sex.* "You're sure you want to do this, kid?"

Worthy lights a cigarette. "I'm a grown man, James. I think I can handle it."

"Okay, kid," he says, leaning back against the booth, "for one, you let your Captain pressure you into taking this assignment you didn't really want. Then, you go drop off that piece of shit truck at home and I hear your wife in their yelling like she caught you in bed with another woman. I didn't hear you speak up for yourself once, kid, but I did see your face when you got in my car." He shakes his head. "Pitiful, kid. At some point you're gonna have to start looking out for numero uno."

Worthy smirks. "Oh, be like you, huh?"

"Naw, you don't wanna be like me, kid. There's no mystery here. What you see is what you get."

The waitress returns with their drinks. She is an attractive young woman with shapely legs and a tight midsection peeking out from beneath her red tank-top. Worthy pegs her to be in her early twenties; *25 at the oldest,* he thinks. He looks to Clarkson. Clarkson's eyes are fixated on the girl's body, moving back and forth with each shift of her hips. *He's like a starving man at a buffet.*

"So what do you plan to do after retirement?" He asks, pulling Clarkson's stare away from the young lady. He taps his cigarette over the ashtray. "You're getting close now, right?"

A slight sigh escapes Clarkson's lips. It's the first genuine sign of vulnerability that Worthy has seen since they met.

"I don't know, kid. This is all I've ever done. The job is all I know. Really, it's all I ever wanted to do. Since a kid, you know, all I wanted to be was a cop."

Worthy nods. He certainly knows the feeling. "Yeah. It was my dream too. Guess it's why I take it so seriously."

The waitress returns and looks to Clarkson. "Excuse me fellas. James, I've got a message for you. Here." She hands him a small note which he reads quickly and tucks it into his pocket. He hands her a few dollars.

"Gracias." He says. "Phone open?"

The young lady smiles and tucks the bills in her bra. "Yeah. You know where it is." She turns to Worthy and smiles. "I can keep you company while he uses the phone. You're cute."

Clarkson gets up from his seat and grins. "Well, kid, dreams can turn to nightmares if you let them. And it'll happen if *you* don't start looking out for *you*. Trust me, kid." He glances to their waitress. "Enjoy the little things."

With that he walks off to the bar, leaving Worthy alone with his cigarettes and his thoughts. He takes a long pull and looks up at the pretty face still smiling at him. She takes a seat in their booth.

Yeah, he thinks, *that's the problem. I'm the only one left standing and it's like we're playing moral musical chairs*

CHAPTER FIFTEEN

After thirty-eight uncomfortable hours, Devin is out of the Santo Domingo City Jail and in the passenger seat of Samantha's Prius.

According to his team of lawyers, the prosecution actually has a case. Since the gunman was fleeing the scene when Devin shot him he no longer posed an imminent threat to his life, which changes Devin's motive from self-defense to vengeance.

"Supposedly they have witnesses saying I shot him after I saw what happened to Saka." He tells Samantha. She missed his bond hearing today, choosing instead to stay beside Sukamaya. Devin notices her face cringe at the sound of his name.

"Any news on the old man?" He asks.

Samantha parks the car in front of the house, beneath the shade of a cocotero and stares blankly ahead. Devin watches her— clutching the gearshift so tight that her knuckles are white—and blames himself for her pain.

"Sam." He calls to her. "Sam. You hear me?"

She turns to him, eyes brimming with tears. "Yeah," she sobs, "it's just, the doctors aren't saying anything. His shoulder and collarbone, it looks bad. And that bullet..."

Devin lays his hand on top of hers. It's all he can think to do. Saying sorry just seems too shallow.

"The doctors say, well, you know, at his age..." A lump forms in her throat, made up of all the fear and anger that she feels right now. She swallows it, forcing it back down with all the grief that she's had to stomach this week and forces herself to smile. A single tear is dislodged from the corner of her eye. Samantha doesn't bother to wipe it away. "It makes sense, I guess. I mean, if he was as young as he acts he'd be okay."

Devin continues to watch her; watching as the tear rolls over the contours of her cheeks and down her jaw where it pauses for a moment, before dripping slowly from her chin like water running off an autumn leaf.

"Come on." She says, unlocking the doors. "Let's get you inside. I know you want a hot shower."

"Yeah." He nods, though no amount of showers can wash away the anguish he feels.

Beneath the steamy shower every droplet of water is but a jarring reminder of Samantha's tears; tears that he created. Her bright green eyes, once a listening pool of jade, are now two stagnant moss- covered ponds and it's all Devin's fault. No matter how hard he scrubs he can't cleanse his conscious. The image of her crying just won't leave his mind. It haunts him with every bead of water he sees.

"Fuck!" He shouts, punching the wall. "Fuck! Fuck! Fuck!"

Shaking his head, he turns off the shower, grabs his towel and climbs out. The mirror above the sink is covered with steam and Devin stares at it, searching for himself behind the mist. He wipes his hand across the glass and beads of water run down from the path he's created. His image is distorted, blurred by the steam covered glass.

A fitting reflection, he muses; a reflection of how he feels: unclear, out of focus, unsure of what to do next.

That's a lie. I know exactly what to do.

Devin opens the door and as the warm mist drifts out the cool breeze brings with it the sweet smell of sautéed shrimp and papaya juice.

In shorts and a tank, Devin stands in the archway watching Samantha work. She commands the kitchen with the confidence of a warrior and moves with the grace of a ballerina.

She's definitely her father's daughter, he thinks, grinning as she grabs the pan of sautéing shrimps, and then, with a flick of her wrist send them flying through the air. She switches the pan to her other hand, quickly catching the shrimps as they fall.

It's the same move Saka would do when he knew me and Sam were watching.

"Guess pigs are fling somewhere," he jokes, "and the weatherman just said the temperature in hell dropped a few degrees."

Samantha looks over her shoulder at Devin and grins. "Shut up, stupid."

Devin smiles back. He continues to stand there, observing her, feeling a strange peace, before sneaking over and snatching a shrimp from the pan.

"Oww!" He shrieks, popping it into his mouth. "Hot! Hot! Hot!"

Samantha chuckles. "While you were in the shower I started thinking about Saka."

She transfers the last of the shrimp from the pan to the platter and takes the plate to the table.

"Grab that." She nods to a bowl of fresh cut fruit. Devin brings the bowl over and then takes a seat. Samantha sits across from him. She places a handful of shrimp and two slices of mango on her plate, and then watches as Devin overloads his.

"You remember Saka would always tell us, 'whatever is is right?'" She asks. Devin nods, his mouth to full to speak. "I'm trying to remember that, you know."

She gazes across the table, watching him take a big bite out of a mango slice, and smiles. "It felt good to cook like this."

Devin lifts his head as she reaches for the juice and catches a glimpse of her smile. "What, Sam? Why're you grinning at me like that? Got some food in my hair or something?"

"No." She smirks. "Just thinking about when we all were living in this house together."

"Yeah. Good times." Devin nods, also grinning now. He pops another shrimp into his mouth and washes it down with the cool juice. "You're gonna turn some guy into a fat old man one day, Sam. Trust me, I know women, and cooking like this..." He pops another shrimp into his mouth. "Rare."

Samantha can't hold back her smile. "If you say so." She watches Devin devour another handful of shrimps, happy to have made him happy, but then, like an accomplished actress, her countenance changes suddenly. Her warm smile disappears, replaced by a straightforward stare.

"So I know a guy that should be able to translate the scroll," she says, "He's a colleague of mine, a professor at the university. He's really good at this kind of stuff. I know he'd do it if I call, but we'd have to fly over there. He lives in—"

Devin cuts her off. "Sam. Sam, hold on." He looks up and there is a twinge of sadness in his eyes. "I've decided I'm going to donate the scroll to a museum. Let them figure out what it says. They have security. We've done enough."

"No, Devin. You can't! Mom kept it hidden for a reason." Her eyes beg for him to reconsider. "You can't just give up like this, Devin! What would Mom think?"

"Mom's gone, Sam. Mom and Dad. And now Saka's in the hospital and I'm being charged with murder. *Murder,* Sam. It's just too much. I can't do this. I don't even know what I thought we were doing anyway."

"Devin, stop it." She reaches across the table and takes a hold of his hands. He lowers his head. "Look at me." She says, and when he look up Samantha gazes into his eyes. She no longer finds the arrogant playboy and daredevil the world knows. All she sees is the man she loves.

"Devin, I swear, since Stacey died I've heard you lie to yourself so many times. You're always telling me what you can't do, then you go and do these crazy stunts that defy all reason. Saka always thought you were special. I know you're special. So stop it, okay. Just stop it. Quit making excuses because you're scared. There is noth—"

"I'm not making excuses, Sam. I just—"

"Look, Saka told me that we honor the people we've lost by living our lives with their memories in our hearts. Is this how you're gonna honor Mom and Dad? You think this is what they'd want, for you to just run away from your responsibilities?"

The weight of the world is bearing down on Devin. His head lowers beneath the pressure. He has been down this road before, chasing a mystery, and he doesn't want to go down it again. He's spent the last ten years of his life and thousands of dollars in therapy to make peace with the unknown and move on with his life.

"This isn't my life, Sam. My life is simple."

He stands and walks off before she has a chance to respond.

Samantha calls out to him but Devin ignores her. *It's for the best,* he tells himself, he has to do what he knows is right.

"Devin, wait!" She calls out to him again. "Where are you going?"

He stops at the archway but doesn't bother to turn around. He can't look into her eyes again. "What, Sam? What do you want?"

Samantha gets up and goes to him. "I want you" She says. "I want to talk to you."

Devin turns around. "Look, Sam, I—"

Her cellphone rings, interrupting him. "Hold on." she says. "Just don't go anywhere. Hold on."

Devin nods but she's not convinced. "Seriously, Devin. We need to talk."

"Just answer your phone. I'm not going anywhere. I promise."

She stares into his eyes, searching for some sign of surety and nods. "Okay, guess you haven't broken a promise, yet."

Samantha takes out her phone and answers the call. The conversation is brief and when she hangs up, those green eyes are once again filled with tears.

"It was the doctor." She says.

Devin doesn't need to hear anymore. He wraps his arms around Samantha and leads her to the front door. They'll take the Lamborghini; they'll need the speed.

Something's wrong with Saka.

CHAPTER SIXTEEN

Heavily sedated, Sukamaya lies on the operating table vaguely aware of the anesthesiologist sliding an oxygen mask ver his nose and mouth.

The chief surgeon stands over him, discussing the procedure with a female assistant. The anesthesiologist tells Sukamaya to begin counting down from ten. He's out before he can get to seven.

In a few minutes, Sukamaya's doctor will begin performing his second arthroscopic surgery since the shooting. The initial procedure was supposed to remove the bullet fragments and bone shards and then repair the damage done to his clavicle and humerus when he tackled Devin to the ground. At the end of the operation the surgical team was satisfied with their work and Sukamaya was expected to be released in a few days.

But with Devin and Samantha sitting outside of the operative room now, it is apparent that something went wrong. A bullet fragment was missed during the initial procedure and has now begun to shift causing severe internal bleeding. It must be removed immediately if Sukamaya is to have a chance of surviving.

Trepidation courses through Devin and Samantha's veins. It is as if time is deliberately slowing down, dragging their pain out like some sadistic torturer. Sharing an uncomfortable bench outside the operation room, Devin wraps his arm around Samantha. She lays her head on his shoulder and snuggles in close. Neither of them speaks. There isn't much to say. Two surgeries, so close together, and on a fifty-seven year old man at that. They know his chances of survival are slim. All they can do is hope and wait.

"Pray with me," Samantha says, her soft voice breaking the silence that has settled in between them. "Pray?" Devin asks. "Since when do you pray?"

Samantha lifts her head from his shoulder and gazes into his eyes. Her once beautiful eyes are now blood-red portals of grief. Devin can't bear her gaze.

"Look at me." She tells him, the despair in her voice almost tangible.

Reluctantly, he turns his head and meets her gaze. In one week Samantha has lost the only mother that she has ever known, her god-father was murdered, and now the man who left his home to make her life better, the man whose green eyes she shares, the man who helped give her life, now lies on an operating table approaching death's door. Her eyes reflect it all.

"There is a power at work here, Devin. I... I don't know what it is. Maybe it's the Tao, I don't know. All I know is it's come into our lives now. It took Mom and Dad, and now it wants Saka." She pauses, swallows. "I don't know if it can hear prayers or if it even cares but we have to try. We have to. We have to because... because—"

"Because we have to." He finishes, taking hold of her hand.

She lays her head back on his shoulder. "Close your eyes."

Devin does as told and listens quietly as Samantha mumbles pleas to some unknown power. The cool dampness of her tears soaks through his shirt. He starts to pray but stops. He hasn't prayed since the day of Stacey's funeral. What's the point? Why ask God to do something else when he still hasn't gotten around to your last request?

But this isn't about me, he muses.

God, he thinks, *or whatever you're called. You took my parents. You took my best friend. And now you want to take Saka, but don't okay. Just don't.*

He opens his eyes and glances down at Samantha, still pleading her case. He closes his eyes and bows his head again.

You know, it just hit me, you probably don't really care what we want do you? Or I guess if you're like the Tao Saka talks about, your job is just keeping balance right? My Mom, Dad, Saka, they were really good people, so you must've took some really evil people too, right? I don't know; just... if you do take Saka, just don't let it ruin her okay. Don't let her be like me. Give her the strength to handle it.

Samantha gives Devin's hand a tight squeeze. "Amen," she says, and raises her head. He tightens his hold on her and she snuggles in closer. Tears slide down her face like raindrops on a child's bedroom window. Devin places a soft kiss on her forehead.

Give her the strength, he prays. *Don't let it ruin her life.* "Amen."

CHAPTER SEVENTEEN

Samantha sits beside Sukamaya's bed watching as his chest rises and falls to the rhythm of the EKG's monotonous beep. It is as if the two have decided to do one last dance before death silences the song. The soft moonlight is the only thing capable of cutting through the thick tension in the room. It has no regard for Samantha, Devin, or the foreboding that they feel. Its only focus is on casting Sukamaya in the perfect light for this final performance.

Samantha closes and her eyes and continues to pray to a god that she doesn't know. Devin can only watch now. Observing someone that he loves in so much agony stirs something deep within him. He wants so badly to ease her stress, *but how? What can I do?* He waits for an answer but there is no response. That is the answer: silence; nothing; and such impotence is but another brick added to an already unbearable load.

He stares at Sukamaya, lying helplessly in bed. Devin has never seen his teacher so weak. There are just so many tubes: the IV running into his arm, the chest tube draining blood from his pleural cavity, the ventilator pumping air into his lungs, the electrodes that connect to the EKG machine—*Saka wouldn't want this. It's too much like fighting against the Tao.*

The Tao, he thinks. Sukamaya's guiding light. As children, he and Samantha would receive daily lessons in their master's spiritual philosophy. Devin thinks back to those lessons now, searching for something that can bring them solace. The manifestation of equality, the harmony that exists between all things, the natural way of life: this is the Tao that Sukamaya taught; the way of life that would lead the true traveler to an abode of peace. All external circumstances merely reflect inner conditions, he would say, and therefore whatever is, is right. The Tao is but the embodying of this principle. Until one frees himself of all conditioned behaviors and preconceived judgments, all thoughts of right and wrong—good and bad—they will never will never be able to be truly free, to live fully in the moment, to exist in the eternal now. The Master, free from the colored lenses of desires, is able to see all things for what they are rather than the illusions they are clothed in. Thus, he can see the harmony in all things and move without thinking.

But where is the harmony in this, Devin wonders as he watches his master cling to life. *I've lost everything, everyone I love. There's nothing right about Sam's tears or Saka's wounds.*

His gaze shifts from Sukamaya to Samantha. Her head is resting in her lap now, probably crying, he supposes, *or still praying.* As much as Devin shares in her sorrow he can shed no tears. Watching her he can only wonder about the future, The Elite, and what they both may bring.

"Samantha-child." Sukamaya's strained voice cuts into Devin's reverie. "Devin-sun. How long have you two been here?"

Samantha lifts her head from her lap. Her eyes are red and swollen and her cheeks are wet and puffy. She tries to smile but falls short. "Oh, Saka," she sighs, caressing his hand. "We've been here since your surgery. I'm so sorry, Saka. I'm so sorry."

"Do not be sorry for me, child." Like his daughter he tries to smile but does not have the strength. "The end comes to us all."

The strain in his voice stabs at Samantha's heart. How many times have his deep bellows beckoned her to the yard for a lesson or to his guesthouse for a chat? And now it hurts him just to speak.

"Dear child. I... I—" A fit of coughing interrupts him. Samantha doesn't know what to do.

"Saka, are you okay? Should I get a nurse?"

"No, child." He grins. "Just water. My mouth is dry."

Samantha disappears to go and find her father a cup and Sukamaya looks to Devin. "And how are you, Devin-sun?"

Devin chuckles. "Shouldn't I be asking you that?"

"I know what awaits me, Devin-sun. It is what awaits you that is my concern."

"I'm fine, Saka. Don't worry—"

"Please, do not lie to me, Devin-sun. I can see—" Another fit of coughing strikes. Samantha returns just in time with a cup of water and a straw. She lifts the straw to his lips and he takes a sip.

"Thank you, child." He tells her, and then looks back to Devin. "Now, you, Devin-sun, tell me the truth."

Devin sighs. "Well, Saka, I guess... I guess I just want everything back like it was before. Before Mom and Dad were killed."

"But this can never be, Devin-sun. All things change. It is the most natural thing in the Universe. Once you realize this there is nothing you will hold on to. You two, both of you." He turns his head towards Samantha. "You must never forget that the Master has no possessions. You must act without acting." He shifts his gaze again. "If you seek peace then you must remember the Way. This is how you honor my memory, as well as the Kings."

His lips curl ever so slightly as he looks to Devin. "Your light is growing. I can see it. The time is coming for you to do great things."

Samantha goes to stand beside Devin. She needs to be close

to him. Her hand slips inside Devin's. He squeezes comfortingly.

"My Samantha. My sweet, beautiful, smart Samantha." Sukamaya smiles. "You remind me so much of your mother—both your mothers. I know that if the two of them had met they would have been inseparable because they are joined together so perfectly in you."

"Oh, Father, please. Don't talk like that." She kisses his forehead just as he would kiss hers when she was a little girl. "You are not going anywhere, Saka. Soon as you get better I'm moving back home and making up for staying away for so long. I won't ever leave you again."

"Samantha-child, why are you apologizing? Everything happens as it should. Did you think I would live forever? You are too smart for such delusions, child. Physically, our bodies must all leave this place, but just as your mother has always been with you, and just as the Kings are with you now, so will I be with you always, child. Always remember, nothing in the world is as yielding as water. Yet for dissolving the hard and inflexible," he winks, "nothing can be better. Wisdom is your twin, Saman—"

A fit of harsh coughs overtakes him. Samantha and Devin can only watch as the man they love slips away, spasming with each ragged cough.

When the episode ends, Sukamaya lays still, gazing at the ceiling through glazed over eyes. He looks toward his children and a single tear rolls down his cheek. Samantha brings the straw to his lips and he takes a sip.

Devin's heads sags with guilt. *This is all my fault,* he thinks.

"No, Devin-sun. It's not your fault." Sukamaya's voice is growing weaker with every word. That last fit took a lot of strength from him and the strain can be heard as he speaks. "Can't avoid...

cycle...Soon, Devin-sun...I see...I see your light...So bright."

Samantha is not sure of what she should do. Should she call a nurse or just stay by his side? He looks so tired. The color has all but drained from his face and his eyes are glazing over. "I think I should get a nurse." She says. "I'll be right back."

"No, don't." Sukamaya insists. "Stay, child. You...watch him...He...watch you...Remember...don't forget...Yes?...Remember the Way."

Devin and Samantha both nod and Sukamaya closes his eyes.

"I'm so tired." He says. "I want to play... I see them... the monkeys."

Samantha squeezes Sukamaya's hand, trying to hold on to the very life he's letting go of. "I love you, Father." She says, placing a soft kiss on his brow. "Don't go."

Devin wraps his arms around Samantha and gazes down at his teacher as he holds her. As crazy as it seems, he never saw this day coming. Somewhere in his mind Sukamaya became an immortal—as wise, strong and fearless as one who's survived many ages– and as he watches his master fading away now, a part of him still doesn't believe it.

"Good-bye, sensei. I love you, Saka."

Samantha looks up at Devin, grabs his forearms and squeezes them tighter around her. The two of them stand like this, gazing down at a slumbering Sukamaya, waiting for the inevitable end.

The EKG's beep is replaced by a deathly drone. Doctors and nurses rush in, flowing around Devin and Samantha like a stream split in two. They stand there, as still as stone, holding each other as they gaze down at Sukamaya. Samantha takes her father's hand one last time. A nurse pleads with her to release him. They cannot use the defibrillator until she lets him go.

"Okay." Samantha says, letting her father's hand fall to the side of the bed. "I'll let go. The Master has no possessions."

CHAPTER EIGHTEEN

For the past two days Samantha has been a symbol of grief.

Her hair is a mess, she hasn't showered and the black bathrobe that she's wearing smells like a bag of onions. Since speaking to the mortician, she's been locked inside her father's guesthouse hiding behind dark curtains and sad music. Devin had suggested that they to move into a suite somewhere but Samantha refused. If the killers came back then she would just have to fight but running was not an option. She needed to be with her father's belongings, with the only parts of him she has left. And so for the past two days she's sat alone in his guesthouse, wearing his bathrobe, going through his things, forcing herself to face the truth: every parent that she has ever known is dead.

And while Samantha mourned, Devin reflected. He didn't have the luxury of grief; there was no time to be weak. The men that killed his parents, the man that got away at the bank, any of them could come back at any time. He has to be ready. And with Samantha out of the picture for now all he has is himself. So for the past 48 hours Devin has sat in his father's chair, staring at the projection screen, replaying his parent's murder. He's watched the recording over and over, searching for any clues that might lead him to The Elite. With a bottle of his father's Scotch next to him, Devin drank and watched, staring at the screen until he passed out, only to awake and do it all again.

Somewhere between drinking and sleeping Devin stopped

trying to convince himself to run back to his old life. His old life was fun but his success was superficial. There was always a better car, a bigger stunt, a more beautiful woman. He never found the peace he sought, the peace he always saw in Sukamaya; the peace he lost when Stacey died.

Devin had never admitted that until yesterday. Staring at the screen, he thought back to a time when his greatest worry was finding someone to do his homework while he partied. That was how he met Stacey. In school, Devin had offered to set him up with girls in exchange for Bs. From that arrangement a friendship soon blossomed and for years the two of them were inseparable. Like the Dick Grayson to his Bruce Wayne, Stacey would eagerly follow Devin's lead.

But where did I lead him, Devin thought, throwing back another shot. He looked at the screen and for the thousandth time that night watched a single bullet pierce his mother's skull.

To the grave, he thought, *and now Mom, Dad and Saka are with you.*

Another night passes and a new day begins. Samantha tosses and turns in her father's bed, fighting the dawn of consciousness. A barrage of memories held her captive through the night: horseback riding through the jungle hills of Samaná, rock-climbing up the Peninsula's jagged cliffs, skeet shooting on the beach; all of the things that her father taught her, all of the fun that she had learning The Way, the science of martial arts—*all of its over now.*

Reluctantly she opens her eyes. It feels like she was just able to fall asleep and the sun is already rising over the horizon. *How long did I stay up last night,* she thinks, pulling off the bed sheet. Sitting up in bed, she glances around at the mess she's been living in. Her father's belongings are scattered all over. The room is still dark but she can see the sunlight dancing at the bottom of her father's curtains, baying like an anxious racehorse at the starting gate. Something about the light is enticing, drawing her out of the bed and over to the windows. She can feel the warmth of the sun on her feet as she stands before the curtains holding the cord in her hand. She pulls down on it slowly and the curtains part, allowing the light to pour in and bathe her body in its radiance. She unties her father's robe and allows it to fall to the floor. It's the first time that she has taken it off since donning it three days ago. The soft fibers tickle her toes and she smiles. The sunrise is glorious and she can feel herself being refreshed as she stares out at Mother Nature's beauty. Wearing nothing but her smile, she strolls off toward the bathroom and a much-needed shower.

"Enjoy this beautiful day while you can." She sings, turning on the hot water. "And what a beautiful day it is."

- -

Devin is passed out in his father's chair when Samantha bursts in the study.

"Wake up, call!" She shouts.

He stirs in the seat. The image of Mrs. King sitting on her husband's lap is frozen on the screen. Samantha can't believe it.

"What's wrong with you? Why are you even watching that? Are you trying to torture yourself or something?" She glances at the screen and shakes her head. Not only has Devin been sitting in here replaying his parents' murder over and over; he's been drinking. *Devin doesn't drink.*

She moves the bottle of Scotch back to his father's mini-bar, grinning. *He hasn't even had half the bottle and he's wasted.* With the liquor back on the shelf where it belongs, she starts to retract the surveillance system.

"Come on, Devin." She kicks him in the leg. "Get up. We have things to do."

"Yeah." Devin mumbles, blinking the world into focus. "I know we have things to do, Sam." The projection screen ascends into the curtain rod and sunlight pours into the study. He sits up, squinting. "Glad to see you're feeling better. What time is it?"

She shrugs. "Time for you to get dressed and get a cup of coffee. I just got off the phone with the mortician's office. Everything's ready to go."

"Yeah." He yawns as he stretches. "But we still have to get the balloon."

"Just go get in the shower. And get some coffee or something—"

"I don't drink coffee, Sam. You know that."

She smirks. "You don't drink Scotch, either. Thought I knew that. Just get in the shower, okay. You stink. I'm going to start breakfast."

She heads out but pauses at the door. "And don't go swimming, either!" She yells. "You know we have a lot to do today."

Devin pulls himself to feet. "Yeah," he mumbles, "and every day after."

CHAPTER NINETEEN

Mister and Missus King's contributions to the Dominican Republic extended far beyond the bounds of Samaná. The two of them were actively involved in improving the country's developing economy, investing in businesses designed to boost tourism and redevelop urban areas. Their commitment to the people of *La Dominica* also made the Kings generous contributors to like-minded politicians.

Judge Fidel Morales' brother was one of those like-minded politicians and without the Kings' contribution to his senatorial campaign he would never have been able to gain his seat. Since the election, Senator Morales has been influential in passing many key pieces of legislature and because of his efforts the people of La Dominica are finally looking towards a bright future. Judge Morales knows the role Mister and Missus King played in her brother's campaign. If hearing the news of their murder broke her heart then Devin's arrest further scattered the pieces. After everything that the Kings have done for the island, Judge Morales felt that the least she could do was grant Devin a temporary furlough to lay their remains to rest.

And so now, hundreds of feet above the Earth, Devin wears a tank-top and shorts as he steers a hot air balloon over Cockpit County, Jamaica with Samantha beside him.

"It looks like a giant green egg-carton." She says, gazing down at the landscape.

"You're right." Devin says.

Steep cone-shaped towers of limestone, covered by a lush green forest, jut up from the rolling hills, making the entire area resemble a green egg- carton turned upside down.

"Out of all the stuff they've seen," Samantha continues, "and all the places that they been, I wonder why they would want their ashes scattered here?"

Devin turns to her, grinning. "So you're saying that you've never heard the story? Really?"

She shakes her head, finding herself grinning back at him for no apparent reason. "Nope. I always tried to avoid their *posthumous* conversations."

Devin thinks back to his first day back home and something Sukamaya had said, right when he pulled him away from Natalie and Clarkson

"Death is a natural part of life, right?" He shifts his gaze to the decorative urn sitting beside Samantha. "That's what Saka would say."

"Yeah." She nods. "That's exactly what he would say. But still," she grins, "I wouldn't want my ashes dumped over egg-cartons."

A refreshing chuckle escapes Devin's lips and it's his first genuine laugh in a while. He isn't surprised that Samantha would be the one to bring it out of him. She's all he has left. "Yeah, well, Dad told me the story. It's kind of cool actually. In that Mom and Dad way, you know."

"Okay, so tell me," she says, forever curious, especially about Mom and Dad. "Come on. I want to know."

Devin smiles again. He feels like a little kid for some reason, like he's sharing some delicious secret that only he knows. "Okay, well, you know how they loved to travel, right? But not just travel, like regular people vacations; Mom wasn't just going to be some tourist. She was always looking for some adventure. And Dad, well, Dad was just always trying to make Mom happy."

Samantha nods again, smiling as she remembers of their love. It's the type of love that she's always imagined for herself: growing old with your best friend and partner beside you through it all. She looks to Devin and shakes her head. "Yeah, guess that apple fell far from the tree, rolled down the block, and then got ran over by an orange truck."

"Yeah whatever." Devin says. "Anyway, so one day, you know, to make Mom happy, Dad agreed to go spelunking in the caves of Jamaica. The same caves that we're floating over right now."

Her face lights up. "So those are caves down there? Wow." She tries to picture the militant Mr. King being strapped into a harness and lowered into a dark cave. She imagines it would look like a mixture of a military operation and that scene from *Batman Begins* when Christian Bale first shows Alfred the soon-to-be Batcave. *Except Dad was probably scared out of his mind while trying to look tough for Mom.*

"Yeah," Devin tells her, "and one of them is called the Smokey Hole. It's over 600 feet deep. Mom and Dad propelled to the bottom of it. Can you imagine Dad cave-diving? I wish I would've seen that."

He starts to laugh and Samantha joins in. "Yeah, I know right? I was just trying to picture it myself. I can't imagine."

"Dad told me that on their way down Mom tried to keep him calm by telling him a story about the Maroons. See, back in the 1600s the slaves that had been set free by the Spanish settlers fleeing the British decided to resist the British occupation and fight for their land. These slaves—the Maroons—used guerilla tactics and their knowledge of the land to their advantage; all right atop those caves. They fought the British for almost 100 years and then finally, in the early 1700s, the British finally signed a peace treaty with the Maroons. The Maroons got like 1500 acres and autonomy from British control."

He grins as he gazes down at the ground below. "You know Dad loved that story. His mother's a descendant of the Maroons."

"Really? I always thought Dad was Haitian."

"Well, he was. By nationality, you know. He was born in Haiti. But his mother's family, my grandmother, was originally from Jamaica. Who knows what else he is. He never met my grandfather."

"Yeah, I know."

"Yeah. Well, Dad told me that by the time his feet hit the floor he was infatuated with Cockpit County. As soon as they got back home they put it into their will that their ashes be scattered here. Dad said Mom wanted to pour them down Smokey Hole but something about their remains being dumped on top of rat-bat dung just never sat right with him."

Samantha glances over at the two urns sitting in the corner of the basket. "You think Mom knew about Dad's descent? Like, could that have been her reason for bringing him here in the first place?"

Devin shrugs. "Who knows with Mom? After this scroll stuff, anything's possible."

She nods and gazes out at the mesmerizing view. The crystal blue sky is clear and cloudless. In the distance a flock of birds soar on a warm updraft. She turns to Devin.

"I think Saka would've loved this place." She says, picking up his urn. "Somehow it reminds me of his waterfall."

"Yeah, me too." Devin says, picking up his parents' urn. "It's peaceful, you know."

The two of them move to the edge of the basket and Devin looks to Samantha. "You ready?"

She nods. "Yeah. I'm ready."

Standing beside each other, the two of them lift the lids from the urns and release the remains of Sukamaya, Derrick and Jacqueline to the winds of fate. The ashes dance in the air, twirling round and round until they're gone.

- -

The balloon drifts through the air as silent as the two onboard and as Devin guides it back to Montego Bay, he avoids Samantha's gaze. But he can't duck her forever. The greens and browns of the shoreline begin to appear in the distance and he takes a deep breath. If he's going to do it he has to do it now.

"Sam...uh... Can I, uh, talk to you for a sec?"

She chuckles. "Devin, it's just you and me up here. I hope I'm the only one you can talk to."

Samantha knows that Devin has been avoiding her. How could she not, when the two of them have been stuck in an 8x8 basket in utter silence? *And now he wants to talk,* she thinks. *This should be good.*

He feigns a smile. "Uhh...yeah, right. Well, look, I've been thinking—"

"Uh-oh." Her smirk grows wider. "That can't be good for anyone."

"I'm serious, Sam." He turns and meets her playful smirk with a graveness she doesn't expect.

"Okay, I'm sorry. No more jokes. What is it?"

"We have to find those guys that stole Mom's book. We

have to find The Elite."

She turns away. *He can't be serious. Just the other day—* "I thought you said you were donating the scroll. What happened to all that stuff about this isn't your thing. You'll let them figure it out."

"I can't do it. I thought about this for the past two days. I realize now that really, I can't trust anybody but you. We don't know how big this Elite thing is. They attacked us not even ten minutes after we got the scroll. And you remember what Natalie said?"

She rolls her eyes. "Guess you can trust somebody other than me, huh?" Devin starts to say something but Samantha cuts him off. "Yeah yeah, I know. Reporter's intuition, right?"

"Look, Sam, you don't have to believe her, okay. But I know and you know—*we know*—that The Elite want that thing." He glances to the satchel. "And as long as we have it they'll want us."

She smirks. Devin's right and she knows it; better yet, Natalie's right and she hates it. But this sudden revelation of his isn't news to her. She had been realized that as long as the two of them have the scroll they will be hunted. It's just commonsense; The Elite have killed for this thing, there is no way that they would give up now. But Samantha is one step ahead of all of them: Devin, Natalie, and The Elite.

She looks out at the cloudless blanket of blue stretching out over the horizon and then turns back to Devin. A resigned sigh escapes her lips. "Look, if we're going to do this then you need to accept that no matter what happens, Devin, it won't bring them back. Not Saka. Not Mom. Not Dad. And not Stacey either."

"Stacey?" He asks. "This doesn't have anything to do with Stacey."

There is no way that you really believe that, she thinks. She tries to look into his eyes—those soft brown portals to his wounded

soul—but Devin can't hold her gaze.

"Look at me." She tells him. She grabs his chin and turns his face back to hers. "You have to face the truth. *Everything* has to do with Stacey. You haven't been the same since he died, okay. Since his death you've been doing this playboy, black Hugh Hefner thing that I've never understood. That's not who you are. That's not the real you. That's you running away from your hurt." She lets her hand fall to her side. "And what if this turns out the same? What if we never get Mom's book back or find The Elite? Can you handle that? Can you handle not finding any answers? I need to know now because I'm not going to help you if you're just going to go down that road again. That's not what Saka would want. Mom or Dad either."

"I never asked for your help, Sam."

She smirks. "Yeah, right. So what was all this leading to then, huh? Tell me. And what's up with all this we stuff then? You need me to contact my friend at the university, don't you? That has to be the next step in this plan of yours, right?"

"Yeah well..." Devin moves over to the other end of the basket. He needs to put some distance between the two of them; not really Sam but the things that she said. *Running from your hurt—or was it heart? It doesn't matter either way; both of them are true.* "I still didn't ask for your help. And I don't need it anyway. Go back to work or whatever and let me handle this, okay."

"Don't be stupid, please. For once." Her smirk grows wider. "You've always needed me, dummy, and you always will." The smirk fades and she looks on with the kind of tenderness that you would expect to see on a veterinarian dealing with an abused animal. She takes his hand. "But Devin, I need you to understand that what happened to Stacey was not your fault. You can't keep carrying that around. You can't keep thinking that everything depends on you. We all make our own decisions, Devin. Stacey made his and he had to deal with the consequences that came with it. It's unfortunate but it's not your fault."

Samantha knows that Devin feels guilty for introducing Stacey to a lifestyle that would eventually get him killed. Devin blames himself for Stacey's death just like he's been blaming himself for Saka's and his parent's deaths. That's why he won't ask for her help: he couldn't live with himself if something happened to her while they were on his quest for justice. But the truth is Devin won't be able to do this without her help and until he lets go of his grief he won't have a mind clear enough to stay alive while they track down book. *It's like Saka said: fixation leads to folly.*

"But—"

"No buts, Devin. You have to let go of the past if you are ever going to move forward. There is no other way."

Devin looks down to his arm and runs his hand over the only tattoo he has ever gotten—a Hindi symbol for 'peace' on his bicep. It was Stacey's idea. They were on their way to an after-party when Stacey saw the design in the window. He wanted to get it but was too afraid of the pain. Devin ended up getting it first, just to show Stacey that it was all in the mind. *If I can do it, you can do it,* he'd said, a line that he'd told Stacey a million times and one that never seemed to take.

At least not like I wanted it to.

Rather than simply continuing to do Devin's homework in exchange for dates, Stacey offered to tutor him instead. Stacey was a very intelligent young man and the ease with which he learned new things always impressed Devin. But, no matter how much Devin praised him, being smart wasn't enough for Stacey. He wanted to be one of the cool kids; one of the guys who was invited to every party and hangout.

He wanted to be like me.

But I was only being myself and that's what he never could get. Stacey was never able to accept that he could be popular just by being himself. Besides, a short, skinny, Jewish kid with freckles and acne was not who Stacey wanted to be anyway—and definitely not someone that girls wanted to be with. He wanted to be the bad boy; the mystery man; the tall, handsome and athletic class clown that all the girls went crazy for; *he wanted to be me.*

Then junior year came and Stacey's prayers were finally answered. He grew four inches over the summer, started playing soccer, and found an acne cream that actually worked. Those popular girls that had once looked passed him, now seemed to notice him everywhere he went. And so did everyone else. When his father's business went under Stacey traded in his car—the only cool thing about him-- for a cheaper model and used the excess cash to purchase large quantities of ecstasy, LSD, and high-grade marijuana. He could not be the man he wanted to be without money and without his family able to provide it he had to figure out a way. Drug-dealing proved to be the perfect fit for a young smart kid like himself. Stacey became a school-wide celebrity overnight.

Devin had watched this change with amusement at first and then pride but that pride quickly became worry once he found out that Stacey was dealing drugs. Devin tried his best to explain to Stacey that this newfound fame was more a product of his confidence than anything. He even offered to pay him for all of those old tutoring sessions to keep him from dealing but this new Stacey didn't want Devin's money or advice.

The Way is about harmony, Devin had tried to explain.

The Tao is the Truth and Truth never changes. Everything else is an illusion. That is why it comes and goes. Money, fame, girls: it all comes and goes. He told Stacey all of the things that Saka had taught him about life and reality but his friend had grown deaf to the sound of reason. A rift formed between them, pulled further and further apart by his Stacey's pigheadedness. It seemed that the more money and women came, the harder Stacey was to talk to.

Angry at Stacey and all of the stupid choices that he was making, Devin gave up on trying helping him and just focused on himself. The end of the school year was approaching and thanks to Stacey's help Devin was close to an early graduation; not to mention he had to figure out who to take to Junior Prom. Devin and Stacey ended up going months without speaking until one night when Devin got an unexpected call. Stacey wanted Devin to come with him to visit two girls who wanted to party. Devin could hear the nervousness in his voice and he knew something was wrong but Stacey was no longer his concern. Stacey had made it clear that he didn't want Devin's advice. Devin hung up the phone without even saying so much as "no."

That was the last time that Devin heard Stacey's voice. The next morning he was found slumped over in his car, dead from a gunshot wound to the head. The coroner's ruled it a suicide. Devin didn't believe it then and he doesn't believe it now.

Samantha lays her hand on Devin's arm and his reverie is broken. He blinks and looks toward her. She looks back at him and sighs. "Devin, there is nothing you could have done. Whatever you're thinking, it isn't true. There is nothing you could have done to stop that night from happening; no matter how much you blame yourself, none of it will change what happened."

Her words are familiar. It is the same message that he's

received from his therapist, from his parents, from Sukamaya.

"Let go, Devin. You have to let it go. You've held on to this for too long. Look what it did to you, to all of us. We have to stop running. It's gotten us nowhere. It's like Saka said, remember: the Master has no possessions."

Remember the Way, Devin-sun. He can hear Sukamaya's voice in his mind as clear as he hears Samantha now. It has always been there. Throughout everything he's been through Sukamaya's voice has always been there. It was only that Devin had chosen to ignore it. Stacey's death marked Devin's rejection of the Tao. None of the things that Sukamaya taught him helped to save Stacey so what was the point? If the Tao was really as powerful as Saka claimed then why didn't it resonate with Stacey?

Life happens, Devin-sun. It is not to be understood; it is beyond understanding. Life is to be lived.

Devin nods. "Okay, Sam. I'll try, okay. It wasn't my fault. Stace made his decision and now I must make mine."

"Oh yeah?" Samantha grins. "So what's your decision?"

"Depends." He says, sporting a smirk of his own.

"On what?" She asks.

"On if you want to go back to your research labs, books and all that stuff, or if—"

She cuts him off. "I called the university this morning and with everything that's happened, they advised that I take some time for myself."

"Well." Devin's grin widens. "Guess it's only one thing left to do then."

She eyes him suspiciously. Judging by that grin he's wearing, whatever it is, she's sure not to like it but she plays along anyway. "Okay." She says, grinning. "What's that?"

Devin smiles devilishly. "We have to get you ready for your date."

CHAPTER TWENTY

The candlelight dances in Gustuv's eyes as he listens to the words of his opposition.

"Doesn't that detective work for your people, Gustuv?" Romano asks. "Why then does he not yet have possession of the scroll?"

"And the grandson," Felix adds, "he was jailed, correct? The scroll was left alone with the girl. Why did your people not make a move then?"

From his seat at the head of their table Gustuv looks down at the insolents before him. He can feel the blood pulsing through his forehead. Massaging his temples, he glares at Felix; that damn accent is so annoying.

He closes his eyes and a small voice speaks.

Why don't you just kill them all and be done with it?

The response comes forth like a mantra. *Because I need them as much as they need me.*

"And what now, brother?" This time it is William adding his two cents. "What of the book? Why not disclose its location to us? Why the need for secrets, Gustuv? We are brothers, are we not?"

Brothers, Gustuv almost laughs at the assertion. *Does the word 'brothers' necessitate trust, loyalty? Do those hoodlums in America not call each 'brother'? Were Cain and Abel not brothers?*

"William," Gustuv smirks, "brother, trust me. I do what I do to the benefit of us all. The grandson has been ordered to stay within the confines of the Dominican Republic. Thus, the scroll stays there as well. He and the girl took a balloon ride today. The house was searched but the scroll was not found. I suspect that they took it with them. Being that they have no allies they are keeping it close."

"Enough of this game!" Romano erupts. "You are getting soft in the chest, brother. Why not just kill the peons and have the scroll? If it is truly what you claim then two lives is but a worthy sacrifice."

Murmurs of approval rumble through the room and Gustuv is far from surprised. *More than the people love a leader, they love to see one fall.*

"Question the cast of my heart again Romano and you will question nothing more." The words are spoken with the calm certainty of a man simply stating his name. The statement was not a threat; it was a lesson on the law of cause and effect.

Romano chooses not to reply and rightly so. He may not believe that Gustuv deserves to be their leader but he has seen enough of his violent displays to know better than to make this a physical battle. Today will not be the day that he deposes Gustuv, but soon. Gustuv Barchulé is digging his own grave chasing myths, ancient books and encoded scrolls; Romano is only awaiting the tombstone.

Gustuv glares at the pretentious buffoon sitting next to him, pompous enough to consider himself to be Gustuv's rival, and hopes that the idiot can muster the courage to speak one more word. How he would love to be rid of Romano once and for all—the man is nothing but an insolent coward hiding behind the prestige of his bloodline—but Gustuv knows that Romano doesn't have the gall to tempt Gustuv again and their stare down lasts but a few seconds before Romano diverts his eyes.

"Brothers," Gustuv bellows, "let us all take a moment to

consider just what it is that Brother Hapsburg asks of me. Two more murders. That is five family members dead within a week's time. Even if their deaths were made to look accidental, there would still be far too much probing. Think of the repercussions. These are not your everyday people. Romano knows this just as well as the rest of you and yet his impatience clouds his reason. As it so frequently does."

He pauses; allowing the memory of Romano's many fiascoes to sink in. Watching as the tide begins to turn in his favor, he smirks to himself. *They are so easy to manipulate because they are so emotional*, he thinks. If any of them would just take the time to look beyond their feelings then they would see that even Romano's failures serve a greater purpose. If they did not they would no longer persist. It is the only reason that he is still enjoying the privilege of living.

In order to bring about their aims it is necessary that the masses of the world become utterly wearied and completely dissatisfied with the incompetence and ineptitude their governments display. Only then will the people's cry drown out the voices of democracy and personal liberty. Only then will they seek out the one king that can unite all nations and religions, and remove all cause for discord. To bring about such an extreme level of discontent, extreme failures like Romano—with their ridiculous schemes and troublesome ideas—are warranted, if not indispensable, to Gustuv's cause. Chaos and confusion must precede peace and prosperity. It is a law as natural as gravity.

"The King family," Gustuv continues, "is renowned for their achievements in business, science, and archaeology. Such accomplishments they have crowned with their philanthropic and humanitarian efforts throughout the world. The death of their entire family in a matter of months would cause a public outcry too loud to silence. If we seek to maintain our anonymity, brothers," he cuts his eyes at Romano to drive home his point, "discretion is key."

Not one present tonight can argue Gustuv's logic. Since the days of Adam Weishaupt's infamous boasts, The Elite has been able to shield its activities from would-be penetrators by taking the name of the exposed—and subsequently defunct—Illuminati. Like a flare expelled from a fighter jet, whenever one draws too close to their organization, the name Illuminati is dropped, sending the threat chasing after a distraction.

The key to the Devil's power is his ability to convince the world that he doesn't exist, Gustuv thinks, *and it is a power I not am ready to part with just yet.*

Romano looks away in shame and Gustuv continues his performance. "How long have we been awaiting a moment like this? What need do we have to rush now? Our journey has surpassed the span of any man's life. We are the luckiest of our brethren to exist here and now. Simply having knowledge of the scroll's location is more than any of our predecessors can boast. Yet, we have also possession of the very book itself. These are causes for jubilation and yet, here you all sit, staring back at me with ungrateful eyes. Have you become the sheep that you are supposed to lead?"

Romano, Felix, and William exchange knowing glances. *Another one of his speeches,* their eyes say; speeches that they have all grown tired of hearing. With each passing day more members of their brotherhood are coming to see Gustuv as they do: an overzealous old man blinded by false mythology. The Elite's power could be utilized to rule the world and, with so much strife spreading about, the time to strike is now. Their Lord is willing it to be. But under the guidance of a misguided old fool they continue to spit in their Lord's face and waste time chasing lost treasures.

Gustuv leans back in his seat and ogles the candle's dancing flame. The enticing light of knowledge has mesmerized him since he was but a boy in a post-World War Germany. It was with his superior knowledge that Hitler stirred the currents of time. There is a power that lies in occult knowledge; the power that lies in the truth. Its seductive sway is what led Gustuv to Yale's Scroll & Key and eventually to this very seat.

How could he, a man of values and intellect, allow heathens such as these to learn the location of the book, to take a step closer to wielding the power of God? It is his duty to protect the ignorant masses of the world, not only from themselves, but from men like Romano Hapsburg—men willing to risk anything to obtain a power they cannot handle.

By any means, this is what Gustuv will do.

CHAPTER TWENTY-ONE

A black sports car zooms pass Detective Worthy's old pickup truck.

His truck, once a shining navy blue, is now a frantic conglomeration of junkyard parts and bad paint jobs. The "Old Lady" was built Ford tough when he first drove her to his graduation from the police academy but now, ten years, two crashes and a promotion later, the "Old Lady" is more commonly known as "The Bride of Frankenstein"—a description so fitting that even Worthy laughs when he hears it.

But it's not a problem under the hood that has Mrs. Frankenstein pulled over to the side of the road tonight. It's that damn ashtray. It's stuck again. Worthy would bet his life that Judith closed it. She's always doing things like this; her little ways of encouraging him to stop smoking. She wants him to quit almost as bad as she wants to get pregnant. Whenever she uses the truck, she'll close his cigarettes and lighter in the ashtray, knowing that it takes nothing short of the will of God to pry the damned thing open.

Nevertheless, the ashtray is only incidental. Worthy's real problem is that he left his lighter on his desk and the cabin-lighter has been broken since that first accident. If he had not forgotten his lighter then everything would be fine. He would have called in that car and continued on his way to Camino Cason. Instead, Worthy was forced to pull over and fiddle with the jammed compartment.

"One day I'm going to fix this damn ashtray." He mutters,

pulling on it with all the strength he was. The slot's indentation is just big enough for him to fit in two fingers, making it that much harder for him to get a good grip. But pull he does, straining with all his effort—one of the many signs that his cigarette habit has reached critical levels.

He contemplates this as he struggles with the slot. *Maybe Jude's right,* he muses, *Maybe I should just—*

The tray flies open suddenly and Worthy smacks his hand on the armrest. "Shit!" He shouts and suckles his sore knuckles.

He gives his hand a quick inspection and shrugs. "No blood; no foul." He says, shaking his head. "Now I really need a smoke."

Worthy flips on the cabin light, digs inside the ashtray (moving his emergency box of smokes aside) and retrieves the lighter. The amount of effort that he put into retrieving an item that he will use for no more than a second before placing it back in the ashtray and risking this entire scene replaying itself doesn't escape him.

But I have to have this back-up, he tells himself, pulling back onto the road with a cigarette dangling between his lips. A familiar phrase creeps up from the back of his mind, in a voice that makes it all the more annoying; annoying because it's right.

You need to just quit smoking those things, Judith's voice says. Worthy takes a long pull of the cigarette then holds it in front of his face as if looking for something on it that will help him decide one way or the other. He rolls down the window and the cool breeze pulls the thick nicotine cloud out into the night.

"She's right. I'm going to quit." He glances out the window, releasing quick puffs of smoke with each word. "And there's no time like the present."

He takes one last deep pull, savoring the tobacco's rich

flavor for one final time, and then flicks the butt out of the window. The glow of the ember is yanked away in the blink of an eye.

"Nothing to it." He says, grinning proudly. "Could've been quit if I wanted to."

Worthy continues to cruise down the empty road in silence (*damned radio went out in again*) alone with his thoughts. His mind has been a jumble this past week. He really needs to clear his head and sort all this mess out.

There's the kid and the girl.

There's Judith as always.

Then there's this new partner, James Clarkson.

Not to mention he wants a cigarette.

That last thought crept through the cracks. Worthy tries his best to ignore it and stay focused on the issues at hand but he can't. No matter how many times he hits decline the nicotine keeps calling. After five minutes of fighting he finally throws in the towel.

"Tomorrow." He lies, grabbing the pack off the dashboard. "You little guys help me think and I need all the help I can get right now."

After a few mellowing puffs the nicotine seeps into his bloodstream and the ringing stops. With his ability to focus restored, he once again ponders the week's dilemmas. Judith's issues are the same ones he's been dealing with since making detective: "*You spend too much time out of the house. You act like you don't care anymore. You aren't as young as you used to be,*" and his favorite, "*I want to have a baby. What type of father are you going to be?*"

Whatever kind gets you off my back. Yeah, that's what he'll say the next time she asks. *Imagine the look on her face.* A grin spreads across Worthy's mug as he pictures Judith's fair skin blushing red.

Now to Clarkson.

Rumor has it that Detective James Clarkson has been with the Peninsula for so long that he'll never get fired because of all the dirt he has on everyone and Worthy believes it. From what he's heard, the reason that Clarkson has so much dirt on everyone is because he's done some dirt *with* everyone.

Everyone but me, Worthy thinks. If there is one thing in this world that Detective Maximus Worthy hates it a crooked cop. Its cops like Clarkson that make doing the job so hard. When they betray the trust of all those people they are sworn to protect the citizens lose faith in the badge. With that faith is gone people start to seek their own justice, perpetuating a never-ending cycle of pain and vengeance. Every time that Worthy sees some young kid dead after trying to stand up to the local gang he blames guys like James Clarkson.

Judith told him to just try to get reassigned (and he had considered that) but in the end he figures he can do more to stop Clarkson by working next to him than he could on some other assignment. *And someone has to do something about him.* If Clarkson is really the guy that he's heard about, he doesn't belong behind a badge, he belongs behind bars. All Worthy has to do is get some evidence that can prove Clarkson's link to criminal activity and his ass is grass (*hopefully the prosecutors aren't dirty too*). Until then, Worthy has no plans on leaving his polyester covered side.

The kid, though—now that's where it gets complicated. It is obvious that the guy that Devin shot had it coming to him. He was trying to kill Devin for Christ's sake. *But law is law,* and according to the law Devin committed a crime. But that isn't really what's troubling Worthy—with all of Devin's million dollar lawyers, he is pretty sure that the kid will walk away with a slap on the wrist, *if that.*

It's just the timing of it all. In one week the kid's whole family was killed and now Worthy has to hit him with a bum murder rap.

To make matters even worse, Detective Worthy knew the late Derrick King. As a teenager Worthy was a member of Mr. King's foundation for wayward youths. Ironically, it was Devin's father that put up the money for Worthy to attend the police academy. Mr. King even purchased the "Old Lady" for Worthy as a graduation present. Worthy refuses to believe that Devin has no clue about the ties that their families share, although he rarely visits the Peninsula from what he's heard. Still, the thought weighs heavily on Worthy's conscious, so heavy in fact that tonight he's decided to make the long drive to the King's estate in hopes of clearing the air.

Ten minutes later, Detective Worthy is pulling his truck up to the King's front gate. He brakes beside the call box, leans out the window and activates the intercom.

"It's Detective Worthy." He calls. "Detective Maximus Worthy, from Precinct 1, Santo Domingo. I'd like to speak with Devin King, please."

He leans back in his seat and takes a few puffs as he waits for the gate's welcoming *CLICK!* He takes a few more puffs and a few more until half of his cigarette is gone and he hasn't gotten so much as a "Hold please." He lets out a sigh of frustration, leans out the window and pushes the call button again.

"It's Detective Wo—" The cigarette slips from his lips and tumbles to the ground in the middle of his sentence. *What a night,* he thinks, shaking his head. *First the lighter and now this.*

"It's Detective Max Worthy," he resumes. "I'm here to speak to Devin."

He opens the door and hops down out of the truck. There

is no way that he's going to let a little dirt and gravel ruin a perfectly good stick--not with the price of smokes getting higher and higher each day. He glances around the driveway, hoping to God his cigarette didn't roll underneath the truck because last thing he wants to do is get down on his knees right now. But with the way his luck has been going, it'll be so far under the truck that he'll have to lay on his stomach to fish it out.

Thank God, he thinks, spotting the glowing ember by the front tire. He retrieves the stick and after blowing some gravel off the filter, it's good as new. With the cigarette once again dangling between his lips, he leans against the hood of his truck and waits.

Five minutes pass and there's still no response. He glances down at his watch. *8:45 pm.*

Too early for the kid to be asleep. Him or the girl. What the hell, then? Why aren't they answering the gate? Either they're avoiding me—I mean I did arrest the kid, for God's sake—or, I guess, maybe the kid could be sleeping.

The filter is the only thing left of the cigarette now. He drops the smoldering butt to the ground and mashes it beneath his shoe. *Probably got drunk with the girl and passed out*, he thinks. *After a week like this, I wouldn't blame him.*

Worthy decides to give the intercom one last shot before heading back home. Judith may still be up and willing if he's in before midnight. He's heading back to the call box, wondering if he can talk Judith into wearing her anniversary gift, when he spots something odd out of the corner of his eye. There, over by the gate, close to the lock, something looks...*wrong.*

Curious, Worthy grabs his pack of smokes off the seat, stuffs them into his back pocket and goes to investigate. *The gate is open but it's looked to left closed.* He unholsters his .38 revolver and, holding it by his side, slowly nudges the gate forward.

"Nothing strange." He tells himself, stepping through the gate. Moving down the driveway he takes note of the surroundings. *No strange vehicles*, he observes. There is just the girl's Prius and Mr. King's old Jaguar convertible. *No visible lights, not even a TV's faint glow in the window. There's nothing to worry about, Max. Everything looks legit. The kid's just passed out on the crouch or something.*

Even as he tells himself this he knows it's a lie. Every nerve in his body is alive, screaming that something is wrong here. He arrives at the house and cautiously ascends the stairs of the veranda, tightening his grip on the revolver as he moves to check the locks on the front door. It's too dark to get a good look but there doesn't appear to be any signs of forced entry. He takes out his cellphone and points the bright screen around the door handle just to be sure. He finds no evidence to support the apprehension churning in the pit of his stomach but if there is one thing that Worthy's learned in the last ten years it's to trust his gut.

He dials the King's home number and presses his ear against the door. *A ringing phone tends to get people's attention,* he thinks, *as long as they aren't so passed out drunk that they don't hear it.* He can hear the telephone's shrill but not the drunken curses of a frustrated lush stumbling for the phone. *At least the phones haven't been disconnected. That's a good sign.*

He hangs up and checks his watch again. 8:57 pm.

"Come on, Max. Just leave. There is nothing here." He paces back and forth on the veranda trying to convince himself to just go home. "Leave now and you can just call back in the morning." He says. "Go home to Jude. Relax for a few and then come check in the morning. There's nothing wrong here but a defective gate."

And as much as he would like to believe that, as much as he would love to go home to his wife and practice making that baby she wants so bad, he just cannot shake the feeling that there is something—

A thought hits him. *Someone is targeting the Kings. That has to be it!* Mister and Missus King were murdered in their home but nothing of great value was taken. Then, only a few days later—*just after the will reading I think they said*—two guys *try to kill their son. But why? And why make the parents' murder look like a robbery gone awry only to attack Devin in public? It doesn't make any sense. Unless the people got desperate, maybe? Is there a time—*

Another thought comes. The morning that the Kings bodies were discovered it was suspected that the killers had somehow disarmed the front gate. *Their bodies had been lying in the hall for hours. What if the—*

Worthy stops thinking and acts. With two powerful kicks he breaks the door's frame and steps into the foyer, his .38 up and ready. "Police!" He yells. "Is anybody in here?" He glances around quickly and then makes his way to the dining room. It's empty. He moves from the dining room to the kitchen—also empty, except for a sink full of dirty dishes. He continues on through the house. His nerves are on end and trepidation lurks at every corner. A closed door is to his left. He stops; hesitates; and squeezes the handle of his .38 tighter. The killer could be—*no, there is no killer,* he corrects himself. *And certainly not behind this door.*

With the revolver held beside his cheek, he uses his left hand to throw the door open, and moves in quick. Heart racing and finger on the trigger, he sweeps the room with his gun. There is nothing but a chair, a desk, and shelves stuffed full of books. *It must be an office or a personal library, maybe.* He takes a deep breath, takes out his pack, and slides out a cigarette. It occurs to him that this is the first time that he's ever been inside the Kings' home. *Hope they don't mind,* he thinks, lighting up.

He takes a long satisfying pull and exhales. "Okay, Max. Calm down. There's nothing here." With every puff he can feel his heart slowing a bit. He takes one last long pull, stubs the stick out on the bottom of his shoe, and tucks it behind his ear. *Okay, now. Back to work.*

He exits the study and ascends the staircase slowly. The wooden planks creak under his weight. Standing at the top of the stairs he gazes down the hallway. All doorknobs and picture frames. Nothing suspicious. He moves down the hall and comes to the first door. He gives it a nudge and it swings open. There is a light switch on the wall. Worthy flips it on and an array of spotless bathroom fixtures glistens elegantly in the light. *It's almost too clean,* he thinks and continues on to the next door: a linen closet, empty except few bath towels. The following door is already open. Worthy steps in and has a look around.

"Have some respect for your stuff, kid." He says, certain that he is in Devin's room. It doesn't take a detective to deduce it; the place has that comfortably messy look that only a young man can accomplish—clothes thrown everywhere, drawers left open, and shoes sprawled out on the floor. He moves around the room and almost trips on a pair of old sneakers.

Everything is everywhere except where it belongs. "Guess that's the problem with having everything given to you," he mutters, a tad more sourly than he would like to admit. "You don't value anything."

He exits the bedroom and continues on down the hall,

hoping that Devin doesn't value his front door. Now that there's obviously no one here, Worthy can't justify kicking the man's door down. He digs out his lighter and takes the cigarette from behind his ear. Lighting up, he heads back down the hall scanning the pictures on the walls. *The Kings looked like a perfect little family,* he thinks, *but could they have been that perfect if they were murdered in the middle of the night. What secrets were they hiding?* He comes to another picture. It's a picture of the King family standing with Samantha and Sukamaya on front of their private jet, probably after some vacation he can't begin to afford.

"Shit!" He exclaims, cursing his stupidity. "Shit! Fuck! Shit!"

He pulls his phone out and sprints down the hall. *I didn't even see it. The bathroom with no toothbrushes, closet with no towels, tossed room, open drawers. The kid bolted! The son of a bitch ran!*

"You son of a bitch!" He races through the door, jumps down the veranda and sprints pass Samantha's Prius. He remembers that black sports car speeding pass his truck earlier. *And you took the Masserati. You little son of a bitch!*

Back inside the truck, Worthy finally gets Clarkson on the line. "You were right," he tells him, backing his truck out, "The kid's running!"

Siren wailing, Worthy flies down the road listening to Clarkson come up with a hundred ways to say 'I told you so.'

"Yeah, yeah." He nods along. "Yeah, I remember the bet. ... Uh-huh, outside El Catey. I'm on my way now. Make sure you have them hold the plane."

Detective Worthy hangs up and tosses the phone in the passenger seat. He opens his hand and finds his cigarette crushed beyond repair. Tossing it out of the window, he digs out his pack and lights up another one.

"But why, kid? Why'd you run?"

CHAPTER TWENTY-TWO

"Devin, slow down!" Samantha screams.

She's been slamming her foot down on the passenger-side brake since they first sped away from the manor. Her screams have been consistently ignored.

"Devin!" She yells again. "Please, slow down. The jet won't leave without us."

But my nerve might, he thinks.

Judge Moralez set very specific guidelines regarding Devin's travel during the course of these proceedings. Rule number one: do not leave the borders of the Dominican Republic without the Court's expressed consent. To guarantee his compliance with said rule, Judge Moralez ordered Devin's passport confiscated and held in the court's custody until the end of proceedings. But with a man with as many resources as Devin King, turning in a passport was like turning in a set of car keys. Devin has had multiple copies of his passport, birth certificate, and every other piece of required identification made since he was eighteen. For someone who travels as much as he does—not to mention with all of his illegal stunts—it was a necessary safeguard.

And now Devin is about to become an international fugitive. The more he thinks about it the more his stomach churns. A few days ago he was faxed a "morals clause" that the board of directors require him to sign before coming on as CEO of his family's business. It was rather loose but still, *what if they freeze all of my assets? Confiscate my property? I could lose everything.*

Staring blankly ahead, he clenches the steering wheel tightly and presses down on the gas. Samantha braces against the door as they round a corner.

"Devin!" She shouts. "Devin! Slow! Down!"

Her shrieks slice into his reverie. He turns to her, blinking like a man just awoken from a dream. "Huh?" He mutters, easing his foot off the pedal. "Oh. Sorry."

The car slows and Samantha releases a sigh of relief. "Uhh, Devin, you sure you want to do this? Maybe I could g–"

"No choice, Sam. We have to." His head bobs with each word like an apple on water. "Your guy can't come to us, right? Can't use the phone or the computer. Could be tapped. Bugged. Can't just beef up security and fly him in. If The Elite have the police—probably had that guy at the bank too—who knows who else is working for them? We have to go to him. This is our only choice."

He looks possessed, she thinks, turning towards the window. An endless stream of cocoteros blur pass. She gazes up at the cloudless night sky, alive with the twinkle of distant stars. The moon is hiding its face tonight. Those stars are all they have to illuminate the darkness, glowing faintly like brilliant halos in some far off heaven. Trepidation engulfs her as she turns back to Devin.

"I mean... about it all." She says. "You know, none of this will bring them back. We talked about that, remember. No matter what we find out, no matter what how it turns out, it won't change anything that's happened. So...just make sure that this is what you want to do. You're risking a lot, Devin. Think about why you're doing this."

Devin turns to her and they lock eyes. He can see her

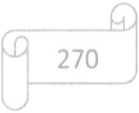

concern, her fear, but he doesn't blame her. On some level he understands—maybe even feels the same way himself—and that's why he loves her. But this isn't the time for love. "Sam. You don't have to come." He tells her and turns his focus back to the road ahead. "You don't have to come but I have to do this."

"Yeah well..." She says, gazing up at those distant lights. "If you have to go then I have to come. You can't do this by yourself."

A slight smirk shows on his face. "Yeah, you're probably right. I don't think me in a dress would have the same effect as you."

"A dress?" She blurts. "Who said anything about a dress?"

Devin laughs and Samantha joins in but her joviality is half-hearted at best. There is still trepidation lurking beneath the surface like a patient crocodile submerged in a swamp's murky waters. She doesn't think she'll be comfortable again until they are back on solid ground.

"You okay, Sam? You look like your stomach hurts or something." Devin knows what that look is and the feeling that accompanies it—his stomach is still churning itself—but he has to at least pretend to be certain of his moves. For the both of their sake.

"I'm fine." She lies. "Just should've eaten before we left."

Devin watches her from the corner of his eye as she scans the radio stations idly. *She always fidgets when she's lying. Right now it's the radio; next it'll be her hair or nails.*

"I know you didn't get scared to fly all of a sudden." He says, hoping to ease the mood a bit. "You know Dad probably just had the jet inspected. Same time every year, you know."

"What?" She asks, cleaning some invisible dirt from beneath her fingernails. "Where did that come from? I *flew* in, stupid."

"Oh. Yeah. Right." He looks her over. "You sure you're alright? This guy that we're going to see, he isn't like some crazed stalker or something, is he?"

Samantha chuckles. The idea that she, Samantha "Bookworm" Matsumi, would have a stalker; *that'd be the day,* she grins. "Yeah. Picture that."

"Yeah. You know what, never mind."

The Masserati makes a right turn onto a narrow two lane road. A security guard nods at them as they drive through a security point. As he drives down the private street he wonders if the jet is ready and waiting. He called ahead while they were packing and stressed the urgency of his departure. The sooner they get in the air the better.

Ten minutes later, Devin and Samantha are climbing aboard the King family's Vrillic twin-turbo luxury aircraft. It has been almost a decade since either of them have stepped foot on the jet. Its luxurious interior, with its carpeted aisles and plush leather seats, were once the site of raucous laughter and wondrous storytelling. Now, with only Devin and Samantha filling the cabin, there is a detectable heaviness in the air.

"So where the hell is Riga, anyway?" Devin asks, the first to break the silence.

"Latvia." She says. "Used to be part of the USSR."

The pilot's voice comes over the intercom and announces that it's time for take-off. Samantha can feel the slight sway of the cabin as the jet accelerates.

Devin gazes out of his window as the jet begins to climb. A car pulls onto the tarmac. *It looks like a Cadillac,* he thinks, and a familiar one at that.

"So how's the weather over there?" He asks. "I mean, over by Russia, it must be cold, right? There's probably some good skiing—" He turns back toward her and bursts out in laughter.

Samantha has her head stuck between her legs.

"It's not funny." She says, trying to make sure that her ponytail doesn't get in the mess. "Stop laughing and go get me a bag."

Please don't throw up, she thinks, willing her body to cooperate. *Please don't. I think I forgot to pack toothpaste.*

CHAPTER TWENTY-THREE

Detective Worthy's truck screeches to a stop and he jumps down onto the tarmac.

"Fuck!" he shouts, gazing up at the Vrillic's taillights growing fainter in the distance.

A Cadillac sedan pulls up beside Worthy's truck. Its eggshell white paint job and shining tires are a sharp contrast to the Old Lady's rusting undercarriage and Frankensteinian frame.

In pointed-toe boots and an old denim jacket, Detective Clarkson steps out of the Cadillac like an old cowboy dismounting his trusty steed. He glances around the airstrip and grins; a smug sort of smile that only grows wider when he looks up at the fading lights of the Kings' jet. He turns to Worthy with an "I told you so" poised on the tip of his tongue.

"Wouldn't keep'em grounded, huh?" He asks instead.

Detective Worthy leans against the hood of his truck and shakes his head. "Didn't even answer the first two times I called." He gazes at the jet's taillights. "When they finally picked up they claimed the plane was already taking off and they couldn't stop it."

"Yeah." Clarkson nods. He's seen that stall tactic before, *might've even been on the other end of a few of them.* "It's the way these private airstrips work. Money talks; bullshit has to call back three times and then gets brushed off."

Worthy chuckles but barely. He can't allow himself to lower his guard. The second that he starts to see Clarkson as a human being—rather than the disgusting rat-worm he is—that is the second that he slips into that gray area where sympathy and compassion can send the strongest moral compass spinning in confused circles. He's witnessed it happen before and he'll be damned if it happens to him.

"Kid's a fugitive now," Clarkson continues, "but he's a famous fugitive, at least. Won't be able to go too far without being recognized."

Worthy nods and pulls out his cigarettes. *Only three left,* he counts, sliding one out. *And now two.* He lights up, trying to remember if he has a fresh pack in the car or if this is it until he makes it to a gas station. *That's not important right now, Max,* he tells himself. There is something odd about all of this. He can feel it just as surely as he feels the nicotine calming his mind. There is some vital piece of information that he's missing. There has to be. There has to be something to tie all of this together. As it stands now, nothing makes sense. Why would Devin flee the country on a bogus murder rap that he has to know won't stick? And where does he even run to? It's like Clarkson said, practically all of Western civilization knows *People's Magazine's "Bachelor of the Year."*

He taps the end of his cigarette and the ashes drop onto his shoes. "Guess we just put out an APB on the worldwide database. Interpol." He takes another drag. "Shouldn't take long for somebody to spot him."

Clarkson dismisses the idea with a shrug. "How 'bout we try and find out where he's going first." He says, scanning the lot. A disheveled young man is crossing the tarmac. Clarkson waves him over. "There's no need in gettin' CNN involved if we don't have to."

Worthy nods begrudgingly. He resents the fact that Clarkson was right about Devin running and he hates that he's right about this

too. There is no point in posting a worldwide APB and plastering
Devin's face all over TV so soon. It will only cause Devin more
trouble and could even add a few more problems to Worthy's own
ever-growing list. If Devin was somehow *not* the person on that jet,
there is only one way that this will end for the department, and that
is in a lawsuit—a lawsuit that would probably demand that Worthy
be fired and the last thing Worthy needs is to be fired right now.

A slim young man in a rumbled red shirt and oil stained
overalls jogs over to the two detectives. His nametag reads: Hangar
Attendant: Juan.

Guess Hangar Attendant doesn't pay enough for a haircut,
Clarkson thinks, looking Juan over, *or a pair of pants that fit.*
Fuckin' kids. "So, Juan, where'd that plane go?" He opens his jacket
and flashes the badge clipped to his belt. "It's okay. You can tell me,
kid. I'm one of the good guys."

Worthy almost vomits in his mouth as Juan shrugs.

"No sé." Juan says.

"Okay then," Worthy asks, "who was on it?"

Juan shrugs again. "No sé."

Clarkson grabs hold of Juan's rumbled collar, yanks him
off of his feet and slams him against the side of Worthy's truck.
"Look kid," he grits, "I don't have time for games today, okay? Tell
me where the hell that plane went or go to jail? *¿Entiendes?* You
choose!"

Flustered, Juan attempts to tell the detectives that he cannot
answer their questions. He wants to explain that he is just a hangar
attendant and all he does in fill the jets with gas. He doesn't even
get to wash them. He wants to beg the detective to let him go and
not take him to jail. He wants to tell them all of this but he's so
frightened that instead what comes out of his mouth is a stuttering

jumble of words that neither detective can understand.

Annoyed, Clarkson throws Juan to the ground and walks off. Detective Worthy reaches down and helps him up. "Look, Juan, just take a deep breath and try to relax, okay. Then tell us where that plane was headed. We really need to know."

Juan takes a few deep breaths and points to a small building across the tarmac. "The guy at the counter. He should know."

Detective Clarkson walks back over to Juan and watched him stiffen with fright. "Relax." Clarkson says, smiling. He pats Juan on the back and smoothes out his collar. "Appreciate the help, kid."

No, Worthy thinks, following Clarkson across the tarmac, *don't you try to act like this was just some bad cop routine. You're on edge about something. You've been acting strange since the other night at the bar, when you got that message. What the hell are you up to?*

They step inside the building and Worthy looks around the luxurious lounge. "So this is how the other side goes to the airport," he mumbles.

Inside the small building a middle-aged man sits behind a cherry wood desk busily typing commands into his computer. To his right two large plush leather couches (*probably as soft as a cloud,* Worthy imagines) sit beside a brass handled door left slightly ajar. Through the small opening he can see more couches and recliners seated around two enormous televisions. Craning his neck, he makes out a wet bar, dart board, billiards table, and some expensive-looking coffee machine. He starts toward the door and Clarkson follows.

"Hello," the man at the desk says, stopping them in their tracks. He nudges his drooping glasses back up the bridge of his nose and smiles. "How may I be able to assist you two gentlemen this evening?"

Detective Worthy introduces himself and flashes his badge. "And this is Detective Clarkson from the Peninsula. We were told you could help us find out who was on that plane that just left and where it went."

"You are the man that called earlier, correct? I am so sorry that I was unable to help you, Detective. The aircraft had already begun its accent, you see. There was no way—

"Yeah, yeah," Clarkson cuts in. "Let's see how sorry you really are. Like my buddy here said, we need to know who was on that jet and where it's going."

The receptionist hesitates. It's a very slight gesture but both detectives notice it. "I am sorry, Detective, but unfortunately I am not at liberty to divulge that information. Our patrons are very esteemed individuals, sir, and their privacy is very important. It is an asset that they place an immense value on."

Clarkson begins to move toward the desk but Worthy intercepts his path. He is not in the mood for another rendition of *Bad Cop Clarkson.*

"Look, I understand that, but we really need your help. This is an official police matter. We're trying to locate a fugitive who may have just fled the country on murder charges."

The receptionist grins. "Well, Detective, if this is an *official* police matter then I'm sure you have an *official* warrant to search our records. And since I am sure that you don't, I can assure you that you are wasting your time. That jet was not harboring any fugitives. There is no way that Mr. King would be—" He stops abruptly, realizing what he's just done.

Detective Worthy grins, takes his wallet from his back pocket and takes out a hundred pesos. He places the bills on the desk and slides them forward. "And where did you say Mr. King went?"

The receptionist eyes the bills, obviously amused. "Sir, if this is a bribe, I feel that I should remind you that we cater to the Elite few. Our patrons are extraordinarily wealthy. I have received tips for keeping the magazines current that were larger than that, Detective."

"You heard'em, kid," Clarkson smirks. "Every woman's a prostitute for the right place."

Worthy shakes his head at the crude—yet accurate—humor and pulls out another hundred pesos. Well, he definitely won't be able to take Judith out this weekend.

The receptionist is not impressed. "Sir, I beg you, please refrain from embarrassing yourself, as well as I, with this foolish spectacle."

Detective Worthy rifles through all of the bills in his wallet: there is a little over three hundred pesos there. *Judith's going to kill me*, he thinks, sliding the bills across the desk.

The receptionist eyes the two detectives suspiciously. He is still unimpressed by the five hundred or so pesos before him. Most of his patrons tip in U.S. Dollars not pesos. Still, Devin didn't tip him tonight and he needs a new pair of glasses. "Okay. You two can have a seat if you like."

He picks the bills up, stuffs them into his pocket and motions to the two chairs sitting against the wall behind them. They both decline the offer and stand at the desk, glaring down on him as he works.

"Mr. King did not really kill someone, did he?" He asks.

Clarkson smiles. "We are not at liberty to divulge that information, sir." His imitation of the receptionist is so perfect that even Worthy has to smile. "Just tell us where the hell he's going so

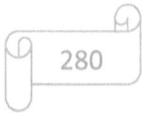

we can get the hell outta here."

Humiliated, the receptionist returns his focus to the monitor and pulling up the Vrillic's itinerary. He doesn't speak again until he's found the information that they are looking for. It is the most uncomfortable two minutes of his life.

"It says here that the jet is headed to the Wagtail Strip, just outside of Riga International Airport." He looks up from the computer. "Is there anything else I can do for you two gentlemen this evening?"

"No, sir," Worthy answers quickly, "I don't think I could afford it." He starts for the door then stops and turns back to the receptionist. "Don't tell anyone about this meeting, okay? You know that, right?"

The receptionist nods. "Same to you, Detective."

The two detectives glance at each other then head for the door. Just before they exit Clarkson stops, turns, and offers a few parting words to their host. "Oh yeah, by the way, Mr. King *did* kill someone. Just thought you should know."

The receptionist's jaw drops to the floor and Worthy shakes his head in disbelief.

"What was that about?" Worthy asks, crossing the tarmac beside Clarkson in the cool night air.

Clarkson turns to him and laughs. "What? Did you see his face? I just thought, hey, you should've gotten more for your money, kid. And the look on that prick's face. Fucking priceless, right?"

Worthy watches Clarkson laugh way too hard considering the circumstance. "You're messed up," Worthy says, rather matter-of-factly. "Something's seriously wrong with you."

Clarkson's laughter ends abruptly and he looks to Worthy again. He watches the young detective—out at midnight instead of being at home with his wife, fishing out a pack of cancer-sticks, heading to a ten year old piece of shit junkyard job he calls a truck— and smirks. *Yeah, I'm the one messed up, kid.*

The two detectives arrive at their cars and Clarkson turns to Worthy. "So where the hell is Riga anyway?" He asks.

Worthy exhales a thick cloud of smoke. "I don't know. Sounds European. Maybe Asian."

"Yeah. Maybe." Clarkson nods. He gazes out at the night, staring at nothing in particular. "Be right back, kid." He slides inside his car (*a new Cadillac, unaffordable on a detective's salary,* Worthy thinks), takes out his cell and dials a number. When he rolls up his tinted windows and turns on some music, Worthy only grows more suspicious. A few minutes later the engine starts and Clarkson's window slides down.

"Call you in a few hours, kid. I got some things to take care of. Better yet, first thing in the morning. It's already past my bedtime."

"Yeah. Okay." Worthy nods. "First thing in the morning." He glances down at his watch. *Oh shit! It's after eleven.*

Climbing into his truck, he pulls out this phone and calls home.

"Hello," he says, lighting his last cigarette. "Hey, babe... No, wait! Honey, please.... Just let me explain."

CHAPTER TWENTY-FOUR

S amantha exits the yellow taxicab behind Devin, adjusting her thin jacket as the brisk night airs whips pass.

She waits on the sidewalk, glancing up and down the quiet street, while Devin pays their driver. Rows of identical brick homes line each side of the curb, accented with well-kept lawns and dimly-lit driveways.

The cab drives away and Devin walks up beside Samantha as another sharp wind rips through her jacket. She cuts her eyes at him, standing there in his beanie and thick coat, wearing the satchel like a sash across his chest, completely unaffected by the gusts. The wind attacks again and she jams her hands in the jacket's thin pockets.

"Should we have called first?" She asks.

Devin shrugs. "We're here now. Let's just stick to the plan. You do remember the plan, right?"

Samantha rolls her eyes. "Of course I remember the plan. It's *my* plan."

It was close to two in the afternoon in Riga and a little before six a.m. on the Peninsula when the Vrillic touched down on the Wagtail Strip. Pumped up on adrenaline and double-shot espressos Devin had wanted to rent a car and drive out to Dr. Bauer's home right away. Once there, he said, they would then show him the scroll, tell him everything that had happened and that was as far as he got before Samantha stopped him. Even jet lagged she could see the utter idiocy in that.

"I've seen enough movies to know that when the police are after you, you never rent a car," she explained. "You know, since you have to use a credit card they can just monitor your purchases to locate you. If Clarkson is really working for The Elite we have to expect that they could have other police, even here, looking for us."

"And as far as Kurt goes," she continued, "It's like you said, the only people that we can trust right now are each other. Unless you keep coming up with dumb ideas like this, then I'm on my own."

Devin glanced over at the book bag full of money sitting on the floor, thinking they could just *buy* a car but whatever. "Okay then," he had said, "So what do you think we should do?"

Samantha's plan was simple. First they get a cheap motel room, making sure to pay in cash, and then they go to sleep. Then, after a hot shower and some food they would discuss just exactly what to tell Dr. Bauer. But first, Samantha needed sleep.

"You're forgetting something," Devin had smirked," You have to buy some new sexy clothes and find something to do with your hair. Ponytails aren't seductive."

Samantha could only shake her head. She didn't know which was worse: having to use her body to entice Dr. Bauer into helping them or having Devin there to watch the whole thing. Now, standing at the end of Dr. Bauer's driveway she hopes that the doctor's curiosity will be piqued enough to get him involved.

"You have to loosen up." Devin tells her, "You know, flirt. Smile. Be sexy." He smiles at her. "I know you say this guy likes a challenge but, just, don't be a Rubrics Cube tonight, you know."

Samantha rolls her eyes. She still can't believe she is going through with this. Something about it feels like prostitution.

"You just remember, we only say enough to get him interested in working with us." She retorts. "Fight the urge to go cry on his couch."

"Yeah, yeah, need to know basis. I got it."

Devin looks Samantha over one last time. Somehow, even shivering, she's still managing to be hot. Her tight hip-hugging jeans showcase her tone legs and slim waist while her low-cut blouse reveals just the right amount of cleavage. Adding to this a form-fitting jacket and knee-high black boots; Samantha could grace the cover of any women's magazine.

Especially with her hair down, Devin thinks. He was struck speechless when Samantha pulled a set of curling irons from her bag and added some volumes to her silky waves.

"Come on." He says and the two start up the driveway, passing a midnight blue BMW 5-series and a forest green Volkswagen Beetle.

"Cute car." Samantha says.

Devin shrugs. "I guess. If you like German."

"You know I meant...you know what, never mind."

A one story brick Tudor, with a three-step incline and small threshold stands before them. They ascend the stairs and Samantha reaches out for the brass knocker on the door.

"Hold on." Devin stops her. "Look at me again."

She turns to face him and the dim porch light accentuates her features. *She's beautiful*, he thinks. He hasn't seen Samantha this made up since their high school prom.

"What?" Samantha asks, girlishly tucking her hair behind her ear. "Why are you staring at me like that? Do I have something in my teeth?"

Devin grins. "I was just thinking how this will probably be the only time you'll look like a girl until you're getting married." His grin grows wider. "Just trying to capture the moment, you know."

"Whatever," she says, trying to hold back her smile. "Let's just get this done."

Devin nods. "Whenever you're ready then, Sam. He wants you, not me."

Samantha murmurs something to herself (It sounds like 'stupid' or 'jackass' or maybe even both) as she takes the knocker and raps the softly against the front door. They wait for about half a minute but no answer comes. She goes to knock again and Devin stops her.

"Let me." He offers.

"Go ahead." She says, stepping aside. "Be my guest."

"See you were too nice about it." He explains, approaching the door like a batter stepping up to the plate. He grins to her and then starts pounding on the door like a madman off his meds, shouting "Dr. Bauer! Dr. Bauer!" the entire time.

Samantha can't believe him. "Stop that!" she says, slugging him in the arm. "Are you crazy?"

"What?" He smirks.

"What do you mean *what*? Look around. This is a quiet neighborhood and it's after nine. People have to go to work in the morning. You can't just bang and scream at the top of your lungs. They'll call the "police"."

Devin looks up and down the slumbering street. *It's like something out of SimCity,* he thinks. "Who sleeps at nine o'clock? And on a Friday night."

Samantha shakes her head but before she can begin to scold him, Dr. Bauer's front door swings open and a salt-and-pepper-haired man stands before them in a partially open robe and slippers.

"Hello," he says, still so preoccupied with something behind him that he is not even looking their way as he speaks. "How may I help you?" He asks.

Samantha smiles at the sight of her half- naked colleague. "Hey Kurt," she says. "Did we catch you at a bad time?"

Recognizing that soft voice the doctor turns to Samantha, smiling suggestively. "Ms. Matsumi," he says, looking her over. "I've never seen you so...so... *stunning.*" The two have rarely ever seen each other outside of the university and the few times that they have Samantha has never been dressed so alluring. "To what do I owe the pleasure, my dear?"

Samantha blushes. Unbeknownst to Dr. Bauer, his robe has inadvertently slipped open, revealing a part of himself she's never seen before. She does her best not to look.

"Uhh, Doc," Devin chimes in, "No offense, but umm, I don't want to see your, uhh, pleasure. Get my drift?" He nods towards the doctor's waistline.

"Oh." The doctor grins, pulling his robe tighter. "Sorry about that. I was about to take a bath when I heard you calling."

"No, it's our fault, Kurt. We should've called first." Samantha apologizes. "I shouldn't have just dropped in on you like this but it's important."

"It's okay," He says, and glances over to her male friend. He looks familiar but Dr. Bauer can't place him.

Samantha can tell that Dr. Bauer is curious about the man she has brought with her. "I hope you don't mind that I have brought someone to your home like this. This is Devin King," She says, "If you didn't know that already. And Devin, this is Doctor Kurt Bauer. The best linguist I know."

The two men shake hands. *Strong grip*, Devin thinks, wondering if Dr. Bauer plays rugby. With his tall, solid build and muscular frame, he'd make a good quarterback.

"Devin King," Dr. Bauer says, his first thought being *how does Samantha know Devin King?* Quickly followed by *and what are they doing at my house?* But the fan in him can only smiles at the man standing on his porch. "The DK." A sudden realization dawns on him and his smile quickly turns sullen. "Sorry about what happened to your parents. I just saw something about it online the other day. Have the police been able to find out anything?"

"No, not yet." Devin says and shoots a quick glance to Samantha, urging her to take over the conversation. The plan was for her to entice him, not Devin.

Dr. Bauer mistakes Devin's glance for something more. He looks back and forth between them "I was wondering how you two knew each other." He says, looking back and forth between them. "Samantha, is this why you've denied all my advances? The best man won out, eh?"

Devin raises his hands in protest. "No, not me, Doc. Sam's like my sister. Her father, he—"

"Kurrrt!" A sultry voice calls from inside the house. "Kurrrt! The water is getting cold!"

"Just a minute darling!" The doctor yells back. He grins at his guests."I don't mean to be rude but as you can see you caught me in the middle of something. Could we do this at another time? If it's not too important, mind you."

"Well, it is kind of important, Doc." Devin nudges Samantha. "Right Sam?'

"Uhh, yeah. Trust me Kurt, you'll want us to stay. That case Devin's wearing, it holds an ancient text, just discovered a few

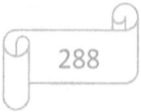

months ago. I think the main body's Sumerian but it's covered in symbols. Some of it looks Egyptian, Hebrew; I think Arabic. I'm not really sure. We need your help."

She gauges the doctor's expression; curiosity dances behind his dark brown eyes.

"And besides me and Devin," she adds, "you'll be the only other person alive who's seen it. I mean, if you help us, that is."

Dr. Bauer strokes his chin in consideration. "So you want my help," He says. "And by help I assume you mean that you need me to translate this text you say you have?"

His face is stark as he stares at the two uninvited guests standing on his stoop in the dead of night. If no one else knows about this text then it is either stolen or dangerous, he figures—two great reasons for him to decline their offer. His third reason is lying naked in a tub of scented bubbles right now. He looks from Devin to Samantha and her eyes meet his. She smiles coyly.

"Well then," he says, "what are we doing standing out in the cold?" He steps back into the house and beckons them to enter. "Come on in. Let's have a look at it."

Devin and Samantha step inside and Dr. Bauer closes the door behind them.

"Wait here." He says. "I'll just be a moment." He leaves them in the foyer and he heads off down a hallway.

"Hope he's going to get dressed." Devin says. "You and me both." Samantha agrees. "Put that turtle back in its shell."

As she looks around the foyer, Samantha gets the sense that Dr. Bauer's home is a reflection of his eclectic nature. His handcrafted rugs, crystal-filled armoire, and assortment of beautiful paintings reflect his appreciation of the finer things in life, while

289

mantle full of collectibles tells of a love for history. The decorative wagon bar besides the couch, the smell of scented candles in the air, and the soft jazz she hears coming from the back are evidence of the more carnal pleasures he enjoys.

That and whoever he has back there, she thinks.

Dr. Bauer returns to the parlor, smiling. "Follow me." He instructs and leads them down a short hall and into a cluttered chaotic mess of a room.

"This is my office." He tells them. "Make yourself at home. I'll be back in a moment."

The doctor disappears out of the door before Samantha can ask just exactly how they're supposed to do that.

"Make yourself at home." Samantha parrots. She surveys the disarray that Dr. Bauer calls his office. He has papers laying everywhere, books strewn about on tables and chairs, with half-empty glasses of liquor sitting atop it all. "I don't think life can exist in this place." Still, despite the mess, the more Samantha moves around the room the more a sense of familiarity settles over her.

It's the smell, she realizes. The sweet stench of burnt tobacco leaves transports her to another time and place, back to when a young pig-tailed Samantha would sit on the floor beside Mr. King's chair reading a book as he puffed away.

Devin can also feel the nostalgia pouring in. The big wooden desk, the way that it's positioned in front of the windows, the smell of old books and cigar smoke—it's all reminiscent of his father's study. Devin forces those memories back, shoving them down into a grave, buried beneath vivid images of his parent's corpses. He stares at the windows behind the doctor's desk and he sees the projection screen descend, playing his mother's last moments over and over. Sukamaya's dying body appears next, followed by a crying

Samantha. A kid lies dead in a car, shot in the head. Devin can see a tattoo on his arm. It looks just like his. The kid lifts his head and Devin turns away.

Dr. Bauer strolls back into the room, sporting wet sleeves and a wide smile. He's still wearing his robe but, to Samantha and Devin's delight, he's also donning a pair of pajama bottoms.

"Sorry about that." He says, moving towards his desk. "I had to tend to the lady." He shoots Devin a sly smirk. "I'm sure you know how it is."

Devin doesn't respond but Dr. Bauer hardly takes notices. He's once again taken interest in the beautiful Samantha and her curvaceous backside. Standing beside his desk now, he ogles her as she reaches up for a book on the top shelf of his case.

"Kurt," she says, giving up on the book and turning towards him, "I never would have pegged you for such a slob. Look at this place." She motions to the jumble of books, folders and files scattered about, "How can you work like this?"

"Organized chaos." He explains. "I know exactly where everything is." A partially finished glass of Scotch sits atop a mound of papers on his desk chair. He downs the Scotch, sets the empty glass on the metallic wagon bar beside him, and moves the stack of papers to the waist-high stack of files on the floor next to it.

"Original Arabic." He says, taking a seat. "I'm doing a translation of the Holy Qur'an for an umm...friend, you could say."

Samantha nods. She'd be surprised if he wasn't doing some type of work while the students are out on break.

The doctor moves some things around on his desk until he's cleared a space he presumes is big enough for the text. Anything more and they'll just have to sit on the floor.

"Okay," he says. "Let's have that look then."

Devin lifts the satchel over his head and begins to unscrew the canister. "Hold on," Samantha stops him. "Before we show you anything, I have a couple questions." She smiles coyly. "Well, if you don't mind, of course."

Dr. Bauer returns the smile. "No. Go ahead." He reaches for a half-finished cigar. "Do you mind?"

She smiles again. "Actually Kurt, I love the smell of cigars. The stronger the better." He offers one to Devin. "They're imports from Cuba. A gift from my father."

Devin once bought his own father a set of Cubans. They were in his study the day he was killed. The murderer even smoked one. His jaw clenches as he pictures the footage again.

"I'm okay, Doc," he says, forcing a grin. "Don't smoke, you know. Body's a temple and all that."

"Right." The doctor nods. "I should've known that. You're an athlete, by God." He moves his gaze to Samantha. "So, you said you have some questions for me?"

"Yes, Kurt." She smiles. "First, are you familiar with Mrs. King's work—Devin's mother?"

"I'm familiar with some of it." He says, clipping the end of his cigar. He reaches in the desk drawer for a lighter. "She was searching for some lost kingdom or something, right?

"Right. Well, we think this was found on her last dig. It may tie into her work, we don't know. What we do know is that for some reason she didn't choose to report the find to anyone. You understand what I'm saying Kurt?"

"Yes, yes, I'm following you," he says, "but what exactly *is* it? That is what I want to know."

Samantha looks to Devin then back to the doctor. "Honestly Kurt, we don't know. That's why we're here. It's very important that

we find out what is it we have. I thought you were the best one to come to for help."

"So can I see this text, then?" He asks, taking a puff of his cigar.

She looks to Devin again, and nods. "Go ahead." She says. "Show him."

"Hold up, Doc." Devin says. "I have a question of my own: how long do you think it'll take you to translate this thing and figure out what it is?"

Dr. Bauer smirks. "Well, I won't be able to tell you that until I've seen whatever it is I'll be translating." He takes another puff as he waits for Devin's response. Devin only glares.

"But since that won't be happening until I answer this question, I'd say..." Dr. Bauer puffs again, thinking. "Well, it's hard to know. If it's cuneiform, that isn't like French or Spanish or something. I'm not fluent in cuneiform, I mean. But I guess, with some help, I—"

"No help, Doc. Nobody but me, you and Sam can know about this." Devin's stare is stern. He needs the doctor to grasp the seriousness of what's being said. "You got that, Doc? No help. Only me, you and Sam can know about this."

Dr. Bauer looks to Samantha, the incredulity he feels is apparent on his face. "So, you come here seeking my assistance in translating some ancient artifact only to tell me that I cannot seek the assistance I need."

He looks back to Devin. It's obvious that he's not budging on this. His fixed stare relays his obstinacy.

"Listen," the doctor continues, "if you expect me to do this on my own it will take time. Time that somehow I don't think you have."

"Well how much will it cost to shorten that time, Doc? What do you need? I have resources."

"That's not the issue. This isn't—"

"Listen, Kurt." Samantha cuts in, swaying her hips as she saunters over to the doctor "This is really dangerous work. People have scarified their lives to keep this a secret. Right now we don't know exactly why that is..." She pauses, gazing seductively into his deep dark brown eyes. "But what I do know, Kurt, is that you're the man to do it. Not because you're an expert in your field but because I know a man like you can appreciate the risk involved here. A man like you can not only accept this challenge but embrace it. I brought Devin here because I thought that's who you are." She leans in now, close enough that he can feel her warm breath on his ear. "If I'm wrong, Kurt, let me know now and we'll leave. We don't have time to waste."

Devin feels like a voyeur watching Samantha's sultry speech. The suggestive gleam in her eyes and the sensual tone of her voice—*it's like she's had a little geisha girl trapped inside her all along,* he thinks. When they came up with this idea it seemed simple enough but as she works him, Devin is not sure if he's disgusted by her ability to manipulate the doctor like this or proud of her for it.

Dr. Bauer takes a few puffs on the cigar, gathering himself. This new feisty Samantha is far from the woman he used to flirt with in the cafeteria, and he likes it.

"You were not wrong." He says. "I have always liked a challenge."

He looks to Devin and the satchel he's holding in his hand. "So, can I see this text now or are there still more questions?"

Samantha nods to Devin and while he's unscrewing the satchel's lid, she slips back around the desk. Fully aware of Dr.

Bauer's stare, she adds an extra sway to each step, enticing him with the womanly curve of her hips. Standing beside Devin now, she tosses the doctor a coquettish grin.

Devin is doing his best to ignore their flirting as he slides the scroll from the satchel and carefully unrolls it on the desk. To be honest, he doesn't like seeing Samantha act this way, even if it is all just a ruse. It cheapens her somehow; makes her more like all the other girls he's been with. *But we're here now,* he thinks, looking up at the doctor.

"Okay, Doc. Here it is. What do you think?"

Dr. Bauer's gaze devours Samantha's image one last time before turning to the scroll now laid open on his desk. He grips the material between his fingers and rubs it gently.

"This is definitely papyrus." He says. "And these are cuneiform." He runs his fingers over the group of wedged-shaped markings in the center of the scroll. "They look pre-Babylonian. Those symbols to the right are definitely Egyptian hieroglyphs. Where did you say this was discovered?"

"My mom found it Iraq, we think," Devin tells him, "about two or three months ago."

"Hmm..." Dr. Bauer takes a puff of his cigar. "Ancient Mesopotamia. The home of Sumer. I think I've seen something like this before."

"Really?" Devin asks.

Bauer nods. "Yes, but not exactly." He takes another puff then sits the cigar in an ashtray.

"It was a creation story. The Sumerians are the oldest known civilization to date." He rises from his seat, walks over to his bookshelf and fingers through the titles. "Well, them or the Egyptians, depending on what you choose to believe. The controversy is really just the legacy of racism extant within the field of anthropology. I'm sure your mother told you how European scholars sought to deny Egypt's African origins because they couldn't imagine a black race achieving so much, especially before Europeans. Many of them attributed Egypt's glory to the influence of outside peoples—of Caucasian, Asian or Semitic backgrounds. It's that same prejudice that's fueling this debate. Since some scholars believe that the Sumerians were Semitic people, they would rather name them the first civilization rather than Ancient Egypt, where more and more evidence is proving irrefutably that the peoples came from Negroid stock."

He selects a book, flips through it, and then places it back on the shelf. "Either way, the Sumerians lived along the Tigris and Euphrates Rivers in Mesopotamia."

"Present-day Iraq." Samantha chimes in.

"Correct." Bauer nods. "I'm not a historian but I have read that the Sumerians supposedly created the first story of human creation. There are some who believe these stories to be profound spiritual treatises and not merely the myths they are generally taken for today. The Sumerians are also purported to have had a system of mathematics so advanced that they were able to map the Earth's skyline."

Samantha nods. She has all about the Sumerians and their achievements. They were one of Mrs. King's favorite ancient peoples. If she recalls correctly it was Sargon I, whom the Hebrew people call Nimrod, that consolidated the regions of Sumer and Akkad into the ancient nation of Babylon. According to the Hebrews, Nimrod was a son of Cush, and the Cushites were descendants of Noah's son Ham. Ham was supposedly the progenitor of the black race which means that the Egyptians,

Sumerians, and all others listed in his genealogy would also be black—which is what Mrs. King also believed. There was also something about a secret school that Sargon may have been a part of and that it was the knowledge that he gained there that enabled him to do his great deeds.

"And," Samantha continues, "Mom told me that about 5,000 years before Christ, the Sumerians had already invented the wheel, discovered that the Earth is round and had somewhat accurate astrological charts."

"Didn't they believe that two of their gods fought for control of the Earth?" Dr. Bauer asks, still looking through his books. "One of them had made humans from clay and then the other tried to kill us all in a great flood."

"Like that story in the Bible?" Devin asks. "Didn't they make a Disney movie out of that?"

"Yeah," Samantha tells him, "It's from the Bible. I don't know about the movie." She shakes her head. "Didn't you listen to Mom at all? That's where the Hebrew story originates. According to Mom that's where a lot of their stories come from."

Dr. Bauer selects another book and flips through it. Still not the one. "An extensive amount of work has been done on cuneiform, actually. It is one of the original languages."

"Original, Doc?" Devin asks. "What'd you mean? Like one of the first languages?"

The doctor grins to himself as he walks back to his desk. "Of course. What else could original mean? The *origin* of *all*, the first, the source— cuneiform is one of the oldest languages known to man."

Devin doesn't appreciate the condescension but he lets it go for the sake of a greater good. Still, this doctor dude only has one more time to try and make him look stupid and something's going to happen. "So, basically, you're telling us what we already know," he retorts. "The scroll's old, duh. We didn't come all the way here for that, Doc."

Dr. Bauer grins. He deserved that. "When you consider the languages that I see here and the fact that it is on this papyrus scroll, yeah," he nods, "it's old. Very old. Could be 10,000 years or more."

Samantha shoots Devin her *I told you so* grin. Dr. Kurt Bauer is definitely the man to help them piece together this puzzle. *What would he do without me,* she wonders.

"What I find unusual," Dr. Bauer continues, "is the mixture of symbols and languages. Some of these languages were not in use until thousands of years after the others had more or less died out. Then symbols have a language of their own. Like this symbol here," he points to a hieroglyph of an Egyptian beetle in the lower right hand corner of the scroll, "its position makes it seem to be some sort of signature. Maybe even a seal."

Devin nods. He can see what the doctor means. If the scroll was a letter the beetle would be positioned just where one would expect to see the author's signature. "Do you know what it means, Doc?"

"Well, you see, the ancient Egyptian way of life was very holistic. No one thing could be taken to be separated from the entire system, so to say. For instance, today the way Western civilization separates religion and government would be unfathomable to them as well as the feud between science and religion. If an idea was presented that did not coincide with their spiritual beliefs, their scientific beliefs, their cultural beliefs, then it would be dismissed or all those other ideas would be updated to reflect this new discovery."

"Soooo....you don't know what it means, then?"

"What I am saying, Mr. King, is that in order for me to give you a decisive answer as to what this beetle represents I would need to understand the entire context of this scroll. But, being that the scroll was found in Mesopotamia, I can speculate that it may have some religious significance of some sort."

"Huh," Samantha says, studying the images on the scroll. "So was that bug a religious symbol? In Egypt, I mean? It was, wasn't it?"

Dr. Bauer grins, impressed. "Yes it was. In Ancient Egypt the scarabeus was used to denote the only begotten or Father, as well as a symbol for transformation, because they erroneously believed the scarabeus to be a self-produced creature, conceived without a female. Now the only-begotten- God was an especial type of mythology in Ancient Egypt involving their *neter*—what we today call a god—Khepera-Ptah. The scarabeus or *khepera* was his emblem. Khepera-Ptah, like another one of their neters, Atum, was reborn as his own son. His son, Iu-em-hetp, is the Egyptian Jesus— the only begotten son of God."

"So you think this is like Jesus' signature in hieroglyphs?" Devin asks. "So, what, is this like a missing part of the Bible or something?"

Samantha had presented the same idea at the bank. Although at the time the evidence she had to support it was the fact that words from the Bible have been found on papyrus before. She smirks proudly.

Dr. Bauer looks at Devin and shrugs. "Could be," he says, "but I doubt it." Samantha's smirk fades. "A lot of the Bible was written in Hebrew, Aramaic and Greek. Coptic too. But you see here," he points to the line on the scarab's back, "that vertical diameter there. Inside that circle. That isn't usually found on khepera beetles. That symbol could completely alter the meaning of the symbol it's a part of. Remember what I said about holism. Everything's connected."

Samantha looks at the figure but can't recall Mrs. King ever saying anything about it. "You ever seen it before, Kurt?"

He shakes his head. "Not that I recall. Symbols were an incidental part of my studies. Hieroglyphs and pictographs, really. They are far from my expertise."

"Okay, Doc," Devin cuts in, "let's get to the point. Now that you've seen the scroll how long do you think it'll take you, you know, working by yourself?"

Dr. Bauer looks at the text again. With all of the different languages, interpolated with various markings and symbols— *it could take weeks just to identify all the symbols' origins*, he thinks. *Then I'd have to put them in the proper context alongside the cuneiform— once that's translated.* "It's hard to say. Maybe, if I work around the clock, I'd say, uhh...about a month."

A month, Devin thinks. *I could be back in jail in a month. And with The Elite after us, I could be dead.*

Dr. Bauer recognizes the look of worry on Devin's face. He hates to lie like this but it is a lie that he must tell. The doctor has had an idea of what the scroll could be since Devin first unrolled it on his desk and the longer he studies it the stronger his conviction becomes. It's that scarabeus and the way it's positioned in the lower right corner.

And it was discovered in Mesopotamia, he thinks. *Surely a fellow treasure hunter as renowned as Jacqueline King would have recognized the possibility. Could it be the reason that she didn't report the find? If so—*

"Sorry, Doc." Devin says, interrupting his reverie. "We can't

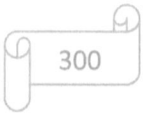

do that. It's too dangerous. For everybody."

"Come on, now. Let's be reasonable, okay. If your mother never reported the find and we're the only people that know it exists then how could it *possibly* be dangerous? Don't tell me you two believe it's cursed or something."

He takes in their solemn expressions and throws his hands up in surrender. "My God! You really *do* think it's cursed, don't you? I can't believe this." He looks to Samantha. "And you're a scientist."

Devin understands how crazy this must sound but that's not what's important. "All I know is that people have been killed over this thing, Doc. And the ones responsible are still out there. So, sorry, but no, Doc. We're not leaving it with you."

"*Killed?* People have been—oh my, you mean your parents, don't you? But I thought—"

"Kurt," Samantha cuts in, "I have an idea that'll work for all of us. Do you have a camera around?"

"Uhh...yeah. A digital one. It's in my bedroom. It records video as well. Why do you ask?"

"Because the solution is simple. You take pictures of the scroll, upload them to your computer, and then delete them from your memory chip."

"But what if something happens to my computer? I won't be able to continue my work."

Devin is getting frustrated. *How many ways do they have to explain to this guy that he is not going to keep the scroll?* "Look Doc, there are people that will *kill you*—do you understand—they will kill you, for a copy of this thing. So be smart and limit those copies. And limit the number of people that know you have them to three—me, you, and Sam. Got it? This is serious."

Dr. Bauer looks into Devin's eyes. *It has to be,* he thinks. *Why else would he be so afraid?*

Unless The Elite also know of this. Could there be something that he's not telling me?

"Okay." He says, rising from his seat. "I'll go get my camera then. It should only take a minute."

The doctor leaves and returns with the camera in hand. Devin and Samantha stand to the side and watch him photograph the scroll from different angles. Once he finishes this he begins to take pictures of each symbol individually.

"Alright." He sets the camera down on his desk, takes out his USB cord, and connects it to his computer. The pictures are uploaded to his hard drive in a matter of seconds. He glances back to Devin and Samantha, shakes his head, and deletes the files from the memory chip. "Now, if it is okay with you two, I would like to go and tend to my lady friend now. She's been waiting patiently but she is starting to grow restless." He looks at Devin and smirks. "I think it was seeing the camcorder that did it."

Devin and Samantha chuckle politely at the doctor's joke. Samantha is just glad that she didn't have to take tonight any further than flirting. She follows Dr. Bauer out of the office and into the foyer, stealing secret glances at Devin. He's been different since they came in the house. She wonders if her performance had anything to do with it.

Standing at the front door, Devin decides to alter the plan and ask a question that has been running through his mind all night. "Hey, Doc," he says, "before we go, I need you to tell me something, alright, and I need you to be honest."

Dr. Bauer nods. "Sure. What is it?"

It's uhh... Have you ever heard of a group called *The Elite?*"

"The Elite?" Dr. Bauer pretends to ponder the name for a moment. "No." He lies. "I can't say that I have." He looks to Samantha. "Do you need me to call you two a cab?"

"Thank you." Samantha says, accepting his offer. She and Devin wait on the landing while the doctor goes to place the call.

He returns, smiling coyly. "I would let you two wait in the living room but the lady is—"

"It's okay, Doc. You already had to miss that bath because of us. What more could we ask?"

The three of them share a laugh that ends too soon and an awkward silence settles in. After a few seconds Samantha takes it upon herself to give Dr. Bauer a courtesy hug. Dr. Bauer takes advantage of the opportunity and holds on a little longer and little tighter than she expected. Devin chuckles under his breath.

"Well," Samantha says, finally free from the embrace, "I guess that's goodbye Kurt. We'll speak again soon."

He nods. "I'll call in a few days with some news of my progress." He extends his hand to Devin. "Good evening to you, sir. It's always good to meet a celebrity you like and still like them afterwards."

Devin chuckles. "Yeah, well, you'll be seeing a lot more of me, Doc. You just stay safe, okay?"

Dr. Bauer nods, steps inside the house, and closes the door behind him, leaving Devin and Samantha standing alone under his porch light. Devin looks to Samantha, grinning.

"What?" Samantha asks.

Devin laughs. "It's just, you know they made us leave so we wouldn't hear them making sex noises, right? And now, after that hug, he's probably picturing you in there with them."

"Ugh!" She exclaims, shaking her head in disgust. "You're

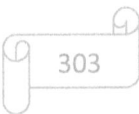

a pervert, you know that right?" She looks down at her watch then goes to wait on the curb. "Come on."

She glances back at the doctor's house one last time. *Be safe Kurt,* she thinks. *Please be safe.*

CHAPTER TWENTY-FIVE

Detective Worthy shakes his head in confused amazement as he staggers out of his quaint one-bedroom home. Behind him, Judith stands in the doorway, toting an oversized duffle bag in her tiny arms.

It's too early for this shit, Detective Clarkson thinks, watching the scene unfold from the driveway. He's been waiting inside of Worthy's truck since nine o'clock and it's going on ten now. He glances down at his watch. *Shit, it's past ten already.*

"Here, Max." Judith calls. "Don't forget your bag."

Worthy stops at the bottom of the stairs and turns to face his wife. *She is more than beautiful,* he thinks, *she's an angel.* Even in an old bathrobe, her glowing skin, flowing golden locks and petite frame belong on the ceiling of the Sistine Chapel, not standing in their doorway fighting back tears. He hates it when she cries; especially when he is the reason why. All Worthy wants to do is make her smile. He thought she understood that but now he is not so sure. Last night he went too far and Judith finally made good on all her threats. Every time he stands her up she threatens to kick him out the house, to get out of the way of him and the thing he truly loves.

What do you love more, Max, she'd ask, *me or your job?*

It's a different kind of love, Worthy would try to explain; an answer that Judith was never really satisfied with. She would yell and fuss and start packing his bag but that was always as far as it went. Worthy would apologize and promise to do better, they would make up and make love, and then Worthy would be off to the work in the morning.

Too much drama for my life, Clarkson muses, chuckling to himself as Worthy climbs back up onto the porch like some love-struck Romeo at Juliette's balcony. *He's going to beg, I know it. I'd bet my car on it.*

"You'll need clean underwear," Judith continues, handing the bag to her husband. "Here. And you can't wear those clothes forever."

Worthy is not sure what to say as he takes the bag from her. "Heavy," is what comes out and he smirks playfully. "How long am I supposed to be gone, Jude? Should I start looking for an apartment?"

Judith smiles and for a moment he is filled with hope. The two of them have been together for too long for all of this. They love each other too much. Deep down inside she has to know that he doesn't want to spend any more nights away from her than he has to. And it's not like he's against having a child. He would love to have a daughter with Judith's soft brown eyes and long sandy hair. It just doesn't make any sense for them to go through all of this. He knows her feelings haven't changed. She made that clear this morning while packing his bag.

"I love you," she had said, "I love you so much that I'm scared that if I don't do this now, this is how it will be forever. It'll only get worse, Max. And then I'll be stuck with you because I love you too much to leave. I don't want to feel stuck, Max. I don't want that for either of us."

He looks at her beautiful face. There is a glimmer in the

corner of her eye. *Maybe she finally understands.*

"I love you, Max," she tells him. She smiles and a single tear falls from her eye. "More than you know."

Worthy drops the duffle bag and steps forward, slipping his hands inside her robe and taking her by the waist. He leans forward as he pulls her in close and their lips meet in a rush of passion.

"No, Max," Judith says, forcing herself to pull back. "You have to stop. We can't. Don't make this—"

Worthy kisses her again and all her protests are lost in his lips. She pushes against his chest, trying her best to break the hold that he has on her knowing that if she doesn't do it now she never will.

"Stop Max. Please. I'll call you in a few days and we'll talk then. Okay?"

Worthy can't believe it. "Jude, honey, don't do this. I love you. You love me. Whatever problems we have, we can work on them together. Just—"

"No Max. If you really love me like you say then you'll just go. I need some time to think about things."

Things, Worthy repeats in his mind. *Is that what our marriage is now—a thing?* He stares into her eyes fighting back tears. What could she possibly need to think about? If she still loves him then there is nothing else to do but work on their relationship. Nobody ever said it would be easy but you have to fight for what you want. *Right?*

He picks the bag up and slings it over his shoulder. "Okay, Jude. Because I *do* love you. That's the only reason I'm leaving."

Judith drops her gaze, wishing that was true. "You're wrong, Max. You're leaving because you love your *job*, and I'm tired of competing. I can't keep staying up late every night, worrying if you're going to come home or if I'll get a call from the coroner. When we got married, this is not what I was signing up for."

"Jude, I'm sorry, okay. I promise, from now on—"

"Stop it, Max. Don't lie to me. Don't tell me that it won't happen again because we both know it will. Just...," she glances over to his truck sitting in their driveway. Detective Clarkson nods to her. "Just go do whatever you have to do and when you're done, *hopefully*, I'll know what we're going to do."

"But, Jude—"

"No. No buts Max. Just leave." She takes a step back into their home. "Please. Don't make me close the door on your face. Just tell me that you love me and then walk away."

He hesitates, wondering if this is a test. Women do that, you know. *She just wants to know that I'll fight for—*

"Say you love me, Max."

"I...I love you, Judy. You know that. I'll always love you."

"Now walk away."

Worthy steps forward. "Kiss me. Kiss me first and I'll leave."

She places her hand on his chest and holds him back. "I love you, Max. I'll call you soon."

He begins to speak again but Judith closes the door on his pleas. For a moment he just stands there and stares at the numbers on the door. This is the only address that he has had since moving out of his mother's house. It is the same address that he has shared with Judith for the last ten years. Could this really be it?

Maybe I should knock? She's probably right on the other side of the door, waiting for me. She can't really want me to—

A blaring car horn interrupts his thoughts. It's Clarkson. "C'mon kid!" He yells out. "Don't be a sucker! You'll only make it worse!"

Worthy glares over to Clarkson—smirking smugly and sitting in Judith's seat. *What do you know about love anyway,* he thinks. *You probably pick up a different whore every night.*

He turns back to the door, imagining Judith on the other side, and raises his arm to knock.

"Stalker! Stalker!" Clarkson's screaming voice rings out through the air. "Somebody call the police! Stalker!"

A group of old women seem to materialize out of nowhere—filling their front porches with fuzzy slippers and tattered bathrobes; every one of them cradling a cordless phone in their arthritic hands. All of their eyes are on Detective Worthy.

"Stalkerrrr!!!!" Clarkson slams down on the horn again. "Stalker! Stalker! Somebody call the police! I think he's trying to break in."

Worthy looks across the street. One of his neighbors is dialing a number on her phone. Shaking his head, he jogs over to the truck, throws his bag in the back and climbs into the driver's seat. He shoots Clarkson a deadly glare as he starts up the engine.

"What?" Clarkson asks, feigning ignorance. "You were set on looking worse than you already did, so I just helped you out." He smirks. "To thank me, we can go and get a few drinks. Looks like you need it."

"Whatever," Worthy says, somewhat shocked that none of his neighbors recognized him. *Am I really gone that much?* "Like you know anything about being married."

"More than you know, kid." Clarkson digs a gold band out of his pocket and slides it on. "Let's go get that drink and I'll give you a few tips on the way."

Worthy backs the truck down the driveway and pulls out into the street. He glances back at his house. The curtains move slightly.

Judith, he thinks. *She's watching. She doesn't want me to leave.*

Clarkson watches Worthy. *The kid's pathetic,* he thinks. *She has all the power now. How can he live like that?*

"See kid, it's like this. Sometimes you have to give'em what they *think* they want, in order to prove to'em that they don't really know *what* they want. Like, right now, you keep on driving. Your wife *thinks* she wants you gone. Give it a day or two, she'll *know* she wants you back. Trust me."

"Trust you?" he parrots, still holding down on the brake. "You just accused me of stalking my own wife. In front of all of my neighbors."

Clarkson shrugs. "It had to be done. Everything that looks bad ain't always bad, kid. You should know that by now, doing this job. Just think of it like this—if she didn't really want you to go, or at least *think* she wants you to go, wouldn't she be out here instead of just standing in the window."

Worthy glances at the house again. Judith's face pokes between the curtains.

"Put the car in drive, kid. Put the car in drive, lift your foot off the brake and let's go get that drink. This is too much for anybody to deal with before noon."

Relenting, Worthy shifts the truck into drive. "I definitely need a drink," he mumbles. "You know any good hotels?"

It's a half past noon and Detective Worthy is pulling his truck up to a cheap motel with James Clarkson sitting beside him, reeking of tequila and cheap cologne. The transmission slips as he slows the truck to a stop. It isn't much but just enough for him to notice. He files it far back in his mind. There is too much going on now to worry about the Old Lady. Not only are Judith and Devin gone but he's just smoked the last cigarette in his pack. He checks the ashtray for his emergency stash. It's gone too.

"You know, you should love yourself more, kid." Clarkson says, feeling the brakes strain as the trucks screeches to a halt. "Get yourself a new ride. I know a guy. He can put you in something nice. Something that says... young tough cop on the scene. Maybe one of those Dodge Magnums or something. Something American."

Worthy unlocks his door and steps down out of the truck. The site is depressing. If it was not for the old pick-up at the end of the lot Worthy would have been willing to bet (and he's certainly not a gambling man) that the place was deserted. It has to be the shabbiest motel in town. Somehow it feels right that Clarkson would bring him here.

He hoists his duffle bag out of the truck bed and chuckles. "A new truck. Look at this place, man. I can't afford a new truck. I can't afford a new anything."

"That's your fault," Clarkson says, grabbing the half-empty bottle of Patrón off the seat. Worthy ignores him and enters the building. Clarkson shuts the truck's door and follows Worthy. The air inside the building is dry and stale, just like he remembers it. He once knew a prostitute that lived here. The owner was her pimp. Rather than put her in jail, Clarkson made her his informant and helped her get cleaned up. The owner is still in prison. *Looks like new management isn't much for beauty,* he thinks, glancing around. *Well, neither was Omar. Christina certainly wasn't much of a looker.*

Detective Worthy steps up to the check-in counter and slaps the bell. The concierge appears from a room in the back. *Isabella,* her nametag reads. She's a young woman, no older than seventeen, with jet black hair and intelligently mischievous eyes.

"Checking' in?" She asks, eyeing him curiously. "We only take cash."

Not surprising at all, Worthy thinks. This place is ragged at best. The old wallpaper is peeling in the corners, the carpet is patchy and stained, and the lobby reeks of furniture polish and floor cleaner. He fishes out his wallet and lays down enough for a single.

"Porn's back here. Pay to rent, you know. There's doughnuts in the morning, and coffee, and if you want quarters for the bed there's a change machine by the vending machines." She slides Worthy his room key. "It's down the hall, on the right."

Worthy sets his bag down. "Uhh... Isabella, you have cigarettes in that vending machine?"

"Yeah, but it's out of stock now. The guy should be here tomorrow. Store down the street has 'em though. Only, they're closed right now, so..."

"Oh, okay." Worthy replies, noticeably disappointed. He glances down at his bag. "No bellboy, huh?"

"My brother Carlos usually does it but he's at school."

Worthy looks to Clarkson and Clarkson grins. "*La familia.* Keep it in the family, you know." He looks closer at Isabella, wondering if she's related to Omar. There is a vague resemblance, around the eyes. He starts to ask her but then Worthy grabs his bag and heads down the hall. Clarkson knows better than to be left alone with some horny teenage girl in a seedy motel. Been down that road before, he thinks, *and I'm not going down it again.*

"Hey!" Isabella calls out. "Hey, I uhh....I know where you can get some smokes."

Worthy stops in his tracks, drops his bag in the middle of

the floor and practically sprints back to the front desk. "You're not joking are you?" He asks, glad to have finally caught a break. "This place is open right now?"

Isabella looks him over again, looking for anything in his body language that says 'narc'. He's stiff, sure, and too high-strung; probably out cheating on his wife. "You're not a cop are you? I mean, my uncle tells me I have to ask. If I ask and you lie then its entrapment. But, you're not, right? You're too cute to be a cop?"

He forces himself not to grin—the last thing he needs right now is some delinquent girl crushing on him—and thanks God that Clarkson is still standing in the hall. Between him 'not looking like a cop' and being 'too cute,' he can only imagine what smart-ass remark he'd make. "No, I'm not a cop." He lies, wondering where in hell that entrapment myth got started any damn way. "Why? What's up?"

"I have smokes. Just, you know, double the price. Gots to pay for the convenience, man. Got every brand too. Interested?"

Worthy doesn't hesitate. With everything going on this morning there is only one thing for him to say and that's the name of his brand. He takes the pack from Isabella, opens it, remembers that he needs to restock his emergency stash, and buys another. With a fresh stick dangling between his lips, he pats his pockets in search for a lighter.

"Shit." He smiles to Isabella. "Got a light?"

Isabella, with a smile of her own, ducks down behind the desk and returns with a shoebox full of lighters in all shapes, sizes and colors. Worthy buys two—a disposable red BIC and an old metal flip-top. He's halfway through his first stick before he picks his bag up off the floor. Clarkson shakes his head in derision.

"You stop smokin' so many of those things, you could

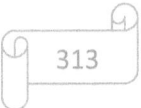

probably get you a new truck." He says, following Worthy to his room.

"It's not the cigarette." Worthy tells him, stopping in front of the door. He slides the keycard into the slot and opens the door. "It's just...I'm on a budget."

He enters the squalid room and tosses his bag down on the bed. A puff of dust rises from the petrified sheets like a mushroom cloud. "Fitting." He mumbles. His new home comes with a TV, a small desk, dilapidated wing chair, lamp and putrid bed. He gazes through the open bathroom door and, sadly, it looks just like the kitchenette: covered with the indelible stains of repeated usage and minimal cleanings. *Mother Mary, please let me never have to use that toilet or sink,* he prays. *But please, not the toilet.*

Clarkson steps inside the room behind him and smirks. "Staying in a place like this, kid, you have to be doin' something wrong." He flops down on the moth-eaten chair. "Something very wrong."

"Actually," Worthy retorts, "the problem is: I do the job *right*." He begins to pull some toiletries from his bag but decides against it. The bag is the cleanest place in here. "Pass me that ashtray."

Chuckling, Clarkson takes the smoke-stained dish from the desk and passes it to Worthy.

"What's so funny?" Worthy asks, dumping the long trail of ash from the end of his cigarette.

"You." Clarkson says, still chuckling. He opens the bottle of tequila, takes a swig and offers it to Worthy. He declines and Clarkson chuckles again. "There you go, kid. Whiz-Kid Worthy. Too good to drink with a friend, even when the world is crashing down around you." He downs another gulp. "You're fuckin' hilarious, kid. A Grade-A clown."

"Because I won't drink with you? Really?" Worthy takes a long drag, tilts his head and exhales a thin stream of smoke to the ceiling. He looks back to Clarkson and smirks. "You're the clown. What are we—dating? You can't be serious right now?"

"Oh, I'm serious." Clarkson replies, deciding to let that clown remark slide. He's punched guys for less but the kid has been having a rough day and it's good to see him have some balls for once. He takes another swig. "Look, I've seen your kind before, kid. You're selfish. And at the rate that you're going, you're gonna lose your wife. Sooner than later."

"Selfish!" Worthy can't believe that James Clarkson, of all people, would call him selfish. *"You!* Calling *me selfish.* Wow, that's new."

Clarkson throws back another swallow then sits the bottle beside the chair. "Exactly what I mean, kid. All you consider is your point of view. I could hear what your wife was saying, back at the door, and I've heard that same thing from a lot of other women too—*divorced* women. But you, your kind is the worst. You're so self-righteous you just can't fathom anybody else being right. Not if it'll mean your black and white world just might have a few shades of gray in it."

"Shades of gray? So that's what it's called now?" He snorts in contempt. "Don't try to sell me on your bullshit, Clarkson. You do what you do because *you're* selfish. I've seen your type before, too. All you care about is getting ahead. Even if it costs you your integrity."

"And what exactly do I *do*, kid? Please.Enlighten me."

Worthy exhales another cloud of smoke. "Don't try to play innocent, now. You know what you do. Everyone knows you're dirty, Clarkson. It's not even," he takes another pull off his cigarette, "I can't even believe I'm doing this right now." He glances around the decrepit room. All he can say is "Wow."

"Yeah, wow, kid. This is your life. You're pretty little wife, she's gone for now. And Devin, he's gone. Your job—that might be gone soon. Oh, and that sense of integrity that you were just throwing in my face—yeah, that's gone too."

"Hold on, man—Judith's not gone. She's just...uhh...taking some time to think. And Devin, he can't run far. Long as I bring him in before that court date, my job's fine. Actually, even if I don't, my job's fine."

Clarkson shrugs. "Maybe. But what about your integrity?"

"What about it? I've never compromised my integrity. *Never!*"

"Yeah?" Clarkson leans back in the chair and smirks smugly. "You sure about that, kid?"

Worthy takes a drag and exhales. "Of course I'm sure. I do the job by the book, all the time, every time. We have rules to follow just like everybody else."

"Really?" Clarkson says, his face showing his confusion. "So that bribe you gave that receptionist guy at the airstrip—that's in that *book* you go by, 'cus if it is, I need a copy. Or maybe buying a pack of boosted cigarettes from a minor—is that in this book and I just missed it?"

The look on the Whiz-Kid's face is more than enough satisfaction for Clarkson. He shakes his head, smirking all the while. "Nobody's innocent, kid. Do you good to remember that."

Worthy stubs out his cigarette and light up another. "It's not the same, man, and you know it. What I did wasn't necessarily a bribe, it—"

Clarkson cuts him off. "What was it then, kid? Don't play more word games. You paid that guy to give you information that he was trusted and *paid*, to keep secret. What? You think God judges any one sin worse than another? Yeah, I know you're a Catholic. I've heard all the murmurs about you too, kid. How you hate cops that work outside your book. Heard you even turned in your mentor when you found out he was letting drug shipments move through the city. But how did you even find out about that anyway, huh?"

A long pull on his cigarette fills Worthy's lungs with smoke. He's stalling. That situation was not as simple as Clarkson wants to make it. Worthy has been haunted by the decision for six years.

"You don't have to tell me, Max. See, I already know. Miguel was a friend of mine."

Miguel. Worthy hasn't spoken his teacher's name in so long it that hearing it feels strange to his ears. "You knew Miguel Santana?"

"I know you were going through some money problems, about to lose that little house of yours, and so a good friend of mine, who *thought* he was a good friend of yours, stuck out his neck for you. And how did you repay him?" Clarkson glares at him accusingly. "You cut off his *fuckin'* head."

Miguel Santana was one of the toughest cops that Detective Worthy had ever met. He was nearing retirement when Worthy joined the First Precinct and was just coasting until his day came. But when Miguel met Maximus Worthy he took an instant liking to the smart young rookie and made it his priority to show him the ropes. Not only did he teach Worthy how to work the streets of Santo Domingo but he also gave Worthy the most important piece of advice that he's ever received: *trust your gut.* "People have more than five senses," Miguel would say, "and intuition is one of'em. So use it, damn it. You use your eyes to see don't you? Wouldn't walk around with your eyes closed, would ya? No piece of tech can replace your gut, Max. And not just on the job, either."

Ironically it turned out to be Worthy's gut that led him to investigate his mentor. It was little things, like Miguel being able to take he and Judith out to dinner with him and his wife every weekend; how they would always frequent the choicest restaurants but never had to wait for a table; and on top of all of that Miguel bought his wife a brand new car. Miguel began to seem more like a crime boss than a detective.

Clarkson watches Worthy mull in his thoughts—his *guilt*. And *he should*. "You know Miguel got involved in that stuff when his daughter got sick, right? How do you think they paid for her medical bills? His pension money? By the time he wanted out, it was too late. Too much had been done. They threatened to ruin him. You know he couldn't lose his family. He loved them too much. And you were like family to him."

He grabs the bottle off the floor, pops out the cork, and throws back a shot, never taking his eyes off Worthy. "You come to him, complaining to him about not having enough money to pay your mortgage and what does Miguel do? He gives you a way to make a couple extra grand for yourself. All you had to do was let a few trucks through a checkpoint. No risk. Instead, what'd you do? You notify the Precinct and help set up a sting operation. Instead of saying *thank you*, you lock up your *friend* and use his arrest to make detective. The mayor spoke to you and everything. It was such a big bust that the city paid off your house for you."

Clarkson takes another swig. "The guys Miguel was helping out, they offered you $250,000 just to refuse to take the stand on

Miguel. *Your friend.* But you couldn't compromise that integrity of yours. The same integrity that let strugglin' tax-payers pay off your house. You sat there and looked Miguel square in the eyes—a man that loved you like a son, that spent every day of four years with you—you looked him in the face and pointed your blameless finger at him. And what happened after that? Where did your integrity get Miguel?"

Initially, Detective Worthy had been assigned to the First Precinct's narcotics division but eight months after Miguel's trial he suddenly requested transfer to homicide.

"Say it, Max." Clarkson downs more of the tequila. "You can't can you? Miguel was *killed* in prison. *Killed* while you were riding around in your piece of shit truck. What did you think would happen to a cop in prison, huh, Whiz-Kid?'

Clarkson leans forward and glares into Worthy's eyes. "You know, that was the first time I saw you. At Miguel's funeral, standing in the back with your pretty little wife. I've always wondered what kind of guy could show up to the man they killed's funeral. Now I know. A self-centered, self-righteous, self-justifying little *puta* like you."

"Whatever man." Worthy says. He doesn't have the strength to defend himself right now. Clarkson can call him whatever he wants. It doesn't lighten the load that Worthy has to bear. Worthy doesn't expect Clarkson to understand. He doesn't expect anyone to understand. "It's not that simple."

"It never is, is it? Not when you're the one being pointed at." Smirking, Clarkson leans back in the chair. "I've heard all the excuses, kid. Shit, I even added a few new ones to the list. You know what I know, kid, after everything I've seen—criminals are the best at justifying their shit. And that's what all this really is. Just two sides of the same coin. We're all just criminals justifying our shit. The cops, the politicians, the kingpins, the working stiffs; we're all the same really. We compromise our morals in service of some *greater good*, whatever it is—family, community, whatever. Trust me, kid, that lil' bribe you gave out, that's just how it starts. One lil' bent rule. Next thing you know, you're destroying evidence, covering up crime scenes, or letting trucks through checkpoints. 'Cus, hey, somebody's gonna do it. I mean, you can't stop'em all, so why not you? But then really it's not even *for you*, right. You'll tell yourself it's for that *greater good*. The wife, the kids, the people, the community—whatever helps you sleep better at night. Whatever helps you live with it."

Another long drag fills the silence as Worthy thinks. He exhales a stream of smoke. "If someone felt like that, why not just quit? That's always their choice. No one can *make* you do anything."

Clarkson looks at the collection of cigarette butts in the ashtray and smirks. "Is quittin' really that easy, kid. How many times you tried to quit those things, huh? Then life's not cheap either and it *damn sure* ain't free. People gotta make a livin'. When somebody's been doin' somethin' for a long time and they're good at it—we're creatures of habit, you know, it's hard to just stop and jump into something else. Habit and security, kid. Once somebody's into a comfortable habit, somethin' they take a lil' pride in, they'll never wanna quit."

Worthy thinks of something Judith once told him. It was back when he first made detective and started coming home later and later. *You always have the best excuses,* she had said, *but they're still excuses. It's not right just because you make it sound right, Max.*

"How much's left in that bottle?" He asks. Clarkson picks

the bottle up off the floor and passes it to Worthy. He raises it his lips and grins. "I don't want to be selfish, you know. People shouldn't drink alone."

Yeah, Clarkson nods, watching Worthy finish off the last of the tequila. *Misery has always loved company.*

TRUE KING

CHAPTER TWENTY-SIX

Gustuv sits at the head of The Elite's table watching the elevator's door slide slowly apart. A blood-red light pours out onto the floor, across the table, and over the faces of his brothers. Two curvaceous figures emerge from the light. They glide gracefully toward the table, presenting their bare bodies as fleshly treats for the group's ravenous stares. Each woman carries a tray of fruit, holding it level with their breasts just as Gustuv instructed. They arrive at the end of the table and separate—one to the left and one to the right— offering their edibles to each member as they pass. Each man takes his fill, dining on the feast of flesh before them.

"Brothers." Gustuv calls, diverting their attention from the naked pair. "You shall soon gratify your carnal desires. For now, let the fruit of Mother Nature be sustenance enough." He lifts an apple from the tray and takes a symbolic bite. "We shall soon dine on manna from the heavens, brothers."

Romano is tired of the spectacle. "Pardon me," he says, "but I wonder, *brother*, how long must we wait for this scroll? Do remember, I have other matters to attend to."

"As do we all." Felix agrees.

Once again murmurs of support ripple through the table like a growing wave. It has been five years since a conclave has lasted an entire seven days. Gustuv's brothers are beginning to grow restless.

"You two look but do not observe." Gustuv replies. He takes another bite from the apple. "Have I not broken our fast?"

Tradition requires that during a conclave all brothers present must abstain from food, drink and sex for the duration of their gathering. Only the head of their order can call an end to the conclave and thus lift the ban. To many of their dismay, today that man is Gustuv Barchulé.

Since the middle of the 20th century there has been an alliance among the four most powerful societies represented here: the Illuminati, Freemasons, Vatican and Black Nobility. After centuries of feuding they finally came to realize that it would better benefit them all to put aside their petty differences and focus on their common goal: the establishment of a new world order. The problem is, with such a tumultuous history behind them, such a goal is tantamount to getting lions and hyenas to hunt together.

The Vatican, once the authority of civilization, not only usurped the power of the nobles but they persecuted and murdered thousands of free-thinking men and women. They not only banned the craft of Freemasonry but excommunicated all who dared to associate with their Lodges. The Illuminati, being made up of scientists and mystics, was always an enemy of the Church, for their teachings disproved many of the clergy's claims. The nobles loathed them for their continual promotion of knowledge to the commoners, knowing well that their power was built on the ignorance of the masses.

Though these feelings still fester behind the fake smiles of fraternity, their forerunners dictated that until their new world order was brought about, the head of their newly formed brotherhood would be the crown of the Illuminati. It was a logical decision, being that members of the Illuminati are by nature the open-minded and critical thinkers of humanity. And whereas the Vatican has their Church, the Masons their Lodge, and the Nobility their Government, the Illuminati has no worldly power structure to protect.

Maybe that is why Gustuv Barchulé, a man with considerable wealth and power, chooses not to actively engage in any nation's politics. He rather enjoys moving in the shadows. There is no need to be *political* when one controls the politicians.

And so Gustuv listens as his brothers chatter amongst themselves, amused by the numerous ploys, policies, and propaganda campaigns they have employed on so many unsuspecting people.

Through the 13 organizations represented, The Elite is able to control every facet of human interaction, from entertainment to economics, schooling to sex. A few of his brothers here hold seats in the United Nations, NATO, the Council of Foreign Relations, while others maintain pawns who fill these seats for them, following a dangled dollar like a horse to a carrot, unaware of the glue factory that lies ahead.

A smirk spreads across his face.

Politics, he muses. *How fitting a word. Poli; Poly; Many; Many what? Many ticks. Too many of you little bloodsuckers for my liking.*

"Brothers," he calls, "I too have matters to handle and the importance of your business is not lost on me. Our goal depends upon all of our activities being successful. This is why I have decided to break our fast."

He shifts his gaze to Romano. "Brother Hapsburg, to answer your question—we should not have to wait for the scroll much longer. Still, I ask for patience, in light of the patience we have already shown. Time is perspective, Romano. You of all people should understand this."

The brothers dart their eyes to Romano, gauging his expression. Gustuv's words were a subtle stab at Romano's obsession with his royal lineage. He is constantly reminding them of his ancestry, what he terms his *natural right to rule*. Even in the dimness of the chamber they can see the anger on his face.

"The boy and girl have taken a jet to Riga." Gustuv continues. "Here they met with one of the girl's colleagues. A linguist by the name of Kurt Bauer. One of the best in the field."

Romano nods. "So they are attempting to have the scroll translated, then. Gustuv, I request that you allow the Families to handle the matter now. Did they not recover the book from the daughter? And who has more power in Europe than we?"

Gustuv makes a show of considering Romano's offer but he had already expected this once he received news of Devin's trip to Latvia. "Okay, Romano. I will allow your people to intercede but your men must follow law. It is forbidden for any brother or their progeny to be—"

"Gustuv, brother, I know better than most the laws we adhere to." Romano glances around the table, gauging the support he's garnering. "How can I not with your constant reminders?"

"I remind only because you so often forget, *brother.*"

"What happened to the daughter was truly unfortunate, but I am not to blame. Those men came recommended by one of Brother Freeman's fellows." Romano's gaze shifts to William. "Isn't that right, brother?"

Spineless coward; William almost yells the words at the ungrateful bastard. *How dare you,* he thinks, glaring back at

Romano.

"Yes. One of my Masonic brothers out of St. Petersburg referred me to those two, in light of their military backgrounds. What he failed to report was that they had been discharged for not following orders." William stares straight into Romano's self-serving eyes. "But like all traitors, they were taken care of."

Gustuv smirks, reveling in William and Romano's exchange. *What a peculiar fellow,* he thinks, *but you cannot straddle the fence for too long William, not when the earth is shaking beneath you.*

"Back to the matter before us, brother." Gustuv looks to William. "The detective assigned to look after the boy is one of yours. He has an interest in seeing the boy apprehended, I believe, and has proven himself a useful pawn thus far. Keep him on board."

William nods. "We have direct contacts with him, brother. And there are many of ours more than willing to assist him."

"Good. Use that worldwide influence to aid and assist them. Our time is nearing."

William nods again. The Order of Freemasonry is said to stretch to time immemorial. According to their lore, ever since the Great Grand Architect—the first Master Mason—the Almighty God Himself, introduced symmetry and harmony to the universe their craft has existed. Throughout the ages their teachings have gone under many names but the goal has forever remained the same: the improvement of mankind.

It is William Freeman, 33rd Degree, who represents the fraternity at this table—a spot that his father once filled and his father before him. William spent his entire childhood being groomed in the ways of the Craft. It has been almost twenty-five years since his initiation, he thinks, reflecting back on his journey to this seat.

Ten years spent mastering the secrets of each degree of the

Scottish Rite; five years of service in the Peace Corps to prove my commitment to humanity before being bestowed the honored 33rd Degree; and a ten year period of patient work and reflection as I awaited father's abdication.

From beneath the hooded cloak, William looks out on the faces of the men he calls brothers— each of them as wealthy and powerful as he or any mortal man. His eyes land on Romano Hapsburg, that pretentious ignoramus with no knowledge of the true powers at work here. His head bows slightly, as if offering a hidden prayer, and he grins to himself. *But equity has never extended to men's mental faculties, has it?*

"Maybe if our leader would have allowed us to assist in the matter sooner," Romano interjects, "we would have the bloody scroll and be done with this business already."

His statement only confirms William's assessment. *Are you forgetting that he allowed our people to retrieve the book and because of this law was violated?*

"Brother Barchulé," Felix chimes in, "I can arrange for diplomatic immunity to be given to William's people guaranteeing them unhindered entry in the country. I am sure of safe passage."

Gustuv grins. He is well-aware of Felix's blatant attempt to divert attention away from Romano and his snide remark but neither he nor Felix is of real import at the moment. The more of these games they play the more they expose themselves for the idiots they truly are. More of their brothers are joining Gustuv each day.

"That is fine, Felix. Ensure that there is no proof that the detective was ever in the country, if you can arrange it. We have to expect that mitigating circumstances may occur."

Felix nods then glances at Romano. It is a look that says,

you owe me. Romano turns away quickly. Gustuv watches it all with amusement.

"Would anyone else like to offer Brother Hapsburg their assistance?" He asks, scanning the table. Not one of them dares to speak. "Well, if that is all then, this conclave is official ended." Gustuv stands and raps the table three times. "In the name of the Father, Mother, Son, and Daughter," he says and raps the table four more times, "and the forces through which they work."

"In remembrance!" He calls.

"In remembrance!" His brothers respond. "Now let us feast and seek union with the Lord."

Across the chamber the elevator's doors slide open once more. A procession of beautiful women pours forth wearing lustful grins and nothing else. Like a living buffet the women move about the room eager to feed the famished fraternity. A mass orgy ensues and the smell of unrestrained desire fills the cavern. Cries of pleasure echo in the darkness.

With the light of a single candle as his guide, Gustuv steps between the entwined bodies coiled together like a ball of mating serpents. He takes notice of each of his brothers and the degree to which they lose themselves to their baser cravings. He has no need for such indulgences. Not at this current time. He is conserving his energy for a far greater work.

Let the others waste their life gratifying the flesh, he muses. *I have things to do.*

Gustuv steps over an entwined couple, moves pass another entangled pair and is just approaching the elevator when the longing gaze of a beautiful young woman catches his eye. She stares at him from atop her mate—*Brother Romano,* he observes— completely lost to the pleasures of her rolling hips.

Something about her eyes feels familiar. A lover from a past life, maybe. It is as if her gaze is calling out to him, urging for him to be the one beneath now. The connection is electric. He can only imagine how it would be to join with her, to feel the rapture that is true union. She continues to watch him. He acknowledges it with a grin.

She waves, a nymphish wiggling of her figures that is as seductive as her stare. Gustuv nods. This is all the time they can share for now. They both have duties to perform.

Her duty lies beneath her, he thinks, *sweating and panting; while mine's lies ahead, agonizing more each day.*

He continues on, moving through his brothers's and their concubines, until at last he comes to the elevator. As he waits for the doors to part, he reflects on the week's proceedings and smiles at the beautiful way it comes to an end.

Romano Hapsburg and Black Nobility will now do what they do best—murder and manipulate— until the scroll is in their hands. Felix will undoubtedly use all of the Vatican's resources to help.

Then they will try to use it as a bargaining chip, he suspects, *and Romano may even attempt to dissolve our alliance.*

The elevator doors slide apart and Gustuv steps into the glowing red light. He presses the button for the 13th floor and enters his key. The doors close, the elevator shifts and the ride to the top begins.

CHAPTER
TWENTY-SEVEN

D etective Max Worthy sits at his desk staring at a lifeless computer screen.

He has been looking for information on Riga all day and at the pace he's going it will be another twenty-four hours before he finds something useful.

The webpage finally updates and Worthy clicks on a link. The little arrow on the screen becomes a spinning hourglass. Rolling a cigarette between his fingers, he leans back in his desk chair (*with lumbar support and message rollers—thank God*) and settles in for the wait. Across from him Clarkson props his legs up on an empty chair and sips cold *café royalé* from a Styrofoam cup.

The two detectives have been glued together for two long and uncomfortable days—filled with cigarette butts, awkward silences, and bottles of tequila. As much as they hate each other's company the coupling is beneficial for them both—Worthy gets to keep his eye on Clarkson and monitor all his behavior while Clarkson gets to let Worthy be the Whiz-Kid and track down Devin for him. Not to mention that since Judith excused Worthy from his marital duties he needs someone around until this is over and even Clarkson beats a zero.

The webpage finishes updating and Worthy sits up in his chair and lights his cigarette. He scrolls down the page, unimpressed. *What the hell made you go here?*

"Those things will kill you one day." Clarkson says. He takes a sip of his coffee and continues to watch Worthy work. "That's what, your third pack of the day?"

Worthy shrugs. "Everything will kill you one day. At least I get to pick the way I go."

All Clarkson can do is grin. "Yeah, whatever you say. You're the Whiz-Kid, right?" He takes another sip of his coffee. It needs more royalé. Tipping the chair back he reaches for his jacket and takes the flask from its inner pocket. He leans forward, adds a bit more Cognac to the mixture, sips it, and adds some more.

"Think we should start calling some of these?" He asks, picking up one of the many print- outs covering Worthy's desk. "Find out which one of these cab companies picked the kid up from the airport. Find out where they took'em."

With their money they probably didn't even get a cab, Worthy thinks. "Samantha works at a university there." He says, still scrolling down the page. "Most likely they'll visit one of her friends. Someone she knows. Maybe even someone from the school. Get them to rent a car for them. Maybe get a room. It's the only thing that makes sense to me. What other ties do either of them have to Riga? We know she's not going to her apartment. Or driving her own car. She's can't be that dumb. But she may contact the school. At least, at the school—"

"It's vacation." Clarkson points out. "School's closed."

Worthy cuts his eyes at Clarkson. *For the students, smart-ass. The faculty can access the grounds all year.* "Like I was saying," Worthy continues, "I doubt that Devin has any friends in the area. It's likely to be her with the contact and most of her acquaintances are likely to be tied to the university."

"Why wouldn't the kid have a connection there?" Clarkson argues. "Everyone knows he's just a rich globetrotting brat. He's probably got some Latvianese model living up in a penthouse suite just in case he's ever in town."

Worthy takes a calming pull of his cigarette. "Yeah," he exhales, "but not in Riga." He turns the monitor towards Clarkson and taps the screen. "Look at this. Riga's not really a big tourism town. It's basically just a port city. And Latvia, Latvia was part of the Soviet Union, then Nazi Germany. Can't really picture lots of sunshine, beaches and pretty women."

Clarkson takes a sip of his Cognac and coffee. It tastes disgusting but he needs the caffeine. He picks up his flask, about to add more Cognac to the mix but changes his mind and sits it back down. *Fuck that. I'm not gonna keep wastin' my liquor in this crap.* He looks at the cup, shakes his head and throws back the rest of the drink in one agonizing gulp.

"Okay." He sits the cup down and wipes his mouth. "I got an idea. How 'bout we get someone at the university to give us a list of the entire faculty's addresses and phone numbers? We can ask them who's friends with the girl too. The ones close to Riga we follow up on?"

Worthy nods, surprised that the old man still has some good ideas left under that comb-over. "Make the call." He says.

Clarkson smirks. "Need the number, Whiz-Kid."

"Oh, yeah. Right." Worthy's cigarette dangles from his lips as he runs a search for Riga Polytechnic Institute. Thin wisps of smoke escape his lips as he waits for the page to update (*like a pompous little toy train,* Clarkson thinks). By the time they find the number Worthy is pulling out his pack for another cigarette.

Clarkson dials the college and gets a recording. He checks his watch. "What time is it over there? It's close to nine here so, like two or three in the morning, right?" He notices Worthy's surprised expression. "What? I went to London once when I was a kid. It can't be that far off, right?"

Worthy nods. "Yeah. I think you're about right. They're about seven hours ahead of us."

Detective Clarkson leaves a simple message requesting that someone from the university contact either him or Detective Maximus Worthy as soon as possible. He hangs up the phone, leans back in the chair and stares at the ceiling. Worthy watches him and can't help but wonder how someone ends up like that. Clarkson has spent the entire day spiking his coffee and obsessing over Devin. If it wasn't for Worthy he probably would have forgotten to eat.

Speaking of food. The detective checks his watch. *That delivery boy should be here any minute now.*

"Hey Whiz-Kid." Clarkson calls. "I got' uh idea. How 'bout we just go over there ourselves?"

Worthy grins. "I know you're hungry but why waste a trip? The food should be here in a second."

"No, not the diner, kid. Over *there.*" He nods to Worthy's desk where a picture of Riga Polytechnic Institute is showing on the monitor. "You know it'll take too much red tape to get their government involved in this."

Worthy stares at him in disbelief. "You're joking, right? We can't just jump on a plane and fly across the world. For one I don't have that type of money. And for what, to chase Devin all over the city? This isn't a movie, man. Oh, and not to mention, we don't have anything *close* to jurisdiction over there." He ashes the remainder of his cigarette and slides another from the pack. "What's the rush anyway? There's no statute of limitations on murder. We'll get him eventually."

Eventually, Clarkson thinks. *I need* him now. "Screw the

jurisdiction, kid. A good cop doesn't always do a good job by being *good.* I thought you understood that, kid."

Unswayed, Detective Worthy stares on. *But maybe Clarkson is right,* he thinks. *Maybe it isn't all good cop and bad cop, black and white, right and wrong; maybe there are shades of gray that fog the road and make it hard it stay on a straight path.*

Maybe, he thinks, but even if that is true it does not mean it applies to him. *Yeah, Miguel was my mentor once but I'm not Miguel. The man that Judith fell in love with is the same man that was willing to turn down $250,000,000 if it meant compromising my values. That's the same man I'll always be. Buying those cigarettes, bribing that receptionist, it might not have been by the book but they were victimless crimes and I did them for the right reasons. I did them for the job.*

He nods to Clarkson, grinning. *But I'll let you believe what you want if it means staying close enough to get that evidence I need to get that badge out of your hands.*

"Not to mention," Clarkson continues, "when that little punk ran, he ran on *us.* I mean, he didn't show no respect for the law, for Judge Morales, and he might as well have pissed in our lemonade."

He grabs his cup in and raises it to his lips but it's empty. *Shit.* Frustrated, he slings the cup across the room and pulls out his flask. "I don't know about you, kid," he takes a swig, "but I can't have that kind of talk about me."

Detective Worthy takes a pull and blows out a cloud. Through the smoke he observes Clarkson— leaned forward in his chair, sweat beads prickling the edges of his greasy comb-over, his flower-print polyester shirt clinging to his flabby chest, topping off his tight jeans and worn-down cowboy boots. Worthy has to take another pull to keep from laughing.

"Hey, Clarkson. Calm down, man. We haven't even eaten yet. The food will be here soon. After we eat then we can figure out what to do. It's hard to think on an empty stomach."

Clarkson nods. Some hot food in his stomach does sound nice. "Okay, kid, I'll eat. But there ain't nothing too discuss. I'm going over there."

Worthy stubs out his cigarette and reaches for his pack. He's on autopilot now—sliding the slim stick from the box, setting it between his lips and sparking his flip-top lighter—allowing his mind to ponder other issues, like Clarkson's true angle. *It has to be something I'm not seeing. I know you're not really willing to risk your pension because of your reputation. Not even you can be that stupid.* He takes a long drag and exhales. *Why is Devin so important to you?*

A knock on the office door pulls him from his thoughts. "Come on in!" He shouts.

A sandy-haired young man, about as tall as Worthy but a lot thinner, strolls in cradling a big brown paper bag in his arms. Worthy recognizes him. It's Judith's nephew Angelo.

"Hey Max." Angelo smiles. "Where do you want it?"

"Over here." Clarkson responds. His stomach growls as the smell of seafood hits his nose. Angelo passes Clarkson the bag and he sets it in the chair in front of him. "Drinks, kid? Where're our drinks?"

Angelo apologizes. "Be right back." He bolts out the door before Worthy can tell him it's alright. Clarkson should be half-drunk by now anyway. What does he need with some iced tea? And the way Clarkson asked for the drinks you would never think that they came free with their order—the order that *Worthy's* paying for.

Oh well, Worthy thinks, chuckling. "He's a good kid.

Probably make a good cop one day. Real honest, you know. Good morals."

Clarkson shrugs. Right now he's not concerned with anything except what is inside the Styrofoam containers he's lifting out the bag. The sweet aroma of steamed crab and grilled shrimp saturates the air. His stomach roars as he cracks open a container.

"Hey Clarkson," Worthy says, grinning, "looks like that open marriage leads to a closed kitchen, huh?"

"Not at first." He replies through a mouthful of shrimp. "But it's not that bad, really. My wife, Amelia, she can't cook anyway."

Worthy shakes his head. Earlier today Clarkson had told him that his wife has a boyfriend that he knows about. It started with Clarkson frequenting prostitutes and now, supposedly, the Clarkson's have an open marriage.

Angelo reappears with their drinks. He apologizes again and sets the two teas on Worthy's desk.

"It's nothing." Worthy tells him and pulls a few bills from his wallet. He hands them to Angelo. "This is for the food," He says and then hands him a few more, "and these are for you."

"Thanks, Max."

"You deserve it, Angelo. Hey, you ever think about enrolling in the Academy? You'll be 18 soon, right?"

Angelo nods. "Yeah. I'll think about it. See you guys later."

"Think about the Academy." Worthy says as he leaves the office. "And tell your mom to tell Jude I love her."

Worthy turns his attention to Clarkson and the containers of food. "So, buddy, how about sharing some of that?"

Clarkson slides over a box without looking up and Worthy has a thought. He is not sure exactly where it comes from but he knows it's true. It was his wife. *It was Amelia who suggested the open marriage.* He can feel it in his gut. It's the same feeling telling him that there is more at stake for Clarkson than just his pride. There is a current running beneath the surface, he thinks, like a warm updraft lifting a young Icarus closer to the Sun.

Worthy takes the box and peers at Clarkson. He watches him ravaging the container of seafood like a starving shark—a shark circling below, waiting on the wax to melt and send a faithful Icarus plummeting to his watery grave.

CHAPTER
TWENTY-EIGHT

A yellow taxicab turns a corner, bouncing slightly as it travels down the old cobblestone road.

In the backseat an attractive woman complains to her smiling boyfriend. *At least I think he's her boyfriend,* the driver muses. His mother had always stressed the importance of him learning to speak English but he never saw the point. For a cab driver with no desire to leave the bounds of Riga, speaking Latvian and Russian is good enough.

Understanding English would make the job more fun, he supposes. *The Americans are very dramatic people.* He glances through the rearview mirror. The young man is still smiling, apparently teasing the young lady about something. She grabs a handful of his long twists and pulls until he submits. The driver watches the young woman. It's the look in her eyes that makes him think that they are a couple; a couple out on a noon date. He doesn't need a translator to understand love when he sees it.

The cab dips in and out of a pothole bouncing the young woman into the ceiling.

"Hey!" She shrieks, rubbing the crown of her head. "Watch it!"

The driver doesn't know what she's saying but he can tell by her expression that she is upset. He offers an apology in Russian and another in Latvian. A red rosary is strung around the gearshift.

He slides it off and discreetly fingers the beads. *Mother Mary,* he begins his prayer, *you know I am a good man. Please do not let this affect my tip.*

In the backseat of the cab, Devin chuckles. "You okay, Sam?"

"Yeah, I'm fine." She nods. "You're the one that needs to get his head checked."

"Come on. It's been three days already. And we've called all morning. Something's up."

"No one's up." She retorts. She checks her watch. "It's a quarter to twelve, Devin. He's probably just sleeping in."

"Guess we'll find out, won't we?" For the past three days, Devin has been sitting on pins and needles anxiously awaiting some word from Dr. Bauer. Samantha tried to explain that it would at least be a week before Kurt had anything substantial to report—Kurt said that it may be at least month before he was finished—but Devin wouldn't hear it. She attempted reading, even going to the gym, to escape Devin's incessant worrying but like a leaky pipe he just continued on until she caved.

"Okay, Devin. If it'll calm you down we can just go by and check on him." She relented.

They were piling in the cab fifteen minutes later.

Devin pays the cabdriver and joins Samantha at the end of Dr. Bauer's driveway. "Told you it would be hot today." He says, pulling his locks up off his neck and into a ponytail. "You didn't want to listen. I don't have to speak Latvian to read the weather forecast."

Samantha looks down at her skintight black jeans and rolls

her eyes. This is one of those times when she hates being a girl. Devin gets to wear cargo shorts and a t-shirt while she is forced to be uncomfortably sexy for Kurt.

Which makes no sense, she thinks. *Kurt already has a girlfriend.* She looks back to Devin, glad that she at least wore a tank-top. "Whatever. Let's just see if he's here. I'm starting to sweat in places I shouldn't."

The two of them start up the driveway and pass a dark blue BMW 5-series sedan. "His car's here." She points out. "Like I said, he's probably just sleeping in."

Devin isn't buying it. "Well, then, if he is it's time to get up. He has something very important he should be doing." He steps up to the porch and knocks. "All this sleeping in is probably why he hasn't figured anything out yet."

Samantha shakes her head. "Or maybe he's at church. It is Sunday, you know."

Practically every driveway on the street is empty, a fact that Devin didn't notice until now. *I'm slipping,* he thinks. *Saka would be disappointed.* Dr. Bauer's car is the one of the few still in the driveway.

He turns back to Samantha. "Doc's religious? Doesn't really seem like the type, you know. Not with that fondness for fornication of his. Plus, his car's still here."

Samantha shrugs. "He could just be out with his girlfriend. Or they could be at church together."

"And what—they took that toy she drives? Not possible."

Samantha's offended. She likes that car. "Wha—why— there's nothing wrong with her car. It's efficient and it's good on the environment. And it's *cute.*"

"Cute?" Devin can't believe his ears. "It wasn't even a car."

"Just knock again." Samantha says, knowing better than to get into this debate. "If no one answers, I'm calling a cab."

"Nope." Devin says. "If no one answers then we're going around back to check it out. It's been three days and no word. Something's wrong."

She rolls her eyes but doesn't object. As she watches him Sukamaya's words fill her mind: *fixation leads to folly.* Devin is on a tightrope walk between commitment and obsession, *and he's leaning towards the latter.* Sukamaya had warned that Devin would need her more than ever in the days to come and after what's happened in the past week his words seem almost prophetic.

Devin goes to knock again but Samantha stops him. "Look." She says, motioning towards the door. "It's already open."

He looks down by the handle and she's right. The door has been left slightly ajar. Smirking, he turns to Samantha and mouths *'I told you so.'*

"Maybe Kurt just forgot to close it behind him." She says. "This looks like a pretty nice neighborhood."

His stare is incredulous. "You can't really believe that, Sam. Not with everything that's been happening."

She can only nod. After everything that has occurred this past week Samantha can't believe that Kurt just forgot to close his door, that the lock is broke, or any of the other reasons that she wants to come up with. But if it is not any of those reasons then there must be another reason why he isn't answering the phone, why he hasn't called in three days, and why his front door is left open. And it's a reason that she is not sure she wants to know.

Devin pushes the door open slowly and crosses the threshold. "Come on. Something's *definitely* wrong."

A rank odor attacks Devin's nose as he steps into the house.
He takes another step and the remains of a broken lamp crunch
beneath his feet. The entire foyer has been trashed. He can't see
the full extent of the damage with the lights off but it's obvious that
someone has been here.

And they were looking for something.

Samantha steps in behind Devin. "Oh my God." She says,
covering her nose. "What's that smell?"

Devin shakes his head as he wades through the mess. "It's
like someone murdered a dumpster, buried it in a sewer, then dug
it up and dumped it here. Be careful," he tells her, "the place's been
trashed. Try to find a light switch."

Instead, Samantha steps through the rubble and goes to
open the curtains. As the sunlight pours in she looks on in shocked
amazement. Dr. Bauer's immaculate bachelor's pad is now ground-
zero. His leather couch had been flipped over and the bottom
slashed open; every picture, lamp, and vase has been reduced to a
shattered rubble; and his armoire—full of his late mother's crystal
knick-knacks—has been toppled over, and the crystal turned into a
pile shimmering shards.

"They were looking for the scroll." Devin says, crossing
through the mess.

"How? No one knew we'd given it to him."

"Come on, Sam. We don't have time to be naive. We both
know who did this."

As much as Samantha would like to believe otherwise, she
knows Devin's right. She hates the thought of fighting an enemy with
so much power. Somehow they knew about the scroll just as soon
as it left the bank, and now, they have managed to find them here
in Riga. Could they be following them somehow, she wonders. Did

someone plant tracers on them? Is it in her cellphone?

Devin nods at the dawning of recognition he sees on Samantha's face. "They must've found out the Doc had the scroll, or, at least they thought he had it."

He shifts the satchel around on his back, glad they didn't decide to leave the scroll with Dr. Bauer. "We need to know if they found those pictures, Sam."

He heads for the hallway, kicking the clutter aside as he does. "I'll go check the computer. See if you can find anything that might tell us where he might've gone."

"Okay, yeah." Samantha says, glancing around the foyer. "Guess I'll start here."

Devin nods. "Yeah, well, good hunting." Shaking his head, he exits the foyer and heads for the office.

A pungent odor—slightly stronger than the first—strikes Devin's nose as soon as he enters the doctor's office. He thinks to hold his breath but what for, he thinks. *I've already been tainted.* He feels along the wall for a light switch and when he flips it, all of his fears are confirmed. Shelves upon shelves of the doctor's books litter the floor; papers are strewn about everywhere; all the lamps (except the one connected to the light switch thankfully) have been shattered; and the two armchairs that he and Samantha has filled just days ago are toppled over and shredded over.

Devin wades through the mess cautiously, his eyes scanning the wreckage for some indication of where the doctor may have gone. A small black object lying on the floor beside the doctor's desk catches his eye. He moves to inspect it and the horrid odor grows stronger.

Standing beside the desk, he uses his foot to spread out the mounds of papers covering the floor. His shoe sticks in a moist black soup. "Ugh." He groans, looking down at his ruined sneaker.

He glances around and spots an ashtray lying beside what's left of Dr. Bauer's wet bar. "Guess I know what that smell is." He looks down at his shoe again and shakes his head. It's destroyed, covered in the unnatural union of tequila, brandy, cognac, the butts of imported cigars, and a mound of ash, all ground together and left to marinate in the doctor's carpet. Holding one hand over his nose, he kicks a few of the files over the tar-pit (as he's come to think of it now), and hopes that it contains some of the smell.

The black object he spotted is lying on the ground. It's a small leather-bound book of some sort. He hesitates to pick it up. It's covered in that same tar-paste that he stepped in. "No way I'm touching that stuff." He grabs a handful of the strewn about files and uses them to wipe the book clean, careful not to get any on his hands. As soon as he's done, he balls the papers up and tosses them as far away from him as possible. He shakes his head again—even with the paste gone the lingering odor is still strong enough to make his eyes water as he unclasps the book's catch.

"A planner." He says, shocked and amused. He browses through the contents quickly but nothing catches his attention; not until he comes to the last entry. It's dated for tomorrow at three o' clock, with "P.D."

"Who's P.D.?" He wonders aloud.

Standing in front of the computer, he sits the planner down on the desk and takes hold of the mouse. The screen awakes from sleep mode. A print-screen task box is sitting atop a picture of the scroll.

"Shit." He mutters as he begins to close out a long succession of windows, each one showing a different image of the scroll. He closes the last scroll picture and another window pops up. It's an image of four strange symbols. *They're from the scroll,* he thinks. *They were under that beetle thing. Doc said they look like some signature or post-script.*

There is a pen sitting beside the keyboard. Devin grabs a piece of paper from the mess on the floor, takes the pen, and starts to copy down the symbols.

I wonder if he figured them out, he thinks, rifling through the disheveled mass of documents, searching for something—anything—that can make sense out of these symbols.

A frightened cry puts an end to his search.

Sam.

He crams the paper into his pocket, grabs the planner, and sprints out of the office. "Sam!" He shouts. "Sam! What's wrong?!"

Devin bolts into Dr. Bauer's bedroom and finds Samantha standing at the foot of his bed, sobbing silently. She hears Devin come in but doesn't bother to turn around. Why? What's the point? There is nothing that anyone can do now. They've done enough already.

From beneath Dr. Kurt Bauer's tattered sheets pokes the face of a man that Samantha had loved to loathe. Each time the two of them would cross paths at the university Kurt would make a suggestive comment or inappropriate joke and Samantha would feign irritation but in reality she looked forward to their hallway meetings. As odd as their relationship was it was still a friendship of sorts. Kurt was her only friend on this side of the world. She liked him because he did not see her as another nerdy girl in goggles and a ponytail but as an interesting and attractive woman worthy of courting. While others may have seen Kurt's crude remarks as harassment, Samantha knew he was harmless and his appreciation was always a refreshing part of her day.

Now, gazing into those lifeless eyes that used to smile when he laughed; looking at the dried blood caked into the corners of the mouth that always had a nice word to say; knowing that she will never again hear that robust laughter as she walks away—it's too much. She turns away and Devin wraps her up in his arms.

"Why?" She mutters. "Why does everyone keep dying?"

Devin can feel the dampness of her tears soaking through his shirt. He pulls her closer. It's all he can do. He cannot answer her question with the tenderness he needs. There is only more anger and more frustration. "Come on." He says, guiding her out of the room.

"We shouldn't have come here." She sobs. "We did this. We brought this here."

"Don't think like that, Sam. You can't think like that. It's not your fault."

Samantha stands in the middle of the foyer staring out at the mess. *Is this what happens to everything they touch? Will everyone they know wind up like Kurt, like Saka, like Mom and Dad?*

Devin takes Samantha by the shoulders and turns her toward him. "Listen Sam, I need you to be strong right now, okay? I know it hurts but you have to push through it. I need you."

In the recesses of her mind Sukamaya's voice speaks. *He'll need your strength.* She takes a deep breath and wipes the tears from her face. "Okay," she says, glancing around at the mess, "I'm calling us a cab. We need to get out of here. What if the killer's are close?" She takes out her cellphone.

Devin grabs her arm. "No. Don't call a cab. We can't risk people seeing us waiting out front or looking out their windows when he blows the horn. If they connect Kurt to you, then you to me..."

"So, what do we do—*walk?*"

"I- I don't—" He scans the room, thinking. There are a set of keys hanging on a hook beside the door. He spots the familiar BMW monogram.

"Come on." He says, snatching the keys. "Let's get out of here."

Samantha stares at him in disbelief. "Are you seriously about to steal his car?"

He shrugs. "I'm already on the run for murder. What's Grand Theft Auto?"

"Right." She mumbles, following him out the door. The two of them slip out of the house quickly and quietly, barely breathing until they are safely hidden behind the BMW's tinted windows.

Devin glances at Samantha as he backs the sedan down the driveway. She's gazing wistfully out at the sky. "Why does everyone keep dying?" He hears her say.

That's easy, he thinks, turning onto the road. *The Elite.*

CHAPTER TWENTY-NINE

The sun is just beginning its ascent over Samaná's horizon, blending last night's blues and purples with the morning's pinks and oranges.

The resplendent rays reach out across the Peninsula, touching the trees with their radiant brilliance. Flocks of snoring birds fill the countless cigua blancas and as the sunlight stirs from their slumber, they kiss the air with their sopranic tweets. One bird, though, is not satisfied with simply singing songs. With a flap of his wings he takes flight, leaving his feathery friends on the branches below.

Standing beside an all black twin-engine turbo jet, Juan watches the bird, wondering how Da Vinci would feel if he could see how far the field of aviation has come. It was probably a day just like, he muses, when Da Vinci first gazed to the sky, watching the flight of a graceful fowl and longed for such freedom.

A white Cadillac pulls onto the private tarmac. A thick speckled paste drops from the sky and smacks the spotless windshield. In the driver's seat, Detective Clarkson turns on the wipers and shakes his head. "Sposed to be good luck." He mumbles. "Guess I'm just lucky it didn't ruin the paint job."

Half-asleep in the passenger seat, Detective Worthy stirs as the car comes to a stop. "We there?" He asks, rubbing the sleep from his tired eyes.

"Yeah." Clarkson replies. "You ready?"

"Yeah." Worthy yawns. "As ready as anyone can be before six."

He opens the door and steps out into the cool early-morning air. The breeze has refreshing chill to it and as Worthy stretches he looks over the top of the Cadillac to a grinning James Clarkson. "I still don't believe that anyone could be this lucky." Worthy tells him. "Coincidence is one thing but this feels like divine intervention."

"Maybe it is, kid." Clarkson gives himself an once-over in the car's window and smiles at his reflection. It's been a long time since he has seen himself in a three-piece suit. "Look at it as proof we're supposed to catch'em."

Worthy looks in the mirror and gives himself a quick inspection. Both detectives are dressed to the nines this morning, wearing suits that neither of them would have been able to afford if not for Clarkson's "hook up."

"If proof of something." Worthy retorts. He glances around the airstrip and spots a kid—*Juan,* he remembers—sprinting towards a hangar. A stern faced man stands in the hangar shouting at him for loafing about staring up at the sky.

He looks back to Clarkson. "So where's the jet?" He asks. "And what exactly are we supposed to be transporting, anyway?"

Clarkson ignores the question and heads toward the check-in building. Worthy follows behind him scanning the hangars as they pass. There is a jet being serviced in one of them. It is the only plane he has seen so far. *Must be the one,* he thinks, though there is nothing that he can see to indicate this. *But then again, I really don't know what does.*

The only thing that Detective Worthy knows for sure is that yesterday evening James Clarkson had a string of luck that a Vegas bookie wouldn't believe.

It all began with a phone call. While the two detectives were busy trying to figure out where exactly in Riga Devin could have gone Detective Clarkson's cellphone rung and started a series of the most fortuitous events that Worthy has ever seen. The caller turned out to be a fellow Mason from Clarkson's Lodge; a Mason who just so happened to have a very unique problem; a problem that he and Worthy were in the perfect position to solve.

According to Clarkson's Masonic brother, not long ago a Latvian ambassador had visited Santo Domingo to meet with President Fernandez. Their meeting went remarkably well and by the end of the ambassador's visit, negotiations for a new trade agreement had been proposed. The problem came when the ambassador returned to Latvia only to realize that he had forgotten a package vital to their dealings. Unforeseen scheduling conflicts prevented him from retrieving the package and all of the ambassador's aides were out on other business. Humbly, he requested that President Fernandez have the package delivered by one of his couriers.

Unfortunately, President Fernandez was suffering from a similar situation. The unscheduled delivery happened to fall at a time when all of his couriers were out handling other matters. Knowing the importance of the ambassador's belongings, the president turned to the only men he could think of to aid him in such distress: the Fraternal Order of Freemasonry.

Detective James Clarkson joined the Brotherhood of Freemasonry for one reason and one reason only—political connections. Being that the political opinions of men seldom agree, political discussion has always been banned from a Freemasons' Lodge, and this ancient statute has made the Lodge a refuge

for senators, congressmen, police officers and even President
Fernandez himself. Where else in the state can the president of a
country be treated as nothing more than a fellow brother if not in a
Freemasons' Lodge? And where else can a simple guy like James
Clarkson get a chance to bond with the president of a country—or at
least a brother that knows him?

It was such a brother that received the call from President
Fernandez and, though denying the opportunity for himself, it was
he who suggested another of their own, a local detective with the
Peninsula.

And where in Latvia, Worthy muses, once again standing
before the receptionist's desk. *Just when we track Devin down, we
get a free trip to Riga of all places.*

Plus compensation.

Worthy smiles at the familiar face. "You must get good
overtime." He says. "Seems like you're always here."

"Ten hour shifts." The receptionist replies. "Trying to save
up so I can buy an engagement ring." He glances down at his watch
and smirks. "I should have been out of here ten minutes ago, but,
you know, teenagers."

Worthy nods, remembering himself at that age but Clarkson
isn't up for reflecting. "Guess my pal's money helped you out
then? Right?" He says. "And I guess we should be expecting our
invitations in the mail too? Max'll be your best man."

The receptionist stirs in his seat, obviously uncomfortable,
and glances beneath the desk. "So I guess you two are here for your
IDs then?"

"IDs?" Worthy was never told that he would need any
new identification. The receptionist pulls a briefcase from beneath
his desk, along with two badges, an envelope addressed to the

detectives, and a document that states the number of official packages they are carrying.

Clarkson takes his badge and smirks. "Glad they used my driver's license picture. Knocks off ten years."

"The jet is taxiing now." The receptionist tells them. "You can wait in the lounge if you like."

"We'll wait outside." Clarkson says, grabbing the envelope and the briefcase. He passes Worthy his badge, snatches the remaining form, and struts out the door.

Detective Worthy stays back to wish the receptionist good luck on his proposal. "There's nothing better than spending your life with the one you love."

"I know. I hate that I have to work these long hours, spending so much time away from Rosy. But once I get her ring, and she says yes, of course, I'll find another job." The receptionist pauses for a second, thinking about the love of his life. "I know you must hate your job, too."

"Why'd you say that?" Worthy asks, caught off guard. "I love being a cop."

"Well, the first time we met it was almost eleven at night and now its six in the morning and here you are again. You can't get to spend a lot of time at home."

Judith's tears flood Worthy's thoughts. He can hear her now—*No, Max, you're leaving because you love your job and I'm tired of competing.*

"Marriage is a job too, man. Remember that and you'll be okay." He tosses a wave. "Good luck." He says and heads out the door.

Clarkson is waiting for him outside gazing out at the sunrise. Worthy walks up beside him. "So what was in the envelope?" He asks.

Clarkson shrugs and passes the envelope to Worthy. He tears it open and scans it quickly. "It's a letter for us?"

"Then read it." Clarkson says. "That is what letters are for right."

Worthy shakes his head, once again wondering what he did to deserve James Clarkson.

"Yeah." He says, and quickly reads over the document. "It is a letter from the president outlining the extent of our diplomatic immunity under Articles 22 and 27 of the Vienna Convention. And then we're thanked for our service."

Clarkson nods. "So basically, don't open the briefcase and our immunity ends when we hand it over."

"That's what it sounds like to me." Worthy glances at the solid black briefcase swinging by Clarkson's side. He expected it to have some sort of government seal or emblem—*something*—but it's just a plain black briefcase with a black handle and numbered lock. "What do you think we're transporting?"

Clarkson shrugs. "Can't say that I care, kid."

Worthy finds Clarkson's nonchalance extremely disconcerting. Any normal person would be at least a little curious about what's in the briefcase. And maybe that's the problem, Clarkson isn't a normal person. Nothing about any of this is normal. "Come on, man. Be serious. It has to seem odd that just when we've tracked Devin to Riga this trip just falls into our laps. As a detective, it has to make you think. Things just don't happen like that."

Another shrug. "Duex ex machine, kid. God's plan and all that."

"Yeah. Well, what about when—"

"Look," Clarkson cuts in, "you should stop asking so many

questions, kid. Haven't you ever heard, 'ignorance is bliss,' or 'more knowledge more misery'?" He starts off towards the jet. "Don't look your gift horse in the mouth, kid. It'd do you good to remember that."

What the hell? Worthy thinks, shaking his head. *Don't look a gift horse in the mouth. What kind of bullshit is that—he read a book of old sayings last night or something? There is no doubt about it—this mutherfucker is up to something and it involves Devin and probably his parents's murder.*

But what? He follows Clarkson up the portable staircase and climbs aboard the jet. It's his first time on a private plane and it makes his one excursion in first-class feel like a port-a-potty.

A young buxom brunette in a tight-fitting stewardess uniform and high-heels wheels a drink cart down the spacious aisle. "We have red and white wine. And there is also Scotch and tequila if you like. I will bring you a menu of our available meals, although I recommend the chicken. It's delicious."

"Double Scotch. Straight up." Clarkson says, unabashedly staring at her breasts.

She looks to Worthy. "And you, sir?"

"I'm fine." He says. "I don't think it's right to be drinking on the job. Especially one as important as this."

The stewardess nods, smiles politely and turns back to Clarkson. "I know." Clarkson says, moving his eyes up from her ass. "He's weird sometimes. He'd be a nun if he didn't have a penis."

She chuckles. "How about I go and get your Scotch and then if her decides that he wants something to ease those take off jitters." She turns to Worthy. "You can tell me when I get back. Okay?"

Worthy nods and she wheels the cart away. Clarkson leans over the seat and stares at her ass until she's disappeared through a

curtain. "She had to know I was watching." He says. "No one walks like that by accident."

Worthy just shakes head. "Yeah, man. It's all for you."

Clarkson sits back up in his seat and looks across the aisle to the up-tight buzz-kill he's stuck with. A part of him feels sorry for the kid. A *very* small part. "You really need to loosen-up. We're just glorified delivery boys, right now. When she comes back, get you a couple shots of tequila or something. Maybe get a shot of her."

"We need to stay focused. There are still too may coincidences. Even if you refuse to care, I can't get over it. I have too many questions running through my head right now." He takes out a pack of cigarettes. "You think I can smoke here?"

"Whatever, kid." Detective Clarkson snuggles into his plush leather seat, lifts the cover on the window, slides on a pair of headphones and activates the monitor hanging from the ceiling in front of him. A selection of movies and music appear. He selects a song—an old blues jam that his mother liked—and settles in. The kid is going to make this difficult—he knows it like he knows Amelia's boyfriend's address—but right now it doesn't matter.

With a grin as wide as the jet's wingspan spread across his lips he turns up the volume and looks to Worthy.

"Why question something as good as this?"

CHAPTER THIRTY

Prime Minister Andris Kratz watches from the back of his all black stretch limousine as a black twin-engine jet touches down on the government's private runway.

He smirks, watching the hangar attendants rush out like a swarm of bees protecting their hive.

Even in an anthill, he muses, pouring himself another glass of champagne, *every ant, no matter how small, has its duty to perform. Just as each bee in the hive serves its purpose.*

The Prime Minister raises his glass and grins; a toast to the two men exiting the aircraft. "And He has created horses, mules, and donkeys, for you to ride and use for show." *How correct you were, Muhammad.* He takes a sip of his champagne and presses a button on the door. The tinted partition descends.

"Yes sir?" His driver says.

"Sergé, call for the other car. These two will need a ride."

"Yes sir."

"Then I want you to call my secretary and inform her that I will be requiring another meeting with Riga's Chief of Police."

"Yes sir."

"Now, come, let me out. I must greet our guests on behalf of the nation of Latvia."

His driver nods and exits the limousine quickly. He holds the door open until Kratz's finished with his champagne. Kratz contemplates a third glass but decides against it and steps out into the cool afternoon air. The two men from the jet are headed in his direction. It would be cordial to meet them halfway, he knows, but making others come to him is one of the many privileges of his station and it is one he enjoys. Almost as much as having Sergé carry his umbrella for him when it rains.

Across the tarmac, Detective Worthy thanks the attendant for pointing them in the right direction, pleasantly surprised that they also speak English in Latvia. *They speak English everywhere these days.* The attendant smiles and walks off. Worthy turns to Clarkson. "Why'd you even ask that guy? It's obvious where we're supposed to go. Look at all the flags on that limo—that's government."

Clarkson nods. "Yeah. But look at that little guy standing there. You expect me to believe he's the guy? I pictured a British Intelligence, MI-5 type, you know?"

You're right on that, Worthy thinks. "He's definitely no Bond." The old overweight man in the black and white double-breasted suit looks more like Mr. Monopoly than the Prime Minister of a country. *And with that slicked back hair he must be from the Grease tribute edition.*

The two detectives walk to the limousine where Kratz is waiting. "Detectives," he says, each syllable coated in a coarse accent—maybe Russian, "on behalf of my country, I thank you for your assistance." He extends his meaty hand. "I trust that you did not open the case, yes?"

"We did not." Worthy assures him. "We were just glad to be of service to our country. And thank for the welcome. But, uhh, sir, if it is not too much trouble, before we continue, can I see some identification?"

Kratz is taken back by the request and the surprise shows on his face. "Certainly." He says, smiling rather smugly. He shows the detectives his ID and, for the sake of formality, requests to see theirs as well. Clarkson and Worthy present Kratz with their official diplomatic courier badges and he nods. Now, satisfied that everyone is who they claim to be, the three of them commence with the delivery.

Kratz looks down at the briefcase and notices Clarkson's ring. "Detective Clarkson, are you a traveling man?"

Clarkson looks Kratz in the eyes. "Yes, I am." He replies.

"And from where do you come?"

"From the West traveling East."

Detective Worthy watches them curiously. The Prime Minister is wearing a ring similar to Clarkson's, meaning that he is also a Mason. Worthy has heard stories about the secret signs and symbols that Masons employ to identify and communicate with one another. *Is that what that exchange was about?*

Prime Minister Kratz and Detective Clarkson nod to each other and Clarkson passes Kratz the briefcase. "Thank you." Kratz says, extending his hand to his brother. Clarkson clasps Kratz's hand firmly, discreetly placing him thumb on Kratz's middle finger. The Prime Minister's thumb touches Clarkson's ring knuckle in return. He grins at the detective. "I have a car coming for you. I apologize for the wait."

"A car?" Worthy asks. "What are you talking about? Why do we need a car?"

"Did you not receive the messages that were sent to the plane?" Kratz looks at the confused faces staring back at him and feigns confusion. "Some people are just imbeciles. Detectives, it seems our local police have found Devin King's fingerprints at the scene of murder. It was not long ago that I received the news. I was told that you two were looking for this man."

Hell no! Detective Worthy is not buying another coincidence. There is something going on here and he's not leaving without getting some answers. He turns to Kratz. "How did you know—"

Clarkson cuts him off. "Hey Max!" He exclaims and slaps Worthy on the back. "We were right, huh? The kid did come here. Good work, man."

Worthy cuts his eyes at Clarkson; he's a long way from excited and nearer to angry. He takes notice of Kratz's smirk and wonders if it's due to Clarkson's jubilance or their naiveté. There is no way that the Riga police force should know that they are pursuing Devin. Even with Worthy adding Devin's prints to Interpol's database, Devin should not have been marked a fugitive—especially a fugitive from the Dominican Republic.

And why didn't they just apprehend him themselves? Why alert us? He looks to Kratz and that smug smirk. *And to top it off, they just happen to find his prints the same day we land.*

A black sedan pulls up beside the limousine. Kratz looks to the vehicle and then back to the detectives. "The driver has been informed of where you need to go, that is, if by chance you two would like to go and see the crime scene yourselves. You are in good hands with Geoff. He is ex-military. All of our drivers are."

Worthy nods. He'll play along for now. His gut is telling him not to trust Kratz but, if the Latvian government is willing to help him find Devin, he'll use them as long as he needs to. Whatever it is they expect in return (and they certainly expect something) is of no concern for Worthy. Once he gets Devin, he's out of here.

"Just remember," Kratz continues, "once you leave

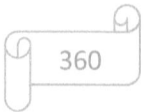

this airstrip, your immunity ceases. I suggest, if you have to do something...questionable, you do not get caught."

"Yeah." Worthy grins. "Thanks for the advice."

The Prime Minister shakes hands with the detectives and climbs back inside the comfort of his limousine. From beneath the tinted windows he watches them debate whether or not they will go visit the crime scene. They reach a compromise, it seems, and climb inside the sedan. Watching their car pull away, Kratz takes out his phone and dials an old Roman church.

"Good evening, Sister." He says. "This is Prime Minister Andris Kratz of Latvia. Could you please connect me to Cardinal Felix Marcellus? He is expecting my call."

"Hold please."

"Yes." He says and glances down to the briefcase in his lap. A wise man once told him that blind faith isn't always the best faith and Kratz has never been one to reject wisdom, no matter its source.

He opens the briefcase and a thousand pictures of Benjamin Franklin stare back at him. He takes out one of the stacks and smiles to himself. "But some will say, 'you have faith and I have works. Show me your faith with works, and I will show you my faith by my works.'"

Guess the idol worshippers aren't that bad either. He looks down at the stack of bills in his hand. *In God We Trust,* he reads. *How can you trust in a god that you do not know? No, I am wrong, they do know their god. I am holding their Almighty now, am I not?*

The Sister comes back on the line. "Cardinal Marcellus is ready, sir. I will transfer you now."

"Graci, Sister."

"Andris." Felix greets. "How good to hear from you."

Kratz has no need for pretenses or small talk. He cuts

straight to the point. "They are here." He says. "Send William my best."

"Then am I to understand that you have received proper remuneration?"

The Prime Minister smiles shrewdly as he reaches for the bottle of champagne. "Oh, how the faithful are rewarded."

CHAPTER THIRTY-ONE

A crowd full of stay-at-home Moms stares curiously at the approaching sedan.

For the last two hours, the house across the street has been alive with law enforcement officials bustling about. Squad cars and crime scene vans fill the street, leaving little space for the sedan to park.

"They're late." A woman remarks. "Things have started to slow down."

Her friend nods. "And they'll have to walk up the street."

"Last to the party always gets the worse parking." Someone chimes in. They all laugh for a moment, until guilt overtakes them and a somber silence settles in.

"Do you really think someone killed Kurt?"

"He was such a nice man."

"Yeah. Nice enough to be seen creeping out your door last Monday night."

"Look." One of the ladies points at the two men exiting the sedan. "Those two look foreign. Who do you think they are?"

"Maybe if we wait until Monday, Mila will tell us."

The crowd erupts in laughter.

Detective Worthy is aware of the curious stares following him and Clarkson across Dr. Bauer's front lawn. Crime scene technicians are always worried about someone tainting their scene with a stray fiber or loose hair.

Guess some things are the same no matter where you go, he thinks.

"Hey! You two!" A deep voice yells. "What the hell do you think you're doing?" Worthy follows the voice to a burly chested man coming their way. *He must be the one in charge.* He has the unhurried stroll of commanding general and his face wears the sort of weathered expression that only comes from a lifetime of police work. It is a look that he has seen on Clarkson at times and one that Miguel would wear with pride. It is a look that says, 'I've seen it all, done it all, and the crime rate has only increased. What's the point?'

He stops in front of them and Worthy flashes his badge. "Detective Maximus Worthy from the Santo Domingo Police Force. This is my, uhh, partner—"

"James Clarkson, I know." The officer extends his hand. "From the Dominican Republic, right? The Chief told me you'd be stopping by." The two men shake and the officer crushes Worthy's fingers in his vice-like grip. "Long way from home, huh, Detective?"

"Yeah, well—"

"Well, we found some prints that turned out to be someone you know. And, as luck would have it, you two were already flying in."

Clarkson grins. "Yeah, the kid here thinks it's divine intervention or something."

The officer stares at Clarkson's ring. *Not a 33rd Degree like the Chief,* he observes, *but still a Mason. And Masons take care of Mason.* "Yeah." He nods. "It's some kind of intervention."

The officer walks off towards Dr. Bauer's front door and motions for the detectives to follow. "I'll show you what we found."

He steps through the door and stops. "Oh, and by the way,

the name's Guntinsky. Inspector Ivan Guntinsky."

Standing in the foyer, Clarkson and Worthy look around at the disaster site that is now Dr. Bauer's home.

"I keep expectin' to see Red Cross workers." Clarkson jokes. "Whoever did this really went to town."

Guntinsky glances around the disheveled room. "Yeah, I haven't seen vandalism like this since '91, back when those Soviet shits tried to overthrow the government."

"'91?" Worthy looks Guntinsky over. "How long have you been doing this?"

"Long enough. I could tell you stories from back—"

"Yeah yeah, I've got stories of my own." Clarkson cuts in. "So how 'bout you just show us where you found those prints?"

Inspector Guntinsky glares at Clarkson, wondering who the hell this guy thinks he is talking to him like that. They're a long way from Santo Domingo and whoever the hell is there, here in Latvia, Guntinsky is the big dog on the lawn. But the Chief gave him orders and he'll follow them, no matter how bad he wants to slug the guy.

"In the office around the desk." The Inspector says. "Around the desk. Some in the bedroom, around the door. And there." He points to the doorknob. "And there." Their gaze follows Guntinsky's finger to a set of hooks mounted to the wall. "That's it." He says, looking around. "Is there anything else in particular I can help you with? If not, feel free to leave when ready. I'm sure you need to get back to your own city."

Clarkson can't help but smirk. "So what's your next move, Gunts?"

"Well, I plan to keep it simple. Have the evening news run his picture. I'm sure it'll flush him out. And then once he's spotted, and he will be eventually, then we'll follow up. And of course," he smiles sardonically, "I'll keep you two posted. That is, unless you're leaving."

"Don't think so." Clarkson says, still smirking. "We'll probably stick around for a while."

"Well, like I said, I'll keep you informed Detective, and I'm sure that you'll do the same, right?"

Detective Clarkson glances to Worthy. "What'd you think?" He asks and then answer his own question. "One, you shouldn't run that picture. The kid has too many resources. If he finds out that you're looking for him, he'll only get harder to find."

"Beisdes," Worthy adds, "I don't think they did it. If they came here it was to seek asylum. Why fly all the way across the world just to kill someone? Someone that there is no evidence to suggest that they even know. It's just not logical."

Guntinsky nods. "And by *they* you mean him and Samantha Matsumi, right? Her prints showed up here too. She is a physicist at Riga Polytechnic, the same place that the dead doctor taught. Maybe those two had some sort of disagreement and she called in her brother to handle it. The faculty says that Dr. Bauer repeatedly made unwanted advances toward her. Maybe he went too far for once. Starting to make sense now?"

"Not if you're suggesting that Devin killed Dr. Bauer for Samantha." Worthy retorts. "That's just crazy. For one, Devin isn't Samantha's brother, and—"

"She has him down as 'brother' in her contact information at the school," Guntinsky interrupts, "and I'm aware of the fact that they were raised in the same home."

"Okay well, even if Devin is her brother, she wouldn't need him to help her kill anybody. Samantha is a trained fighter. Her

father used to teach martial arts back home. I'm sure she could've handled the guy by herself."

Guntinsky relents. "Look kid, whether it makes sense or not doesn't matter. It doesn't have to make sense. Not around here. I've seen all kinds of crap that doesn't make sense. You know what I learned? Criminals are stupid. They do things that don't make sense." He takes a moment to chuckle at his wit. Clarkson and Worthy look on, annoyed.

"So, I'm sorry Detectives," Guntinsky continues, "but Devin King and Samantha Matsumi are now wanted as suspects in the murder of Dr. Kurt Bauer." He glares at Detective Worthy. "Hope that *makes sense*."

With that, the Inspector turns to leave. "Hey." Clarkson calls out, stopping him. "You said there were prints found by that rack?" He looks to the set of hooks on the wall. "And that's probably a 'anything' rack, you know? Right by the door like that. Come in, hang up your coat, hat or whatever. But Dr. Bauer was at home when he was killed, of course, and there's no hat or coat laying around. What would have been on those hooks then?" He rubs his chin as if contemplating. "Inspector, Dr, Bauer's car's missing isn't it?"

Guntinsky nods. "The girlfriend, the one that first called in the report, said that he drove a black BMW, but there was not a car in the driveway when we arrived. She also said that a man and a woman came by, unannounced, a few days ago. She didn't see them but I'm willing to bet it was your two runaways."

"Would explain the prints." Worthy mumbles.

Clarkson agrees. "The kid and the girl, they're close. Probably still in the city. Put some people in plain clothes and have them watch her place. If you run those pictures they're just going to run again. I have a better idea."

"Okay." Guntinsky says. "I'm listening."

"You put those men on her house and keep all of this under wraps for as long as possible. If you have to give them something then you just say that you don't have any suspects yet but you're pursuing leads. Then you put out an APB on that car. Get the plate number and make and model to every officer you have in the street. If one of your men spot it, have them follow it to their hideout. Once we know where they are, we can move in at night, catch them while they're sleep. Nice and quiet."

"*Sleep?*" Guntinsky doesn't like the sound of that. It's too cowardly. "My men can bring him in as soon as they locate him. We don't have to sneak up on him while he's sleep like...like we're scared of him. He's the one that should be sneaking around."

Detective Worthy grins. "Clarkson's right, Inspector. Remember what I said about Samantha and her father. Well, Devin was trained by the same guy. They're like ninjas, Inspector. So if I were you I would put my pride to the side and think about the safety of my men. Tell them to follow him, then call for back-up and wait before moving in. Trust us on this."

"What is he—ex-military?"

Clarkson laughs. The Inspector's doubt is understandable. He'd probably feel the same way if he hadn't seen what Devin did to that kid outside First Bank or hadn't seen all those sparring videos Worthy found online.

"Just trust us, Gunts. Tell your guys that if they do move in, they better bring lots of back-up or lots of bandages."

CHAPTER THIRTY-TWO

Standing outside of a second-floor motel room, Samantha balances a bag of groceries in one hand while she digs in her pocket for the room's keycard.

"This looks so much cooler on TV." She grouses. Shaking her head she manages to pull the card from the pocket of her jeans—*jeans that are too tight to even have pockets,* she thinks— and slides it into the lock. The red light turns green and she opens the door.

"Finally." She says as she enters their tiny room and heads for the kitchenette. Devin is sitting on the edge of their bed with the TV on, flipping through Dr. Bauer's planner. He doesn't bother to look up. "Hello to you, too." She says, setting the bag down on the small space between the sink and stovetop. Devin nods and flips to another page.

"What if I was here to kill you, Devin? You'd be dead right now. You know that right?"

Now she has his attention. He turns to her, grinning. "Okay, I'll play. Let's say you were an assassin sent by The Elite. Why would you make your move at," he checks his watch, "four forty-eight in the evening, in a motel room with thin walls and lots of people coming and going who could be potential witnesses? Plus," Devin moves the book from his lap to reveal a small knife, "I'm always prepared."

"Whatever." She rolls her eyes and starts emptying the bag.

*What you fail to realize, Superman, is that if I was an assassin I
wouldn't care about thin walls and witnesses. We were attacked in
front of the bank with all those people around, dummy.* "Anyway, I
brought food. You were sleeping when I left. You see my note?"

He nod and turns his attention back on the planner. Even
after four days, it still stinks.

"I got some fruits, bread, turkey, cheese, lettuce, tomato, and
a few extras." She takes a bottle of ranch dressing from the bag and
sits it next to the pack of deli meat. "I'm starving. Want me to make
you something?"

"No thanks." He says and flips the page.

Yeah right, she thinks. While Devin reads, Samantha makes
two sandwiches—one with an extra slice of cheese—then pops them
in the microwave. Now warm, she adds lettuce, tomato and ranch
dressing to them both, sets them on two paper plates and heads to
the bed. She sets a plate down in front of Devin and flops down
beside him.

"Told you I wasn't hungry." He says, picking up the
sandwich. "You put ranch on here, right? And two slices of cheese?"

Samantha grins. "If you're not hungry then why does it even
matter?"

He scarves down half the sandwich in two bites. "Just
saying." He swallows another bite. "If you're going to do something,
do it right."

Samantha smiles. Watching him eat like this triggers her
nostalgia. Thoughts of better days torture her with bittersweet
memories. She cannot begin to count the number of times this
scene has played itself out; always ending the same—with Devin's full
stomach and her empty heart.

Samantha has been taking care of Devin for as long as she

can remember and if she were ever to see a therapist they would probably tell her that it is this deep-rooted sense of guardianship that has always made her oppositional to any of his girlfriends. *They don't really get him.* The majority of Devin's romantic partners have never known that he collects comic books, that he is allergic to chocolate, or that he chews his tongue when he is deeply focused on something. All they knew was the handsome, rich, and charming Devin.

Which he is, she thinks, captivated by the way that his jaw clenches as he chews; the graceful flow of his locks down his strong broad back; and the intensity hidden in his dark brown eyes, smoldering like a pair hot coals—until he releases an earth-rattling belch.

"Excuse me." He says, patting his stomach. "Couldn't help it. Think you could make me another one of those? It really hit the spot."

"Here." She says and passes him her plate. "I'll make me another one later."

Devin grabs the sandwich off the plate and goes to bite into but stops. "You're sure?" He asks. "I can make my own, you know?"

"What?!" She scoffs. "No! Uh-uh! I don't think you've been allowed near a kitchen since the great fire of '01."

He smirks. "I thought we promised to never speak of that again."

"Then you should've started talking about cooking."

"Making a sandwich isn't cooking." He takes a bite of the sandwich and the crisp lettuces crunches between his teeth. "Is it?" He asks between chews.

Samantha shakes her head. "For you it is."

He flashes her that enchanting grin. "Whatever. That's why I have you."

Samantha looks away. Devin's right, he does have her, but when will she have him? This question has been coursing through Samantha's mind like a cord of rope tying together the last ten years of her life.

It was the night of her senior prom that these questions first began. It was that night when Samantha decided to be honest about her feelings and tell him the truth. *It may be my last chance*, she had thought, with him going to Harvard and her going to Europe. *Tomorrow may be too long.*

She wasn't sure if it was the alignment of the stars or the spiked punch in her veins but as Samantha and Devin sat in the back of their limousine, heading home for the night, she could think of nothing else but being in his arms. She walked down the second floor hall wondering if he could feel the same sensations in the air. Standing outside her bedroom door, she decided to find out.

"Goodnight." Devin had said. "Uhh...guess I'll see you in the morning." Then he flashed that familiar grin and her heart fluttered. He turned to leave but she couldn't let him walk away.

"Wait." She had said, grabbing his hand. "This night has been perfect. I had the perfect dress, the perfect shoes, the perfect hair and the perfect date." She paused then and gazed deeply into those smoldering dark-brown eyes. "Now all I need is the perfect ending."

Devin parted his lips to speak but the delicate press of Samantha's kiss distracted him. Instinctively, his hands grasped her waist, pulling her closer. With each exchange of breath their desire grew until, somewhere in their thrall, her bedroom door was opened and they stumbled inside, lost in passion. They collapsed onto her bed and in that moment of separation they both paused, unnerved by the same thought: *is this the right thing to do?* But as they looked into each other's eyes they knew it was. With a coy grin, Samantha laid back on the bed and invited Devin to behold her most precious gift.

That next morning came too fast for Samantha. She could have spent the rest of her life with her smaller frame nestled snugly in the arc of Devin's back like two perfect puzzle pieces. As her eyes fluttered and the warm sun smiled down on her bare skin, she rolled over to place a kiss on her love's sweet lips but he was gone. The spot where Devin had laid beside her, snuggled close, keeping her safe from the world, was now empty and cold.

It was Sukamaya that had broken the news to her: Devin had gotten up a few hours before and left to take his then-girlfriend on a make-up date (since he didn't take her to his prom like she wanted). Heart-broken and confused, Samantha couldn't stay in the Peninsula any longer than she had to; she left for Europe as soon as she could. After college she made sure to take a position as far away from Devin, the Peninsula, and that day as possible.

It's been almost ten years now, she thinks. *And neither of us has ever mentioned that night.*

"So now what?" She asks. "They have the pictures of the scroll. Is it over?"

Devin sets the empty plate aside and shakes his head. "Naw, I doubt it. You saw how they tore up the place. They're still looking for something— and it's probably the *real* thing. This scroll. And *we* still don't have Mom's book back."

They both glance at the satchel. It's leaned against an empty chair in the kitchenette. Samantha looks back to Devin. "But, then, why kill Kurt?"

373

Devin shakes his head again. "I don't know, Sam. Probably to keep him from telling anybody about what happened. They didn't know who or what he knew so..." His words trail off as he thinks something so horrible he's not sure if he should say it. "Or maybe it was a message to us."

Flashes of Kurt laying stiff beneath his blood-soaked sheets force their way into Samantha's mind. She gets up and turns on the TV, looking for some sort of distraction.

A man and woman argue in Russian. It looks like the woman caught the man cheating but she can't understand what's being said. Samantha cannot speak Russian or Latvian, though the latter she can understand fairly well. She goes to change the channel but stops as the show ends. *Maybe I'll be able to understand the next one,* she thinks, sitting back down.

"So what's that book you're reading?" She asks Devin. A car commercial is on the TV now and car salesmen are annoying in any language.

"The Doc's planner. I've been browsing through his contacts and appointments. He had a meeting scheduled for tomorrow in Riga."

"Really? Kurt still had a day planner." Samantha can't believe it. "What's the point? You can just put everything in your phone?"

"Don't you remember how he complained about not having the real scroll. Everyone doesn't trust technology like you, professor."

"I'm not a professor, stupid. I don't teach." The news comes on the TV but Samantha ignores it. "And F.Y.I., the only people that don't trust technology are backward terrorists, conspiracy theorists, old people and anarchists."

"Bullshit. What about Morpheus, Neo and John Conner. You're just a nerd."

"Devin, you collect comic books." She retorts. "Who's *really* the nerd?"

"Those comics will be worth hundreds of thousands one day. It's a smart investment that—"

"Whatever."She's heard this argument before and it's BS. He reads his comics too much for them to ever stay in good condition. "Who did Kurt have an appointment with tomorrow?"

He hands her the planner. "Look. It's the last entry. It just says 'P.D.'"

"So then who's P.D.? Police Department? You think he was going to meet with the police?"

Devin shrugs. It's as good a guess as any. "Guess it would explain why they killed him. But check this out." He digs into his pocket, pulls out a couple pieces of paper and spreads them open on the bed. "I found these on his desk. Know what any of this is? It's from the scroll."

Samantha studies the drawings. "You said these are from the scroll? Where?"

"Beneath that bug thing. Hold on." Devin goes to get the satchel and slowly unrolls the scroll on the bed. "See, it's right there. Beneath the beetle."

She nods. "On Kurt's notes, here, that says 'signature.' Remember he had said that the scarabeus could be like a signature? Maybe those drawings are part of the signature, too."

"Like what? A return address or something? I guess they could be numbers. Shit, they could be anything."

"Yeah." Samantha continues to study the drawings, trying to recall something—*anything*—that Mrs. King may have told her.

"Could be anything."

A breaking news update flashes across the television screen. Samantha recognizes the familiar music and turns up the volume. Fortunately the anchor is speaking in Latvian.

Breaking news report coming out of Riga.

The body of local Polytechnic professor, Dr. Kurt Bauer, was found dead in his home today. Authorities arrived at the scene at approximately two o' clock this afternoon after a call from a woman claiming to be his girlfriend led him to his home. According to her she had not heard from him for two days, which was very unusual behavior. Sources report that the authorities have yet to identify a motive for the killing but they do have two suspects, a Mr. Devin King and Ms. Samantha—

A picture of Devin is juxtaposed beside a mugshot of Samantha—taken after her arrest for disorderly conduct at an environmental protest.

Devin can't understand what the anchorman is saying but when he hears his name and sees their pictures on the news he understands enough. "Grab your stuff." He says, scrambling around the motel room. "We have to go, now!"

Samantha moves quickly, bouncing around the room, scooping up everything that they have and sliding it into her bag. "What about the food?" She asks.

"Grab it. We might not be able to go out in public anytime soon."

She slings the backpack across her shoulder, grabs the brown bag from the counter and heads towards the door. "You think someone called us in already?"

Devin shrugs, glancing around the room. He has his bag, the planner is in his pocket, and Samantha has everything else. Why does he feel like he's forgetting something?

The scroll. It's still lying open on the bed. As quickly as he can manage, he rolls it back up and slides it into the satchel.

"Okay, let's go." He says, slipping the satchel's strap over his shoulder. "You know we don't exactly blend in, so avoid eye contact and just head straight for the car."

"Okay, but, Devin—where are we going to go?"

"I don't know yet, Sam." He cracks the door open and peeks outside. There aren't many people out right now. "But we're getting the hell out of here."

CHAPTER THIRTY-THREE

We can't just ride around all day, Devin. We need a plan."

Samantha is right. The two of them have been driving through the city for twenty minutes now and they are no closer to a destination than when they left. Devin is going nowhere fast, and as he makes another directionless turn, he kicks himself for not having a Plan B.

"There aren't any more plans." He tells her, "Kurt's dead and The Elite have pictures of the scroll. I'm wanted for murder in two countries now and you're an accomplice to one."

The gas gauge sounds and a red-light on the dashboard glows.

"*And we need gas.* All we can do now is play the hand we're dealt."

A gas station is coming up on the right. Devin switches lanes and pulls in beside a pump. "Just keep looking through that planner while I fill up."

"That appointment that Kurt had for tomorrow," Samantha says, "with 'P.D.' I checked his contact list. There's no 'P.D.', but there's a number here for 'Poppa Doc.' I mean, that has to be 'P.D.' right? Think we should call?"

"I don't know, Sam. Doesn't sound real safe."

"But he might be our only chance and we have to do something. Kurt was probably looking for some help. What are the odds that he would set up a meeting four days after we come over?"

"Exactly." Devin retorts, "Didn't we tell him not to do that? We don't know why he set up that meeting. He could be in on this too and his people just betrayed him or something. What if this is a set- up? And now we're wanted by the police here too. Poppa Doc might turn us in for a reward."

Samantha rolls her eyes. "If it was up to me, we'd call him," she persists, "but whatever, you're scared. Just get me a juice and some candy, okay. Somebody ate my lunch so now I'm starving."

"Yeah, okay." Devin reaches in the backseat ad digs an orange out of the grocery bag. "Here. Eat this."

He tosses Samantha the fruit and exits the car. A red Mercedes rolls pass and pulls out into the flow of traffic. The driver didn't seem to notice him, *thank God*, and now their BMW is the only car left on the lot. Still, Devin moves quickly, eager to get away from traffic and the curious glances it may bring.

That's all it'll take, he thinks, *one stray glance and pumping this gas will be—*

He stops in his tracks. "Aye Sam," he calls, "What pump is that?"

"Seven!" She yells.

Lucky number seven. He smirks. *We definitely need all the luck we can get right now.*

Stepping inside the store he's amazed at the familiarity he feels. A BP is the same in New York, in Santo Domingo, and it seems in Riga.

"Guess I know where everything is." He mumbles. Walking down the snack aisle he browses the selection, immediately eliminating with peanut butter or chocolate in it.

"Here we go." He says, grabbing a pack of sour Gummy

Worms® and two boxes of MikeN'Ikes®. What the hell, he thinks, taking a few bags of Skittles® and some Starburst® too. Cradling the assortment in his arms, he carries it to the front counter and the clerk begins to ring it up. He does his best to keep his head down and not draw any attention to himself, though he doubts the middle-aged man behind the counter watches the news much.

"Oh, shit. I forgot Sam's juice." He blurts out. The clerk looks up as Devin jogs down the aisle. Unsure of what's going on, the clerk stops ringing up the items and goes back to flipping through a magazine.

In the back of the store Devin grabs the refrigerated door and a chill shoots up his spine as he watches two uniformed officers—one short and blond guy and the other tall and dark—stroll in. They nod to the clerk and head down the snack aisle, coming straight towards Devin.

Devin sticks his head deeper into the cooler as they draw nearer. They slow down as they close in on him. Devin takes a deep breath, preparing for the worst.

The officers stop behind him and the short blond one reaches out his hand. Devin readies himself to strike.

"Excuse me." The officer says, taking a juice off the shelf.

"Uhh...yeah." Devin says, grabbing one too.

The two officers continue on about their business and Devin exhales. He closes the door and starts up the aisle, looking to get out of this store as fast as possible. The tail dark-haired officer spins around.

"Hey you." He calls out. "Wait."

Ignoring him, Devin continues up the aisle and the officer calls out again. "Hey sir. With the long hair. Wait up!"

"Me?" Devin asks, stopping beside a broom. He glances at

it. It's the best weapon in range.

"Yeah. You."

The two officers close the distance quickly. The blond one studies Devin. "You okay?" He asks. "Look tense."

"I'm fine," Devin replies, positioning himself nearer to the broom. "So how can I help you two today?"

"Well," the blond begins, "me and Hanz here, we were having this argument when we saw you. And you, uh, look like a guy that knows how to deal with women, so—"

"So tell Arnie that we should get beer and not vodka." His partner cuts in. "We're double-dating tonight."

Devin lets out a sigh of relief. "It depends on the situation." He explains, feeling like Neil Strauss in a room full of nerds. "It's about the intent. If you intent on this being a first *date* then you go with beer. Hard liquor will make a woman assume you're trying to get her drunk and take advantage of her. But if this is only supposed to be a one-night stand, she might want that, and so vodka would be the way to go."

Hanz smirks. "Told you, Arn."

"Okay." Arnie relents. "Just get the beers."

Devin walks off, grinning to himself. Back at the counter he sets down the juice and tells the clerk "100 on pump number 7."

The clerk rings up the juice and adds it to the bag of snacks. Devin repeats "100 on seven." The clerk shakes his head.

I don't have time for this, Devin thinks, wishing he spoke every language in the world. He points out at Dr. Bauer's car and tries again.

"100...on...pump...seven."

"No fuel." The clerk says, though his limited English and thick accent don't do much in the way of helping the situation.

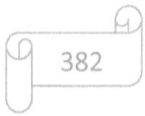

"No fuel." He repeats. He holds up seven fingers and shakes his head again. "No fuel." He holds up nine fingers. "Yes, fuel."

Officer Hanz sets a case of beer on the counter. "What's going on here?" He asks, taking notice of the clerk's exasperation.

"Yeah," Arnie says, backing him up. "Is everything alright?"

Devin and the clerk both begin to explain themselves. The jumble of English and Russian is too much to bear.

Hanz turns to Devin. "Hold on." He says and switches his attention to the clerk. The two of them go back and forth for a bit and when the conversation is over, Hanz and Arnie are both smiling.

"Frederick here says that he understands English," Arnie tells Devin, "but he can't speak it very well. The pump you want, it's out of service right now. That's why he kept saying 'no fuel'."

Devin glances at Frederick. He's nodding along in agreement.

"He held up seven fingers, like you did, to show you pump 7, and then nine fingers, thinking you'd think pump 9."

Devin grins. "I thought he was saying 'fool.'"

Hanz nods. "He says he's happy to put your money on any pump besides 5 and 7."

"Okay, tell him to put 80 on nine, take out the candy, and he can keep the change. "Frederick nods. He doesn't need anyone to translate free money. *Smiling*, he activates pump 9 and hands Devin his bag. Devin takes it and heads for the door.

"You said pump 7," Arnie asks, gazing out into the parking lot. "So that's your 5 series out there?"

Standing at the door, Devin nods "Yeah, but I have to go guys. Got someone waiting. Have fun on that date."

He slips out the door quickly, before they can ask him

anything else.

Samantha watches Devin exit the store carrying a plastic bag. She decides to help out and pump the gas but the pump won't turn on.

"My juice better be in that bag." She shouts. "And the pump's broken!"

Devin can't yell, not when those two nosy cops are probably staring at him right now. He mouths the word 'police.'

"Get back in the car, Sam, and move the car to pump nine."

Did he say '*police*', she thinks, scanning the lot. A white and blue City of Riga squad car is parked right in front of the store. She can't believe they pulled up without her noticing.

Reading that planner, she thinks, *fixation leads to folly.*

"Hey!" A raspy voice calls out to Devin. "Hey, buddy! One more thing."

Devin turns to find Arnie and Hanz approaching quickly. They catch up with him in the middle of the lot.

"Arnie's been thinking about getting a new car." Hanz says. He slugs his Arnie in the arm. "Go on. Tell him."

"Well, yeah, see... I've been saving up all of my bonuses and—"

"Sorry to be rude, guys," Devin cuts in, "but I *really* have to go. Trust me, man, if you can get one, get one. Okay? See you later."

He turns and heads for the car. Samantha has already moved it and is connecting the pump's nozzle to the gas tank now.

Devin shakes his head. "Damn Sam, why couldn't you just wait in the car like a normal girl?"

"Guess if I had a girl as pretty as her I'd run off too." Arnie says, watching Samantha pump the gas.

"I don't know," Hanz replies, "I'm not really into black girls. And why are you worrying about her anyway? We have Mila and Natasha coming tonight."

"I'm not worrying about her. She's just an attractive woman. An Asian woman, by the way."

"Whatever." Hanz says, turning towards the squad car. He stops. "Hey, you remember, right at the end of our shift, wasn't there an APB put out on a dark blue BMW? And something about a black guy and an Asian girl?"

Arnie shrugs. "Maybe. Why? You think it's them? Come on man, not now. It's like you said, Mila and Natasha."

"Better safe than sorry."

Devin is standing beside the driver-side door when he hears Hanz call out to him. He looks to Samantha, still pumping the gas, and mouths, *be ready.*

Arnie and Hanz stop beside hood of the car. Somber faced Arnie asks for Devin's name.

"And also, where are you staying?" Hanz adds.

"With me." Samantha answers. "What is this about?"

"Ma'am, calm down, okay." Hanz unclasps his holster. "I just need to see some type of identification. This car was reported sto—"

Samantha yanks the nozzle from the tank and sprays Hanz in the eyes. Disoriented, he stumbles backward, reaching for his gun. Before he can get to it, she flips the nozzle over and smacks him with the handle hard across the jaw. Hanz crumbles to the ground, unconscious.

She moves quickly now, jumping to the left and using her momentum to kick off of Dr. Bauer's car. With all weight behind her she lands a brutal right across Arnie's jaw. He collapses in on himself like an imploding tower.

Devin smirks. "Why'd you waste that gas? I had those two."

"There was only a few dollars left." She picks up the pump and sticks the nozzle back into the tank.

"Why didn't you just stay in the car anyway? You know you stick out, especially with me."

"What?!" She removes the pump from the gas tank and steps over Hanz. "You're not blaming this on me. I live around here, remember?"

"It's your fault, Sam. You should've just—"

"Whatever." She says. "You get my juice?"

"Here." Devin tosses her the bag. "Get in the car."

Samantha catches the bag and sifts through the contents. "I said juice, not tea." She continues digging and looks up smiling. "Oooh, you got Gummy Worms."

"Sam. Get in the car. We need to get out of here." He looks toward the store. Frederick is standing in the window watching them and it looks like he's on the phone. "Now!"

The two of them slide inside the BMW and Devin pulls out into traffic.

"The car's been flagged." He tells her. "We're going to have to ditch it."

"Yeah," Samantha says, swallowing a mouthful of candy, "but we need a new one first."

"Right. So, question is, where do we get a car?"

Neither of them can come up with an answer that won't draw

more attention to themselves. Devin isn't a car thief and Samantha couldn't steal a kiss, never mind a car. They ride around in silence heading nowhere in particular. Devin makes a right and they come to a stop at a red light.

Samantha's cellphone rings. The number is unfamiliar but local. She's not sure if she should pick it up or throw her phone out of the window. She's heard about people being tracked through their cellphone.

"Answer it," Devin tells her. "Just, you know."

"Yeah, I know." She connects the call and a male voice comes through the line.

"Samantha Matsumi?" The caller says. "Samantha Matsumi, is this you?"

"Who is this?"

"Listen to me. I can help you. Leave the car somewhere and go down to the boatyards. There is a ship there. *My Little Secret,* find it and wait there."

"What? Who are you? Why should I trust you?"

"I don't have time to explain. Just go there. Tomorrow at three, I'll come for you. Trust me. It's the only way you won't go to jail."

"Tell me who this is?" Samantha persists. "If you want me to trust you, trust me."

There is a moment of silence and then the man agrees. "Okay, he says, "but you have to do what I say."

"Tell me who you are."

Devin watches Samantha and her face goes blank.

"You okay, Sam? Who was that?"

Samantha turns to Devin fighting back tears. She has cried more this last week than she has in her entire life. But these are not tears of lost; these are tears of anger; tears that spring up quickly in response to an unsuspected pain, like snatching the bandage from a wound that has just began to heal.

"Sam, who was it? Tell me."

Dr. Bauer." She sobs. "His said his name was Dr. Bauer."

CHAPTER
THIRTY-FOUR

nspector Guntinsky is the first to notice the black sedan pulling into the gas station.

He checks his watch. It's only been fifteen minutes since his office got the call.

Whoever's informing these two, they're close to the action, he reasons. *Those Masons always take care of their own.* The Inspector has never been fond of the Masons that serve in Latvia's public offices and as far as he's concerned, the Church was right for condemning the brotherhood. Any society that keeps secrets must have something to hide.

He scans the lot for a familiar face and spots his guy—a young man in uniform standing around idly. "Hey you!" He yells. The officer points to himself. "Yes. You!" Guntinsky bellows. "Come here!"

Guntinsky has a discouraging thought watching the scrawny, pocket-faced young man trot over to him: *If this is the future of Riga's law enforcement then we might as well save the people some money and turn the city over to the Russian Mafia now.*

The young man stops in front of him and stands at attention. "Yes sir!" He reports.

Guntinsky grins. The kid is obviously a fresh discharge. His blond hair is cropped close to the head, his face is clean shaven and his posture is impeccable. *Is this what I looked like when I got out?* Guntinsky wonders. He looks the kid over again. *Doubt it. I was never that dopey.*

"Listen, uhh... what's your name again, officer?"

"Stein, sir. Henrich Stein."

"Okay, Stein. I know you're the one who relayed the situation to me, right, but I don't know who else you told about what happened here. Who else did you tell, Stein?"

The officer looks confused. "Just you, sir."

"You sure about that?" Guntinsky presses on. "It's okay if you did. You were just following orders, right?"

Stein looks down at the ground. "Yes sir. And well...uhhh." He hesitates. "Well, you're right, sir. I had orders to report any information regarding the two fugitives directly to the Chief, sir. Besides you and the Chief there was no one else, sir. "

The Chief, Guntinsky should've known. *Another Mason.* "You just started here last week?"

"Five days ago, sir." Officer Stein takes notice of the Inspector's furrowed brow. "Did I do something wrong, sir?"

Guntinsky looks over Stein's shoulder and watches Detectives Clarkson and Worthy exit the sedan. He looks back to Stein. "You're dismissed, Stein. Go finish taking Kohl and Oder's statements."

"Yes sir." Stein says, relieved to be sent to do something less nerve racking. He performs a crisp 180° turn and trots off to the medic van.

Inspector Guntinsky suspects that the Detectives are going to want to speak to him about what happened here. He doesn't really feel like entertaining them, especially Clarkson. It's obvious the Chief is feeding them information, so why keep up the pretense by coming to talk to him? *Just to waste my time,* he thinks.

He goes to intercept their path but they change directions

and make a bee-line for the curb. The store clerk is sitting there alone, having already been interviewed by Riga's finest. Curious, offended, and slightly annoyed Inspector Guntinsky moves to join them. By the time he gets there, the detectives have already started their questioning. Worthy stops in the middle of a sentence and turns toward him.

"Inspector." He says, extending his hand, "Just who we need to see. This guy doesn't speak good English and I'm sure he no *hablé espanol*."

Clarkson looks the Inspector up and down and grins smugly. "Yeah, Gunts. So tell me, how do you say 'I told you so' in Russian? No wait, or is it Latvianese? Whatever you speak over here."

Guntinsky returns Clarkson's grin but he's far from amused. Bridling his tongue, he says something to the clerk that neither detective can understand. The clerk stands up and heads inside the store.

"Hold on." Clarkson protests. The clerk stops and looks at the Inspector, confused. Guntinsky waves him on.

"Wait." Clarkson says. "We were talking to him."

Now it's Guntinsky's turn to smile. "Thought you didn't speak *Latvianese*." He says, smugly. "How can you talk to someone and neither of you speaks the others language?" He watches Clarkson, waiting for a reply, and then shakes his head in disappointment. "I already spoke to him, Detective. He's going to get the security footage."

Detective Worthy looks through the store's window and watches the clerk walk behind the counter and then disappear through a door. He looks back to Guntinsky. "So what'd he tell you? Did they use a credit card? Did he see anything that might suggest where they're staying?"

Guntinsky half shrugs and half nods. It's a gesture that says, *yeah, he said something but it wasn't anything important.* "He claims that after your guy paid for his stuff, the two officers—the guys over there," he points to the back of the ambulance where Kohl and Oder are still talking to Officer Stein, "Kohl and Oder, went to ask him something. Then he says he looked out the window to make sure that your guy was using the right pump. That's when he saw a darker complexioned woman, in a jacket and jeans, take out the officers. He says that after that the man and woman drove off in a black BMW 5-series—the doctor's car, probably; we're going to check the camera for a shot of the plates— and sped off that way." He points down the street towards an intersection. "They made a right at the light."

Clarkson and Worthy both nod. "Told you to have your guys call for backup." Clarkson teases.

Guntinsky isn't in the mood for jokes. "This isn't amusing. Those two are officers and they were off duty, probably on their way home to their families." He glances to the ambulance. "Now look at them. One has a broken jaw and the other may have permanent eye damage. They should have just shot them both."

"Broken jaw?" Worthy smirks. "Guess Samantha has a mean right, huh?"

"What?" Guntinsky says. "You two just don't respect—" Before Guntinsky can give the little smart-ass a piece of his mind, Officer Stein jogs up and interrupts him.

"Sorry, sir. But I've just been informed that Dr. Bauer's car was found abandoned not too far from here. It was empty except for some candy wrappers. The crime scene people are on their way now."

Worthy nods. This is good. They can work with this. "So

either they are on foot or in a cab." He says, thinking aloud. "But with the city on alert I wouldn't take a cab. And walking around in broad daylight is too dangerous looking like them. Their best bet is to steal another car."

Clarkson agrees. "But to go *where?* That's the card we need to draw."

Guntinsky asks the obvious question. "Do they have any friends or family in the area? Any contacts that you know about?"

Clarkson shakes his head. "You don't think we thought of that? Far as we know, it was just the dead guy. But the girl with that mean right hook, she does work around her. Could have some contacts that we don't know."

Guntinsky bites his lip. "Yeah, well, according to the school's faculty she pretty much kept to herself." He says, doing his best to stay focused on the case and not punch Clarkson in the face. "It seems Dr. Bauer was her only friend. I've already put some unmarked cars at her place in case they decide to go there for anything and I'm going to get some more of her co-workers interviewed; make sure no one's hiding anything. In the meantime, we'll keep watching the airstrips and Riga International in case they try to run."

They aren't running, Worthy thinks. *If they were they'd be out of the country already. Devin has too many resources and too much money to stay around unless he wants to. But why would he want to?* "Aye, Inspector, find out exactly what it is Dr. Bauer does at the University. What does he teach? I have a feeling that he might've been helping them with something. They had to have come here for a reason, right? With their money and Devin's connections, they could have hid out anywhere in the world. So why come here, to Riga, and meet with Dr. Bauer?"

Clarkson nods. *The kid is one hell of a detective. A cowardly little bitch,* he thinks, *but one hell of a detective.* "Yeah, and see if you can get a trace on her phone. You'll probably have to get some type of court order before the cell company gives it to you but it's worth a shot. The kid's already dumped his."

Guntinsky glances over at Stein. He's been standing there quiet for a while now. Too quiet, actually. "Why are you still here?" Guntinsky asks. "Go finish taking those statements. This conversation is above your pay-grade."

He glares at Stein and Stein does one of his perfect about-face turns and jogs back over to the medic van. The last thing Guntinsky needs right now is little Officer Stein soaking up all of their plans and parroting them back to the Chief so he can help these two island idiots. It's obvious that the Chief cares more about being a Mason than serving the people Riga but Guntinsky could care less about whatever it is that Samantha Matsumi and Devin King did in the Dominican Republic. Here, in Riga—the place that he is sworn to protect—they killed a man and injured two officers. And even if those detectives are right and they didn't kill Dr. Bauer, they probably know something about the person that did. Why else would they flee the scene?

The Inspector glances at the detectives— he'll keep working them until they give him what he needs to find Devin and bring him in for Kurt Bauer's murder—then glances to Stein. *But how can I do that if they know every single move he's going to make?*

"You know what's bothering me?" Worthy asks. "How did they know we were on to them? If they had somewhere to lay low already, what made them decide to just up and leave?"

Clarkson shrugs and looks to Guntinsky. "Don't mind the Whiz-Kid, Gunts. We don't know for sure they were running.

Probably just needed some gas and nibbles and stuff, saw your guys and got spooked."

Guntinsky doesn't agree. "I don't know. He might be right. We received a call from a motel where some lady thought she had saw our suspects. I sent some people over and the room was abandoned. The attendant says they left but never checked out. Then I found out that somebody leaked their names to the press. Their pictures were on the five o' clock."

"And twenty minutes later they show up here." Worthy mumbles.

"Any idea who leaked the news?" Clarkson asks.

Guntinsky darts his eyes toward Stein. "No. There are some things in my office I need to sort out, if you don't mind, Detectives."

The three men shake hands. Guntinsky yells for Stein to come and join him, then turns back to the detectives one last time.

"I'm sure we'll be seeing each other again, Detectives. Until then." He raises his hand in a half- wave then walks off to intercept Stein.

The store clerk emerges holding a security tape. He looks for Inspector Guntinsky but him and Stein are already inside the car.

"We'll take it." Clarkson says, reaching out his hand. The clerk hesitates and Clarkson snatches the tape from him. "You should go and talk to them." He looks to two officers still sitting in the back of the medic van.

The clerk eyes him suspiciously but decides it's better to just cooperate and walks off.

"Think we can trust the Inspector?" Worthy asks. "Seems like he's keeping secrets."

Clarkson smirks. "You can't trust anybody but me, Maxy."

Worthy grins. "I hope that's not true."

CHAPTER
THIRTY-FIVE

A sharp gust of wind rocks the docks, swaying the rows of slumbering ships tucked in the harbor for the night. Samantha hunches her jacket up around her exposed ears, once again regretting her choice of wardrobe. She can't wait to find this boat. Besides being cold, she's starving, and there has to be something to eat on-board. A hot meal and a warm bed is just what she needs.

With their backpacks slung across his shoulders and the satchel in hand, Devin walks alongside Samantha scanning the name of each ship in the docks. Most of them are just small fishing boats but every so often a luxury cruiser breaks the line. They come upon one now; a sleek mid-size vessel that Devin hopes is built for speed. If he's right and this is a trap, he and Samantha will have to capture the ship and set sail—*where*, he has no idea.

"This is it."He tells her, stopping beside the ship's dingy white hull. "My Little Secret."

"Well let's go then." She replies, aware that they don't really have any other choice but to trust that this works out in their favor. *Trust in the Tao, Sam. Remember The Way.* Her stomach growls and she smiles. "I just hope the secret not that they're out of food."

"Right." Devin says. The two of them climb aboard the ship and scan the deck. Finding it empty, they head for the cabins below. The area is spacious enough. There is enough room for two separate living quarters, a shared bathroom, and a small antechamber that's being used as a storing space. It could be an extra sleeping space, Samantha thinks, and as she does so her stomach growls again. They search the area quickly. Satisfied that they are alone, Devin flops down on the bed and stretches out.

Samantha looks at him and smiles. As paranoid as Devin's been, for him to lay out like that means he actually feels safe for a moment, and if he can relax then maybe she can too. After today, God knows she needs it. *Almost as much as I need to eat.* "I'm going to find food. That looked like a mini-fridge back there."

"Yeah, okay." Devin sits up. "It'll probably be full. You saw all those clean towels in the bathroom and these new sheets on the bed. Whoever our savior is, he left this place ready for us."

Samantha had thought the same thing. While they were ensuring that they were alone she noticed that there was a running generator in the anteroom. "I'll be back with some food. Look around for a heater. I'm freezing."

She disappears into the backroom and Devin gets up and roams around, searching for a space heater. He finds a slim electric one in the second bedroom and by the time Samantha returns with two streaming microwave dinners, the room is nice and toasty.

"Let's take these up to the deck." She suggests. "The moon's out and the view on the water is too beautiful to miss."

Devin looks at her quizzically. "Thought you were cold."

She shrugs. "Just grab a couple blankets from that closet and come on."

On the boat's deck, Devin spreads out a thick blanket and he and Samantha take a seat. For a while they eat silently, gazing out at the rippling water glistening beneath the man's glow. Devin notices Samantha shivering slightly and lays another blanket across their laps.

"Thanks." She says, snuggling up. "You know what this is missing?"

He glances around. "Guess it depends on what you're going for. Me, personally, I'd add a piñata."

Samantha can only shake her head. "Well, I was thinking a bottle of wine. I saw one down there in the fridge. Should I go get it?"

"Naw." Devin replies. "You stay bundled up. I'll get it."

"Alright." She sets the empty tray aside and snuggles further beneath the blanket. "There were glasses in the closet."

With a quick nod, Devin disappears down the cabin's steps. He's back within minutes, carrying a bottle of wine and two glasses. Back beneath the blanket, he pops the cork and hands Samantha a glass.

"Thanks." She says, taking a sip. "What is this?"

Devin fills is glass and then examines the label. "A '67 Pinot-Blanc." He says. "Our benefactor has taste."

Samantha takes another sip, imbibing all the flavors of the moment. There is something intoxicating about it all: the moon's soft glow, the shimmer of the sea, the ship's slight sway like the rhythmic rock of a mother's arms, and Devin— sitting so close and, yet, still he can feels so far away. She turns her gaze his way. He's staring up at the sky, *probably at the moon*, she thinks—*he's always had a thing for full moons.*

She turns her face to the sky and grins. "It's beautiful, right? Just takes you away?" Someone once told her that our lives are written in the stars and for some reason she thinks of that now. She closes her eyes and pictures a wise old man with a beard down to his lap sitting in a rustic cabin— Father Time, she supposes—writing the fates of all his characters when he spills a bottle of the purest ink onto his table. Rather than get upset he smiles and calls in his daughter, Little Lady Luck, and has her sprinkle glitter all over his mess. That is what the sky looks like now. Like a child's perfect piece of art.

"Yeah." Devin says. "I was just thinking about how we'd go camping and just lay on our backs, staring up at the stars. You remember? I think we were like 10 or 11 or something. Remember that goat wandered in your tent?" He chuckles. "You were so scared you ran in mines and woke me up."

Samantha chuckles too. "That's not funny." She retorts. "I didn't know what it was and we had been up all night telling scary stories. You know how scary Saka's stories were."

Devin smiles. "I wasn't scared."

Samantha looks at him and rolls her eyes. "Whatever, Superman."

"No, but seriously, it was a *goat*, Sam. A *goat!*" He can't restrain his laughter. He doubles over in a fit of raucousness that Samantha attributes to the wine. Devin doesn't drink very often and he's obviously feeling inebriated. He regains a bit of his composure, just enough to continue. "You ran in my tent like it was going to eat you or something. Remember, you tried to climb in my sleeping bag? Why'd you run in my tent, anyway?"

"Why do you *think?*" She slugs him in the arm. "You were supposed to protect me, that's why. Saka was off meditating somewhere and you were all I had left."

"Oh, yeah. Saka was gone. Remember when we peeked out? The goat was in Saka's tent."

Samantha pours herself another glass of wine and takes a sip. "You know, Devin, I was so scared that night. Really. I didn't know it was a goat and I thought that whatever it was it was going to come and get us next." She takes another sip and gazes deeply into Devin's eyes. "But you were there. You held me all night until I stopped shaking. You even gave me your sleeping bag."

Devin smirks. "I didn't have a choice. That goat ate yours."

"You could've let me sleep in the cold." She points out.

He smirks again. "Naw, I could never do that, Sam."

There is an attraction in their eyes, pulling them deeper into each other's gaze. The connection is palpable, magnetic; it is as if the entire universe desires their union. Neither of them can feel themselves leaning forward and even if they did they wouldn't pull back.

Their lips touch softly at first, a delicate meeting that Samantha savors. Devin's lips taste sweet on hers, bathed in the fragrant wine, and she can smell its sweet aroma on his breath. She parts her mouth invitingly and feels the warmth of his tongue on her own. She can feel her body shifting now, giving in to its desires as it slowly descends towards the deck.

Devin is atop her; his hands exploring her breasts, her waist, and her thighs. His fingers find the clasp on her belt and unhook it. A sigh of anticipation escapes Samantha's lips. He finds the button of her jeans in between kisses. He slips it through the hole in the fabric and kisses her again.

"No." Samantha says and pushes him back. "Stop. Not like this."

Devin hesitates, confused. "Wha—what's wrong, Sam? Did I do something wrong?"

She sits up and Devin moves aside. Befuddled, he gazes out at the water, not sure what to say. Beside him, Samantha too gazes out at the sparkling sea, just as confused as he. *What if this is a mistake,* she thinks. She's wanted this for so long now she has to be sure. She can't—no she won't—let this be another prom night. She has to know that he'll be there in the morning.

She stands and her hair shimmers as it dances in the cool breeze. Devin looks up at her, bathed in the moonlight's radiance. She's beautiful, more beautiful than any woman Devin has ever seen. She looks down at him with eyes like pools of jade.

"Come on." She says.

Devin doesn't hear her. He's too lost in her splendor. But whatever he did—"Hey, Sam." He says. "I'm uhh...sorry, you know."

"Sorry? No, Devin, it's not you. Not now. It's just—"

"I'm sorry for not noticing just how gorgeous you really are. You know, I make jokes but, right now, Sam, you look so much like your mother. Like that picture that Saka kept by his bed. I just—"

"Devin." She says, reaching out to him. "Stop talking and just come on."

Grinning, Devin sets the glass on the deck beside him and takes Samantha's hand. The two of them head down the stairs and into a cabin.

"I'm going to take a quick shower." She says. "It's been a long day and I need to get out of these clothes." She flashes Devin a coy grin and disappears into the bathroom. Undressing hurriedly, she pulls her shirt over her head and wiggles out of her jeans. She doesn't want to leave

Devin wanting for too long but she needs everything to be perfect.

The shower's spray is just the right temperature—*a sign,* she thinks-- stepping beneath the warm stream. There's lavender body wash in the receptacle hanging from the shower curtain rod— another sign that this is meant to be. She squeezes a copious amount onto the wash towel and the soothing aroma of lavender wafts through the room. She smiles as she washes, absorbed in the surrealism of the moment—a moment that she still can't believe is actually happening. She thought this day would never come and now that it is here, it feels...*right.*

Feeling refreshed, she reaches out from under the mist, grabs a towel off of the rack, and shuts off the water. There is a mirror above the sink, just big enough for her to check herself from the waist up. She has always had a nice body (at least that's what she's been told) and she works out regularly—she twists around trying to get a glimpse at her backside—but Devin is used to supermodels. Will she be enough?

She wraps the towel around her breasts and looks at herself again. *Should I just go out naked,* she thinks, and then decides against it. It's just not her style. She isn't some vixen and Devin isn't just some hunk. This isn't a fling. This is the love of her life.

Okay, she tells herself. *This is it.* She takes a deep breath, smelling the fading lavender, and opens the door.

"Sleep?" She says. She can't believe it. Devin is lying on the bed shirtless and slightly snoring. It must be the wine, she supposes. "I know I didn't take that long." Shaking her head she discards the towel, slides on a t-shirt and panties, climbs into the bed and snuggles close. She can feel his strong chest through the thin t-shirt. Aroused, she wiggles back against him, hoping to rouse him and resume their plans. Partially awakened, Devin wraps his arms around her and pulls her back into him. His body feels so good pressed against hers— like two puzzle pieces, she thinks, and that's good enough for her. She closes her eyes, takes hold of his hand and kisses every one of his fingers.

"Be here when I wake up. Please don't leave me again."

403

CHAPTER THIRTY-SIX

A n all-black AH-64 Apache attack helicopter lands 15 feet from an Afghan rebel camp.

Swirling clouds of sand and dust sail through the stark night air. Ten armed guerillas rush to the site and draw their guns on the unfamiliar aircraft. As anxious as a firing squad they wait, watching the propeller's slow to a still. The bulletproof doors slide open and Gustuv Barchulé exits the craft.

"Tell General al-Yadani I have arrived," he commands, speaking in the local Pushtun tongue, "and tell him that I have brought gifts."

The fighters look on as the helicopter's pilot climbs down and begins to unload several large crates from the back of the chopper. They do not recognize either of these men, though they must be allies, they reason, if the General is expecting them.

"Shoo ismak?" A fighter calls out, seeking the visitor's name.

"Jabril." Gustuv replies, helping his pilot unload the third of five wooden crates. "Tell him that Jabril has come bearing revelation."

The young rebel jogs off into the camp, leaving his comrades to keep an eye on their visitor. Tracing his every movement with their rifles, they follow Gustuv as he unloads the crates.

Gustuv pays the fighters little attention. He knows that they will not shoot unless provoked, and they are smart to do so. Their band of rebels cannot afford to expend valuable ammunition on uncertain threats. Their limited resources will not allow it.

Just as the last crate is unloaded and Gustuv takes a seat atop the box, the rebel fighter returns. "Ta'aal ma'ee!' He says, though it comes out as more of a question than the command it was meant to be.

"Okay." Gustuv replies, rising to his feet. A quick breeze skips over the land and his billowing trousers flap around his stocky legs, slapping against the knee-long shirt he's adorned for this meeting. Gustuv is but a turban short of being a native and if not the seclusion of General al-Yadani's camp he may have even donned the customary head wrap this evening.

Collapsible tents and small camp fires form the aggregation that Gustuv is led through. His eyes dart across the desert terrain, surveying the slumbering encampment. Men of all ages are scattered about, some stealing a few moments rest, others tending to their weapons, the majority staring brazenly at the guest moving amongst them. *Jabril,* they heard him call himself, *the angel responsible for delivering the word of Allah to the Prophet Muhammad (May peace be upon him). What revelation could this old white man bear?*

"In there." Gustuv's escort directs him toward a grandiose tent, the largest of all the dwellings here. "General al-Yadani is waiting for you."

The young fighter standing guard steps aside and allows Gustuv to pass. Gustuv glances back at him and smirks.

Do you know what you are risking your life, his grin asks, *or are you just another sacrificial lamb standing before the altar?*

Though sacrifices must be made, he muses, pulling the tarp aside. *The cost of freedom is blood.*

"As-salaamu Alaykum." He greets, entering the general's

parsimonious chamber.

Gustuv takes a seat across from him and the two men study each other, not from a lack of familiarity but rather from an honored custom. It seems General Mustafa al-Yadani has changed nothing but his title in the past decade that Gustuv has known him. His tawny complexion is still the color of sand and just as coarse. His beard is still as scraggly as the bushes outside the camp, although— Gustuv notices—since becoming leader of the resistance that beard has been overrun by an onslaught of gray hairs.

And he's still cheap, Gustuv observes. The General's unwavering frugality makes it near impossible for him to succumb to the weight gain that typically accompanies such a rise in station or decorate his tent with more than the bare necessities.

A Holy Qur'an resting atop a small table, these two uncomfortable chairs, a flickering lantern, his sleeping bag, an old AK-47, an a tea set; this last item makes him smile. Some things never change.

As if reading Gustuv's mind, General al- Yadani prepares two cups of tea. He pours very carefully, filling the two ceramic teacups just below the rim. He passes one across to Gustuv.

"Wa-alaykum salaam, brother." The General replies. He raises the cup up to his nose and wafts the warm stream toward him, reveling in the sweet aroma of the black Indian tea, imported from one of his favorite *tchani khans.* "Though I am disappointed, Mr. Barchulé. I was told that the archangel Jabril had appeared here and had brought with him divine revelation."

Gustuv takes a sip of his tea. Like always it is very sweet— too sweet actually—but he doesn't mind. The excess sugar is meant to prevent dehydration and loss of energy. "I did not mean to disappoint," he grins, "although I do come bearing revelation."

The General nods. "And gifts, I was told."

"Yes. And gifts." Gustuv takes another sip and sets the cup aside. "But we will get to that in due time. Is not the revelation, in itself, a gift from Allah?"

Annoyed, General al-Yadani sips his tea and waves Gustuv on. Despite Gustuv's extensive knowledge of the Islamic faith, he is still a *kafir* and so the General strives to avoid any unnecessary discussion that could lead one to blaspheme.

"Do not act that way, Mustafa. Just because I have not taken my physical *shahadah* does not mean I lack faith in Allah."

The General takes another sip and peers over the rim of the cup. "You did not come here to discuss issues of faith, Mr. Barchulé." He sets the cup down in front of him. "So let us handle first things first, please?"

Gustuv nods. "Spoken like a wise man." He picks up his cup and finishes off the remainder of the tea before it cools.

"More?" The General offers.

"Please." Gustuv accepts. With his cup once again filled just below the rim he finally reveals the reason for his sudden arrival. "*Shakran.*" He says. "Now, General, I have just recently received news that tomorrow morning the Islamic Republic of Afghanistan—the government that you are currently fighting so vehemently—will be authorizing its military to purchase 5,000 RPGs and 10,000 Soviet AKMs with a million rounds of ammunition. Such a small buy seemed rather suspicious until I thought of your resistance. I reason that they intend to use such an arsenal in a very specific campaign."

General al-Yadani finishes his tea. "Say, for instance, eliminating the rebels that have been burning your poppy fields."

"Exactly." Gustuv smirks. "But that is not all."

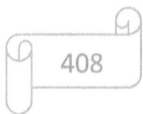

The General's solemn countenance grows dimmer still. "What more could there be? If they unify their forces, with that arsenal, the majority of my men will be slaughtered. I know that my troops will fight but if I send them to a certain death then I am more of a murderer than those we are resisting."

"Heavy is the head that wears the crown, Mustafa. You knew this when you assumed the position."

Dejected, General al-Yadani shakes his head and sighs. "What more do you have to tell me, Mr. Barchulé?"

"I am no longer sure." Gustuv sneers, disgusted by the General's cowardice. "It is of no import if you have already conceded?"

"Conceded." He spits the word out like a taste of spoiled milk. "I do not *concede*, Mr. Barchulé. If I did our dealings would have ceased long ago."

Gustuv is not impressed by his bluster. "You look as if you have been defeated, General; as if you know that your end is imminent and are merely waiting for the sword to fall upon your neck."

Gustuv's words spark a fire inside of the General and as it rages it engulfs him with a burning desire to show his guest exactly how much fight he has left. To concede defeat before the battle has begun is to be a coward and as an Afghan warrior, a coward is a thing that Mustafa al-Yadani can never be.

"Let me tell you about my people, Mr. Barchulé. We have a saying: *if glory is to be found in the jaws of a lion, go tear it out of his mouth. You will have prestige and honors. If you fail, die like a man.* Do you understand? This is what I believe. The tradition of my people does not even permit a coward to be buried properly, Mr. Barchulé and do you know why this is?'

Gustuv knows exactly why this is so but he shakes his head nonetheless. "No." He lies. "Why is that?"

"Because then the coward cannot reach paradise, Mr. Barchulé. I fear nothing but Allah. I am fighting to free my people from the corruption and oppression that they are under here. Look at the state of my people, my country. In the cities, decrepit buildings fill our skylines; our elders, who should be imparting wisdom to the young, instead stagger about in a drug-induced daze; children, rather than play games, chose to get high, while their parents neglect their duties to do the same. Heroin is destroying my people, Mr. Barchulé. But the men I am fighting against pretend not to see this. All they appear to see is the profit that can be made from exporting the drug. Do you know that my country supplies 80% of the world's heroin, Mr. Barchulé? They see the problems that the drug causes, at home and abroad, but because of their greed they pretend not to notice. They condemn me and my brothers, call us rebels and terrorists, when we are the true patriots, and for what—for burning their poppy fields. These are the men with the power to buy 10,000 new rifles, 10,000 new missiles, and a million bullets to kill off their own countrymen. That money could be used to develop better treatment programs, to build new schools, new hospitals, and roads. These are the men that I am willing to fight to the death, Mr. Barchulé. So, please, for your sake and mine, do not ever again suggest that I am a coward."

Gustuv grins to himself. He has finally found the precious stone he had been digging for. "I am glad that you are not a coward, Mustafa, because, as I said, what I have left to reveal is not for the faint of heart."

General al-Yadani nods. He can feel the rapid thump of his heart beating strongly against his chest. Gustuv's words have excited him and this impromptu flood of adrenaline is mixing with the sugar from his tea, producing an intrinsic euphoria like nothing he has ever experienced. "Mr. Barchulé, you are a learned man. I wonder, are history and politics of any interest to you?"

A sly smirk spreads across Gustuv's face. The General notices but mistakes it for interest. "Without knowledge of where we have been we cannot know where we are, therefore we cannot know where we need to go, General. So, yes, history is a favored discipline. As for politics, due to the nature of my business, I stay abreast of what I must."

"That is understandable. If you truly care whose hands your weapons fall into."

"It is my responsibility." Gustuv retorts. "And I do not shy from my responsibilities. Only those who I desire to have my weapons, have them."

The General nods. "Now, the reason that I asked about history is because I would like to share some historical precedents for what is happening in my country today. If you have the time to listen."

"Go on, Mustafa." Gustuv says and, with a knowing grin, listens as the General compares the Iran-Contra affair that plagued the Reagan Administration to the situation currently troubling Afghanistan.

"And it has happened in other countries." He continues. "The Opium Wars in China, for instance. Corrupt governments are sacrificing their own people to make a profit." General al-Yadani glances at the Qur'an sitting on the table. "You can only worship one Lord, Mr. Barchulé, and it seems that the world has chosen the dollar as its Almighty."

Gustuv nods. "You do not have to plead your case to me,

Mustafa. I know well what motivates your cause. I support your struggle. I, too, understand the fallacies of the world's governing bodies. I supply your resistance with as many arms as I can spare, at virtually no profit, for I *do* understand that the age of reason has passed and the time for action is now. Your movement is but one of many more to come, all throughout the Earth, if true change is to be brought forth."

"Ishallah, Mr. Barchulé. Without your arms we would not have made much progress—your arms and your aid. Your hand may be what tips the scales in this war of attrition."

Gustuv smirks. "Which brings me to my gift."

Guerilla warfare is as old as man. Traditionally, it is characterized by the avoidance of frontal assaults in exchange for surprise attacks and the repeated harassment of enemy forces. Politically, guerilla movements have been the rebellious response of a desperate and despondent proletariat class seeking reformation— at times, revolution—of an oppressive system. Whether the war is one of religious uprising, peasant revolt, or resistance to foreign occupation, it is never manpower that guerilla movements lack, but weaponry. And on today's technological battlefield, modern munitions can mean victory or defeat.

"Come with me, Mustafa. I have something to show you."

The general follows Gustuv out of the tent and through the encampment. The young fighters watch their leader in awe as he moves amongst them. A man of adamantine principle, ardent convictions, and Herculean will, General al-Yadani's rule is one of mutual respect and reciprocated trust, gained not through force, but by his character and merit alone.

A man after my own heart, Gustuv thinks. He and the general come to a clearing about 15 feet outside the camp. Rebel fighters are still standing guard with their weapons fixed on Gustuv's pilot. The pilot sits on a crate, smoking a cigarette, unabated.

He looks up. "About time." He says, flicking the cigarette into the darkness as he hops down. "These guys aren't great hosts."

General al-Yadani takes notice of the five crates. "What is this? IS this your gift, Mr. Barchulé?"

Gustuv nods. "A resistance must first have the ability to resist."

"Ishmail." The General calls to a young soldier. "You and Akbar, see what Allah has blessed us with."

The two fighters jog over to the crates and that pilot hands them two crowbars. They pry open the first lid and dig into the box. What they find is enough to make them cry out in jubilation.

Five hundred brand new M-16 assault rifles with one hundred thousand rounds of armor- piercing ammunition fill the crate. They wave one towards the General. He steps to the side and turns to Gustuv.

"Thank you, Mr. Barchulé, but I have to ask, what is your price?"

"Have them open the other containers first, General. Then we will negotiate a reasonable recompense."

General al-Yadani relays the orders to his men and they start prying the lids off the remaining four crates. None of them speak as they unload the contents, amassing a pile of ordinances beyond any they have ever seen. With the crates now emptied, they step back and take in the mass.

Fifteen rocket launchers, a hundred frag grenades, fifty Claymore mines, ten RPGs and six cruise missiles.

"Mr. Barchulé," the General cannot believe his eyes; Allah has truly favored their cause, "with this...we---"

"Your resistance can resist." Gustuv smirks. "And maybe your movement can grow. You need to be the one leading this country, General, and I think your men will agree with me. We need you to lead Afghanistan into the light."

Cheers of support erupt from the crowd that has now formed. General al-Yadani smiles at the display. He had never considered such a thing as him running for President; his aspirations have always been to help the people.

And I could help so many, bring about so much change, if were the President. Imagine what I could do—

The roar of an engine drowns out his thoughts and a hard wind kicks up dust into the air. Shielding his face he gazes skyward. A helicopter is attempting to land not far from them. The rebels immediately take aim.

"It is mine." Gustuv says, checking the time on his watch. "My ride."

General al-Yadani orders his men to lower their guns and then turns back to Gustuv. "I don't understand, Mr. Barchulé. You have this helicopter here."

"That is my gift, General. What did you think those missiles were for? And as recompense goes, if you ever to make it to office, General, just be the man we all need you to be."

The General shakes Gustuv's hand. "That I will do, Mr. Barchulé."

"Good-bye friend." Gustuv says. He climbs inside the helicopter and the General watches him fly off. He doesn't notice that Gustuv has left his plot behind until the man comes marching up.

"General." He says. "Sergeant John Burgundy. American Air Force. Served two tours in Iraq. Paratrooper, pilot, tactics, pretty

much can do it all, sir. Mr. Barchulé is a friend of mine. He thought you might need some help training and organizing your men."

He glances back to the attack chopper. "And somebody has to learn how to fly that thing."

CHAPTER THIRTY-SEVEN

How long has it been since My Little Secret escaped to the sea; since the hawser was freed and she voyaged out into the endless waters she was built to explore? Long enough that all of the dockworkers have grown accustomed to her sitting in the harbor, rocking back and forth like a depressed dowager. They even have changed her name from My Little Secret to the apt Old Maid.

But today will be different. The Old Maid's husband has finally returned and as he approaches her hull glistens for him welcomingly. Curious glances follow the forgotten fellow—once a slim and strong young man—now stout and sagacious in his old age.

He climbs aboard the vessel and the boat rocks slightly. He looks to the sky and sighs. It feels good to be on the deck once again, staring out at an endless horizon. His khakis and windbreaker flap in the cool breeze and he stands still for a moment, taking it all in: the chop of the waves against the hull, the ship's responsive sway, the squawk of soaring seagulls, the smell of salt in the air; he's transported to another time—a better time.

In that brief moment the old man is able to forget what it is that brought him back here after so many years but then, like a rude patron cutting the line, reality comes, shoving all other thoughts away as it rushes to the forefront of his mind. And so he moves, as quickly as his old bones will allow, down the cabin steps and into the sleeping quarters. A bare-chested man lies on the bed, snoring lightly and he can hear the faint sound of a woman singing to herself in the bathroom. *And she's not too bad, actually.*

He moves toward the man, certain that this is the one he is looking for. "Sir." He says, leaning in close. "Sir. Please wake up, sir."

He reaches out for the stranger's shoulder, hoping to stir him to life. His fingers graze the man's skin and the stranger's eyes shoot open.

Moving on instinct, Devin brings his right leg up and drives his foot into the old man's burly chest. He's up and standing over him before the old man can even register what just happened.

"Who are you?!" He demands to know.

"I'm—I'm Dr. Bauer." The old man replies, somehow managing to smile in spite of the throbbing pain in his sternum. "This is my boat, sir. I am the one that invited you here."

"What?" Devin gawks, dumbfounded. He doesn't believe him; he *can't* believe him. "The Doc's dead, old man. I saw his body. Try again."

The old man closes his eyes and his smile fades. "Yes. I know that, Mr. King. Kurt is my—was my son."

What?! Devin can't hide his shock. There is no way that the man lying on the floor—this gray- haired, stoutly built, *black* man—is Dr. Kurt Bauer's father. The more he thinks about the absurdity of the claim the angrier Devin grows. *He must think I'm an idiot.*

He snatches the man up by his collar and slams him into the closet door. "Who are you?" Devin asks again. The tone of his voice carrying a subtle warning: *tell me the truth or die.*

The old man looks on with begging eyes but Devin's glare

only intensifies and he shoves the man against the door again. "This is the last time I'm asking—who... are...you?"

The bathroom door swings open and a half- naked Samantha steps out. "What's going on?" She asks. Her gaze shifts from Devin to the old man he has pinned against the wall. "Who is he? Devin, what's going on?"

"I'm Dr. Bauer." The man says, hoping that she will be more reasonable than her beau here. "You must be Samantha. My son told me that you're beautiful. He was not wrong."

"Son?" Samantha parrots. "Who's your son?" She looks to Devin again. "What's he talking about?"

Devin sighs, exasperated. "He says Kurt's his father."

Samantha chuckles. The idea that this man could be Kurt Bauer's father is so ridiculous that Samantha can't help herself. Other than the undeniable fact that Kurt is white and this man is obviously of African ancestry, he and Kurt do not share any similarities—Kurt's eyes were gray, this man's are dark brown; Kurt was tall and slender, this man is small and compact; and, well, he's *black* and Kurt's *white.*

"Exactly." Devin says, throwing the man to the ground. "He's lying. He brought us here to set us up." He glares down at the stranger, whoever the hell he is, and his eyes glow like fire. "You're working for The Elite, aren't you? Are they on their way here now?"

The old man struggles to stand and Devin throws him back to the ground. Unabated, he grins and begins to rise again. There is something about the man's lack of anger that just doesn't make sense. *He should be resisting a little, right? Even if he's not setting us up. Who just grins through this? Is he a masochist or something?*

Devin throws the old man down again but this time Samantha moves to help him up. Devin grabs her by the arm. "Go put some clothes on, Sam. We don't need this guy having a heart attack before he tells us who he really his."

Samantha looks down at herself and blushes. In all the confusion she had forgotten that all she's wearing is a bra and panties. "Yeah, uhh...okay. I'll be right back. Don't do anything, okay?"

Devin nods and she disappears into the bathroom. He turns his attention back to the old guy and watches as he struggles to his feet. "Those old bones aching?" He teases. "If you keep lying, I'm going to do a lot more than just shove you around. Understand?"

The old man grins and looks towards the bathroom. "I can see why my son was so taken with her." He says. "She is a very attractive woman."

In her rush to get dressed, Samantha has left the door slightly ajar. Devin looks through the opening and watches her wriggle into a tight pair of cargo shorts, admiring her fit form. *She still looks the same way she did in high school.* He grins as she pulls her hair back. *All the way to the ponytail.*

He turns back to the old man. "Yeah, I guess. But we're talking about you, not Sam."

"I told you already, son. I'm Dr. Bauer. Kurt was my son."

Samantha strolls out of the bathroom, pulling a tank-top down over her head. "I think I remember

Kurt saying something to me about his father before but he never said that you were *black*."

Moving cautiously, the man steps around Devin and takes a seat on the edge of the bed. "He never does. It's not that he's ashamed, he just...he forgets that it is not as normal as he thinks." He pauses. "Well *thought*. Kurt was adopted, you see."

"Adopted?" Devin can't believe this guy. "I didn't even

know that there were black people *in* Latvia. Not to mention adopting *white* kids.'"

"Devin!" Samantha slugs him in the arm. "You sound like a racist. You didn't know Latvia existed last week; of course you didn't know there are black people here.'

"It's okay." The man grins. "Let me explain a few things first and then maybe you will understand why it is I called you here."

Skeptical, Devin leans against the wall and folds his arms. "Go ahead. I'm listening."

"Well, my grandparents were slaves in America." He begins. "Like most slaves, they dreamed of escaping to Europe where the trade had been abolished and racism was not as harsh. Unlike most, though, my grandparents got their chance. When they were still young my grandmother, being light enough to pass and able to read, claimed my grandfather as her servant, and the two of them snuck aboard a ship headed to London. Soon after landing there, my grandfather found work as a blacksmith and later became a successful entrepreneur, owning not just his business but his house and land as well."

He stops to survey his audience. Devin stares on, unconvinced. "You have to keep in mind that this was beyond imaginable for two former slaves. They felt that they owed their prosperity to Europe and so, when the Great War came knocking, my grandfather aided the Allies, using his skills to help produce munitions. Knowing how badly his father wanted to fight, he enlisted in World War II. When the war was over, he took my mother as his bride and the two of them moved here. Latvia's is my mother's native land, she had only left to be a nurse in the war, and with her family's wealth she helped turn the business that Grandfather Bauer had started into a major manufacturing company."

"So your mother was rich?" Devin asks.

"My mother was a *kulak*, son—a wealthy Latvian that opposed the Soviet rule of their country. I recall being very young and fearing that my family might be deported to be Siberia. It had happened to many of my mother's friends."

"But you weren't?" Samantha asks.

"No. We were lucky. My family was able to avoid the deportation and remained in Riga. Though, I admit, growing up in Riga didn't feel very lucky. Having my father's complexion in a society where the minorities were criminalized more every day, I was often teased and taunted by the school children. Understand, the Latvian army had participated in the Jewish Holocaust and some of that institutional prejudice was still extant. When I was a child an extensive program was instituted limiting the use of my mother's tongue in favor of the new official language of Russian. A lot of the minority schools were schools were closed, leaving only two languages to be taught: Latvian and Russian.

This is where the seed that blossomed into my love for language was first planted. My mother had told me that when you lose your language, you lose your culture, and eventually, you lose yourself. It was the same thing that happened to my father's people in America, she told me."

"You mean, like, during slavery." Devin thinks back to his own mother and the similar feelings she had expressed. "The indoctrination phrase. My mother used to tell me about that."

He nods. "Yes, son, and as I grew older I always wondered why someone would desire to destroy another people's history, identity—their entire culture. I dedicated my entire life to the search actually."

Devin isn't sure what the old man's trying to tell them and

he's been going on for a while now. It's getting annoying. It's time to get to the point. "What the hell are you talking about?" He asks. "I mean, okay, cool story. And let's say that Kurt is your son.

What does any of that have to do with why you called us here?"

The doctor looks surprised. "Oh. I'm sorry, son. I thought it was presumable enough." He stands up and offers Devin's his hand. "I am Oliver Bauer, arguably the world's best linguist and a self-taught student of the occult. I am here to help you in this mystery."

"Occult?" Devin laughs. "Like witches and pentagrams and stuff?"

Dr. Bauer grins. "That is the common idea, isn't it? The world 'occult' *actually means something hidden or concealed from plain view.* It derives from the Latin 'occultus,' the past participle of 'occulre,' which itself is made of the verb 'celare' or 'celo' meaning to conceal or hide."

He glances at the satchel sticking out from beneath Devin's pillow. "My son was translating an ancient text for you, correct? He had reached out to me for help before he was murdered. I take it that's it there?"

"You're Poppa Doc." Samantha says. "I should have known. Kurt had told me his father was the reason he went into linguistics."

"Yes." The doctor nods, looking towards Devin. "Parents do have a way of influencing their children's paths, don't they?"

"Tell me about it." Devin replies. "My parents were always trying to—"

"Not you." Bauer cuts in. "I meant your mother, Jacqueline St. Clair."

"Mrs. King?" Lines of confusion wrinkle Samantha's brow. "What would Devin's grandparents have to do with this? Mom just found this stuff a few months ago."

Dr. Bauer grins. "Do either of you know how to sail a boat? It's been a long time since I have taken the old girl out."

Devin and Samantha exchange knowing glances. "Yeah, I know how to sail." Devin answers. "But what were you saying about my Mom and my grandparents?"

"Soon enough, son. You'll learn more about your family than you would probably like to, I guarantee. It is times of trial that teach you who really cares; in triumph the world is your family."

Devin stares at him skeptically. "And you care, huh?"

"Soon enough, son, you'll have your answers."

Dr. Bauer's cryptic response only leaves Devin with more questions. He presses on until the doctor begs him to stop.

"Let an old man enjoy an evening on the water before we dive into this, please. Come. Join me up on the deck." He offers an assuring smile and heads up the stairs. Devin and Samantha hang back.

"So what do you think?" Devin asks her. "You trust him?"

Samantha shrugs. "I think he is actually Kurt's father and he did help us out yesterday. Not to mention that he's really the only choice that we have right now."

Devin nods. "But he seems crazy or something. And what do you think he knows about my family?"

Before Samantha can respond Dr. Bauer's deep voice comes bellowing down the stairs. "Come on up!" He shouts. "I need some help with the moorings."

Samantha smirks. "Come on, Devin. Let's go help him. This whole situation is crazy. Crazy might be just what we need."

Devin nods. "Hope you're right, Sam. 'Cus he's definitely crazy."

The two of them head up the stairs laughing to themselves. Halfway up, Devin realizes that he's left the satchel. He goes to get it off the bed and then joins the others on the deck.

"Couldn't leave this unattended." He says, motioning to the strap now draped across his chest.

Dr. Bauer looks up from his work. "Are you sure that you do not have any idea of what it is that you possess there?"

Devin grabs one of the thick ropes tying the ship to the dock. "Just that it's old and obviously valuable."

The doctor grins. "Then you have good instincts, son. Protect that scroll with your life."

"Is it really that valuable?" Samantha asks. "No." The doctor smirks. "It's priceless."

CHAPTER THIRTY-EIGHT

R iga is not a very violent city and—with the Red Mafia controlling the underworld—what a blessing that is.

The Police Chief has been doing a lot of that lately—counting his blessings. Sitting behind his desk, he contemplates the relatively smooth career that he's had thus far. A glass of vodka sits to his right, directly beside a stack of documents relating to an open murder case. He raises the glass to his lips and downs the tonic.

Why am I even thinking about the Mafia now, he wonders. *Those idiots are the least of my problems.*

Late last night the Chief received an unexpected call from a fellow Mason. He was told that a brother would be requiring further assistance in tracking a fugitive and was asked to aid him however possible. He agreed and the caller—to his surprise—guaranteed that he would surely be rewarded for his service. Too tired to think much of it, he simply hung up the phone and went back to sleep.

When he finally did make time to think about it, he assumed that by "reward" the caller meant that the reciprocal nature of the Grand Architect's design would return his act of service with good peace of mind and fulfillment. He never expected that a briefcase with $50,000 and a note would be waiting outside of his door this morning.

He fishes the note from his desk drawer again and reads it again.

*You have proven yourself a useful brother. Enjoy the fruits
of your labor and be always ready to aid in the building of
Solomon's Temple. We will speak again soon.*
    -W.F. 33°

He looks at the stack of documents on his desk. This mass
makes up everything that his office has been able to find on Dr.
Kurt Bauer, a recently decreased college professor. Most of this
information the lead inspector—Guntinsky—has already seen; most
but not all.

"Do I impede the inspector's work to aid a brother?" The
Chief asks himself or maybe the Universe. He looks at the stack
of documents again and sighs in exasperation. "Or do I follow the
suggestion of the mysterious W.F.?"

He finishes his vodka as he waits for the Universe to give
him an answer. None comes and he pours himself another glass.
"A man with the ability to give away $50,000 would not have much
trouble punishing me for disobeying orders, would he?" He waits
for an answer. "But were they really orders? No true Mason would
force another brother to behave unjustly. Certainly not one who has
attained to the glorious 33°."

The Chief throws back the vodka and yells for his assistant.
While he waits for her to appear he removes a few documents from
the stack and sets them aside. His assistant pokes her head through
the door.

"Yes sir?"

"I need you to take these files here," he places his hand on
the stack of documents, "make copies, and send them to Inspector
Guntinsky. When you're finished with that, I need you to bring me
those copies. I have a few papers to add to them and then I need you
to hand deliver those to that detective from the Dominican Republic—

James Clarkson."

She nods. "Okay sir. What's the address?"

"Just take care of his first and I'll have the address for you when it's done."

"Okay." She says. She walks into the office and grabs the stack off his desk. "I'll let you know when I'm ready for that address. This shouldn't take long."

The Chief pours himself another shot as he watches his secretary carry the stack of papers away. It feels like a weight is being lifted from his chest.

"Better safe than sorry."

TRUE KING

CHAPTER THIRTY-NINE

There is a smile on Dr. Bauer's face as he stands behind the wheel of My Little Secret, steering her farther out into the Gulf of Riga.

Lost in the calm sway of the sea, he fails to notice the impatient glare on Devin's face. In his mind he's back in a better time—a time when he, Kurt , and Sophia would sail out, anchor the ship and scuba-dive in the Gulf's cool waters.

"Come on, Doc." Devin blurts out. "We don't have time to be sitting around watching the seagulls. Can you help us figure out what this thing says or not?"

"Devin!" Samantha shrieks. "Don't be rude."

"No. He's right dear. It is time that we drop anchor. I did not invite you here to go diving." Dr. Bauer kills the engine and the ship cruises to a stop. "I called you here because I believe my son would have wanted me to help you."

He flips a switch on the panel and the clanging of gears can be heard below. There is a sudden jerk as the anchor strikes ground, tethering them in place. "Come." He says, moving from the wheel to a small table in the corner of the room. There are rolled up maps in containers on the floor and an encased map of the Gulf of Riga posted on the wall. "This is usually where me and Kurt would plot the day's course. I guess it's only right that you spread the scroll out here."

431

"Why is it '*only right*,'?" Samantha asks.

Devin also wants to know what that was supposed to mean. "And don't give us any of that '*in due time*' stuff, either. We need to know exactly what we're dealing with."

"Okay." Dr. Bauer nods. "But before I tell you what I *think*, let us have a look at this text and see what I *know*."

With a reluctant nod, Devin unscrews the satchel's lid and, very carefully, slides the scroll out onto the table. Samantha begins to unroll it.

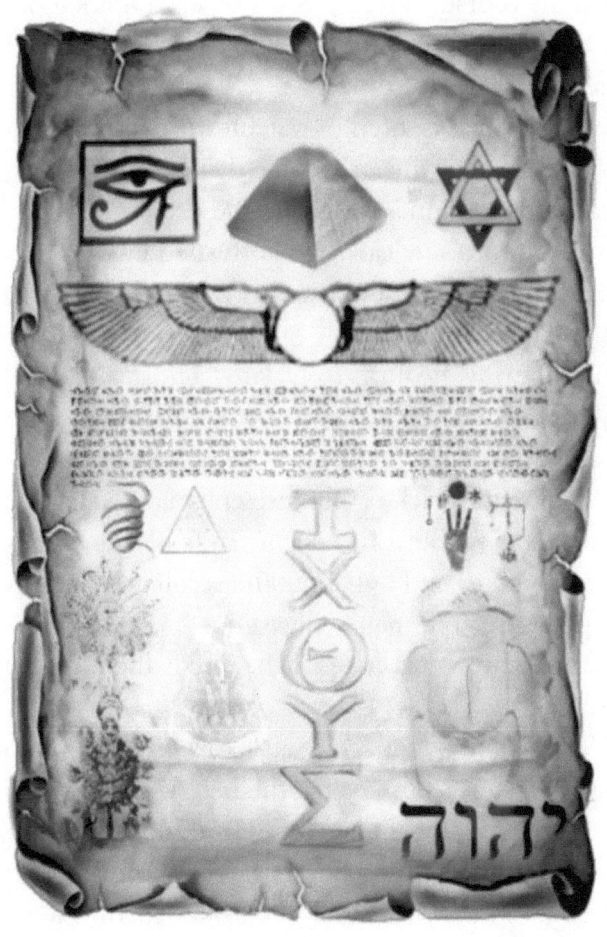

A myriad mixture of signs and symbols from schools long
forgotten—nations of antiquity whose work laid the cornerstone
for every modern marvel— sit before the doctor now. He runs his
fingers along the coarse papyrus, caressing each mark tentatively.
Devin and Samantha are waiting for him to say something but all he
can manage is a reverent, "Wow."
"Okay, Doc." Devin says, tired of watching the old man drool.
"What is this thing and why are people dying for it?"

Dr. Bauer continues to stare at the text, astounded by the
multiplicity of messages he can see intertwined into one document.
Whoever authored such an intricate work would have surely been
a member of The Mysteries, he is certain of it. *Could this really be
it?* Grinning shrewdly, he turns to Devin. "Those are actually two
different questions, son, though I do believe that the former shall
cover the latter."

Devin is getting sick of all these enigmatic statements and
open-ended answers. If anyone is being rude it's the Doctor, not
him. They are here to find out about the scroll and find his mother's
killers; not play some old man's silly game.

Devin releases a frustrated sigh. "Okay then, Doc. What's
the former?"

"Well, I can't say for sure. I just have my assumptions."

Devin grits his teeth. "What the hell do you *know*, Doc?
Please! Just give me a straight answer before I lose my mind. No
assumptions, no riddles. Just tell me what you *know!*"

"Well..." The doctor swallows. "Okay then." He takes a pair
of reading glasses from his pocket, puts them on, and takes a seat
in front of the scroll. "I am certain that it is a scarab, an Egyptian
beetle. Below it, that's Hebrew. It means Yahweh or Jehovah. The
Tetragrammaton, it's called. Above the scarab, well... those symbols

above the fingers would make me assume it is—"

"No." Devin stops him. "No assumptions, Doc. Not now. Right now just stick to the facts."

Samantha slugs Devin in the arm. "Let him work his own way. You don't—"

Devin stops her too. "His way doesn't lead anywhere, Sam." He looks back to Bauer. "Go on, Doc."

"Well, that there." The doctor points to the symbols to the left of the scarab. "That is a Greek word for 'fish.' Inside that tree, those are zodiac signs. The main body of text is definitely cuneiform— Babylonian or Sumerian. I cannot tell without further examination. And the rest are symbols—the pyramid and capstone; the rose and cross; the hexagram; the tetracyts; the eye of Heru. Symbols have various layers of meaning."

Samantha nods along but as she watches the doctor she can't shake the feeling that he's not telling them everything. The question is: is it because of Devin's impatience or something else? If it's something else, then what? Can they really trust him?

"Do you know what any of these symbols mean?" She asks. "Or the cuneiform—can you translate it?"

Dr. Bauer looks up at Devin then back to Samantha. "Well, I have an idea about some of those symbols. As far as the cuneiform is concerned, I'll have to translate that at home."

Devin shakes his head. *This guy is just not getting it*, he thinks. *Like father like son.* "You know, we might not have that kind of time, Doc. The Elite could be watching us right now."

"Yes, you've mentioned them before—The Elite. What do you know of The Elite, son?"

He shrugs. "I just know they're the ones responsible for all this. And I know you know who they are, at least you've heard of them. When I first brought them up you didn't even flinch."

"True indeed." Dr. Bauer nods. "True indeed." He
turns his attention back to the scroll and its markings. A look of
recognition dawns on his face. Samantha sees it.

"What is it?" She asks.

"It is everything, dear. The scarab, for instance. It is the
symbol of Khepera—"

"Khepera-Ptah." Devin cuts in. "Yeah, Kurt told us about
the beetle and the Egyptian Jesus."

"Right," Bauer responds, "but then there is this circle on its
back with a vertical diameter." He points to the circle encompassing
the beetle's shell. "That is one of the oldest symbols known to man.
It is part of a trinity."

Samantha nods. She has heard of the trinity before. "Like
Father, Son, and Holy Ghost?" She confirms.

Dr. Bauer smiles. "Not exactly, dear. A trinity is technically
any unit of three. This trinity consists of three phases represented by
three symbols." He looks to Devin. "Can you hand me that pad and
pen, please?"

There is a small notepad and an old fountain pen sitting on
a counter. Devin retrieves them and hands them to the doctor. Dr.
Bauer takes them and quickly sketches three pictures.

TRUE KING

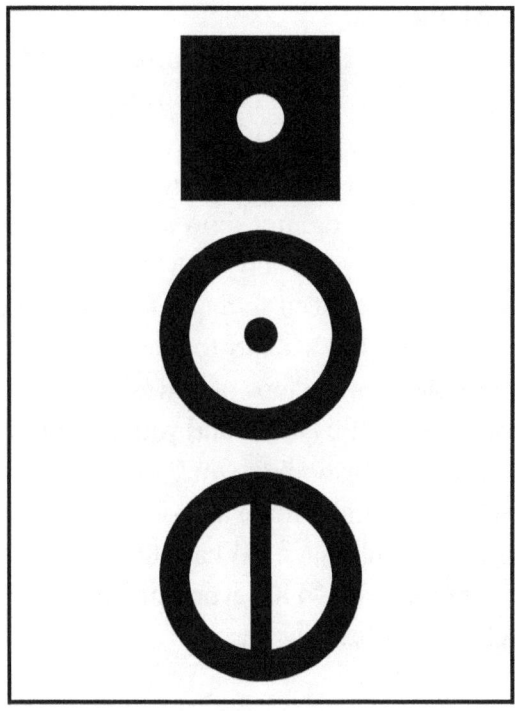

"The first symbol is a circle surrounded by darkness on all sides." He explains. "It is left white to contrast against the darkness it is within, to show its luminescence. That circle is meant to represent God in his first state as an all-powerful, yet still dormant, slumbering, life energy. The darkness that encompasses it is the womb of space, the Universal Mother."

Devin looks on in disbelief. *Slumbering gods, wombs in space—Stan The Man couldn't have wrote it any better.* "You serious, Doc?"

Dr. Bauer expected some skepticism. Actually he would be more worried if Devin did not show any resistance. The nature of God is a subject worthy of deep thought. Throughout history many lives have been sacrificed so that humanity can enjoy spiritual liberty. To not exercise one's ability to reason on such matters would be to trample upon billions of graves.

"Before I continue, Devin, and you too, Samantha, one thing must be accepted by both of you."

Devin and Samantha share a curious glance.

"Okay." Samantha says. "What's that?"

The doctor smirks. "That everything that you think you know about God is probably wrong."

CHAPTER FORTY

D r. Bauer had assumed that he was speaking to Christians. With close to two billion Christians in the world, it is a logical assumption but an untrue one nonetheless. For Devin and Samantha—who are far more spiritual than "religious"—the notion that their conception of God may not be accurate has the impact of a fly's fist punching an elephant's hide. They respond with a dry, "Okay."

Grinning, Dr. Bauer continues. "This trinity relays the story of creation. All life began in darkness; the universal womb. The Egyptians saw this as the primeval waters of Nun. That first symbol, the bright circle surrounded by darkness, is the Creator first becoming aware of Itself. In one of Egypt's creation tales, the priests of Khemenu say that Tehuti, the god of wisdom, was hidden within the primeval waters of Nun. Using his serpent- wound staff, Tehuti stirred this swirling vortex of energy and called forth light. True to the nature of the ibis bird—whose head he is often depicted as having—Tehuti then peered inside Nun and saw the potential that lied within. He saw four pairs of opposites, eight gods all twisted together; the males taking the form of frogs and the females of snakes."

Devin laughs. "Frogs and snakes? Really?"

Bauer nods. "See, to the ancients, the snake was hardly ever a symbol of evil as it is today. Serpent worship, in some form, has been found all over the globe. Moses raised he brazen serpent in the wilderness. The Hindu goddess Kundalini, which literally means *'coiled one,'* is depicted as a snake. The Gnostic Agathodaimon was symbolized by a snake. There are also the North American serpent mounds and the carved stone snakes of Central and South America. Scandinavia had the Migard snake. India revered the hooded cobra. I could continue on and on. Personally, I believe it is a misunderstanding of Christendom's Garden of Eden tale that is to blame for all of the ophiciophobia plaguing the world today."

Devin vaguely recalls his mother telling him something similar. "You mean, how the devil became a snake a tricked Eve into eating a forbidden apple, right? Then she gave the apple to Adam and he ate it, and because of that now all people must die."

"And all women have labor pains."Samantha adds. "Patriarchal misogynistic propaganda."

Dr. Bauer holds back his laughter. "Yes, that is the common misconception. When the tale is understood to be more symbolic than literal, though, a much deeper and far more profound meaning—and certainly more rational than walking talking snakes—presents itself. But I am getting off of topic."

Samantha would like to hear more about the actual meaning of the Garden of Eden story. "It sounds like something that Mom would've told me over a glass of hot chocolate."

The doctor glances at the scroll. "Later, dear. For now let's just say that this first symbol represents God coming into awareness of Itself. With the creation of light, It can now see that he is everywhere and everything. It recognizes Its omnipresent state of being, though he has yet to put it to use.

"This second symbol is the point within the circle." He continues. "At this stage of the story Tehuti stirs up the bubbling cauldron of Nu, bringing forth four pairs of opposites. Tehuti then spoke the word of power—the *heka*—and the cosmic egg exploded, spewing forth all the makings of the universe. It is as if Tehuti, having now seen the potential that lied in the primordial waters had the desire to bring it forth. This desire for self- manifestation is the cause of all existence in the universe."

"Hold on, you said it exploded?" Samantha asks, wondering if he can see the implications of that statement. Somewhere in the recesses of her she always knew that the study of physics would be able to unveil the mystery of the universe. It appears the Egyptians saw this too. "This sounds like the Big Bang, Doctor. All matter was condensed into one vibrating mass of energy and then that mass exploded, expanding rapidly. This explosion—the Big Bang—released various particles that spread out at supersonic speeds, under intense heat and pressure."

"Yes." Dr. Bauer smiles. "It is exactly like the Big Bang. Once the Divine Mind, in this case Tehuti, comes into knowledge of Its omnipresence It then recognizes Its omniscience. Logically if you are all things then you must *know* all things. Notice the four pairs of opposites or eight beings that Tehuti perceives within Nun. The symbol for an eight is but a vertical infinity sign, an ongoing intertwining of spheres, and representative of the limitless nature of the All. This intertwining nature of duality is what allows for creation. All of this is represented by the second symbol, the point within the circle."

The point-atom, Samantha thinks. "Doctor, have you ever heard of a quark?"

His smile grows wider. "Yes, I have, and I am glad that you see the resemblance."

"What are you guys talking about?" Devin asks. All of this scientific mumbo-jumbo is foreign to him. The two of them may as well be speaking Klingon as far as he's concerned.

Now it's Samantha who smiles. "Well, to put it in *layman's terms*," she ribs, "a quark is basically a positively charged sub-atomic particle that, when paired with the negatively charged lepton, can produce anything in the universe. Sometimes it's called the point-atom or a geometrical point."

"Right again." The doctor says. "The next manifestation of that all-powerful force, the Divine Energy polarized into negatives and positives, quarks and leptons, is the point within the circle— the second stage of God's evolution."

"Evolution?" Devin parrots. "So you're saying God evolved, Doc? From what? And then, you're telling us that all of this stuff was already known a hundred thousand years ago? Before any microscopes or computers or anything?"

"I told you that you would have to keep an open mind, son. The evolution that I speak of is not Darwinist. It is simply growth and manifestation. This energy always was and always shall be. It is everything and *no* thing. This is the same energy in the first stage only being manifested differently. You know that water's chemical make-up does not change whether it is in the form of a solid, liquid or gas. Think of this the same way."

"The law of conservation of energy." Samantha mutters.

Dr. Bauer nods to Samantha then turns to Devin. "As far as how the ancients received their knowledge, well, there are a multitude of theories— angels bringing revelations, gods speaking with men, aliens visiting Earth—but what is never disputed is the fact that they *did* know these things to be true. Actually, they may have known a lot more and we are just beginning to catch up."

Samantha runs her fingers across the image of the scarab. "So this symbol here—the one on the scarab's wings—what is this?

It's the last of the trinity?"

"Yes it is. That symbol there represents mankind. See, in the second stage, with the manifestation of quarks and leptons, of duality, came the ability to create. Quarks and leptons create atoms, which in turn create everything else. The second stage is the creation of matter. Man is the perfection of matter; the perfection of atoms. The Divine Mind alive within material substance is seen nowhere to the extent that man displays. This is why the Bible states that man was made in the *image and likeness* of God. We display the same traits as God, namely a free-will. Man is the child of mind and matter."

"Okay, Doc, let me get this straight." Devin says, trying to understand all of this. "You said the first symbol is the self-awareness of God. The next is the desire to manifest, right, and this means duality. And now this last symbol is the perfection of creation, which is man. I don't get it."

Dr. Bauer points to the symbol. "This vertical diameter here, this represents man's upright posture, separating him other animals. Vertical bars also reflect the spiritual or higher parts of reality."

"So then that means that we're all just another manifestation of God, then?" The look of doubt Devin's wears is unmistakable. Yet and still, Dr. Bauer persists.

"I'm only telling you how these symbols are to be interpreted." He replies. "Although my own findings do coincide with that theory."

"Findings?" Samantha asks. "What findings?"

"Take, for instance, the name of the first man in the Bible: Adam. Well, in ancient Egypt, the creator god Atum was also the first man. Atum means self-created; everything and nothing; the all— which is significant because Allah has been said to mean 'All in All.' The word Atum is where the Greeks derived their 'atom,' just as I suspect the god Nun is where we get the word 'none.' Notice it is only the vowels that have been changed. The word Atum is actually spelt A-T-M. The root of A- T-M is T-M, which can either be T-E-M or T-U-M, and it has several different meanings. Two of these are '*completion*' and '*people.*' In the Bible, Adam— the first person—represented the completion of God's work. Then there is the fact that the cognate root of *Tem is Dem*, which means 'to name,' and Adam was also the namer of all the animals. Not only, then, do we have the characteristics of Adam found in the word 'Atum,' the Egyptian God-man, but the name Adam itself is a clue.

Adam is a compound of *AD* and AM. 'AD' is the Syrian name for God and it also means 'holy,' while 'AM' is the ancient *OM*, the unspoken name of God. 'Om' was never uttered unless it was attached to the beginning or ending of another word. So 'Ad-Am' also means 'God am' or 'Holy God.' Adam was a holy god. This could be proof enough that the ancients were attempting to tell us that man was but—as Devin put it—another manifestation of God."

He surveys Devin and Samantha's faces, hoping that are able to accept the truth. These teachings must be grasped if the scroll is what the doctor believes it to be. This knowledge is the only way for them to guard themselves. If he is right then as long as they have the scroll The Elite will stop at nothing to get it. They cannot allow that to happen.

"I guess it makes sense." Samantha says. "It's like art to the artist or, better yet, a child. A child is simply the extension, another manifestation, of their parents. In this case, God. It's like Saka would say, the Tao is All and All is the Tao."

444

It's not that simple for Devin. If man is made in the likeness of God—this all-powerful energy—then he cannot help but wonder why mankind suffers from so many limitations. Humans can't fly, make things appear out of thin air, teleport from place to place or do anything else that might resemble omnipotence. There must be something that he's missing.

"So by placing that circle on the back of the scarab." Dr. Bauer continues. "I am lead to believe the allusion to Atum as a God-man is correct. Also, having the symbol located on the wings may have relevance. Being that the scarab's wings where hidden beneath its shell, the wings represented the soul of man, believed to be hidden with the body, our physical shell."

He points to the four letters beneath the scarab. "Those letters—Yod, He, Vau, He—read from right to left and spell out the name of the Jewish Demiurges, the lord of the material realm. It is the Demiurges that mankind is said to directly descend from. Once again the idea of a God-man shows itself."

All Devin can do is take the doctor's word for it. He has no clue as to what any of these signs may mean. A part of him knows that if he had only spent more time with his parents he would have something to offer. Instead, all Devin has in this intense churning in the innermost part of his being that Dr. Bauer is on to something.

The notion that everything is connected isn't new for him. Since he was a child he has experienced recurring moments of *déjà vu*, vivid dreams that would wind up coming true, amazing feats of strength, or times he could just seem to intuit the right thing to do without thinking. The problem was that if he ever tried to make one of these moments occur on his own, it wouldn't work. Sukamaya had instructed him in the discipline of meditation and that helped some but it has been years since Devin's meditated.

Could I have been tapping into some dormant place—the God within—all along?

He looks to Dr. Bauer. "So, do you believe it, Doc? You think there's a piece of God in us?"

Dr. Bauer smirks. "Son, it doesn't matter what I believe. What really matters is what the rest of these symbols mean. To figure that out, we'll need to go back to my home, my library."

"Is it close?" Samantha asks, worried about the two of them being seen and what my happen to the doctor if he's caught with him. "With everybody looking for us, it may not be safe to be riding around."

"I have a place in the city." He says, rising from his seat. Dr. Bauer moves to the steering panel and raises the anchor.

"Devin, son, if you'll steer, I'll explain to you what it is that I believe."

CHAPTER FORTY-ONE

F encing is a peculiar sport. Technically, it is a combat sport—that of sword fighting—but, unlike the martial arts or boxing, there is no risk of injury in fencing.

The light weighted foil, heavier epée, and saber are tools that are not used to maim but to score points; points that are registered electronically by the protective clothing that each combatant must wear.

Fencing is a lot like politics. The speeches that opponents give, holding no real weight, are like the foil: they are not employed to cause any substantial damage but rather to score points in the minds of voters; points that will later be registered electronically by this and that poll.

Fencing, like politics, has always been the sport of noblemen; a perfect opportunity to reveal one's superior intellect and cunning.

A way for the coward to feel strong, Gustuv thinks as he parries, spins and lands a vicious elbow to his opponent's head. It's an illegal blow, true, but one with a definite purpose. Gustuv is in dire need of a worthy sparring partner. In this past week alone he has had three men come to his mansion for training sessions that were lackluster at best. Sure, they were all proficient swordsmen but only when the rules were in place. The instant that those protective regulations went out of the window so did their courage. One elbow, one punch, or knee is all that it took for them to abandon the fight and cede defeat.

But it seems that today may be the day that he's found what he's looking for.

"Good one." The fighter says, his foil hanging at his side. "Hope you take it as good as you give it."

Gustuv nods and a sinister grin spreads beneath his mask. "We shall see, Alex."

The fighter, Alexander Dumont—a young man in his late twenties—walks to the middle of the mat and readies himself, foil at guard, waiting for Gustuv to be the natural aggressor that he is and make the next move. That elbow shocked him but only because he didn't' expect such an underhanded move from an old guy like Gustuv. He's been making a living helping old rich guys train for about two years now and they're all the same: wealthy aristocrats suffering from delusions of grandeur. They all have a secluded mansion with a vast hall or study that they have had converted into an arena of sorts—complete with scorer's tables, mats and seats for views. Gustuv is no different in that regard. What sets him apart from the others is his edge. None of Alexander's other clients would have ever tried a move like that. This might actually be fun.

Just as Alexander is thinking of fun and games Gustuv fakes a step forward, putting him back on guard. He thrusts his foil quickly, gauging his opponent, feeling him out, waiting for his moment. He moves in closer and Alexander moves with him, keeping their distance equal as they circle each other. Gustuv thrusts again.

Alexander parries quickly. He can see what Gustuv is attempting to do: feeling him out, hoping to coax him into a pre-emptive strike that will be easily countered but he's too smart to fall for that. Just one more of those half-thrusts of his and Gustuv will learn exactly how smart that is.

"C'mon old man." Alexander taunts. "You land a cheap elbow and now you're scared to move in. I think you're nervous. What?!" He lunges forward quickly, thrusting his foil into Gustuv's breastplate and scores a point.

Beneath his mask, Gustuv grins. "Nervous, you say? No, I am not nervous." He chuckles at the thought of it. "Actually, I am rather bored. What is the thrill of sword fighting when you do not fight with actual swords?"

Gustuv drops his foil to the floor and walks off the mat. Trepidation creeps in under Alexander's chest pad as he watches Gustuv unhinge the two swords forming an X over his mantle.

The old man's crazy, he thinks.

"Are you familiar with the samurai?" Gustuv asks, removing the swords. "They were the warrior- lords of feudal Japan—protectors of the shogun—but were eventually eradicated. Do you know why?"

Alexander shrugs. He didn't know that he came here for a history lesson. "I don't know, man. Imperialism."

"If you are the type to blame their eradication on externalities, then yes, that would be correct. I have always felt that it is the slave, not the captor, who should bear the butt of the blame for his state, for it is the slave that allows himself to be enslaved. I, personally, place the blame the Japanese people. Had they stood firm in their culture and supported their samurai and shogun instead of so readily embracing foreign ideals, imperialism could have been thwarted—possibly. First and foremost, though, the samurai should not have allowed their ways to become so outdated."

"Nevertheless." Gustuv steps onto the mat and tosses

Alexander a sword. The sunlight glistens off of its sharp edge. "These are not samurai swords. The samurai's main weapon had a much longer broader blade than these. No, these are similar to their side arm—a shorter lighter weapon— the katana."

He removes his gloves and runs his finger along the katana's blade. Blood drips from the cut. "The katana was adopted by the ninja clans, who would use—"

"You talk too much, you know that? You're like that evil villain that always lets the hero get away because they have to give a speech first." Alexander takes off his gloves and mask and tosses them aside. "Just show me what you got."

Tossing his sword back and forth between hands, Alexander peers at Gustuv, waiting. "C'mon grandpa." He says, waving him forward, tauntingly. "C'mon."

Alexander moves in quickly, closing the gap between them with one long stride. Gustuv shoves him back and raises his blade. He attacks, striking high then low, with Alexander defending them all. Their swords lock hilts and Alexander attempts a leg sweep. Gustuv steps back over his foot. Alexander tries again. Gustuv dodges a second time, countering with a jarring head-butt that sends Alexander stumbling backwards.

He shakes off the blow and moves in again. The clang of the blades resound as they strike and thrust, block and parry. It is Gustuv that finally gains an advantage, slicing Alexander's arm in a counter- attack. The razor sharp blade easily slices through the suit's padding. He watches his opponent's blood seep through, staining the white suit like pasta sauce on a paper plate. Gustuv seizes the opportunity and moves in for the finish, directing his every attack at the injured arm.

Alexander's grip is weakened by the loss of blood. If he

wants to beat this old man then he needs to do something quick. Gustuv strikes again— a high arching blow that crashes down like a fallen plane. Alexander gets his sword up in the nick of time but the force of the blow knocks the sword from his hand. Unarmed, he backpedals frantically.

"Concede." Gustuv tells him. "You have impressed me enough. The job is yours."

"You still haven't won yet, old man. Not until I'm on my back and that blade is at my throat!"

Gustuv grins. "As you wish." He attacks fast, slashing at the bleeding arm. Alexander sidesteps quickly, slipping behind Gustuv, and kicking him in the rear.

"Catch me if you can." He taunts, moving off of the mat. Gustuv follows him, grinning like a hyena after a wounded calf. He lunges forward and Alexander jumps out of the way, barely avoiding the sharp blade. A spinning heel-kick comes hurling at his head. He ducks. A shin comes, barreling towards his face. He throws his hands up to block and is sent sprawling backwards. Rolling with the momentum, Alexander is back on his feet quickly. Gustuv wastes no time and charges in again.

Alexander doesn't wait around. He moves fast, making his way to one of the empty scorer's tables. Gustuv closes in on him, backing Alexander up with the point of his blade.

"There is nowhere left to run, boy." Gustuv warns. "Concede or bleed—the choice is yours."

Thinking quickly, Alexander braces his hands on the edge of the scorer's table and mule kicks Gustuv in the chest. It knocks him back a few feet but not enough and Gustuv comes rushes forward again. He swings the sword low, aiming for his opponent's legs but Alexander backflips over the blade and onto the table. The move surprises Gustuv and that shock costs him. An explosive heel-kick smashes into the side of his face and he crumbles to the floor. The katana rolls from his hand. He reaches for it but Alexander hoops down from the table, landing one foot on Gustuv's arm. He picks the sword up and places the tip at Gustuv's throat.

"Concede or bleed, old man."

Gustuv takes off his mask and tosses it aside. Glaring into the young man's eyes, he smirks. "There are many worthy reasons for a man to shed his blood. This is not one of them."

He extends his hand and Alexander takes it, moving the blade away from Gustuv's throat.

Gripping the young man's hand firmly, Gustuv's eyes come ablaze with fury. "Though I never said I conceded."

In one swift motion Gustuv takes Alexander down, tosses the sword aside and straddles his chest. Pinned to the floor Alexander is forced to concede defeat. Victorious, Gustuv stands.

"Good workout." He says, helping the young man to his feet. "Same time tomorrow? You are familiar with long swords, I presume."

Alexander nods and Gustuv strolls off. "Someone will come and let you out." He calls back over his shoulder.

"Hey Mr. Barchulé." Alexander calls out. "You know I beat you. That fight was over. You cheated."

Gustuv laughs. "There are no rules in war, boy, so how could I cheat? You cheated yourself by believing that there is such a thing as playing fair."

CHAPTER FORTY-TWO

Gustuv steps out of the shower and enjoys the cool feeling of the air on his bare flesh.

Bypassing the thick towels hanging on the door, he slips his feet into his slippers and crosses the cold marble floors.

That was a good workout, he thinks, clenching his sore jaw. *One of the best that I've had in months.* In fact, the session was so invigorating that afterwards Gustuv not only decided to run a few miles, he also did some weight training and ended with twenty laps in the pool. All that remained was a relaxing round in the sauna and a cool-down shower.

He twists his decorative gold door handle and pushes the door forward. An immaculate chamber of comfort lies before him. High vaulted ceilings, an enormous plasma television mounted to the wall, a custom-crafted bed; all the luxuries that a modern man can possess, Gustuv has here in his fifth floor bedroom. He glances to the antique masterpiece that he uses for a desk. Handcrafted by Leonardo Da Vinci himself, the cedar wood piece now holds a mound of unattended to forms. He moves to his dresser, feeling no rush to sort through the documents. He's pretty sure he knows what the mass contains: contracts to be signed, a few eight- figure proposals to review, and one payment from the Islamic Republic of Afghanistan to cover the cost of 5,000 RPGs, 10,000 Soviet AKMs and one million rounds of ammunition. What he doesn't know is what the hell the man currently sitting in his armchair is doing inside his home.

"Romano," he says, selecting a pair of undershorts from his dresser drawer, "what brings you here now?"

Romano smirks. Gustuv's disrespect knows no bounds. Not only does he speak to him with his back turned, he has the gall to do it naked. Always the politician, Romano pretends not to notice. "You did not return my calls." He responds, diverting his gaze.

"Then obviously I did not want to speak with you. Did that thought ever cross your mind?"

"You will want to speak with me after you see what I've brought here, Gustuv." He taps the manila envelope he's holding.

Moved beyond mere annoyance, Gustuv pulls on his boxers and goes to his closet. "I hope it is not more unwarranted attention. You do understand that are reasons why we meet as we do?"

"Why are you concerned with the suspicions of a few reporters when we own the media, brother? Do not let fear consume you."

Romano rises from his seat and walks to the closet. "See for yourself." He says, shoving the envelope into Gustuv's chest. "I have done what you could not."

Gustuv lets the envelope fall to the ground, selects a pair of socks from his drawer and puts them on. "Nothing is impossible, Romano, although there are occurrences that are so improbable as to be labeled impossible." He steps over the envelope and pushes pass Romano on his way to his desk.

Romano picks up the envelope and follows Gustuv to his desk. "Here, brother." He tries to hand the envelope to Gustuv again and Gustuv glares at him, wondering how long Romano will leave his arm out like the human road sign he truly is. Romano goes to retract his arm and Gustuv snatches the envelope from him.

Romano grins. "Go on, brother. Open and see. I have done the impossible."

There is a letter opener on Gustuv's desk. He picks it up and slides the blade beneath the envelope's seal and a thought crosses his mind—one that involves testing the sharpness of the blade against the thickness of Romano's skin. He puts that aside for later. Right now he must learn what has brought Romano Hapsburg to his home.

He turns the envelope over and five pictures fall out onto his desk. He selects one and studies the image closely.

"They were retrieved from the late Kurt Bauer's home computer." Romano informs him. "You see now, brother. I have done what you could not."

Gustuv tosses the picture aside and takes a seat. "I am sorry, Romano, but it appears that all you have done is cause another fruitless murder and, of course, further irritate me."

"No." Romano refuses to accept what he is hearing. "You said that we needed the scroll and there it is. Whatever it says we can learn from those images. All we must do now is have the text transl—"

"Stop." Gustuv orders. "Do you hear yourself, Romano? How could you have decided on such an idiotic course of action. I told you that I needed the scroll Romano, not pictures of the scroll. A part of me feels that you must have done this intentionally, for no one could be so foolish, but when I consider what your motive could have been, I realize that you do not have the intelligence for such far-reaching machinations."

He peers at Romano, piercing the man's soul. "Have you forgotten what it is we are searching for, brother?"

"No, I have not forgotten, but—"

"You must have forgotten or else you would not presume that mere *pictures* are suitable to our brotherhood's endeavor. Have a seat, Romano, please, and allow me to remind you of what exactly it is we are searching for."

Like a scolded child, Romano reluctantly takes his seat and looks on listlessly as Gustuv speaks.

"Our order was entrusted with the divine task of protecting the knowledge of God until there came a time when mankind was ready to learn the truth. Since the beginning of history, we had recorded and kept safe those priceless treasures, only to be betrayed by members of our very own. The *Book of Immortality,* the very book that holds all we need to save mankind was stolen. Along with it, the betrayers took the key to unlocking the magical work."

He glares into Romano's insolent eyes. "And so I ask you brother, if we are seeking a magical scroll, created thousands of years ago by the wisest minds of the ages, do you truly believe that we only require *pictures* to decode its cryptic messages?"

Romano tries to speak in defense of himself but Gustuv will not allow it. "No." He barks. "What you mean to say is, *'I was wrong, brother. I will have my people locate and retrieve the scroll. The scroll brother. Not pictures of it.'*

Romano nods. "Do not worry, brother. We will recover the scroll. I have already had the boy's and the girl's pictures put on the news in Riga. They will be forced out of their hole and when they surface they will have an entire city looking to turn them in."

"I pray that you are right, Romano. Six sextillion tons rests on your shoulders. I only wonder if you are capable of bearing such a load." He picks the phone up from his desk. "You are dismissed." He says, dialing. "I have business to attend to."

Romano rises from his seat and heads for the exit. He stops at the door. "The weight of the world presses down on us all, Gustuv. We must divide the load up amongst each other if we are to fulfill our duty. Remember that."

Romano exits and Gustuv watches him, amused at the subtle threat in his throne. A cheerful voice comes through the phone. "Well, hello to you too." Gustuv replies, smiling. "Listen William, the scroll is yet to be retrieved. I do not care what you have to do or who you have to pay, you must retrieve it before Romano's imbeciles get a hold of it. We cannot allow him to possess bargaining power of that magnitude. A hammer in the hands of a fool is a dangerous weapon."

Ignoring the threatening glare of Gustuv's guards, Romano pulls out his cellphone and makes a call. "We need the original." He says, strolling down the hall. He nods as he listens to the man's reply.

"Yes, yes." He says. "And you should have known that. Do you not know what we are working for?" He laughs. "No, I do not care how you get it just do what it takes. If he truly possesses the Book we cannot allow him to get his hands on the scroll. If so, we will never ascend to our rightful seats. Our destiny is to lead, brother."

He nods again, smiling as he enters the elevator. "Yes. Happy hunting brother."

TRUE KING

CHAPTER
FORTY-THREE

Sitting in the passenger's seat of Inspector Guntinsky's town car Officer Stein takes a hefty bite of his juicy bratwurst. A stream of grease squirts onto the dashboard.

"Sorry, sir." He says, looking around for a napkin. "Feels like we've been here forever."

Inspector Guntinsky checks his watch. He and Stein have been parked across from Dr. Bauer's home for exactly one hour and thirty-seven minutes now. "Didn't you ever have to lay in the trenches and wait on the enemy when you were in the army, Stein?"

"No, sir. We never had to fight while I served." He takes another bite of the sloppy sandwich.

Guntinsky takes a handful of napkins from the armrest and hands them to Stein. "Well, this won't be like those TV shows you watch. Oliver Bauer has not committed a crime and he is not a suspect in his son's death. We are only here in case the boy and the girl—"

"Devin King and Samantha Matsumi, sir."

"Yeah, Devin and Samantha. They might try to contact the doctor for help and when they do, we'll be here waiting."

He looks out the window and watches a thin stream of pedestrians gathered in front of the doctor's building. Most of them are teenagers, probably headed to someone's house, he thinks. These kids today rarely ever spend time outdoors. Guntinsky glances up to the gray skies coming their way. *Definitely not today*

"Sir, you don't believe they really killed him, do you?"

Good question, kid. As much as Guntinsky hates to admit it, that detective did make a good point: why would Devin fly halfway across the world to kill his sister's colleague? What is the motive? Could there have been some type of perverted love triangle going on?

The Inspector's phone rings before he can give Stein an answer. "Hello." He says. "Who is—" The caller cuts Guntinsky off and Guntinsky listens intently as the man speaks.

"Yes, Mr. Kratz. No, I'm sorry. Prime Minister—"

Officer Stein looks over to Guntinsky, not sure if he heard him correctly. Could he really be speaking to Prime Minister Andris Kratz. *And if so, about what?*

He sips his drink, watching the Inspector; he appears slightly irritated yet intrigued. Stein hears him mutter something about terrorists and a scroll.

"I'll be right back." Guntinsky says. "Stay here, Stein."

"Yes sir." Stein finishes his sandwich and watches the Inspector through the car's window. Guntinsky stands outside of the driver's door staring at Dr. Bauer's building with his phone pressed to his ear. The call ends and he crosses the street, pulling out his badge as he approaches the doorman. Stein watches him question the man and when the doorman seems hesitant to answer Guntinsky's face tightens into a furious scowl. After a few more exchanges the doorman is smiling and shaking the Inspector's hand. Guntinsky strolls back over to the car and slides into his seat.

"He went to the docks." He tells Stein. "He was excited about taking the boat out. The doorman said it's been years."

Stein doesn't follow. "So will he be back soon, sir?"

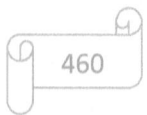

Guntinsky shoots Stein a look of disbelief as he starts the car. "What has recently changed in Oliver Bauer's life that just so happens to coincide with this boating trip?"

"His son just was murdered. Maybe he wants to go out on the water for some peace and quiet. Nobody around. Just you, the sea and your thoughts."

"Exactly Stein." Guntinsky hits the siren, slams on the gas and the car speeds away from the curb. "Let's go make sure that those thoughts don't include aiding two fugitives."

"This tape was useless." Clarkson says, shutting off the television.

"And I think Gunts knew that." Worthy adds, smoking a cigarette on the edge of their king- size bed. He's not a big fan of the local brands but they'll do for now. It's not like he's in a position to complain. This hotel room is definitely better than the rat-motel he left back home and nicer than anything he could afford on his own. Not only did the Prime Minister provide them with a personal escort, he also set them up in this plush presidential suite.

Jude would love something like this, Worthy thinks, glancing over at Clarkson—leaned back in the recliner, cracking open one of those tiny bottles of vodka from the mini-bar—*and I'm stuck here with you.*

He shakes his head, displacing all thoughts of Judith and his teetering marriage. A few hours ago a courier delivered an imposing mass of documents on Kurt and Oliver Bauer —supposedly from the desk of the Police Chief—and he has been sorting through it ever since. The more he sifts through it, the more he wonders just how the Police Chief was able to acquire such spy-like intelligence.

"Think he's hiding something?" Clarkson asks. He drains

the bottle in one swallow. "These Lats got some good liquor."

Worthy takes a puff and shrugs. "Somebody had to tip off the news and it definitely wasn't us." He looks from the empty vodka bottle to the open mini-bar. "Isn't it too early to start drinking?"

"Naw." Clarkson grins. "Just a little something to get the blood flowing. You should try it. Good stuff. Real smooth. *And free.*"

Worthy shakes his head. "No thanks. Too much to do. You should watch that tape again. Maybe you missed something." He picks up another document from the mass of papers and continues to read.

Clarkson ignores him and looks to the mini- bar. What he should do is get another bottle of vodka. He's watched that tape three times already and hasn't seen anything substantial yet. He looks to the mound. "Anything good over there?"

"So far it's just been property listings. Kurt— the son—had a house, his car and that's pretty much it. His father—Oliver—has his apartment in the city and a boat, and a car, of course. There's a family business—couple manufacturing plants. Nothing unusual."

Speaking of unusual, Worthy's mind shifts to all of these coincidences that keep happening. "Let me ask you something, though? Unrelated, I guess."

Clarkson leans forward in his chair and nods. "What you wanna know, kid?"

"Just, why the hell are you willing to risk your career chasing this guy all over the world? We both know that he would have been acquitted on that murder, which also makes me wonder why did he run in the first place? And to Riga, of all places. Then, how does Kurt Bauer fit into all of this? And there's all *divine intervention* crap that got us over here. And the Prime Minister. What's really going on, man? That many coincidences can't be coincidental. Something's up."

Clarkson gets up and heads for the bathroom. "That's too many questions for me. You're the Whiz-Kid. You try and figure them out while I go take a piss. Vodka ran through me."

Clarkson's phone rings. Worthy grabs it from the table beside the bed and tosses it to him.

"James Clarkson." He answers. "Okay. Hold on." With his hand covering the receiver he looks to Worthy. "Keep looking through that stuff. Maybe we'll head to Samantha's place, then Kurt's, then his old man's."

Worthy nods and goes back to work. He's rifling through the papers when hears Clarkson say something about a scroll just as the bathroom door is closing behind him. *A scroll?* He thinks. *What the hell is he up to now?*

He files that thought away for another time and keeps at the search. *Of course they didn't go to Samantha's place,* he thinks, scanning the documents. *If they're smart enough to not use a credit card then they can't be dumb enough to hide out at home. But that brings me back to my point: why run to Riga if not to go to her place? Who was Kurt Bauer? Could he have really been her boyfriend? People at the University said they would flirt but I don't know. Maybe Kurt was supposed to hide them? No, the girlfriend called it in. Right, he already had a girlfriend. You wouldn't hide one of your girls in the house while the other is there. Maybe Samantha was his ex or just a good friend? But the girl said Samantha and Devin showed up unexpectedly. Kurt couldn't have known about Devin's situation then or he would have been expecting them. Maybe the connection isn't personal. And what about that girlfriend? Why is no one considering her as a suspect?*

The toilet flushes and Clarkson strolls out of the bathroom drying his hands on his shirt. "Find something?" He asks.

"Nothing exceptional." Worthy looks over the page he's holding. The Bauer's business has some tangible holdings, he learns, including some warehouses and a house in the country. "I was thinking, there is no way that they went to Samantha's place. That's just stupid. But then, why come see Kurt Bauer? Who was this guy really? That's the key to this."

Clarkson takes a seat in one of the many plush armchairs filling the suite and leans back as he mulls over the question. *Could the professor's murder be related to the Kings' murder,* he wonders. That was one job that he hated to do. The Kings were exemplary people and they didn't deserve to go out like that. If he had known beforehand that someone was planning on killing them he would have made sure that it didn't happen anywhere near the Peninsula. Unfortunately, the first he heard of it was when he was being asked to do a favor that he couldn't refuse.

"How about his old man?" He suggests, sitting up now. "He hasn't done anything and I'm sure he'll want to help find his son's killers. We should go talk to him."

Detective Worthy nods. Letting Oliver Bauer believe that Devin and Samantha killed his son would give him an incentive to help and his helpfulness may be just what they need to figure out who Kurt really was. "What if we're looking at this all wrong?" He says, lighting up another cigarette. "If you consider that two weeks ago the King's house was burglarized and Mister and Missus King were killed, and then a few days later Devin, Samantha and her father get attacked outside of a bank after a having just left a will reading and that ended with Devin's murder rap and Sukamaya

Matsumi's death. I spoke to the bank manager that day. Devin had picked up something from his mother's safety deposit box. You worked the King's murder. Didn't it seem odd to you that there were so many valuable items left in the house?"

Clarkson shrugs. "A lot of that stuff's hard to move, kid."

"Yeah, well, it seems like they might have been looking for something specific. The burglary may have just been a cover. But they didn't get it and so they—whoever *they* are—followed Devin to the bank. Whatever he got from that safe deposit box must have been what they wanted. The security footage showed Devin leaving with one of those cylinders you put paintings in. He didn't come in with it, though. And what addicts would try to rob Devin King in broad daylight in front of First Bank—all that security. Just doesn't make sense. So I'm thinking, maybe they aren't running from Devin's murder rap. What if someone's after them and they came to Kurt for help? Whoever they're running from found out about it, killed Kurt and tried to frame them for it. Flush them out. It would explain—you know, if the people after them have someone in the media leak the story; maybe some police help too."

He shoots an accusing glare at Clarkson. "They would have needed someone to cover up the evidence at the mansion, too. And that kid that attacked Devin, his heart attack was very fortunate. And, now, here—"

"Okay, enough Whiz-Kid." Clarkson interrupts. "You're reaching. Starting to sound like a conspiracy quack. We arrived here on government jets with diplomatic status. These killers that you think I'm working with, they got that much clout? And, by the way, I didn't know about the Kings' death until that morning and I got took off the case to work with you, remember?"

"Yeah." Worthy concedes that point. "It does seem

conspiracy-theoryish but we both know they didn't kill Kurt Bauer. Something else is going on."

Clarkson shrugs. "Doesn't matter anyway, kid. It's not our case. Right now we don't have any idea where he's at and no way of finding out. All we can do is hope some citizen recognizes them and calls the police. And that's today. We can't stay here too much longer."

"So what about calling Oliver Bauer? Maybe Samantha and Kurt used to date. They had to have some other connection than work. Maybe Dr. Bauer has met her or knows where she might be."

Clarkson nods. "Make the call, kid."

Worthy finds Dr. Bauer's home number in the files but no one answers. He calls the building's front desk. "Can you put me through to Dr. Oliver Bauer?" The receptionist tells him that the he isn't in but Worthy persists. "Ma'am this is a serious matter. A *police* matter. We need to speak with him about his son's murder."

"Kurt." She sighs. "Oh, it is so terrible. I saw it on the news yesterday. It is just so sad. First his wife and now his son. Kurt was such a good boy. He hated it when they moved to the city." She sniffles. "I'm sorry, Officer. I believe that he went sailing to ease the pain. He and Kurt used to go together after Sophia's death. That's his wife, Sophia." She sniffles again. "It's just so sad. Such a sweet man losing his entire family."

"Uhh..." Worthy stammers, not sure how to end this conversation politely. He grins at Clarkson. "Yes, it is sad. No one deserves that. You, uhh...you take care of yourself."

The receptionist begins to speak but Worthy hangs up. He has what he needs. "We have something." He says, grabbing his gun and badge from the nightstand. "Oliver's not at home. He took his boat out today. Maybe he's still—"

"C'mon." Clarkson says, hopping up quickly. "It's all we got."

The two detectives head for the door.

"So who was that on the phone?" Worthy asks, stepping into the hall.

"No one." Clarkson says, pulling the door shut. "Something about a early retirement package."

- -

Ivan Guntinsky has watched crooked cops and low-life thugs run his city since he was a child. He became a police officer so that he could make a difference but unfortunately the only thing that's changed since he joined up is his pant's size. One man cannot fight an entire system, especially when that system is as all-encompassing as the corruption plaguing Riga. It's not only groups like the Freemasons but an entire world of secret-keepers. How can you trust anyone when no one is honest? In Guntinsky's world if a person has a secret it's because they are doing something that they shouldn't. That's why, even after all these years on the beat, he's never had a partner and never will. And it's also why he grimaces at the sight of a black sedan pulling into the boatyard.

How could they know to come here? He glances at the idiot standing beside him. *You were with me all day. It has to be the Chief. Fuckin' Masons.*

Guntinsky looks around, thinking. He cannot allow these two to get to Devin first. This is much bigger than whatever it is they are after— according to the Prime Minister, Devin's capture is now a matter of national security.

"Sir." Stein says. "The two Dominican detectives are here."

"I can see that, Stein. The question is: why are they here?"

"Maybe they want to speak to Oliver Bauer, sir. It's why we

are here."

Guntinsky rolls his eyes. "But how did they know to come *here*, Stein? We didn't know until I talked to the doorman and I didn't tell anyone. Did you?"

"Umm..no sir." He says, not sure if that is a good or bad thing. "I would have told the Chief, sir, but it all happened so fast."

Guntinsky isn't sure who is dumber: Stein for thinking that he could be a police officer or whoever it was that gave him his badge. He looks at Stein—*it was the guy that gave him the badge.* "Listen, how about you let me take care of that from here on, okay?"

Stein looks confused. "What sir?"

"Informing the Chief. I'll do it."

"Okay." Stein nods, glad to be relieved of the burden.

Clarkson and Worthy have exited their vehicle and are approaching the entry to the docks now. The Inspector needs to get rid of them and quick. There is too much at stake for them to get in his way. He looks to Stein and grins. "Besides, I have a new assignment for you. Stein, I need you to be the detectives' official guide around the docks. Whatever they need, you take care of it. Stick to them like glue. Okay?"

He nods. "Yes sir."

Guntinsky stares at him. "I meant now Stein.Go!"

"Oh, sorry sir. I'm going sir." He runs off to intercept the duo.

"Okay." Guntinsky mumbles. *Now that should keep them out of my way for a while.* He looks around and starts towards the piers. "Now where the hell is this boat?"

CHAPTER
FORTY-FOUR

Despite Devin's adamant protests, the crew of My Little Secret has once again dropped anchor and now sit aboard the deck enjoying a late lunch.

With so much awaiting them ashore, Dr. Bauer had suggested that they take some time to revel in the peace of the bay's waters. Captivated by the doctor's lore, Samantha quickly agreed and after shooting Devin a few reproving glares, so did he.

"So, Doc, what you're saying is all that conspiracy stuff's true? I mean, secret brotherhoods, magic books, new world orders— it sounds like a bad novel, Doc."

Dr. Bauer knows how it sounds. The ability to discredit their accusers' claims is one of The Elite's best defenses. They make films that fantasize their actions, create stories that dilute the truth and use their publishers to disseminate "authoritative" works that '*prove*' their alleged activities are impossible to perform and absurd to believe.

"Regardless of how it may sound son, it is true. I have spent the better half of my life researching conspiracy claims, secret societies and occult lore. Do you know what I have learned? I've learned that the things that seem the most absurd, far-fetched and even impossible are usually the things that are true."

Samantha takes a small bite of her sandwich. "So when Kurt contacted you it was because he knew about all this conspiracy stuff?"

A proud smile spreads across his face. "My son was an extraordinary linguist, dear. He could have translated the cuneiform with little difficulty. Kurt only reached out to me because once he saw those symbols and you mentioned The Elite—you must understand, I had told him all the tales as a child. He did not intend to betray your trust. It was necessary that—"

"Doc, Doc." Devin stops him. "Nobody thinks your son was evil. I just want to know what this thing is." He plucks the satchel's strap. "I need to know what my mother was willing to die to protect."

The doctor nods. "All I can tell you now derives from the same stories that I would tell Kurt."

The echo of distant thunder rumbles through the air. Dr. Bauer looks up at the gray clouds approaching—*an omen perhaps.*

Devin isn't worried about the weather. He stares at Dr. Bauer impatiently. "If it explains what this thing is then go ahead, Doc. I need to know something."

"Well," he begins, "the story starts with Hermes Trismegistus, Thrice Greatest, Master of all the crafts, Ruler of the Three Worlds, Scribe of the Gods and Keeper of the Book of Life. The ancient Egyptians regarded Hermes—whom they called Tehuti or Thoth—as the embodiment of the Universal Mind. Tehuti was the neter, or god, of wisdom. He was known to the Jews as Enoch; Mercury to the Latins; and Hermes to the Greeks. The planet Mercury was one of his symbols because just as it is the nearest planet to the Sun, so is Tehuti or Hermes the nearest to God. The archangel Metatron is another one his counterparts, through Enoch's apotheosis, representing his role as Divine Scribe and Messenger to the Gods. In this capacity Tehuti is said to have brought mankind medicine, chemistry, law, art, astrology, music, philosophy, mathematics, anatomy, and geography, along with other arts and sciences. The caduceus—his serpent- wound staff—is still used as the emblem of the medical profession today.

A series of forty-two ancient Egyptian books are attributed to Tehuti. Some believe that the knowledge in these books is the cause for the advancement of the Egyptian civilization which, if you believe it, would also explain its decline. Understand that the Romans— and later the Christians—knew that until these great works were destroyed they would never be able to bring Egypt under subjection. So when the city of Alexandria was burned down they made sure that the collection was consumed by the fire."

"Alexandria, Doc?" Devin has no clue what Dr. Bauer is talking about.

"I've heard of it." Samantha tells him. "It's a city in Egypt right, built by the Greeks?"

"Yes, dear. Alexander the Great is said to have drew the blueprints in the sands when landing on the coast. It was a magnificent city. Before the Christian era, seven hundred thousand books were gathered together from all over the ancient world and kept in the city. There were special libraries built explicitly for this purpose. Legend has it that there were books in Alexandria over two hundred and fifty thousand years old. The library that Cleopatra had given to Marc Antonius, along with the collection he gave her to compensate for the part destroyed in the fire of 51 BCE, was stored there in Alexandria."

"And that was the fire that destroyed Tehuti's books?" She asks.

"No, dear. It took three fires to actually annihilate the library. But the story gets interesting here. The volumes that were not consumed in that first fire lit by Caesar were said to have been destroyed later, in 389 CE, by the early Christians.

The Roman Emperor Theodosius' edict had ordered that the Serapeum—which housed the volumes—be destroyed. Later, the Arab General Amru is said to have completed the deed.

The thing is, that first fire lit by Caesar took several hours to spread from the burning fleet to the buildings by the harbor. According to the legend, in this time-frame the librarians, along with hundreds of slaves, removed the most precious of the seven hundred thousand scrolls and books. It is believed that these books are buried somewhere beneath India or the sands of Egypt."

Samantha looks to Devin, wondering if he's thinking the same thing that she's thinking. "So, the scroll and the book that Mom found..."

Devin finishes her thought. "They escaped the fire, right Doc?"

Dr. Bauer nods. "In all likelihood, yes, although there is no way to say that they were ever in Alexandria. While Tehuti lived he is said to have entrusted his chosen successors with a sacred book. This book contained the secret steps that mankind was to take to bring about its regeneration. It was also the key to all of his other works. According to legend, this book was kept in a golden box, guarded by a coiled serpent, and encased within six other boxes, hidden within the inner sanctuary of the temple. There was only one key to this box and it was held by the Master of the Mysteries—the highest member of the Hermetic Arcana. This book is the fabled Key to Immortality, in which Tehuti revealed to mankind the One Way."

The *Way*, Devin thinks, attempting to reconcile this puzzle. "So you're saying, the book Mom found—"

"What I'm saying, son, is that I believe that the book your mother found is the same book that Tehuti left to his successors, and this scroll, I suspect it is the Master's Key."

CHAPTER
FOURTY-FIVE

Standing at the edge of the pier, Stein points towards a group of ships approaching the docks.

"Sir, there's a boat there, sir. Maybe that's him." Inspector Guntinsky cuts his eyes at Stein. His patience is nearing its limits. It is bad enough that Stein could not keep Clarkson and Worthy busy. Now he's pointing out every ship with sails.

Guntinsky lifts a pair of binoculars to his face and peers out at the ships. "That's a fishing boat, Stein."

"I think he means the one to the left." Detective Worthy interjects.

"Yeah." Clarkson adds. "That big white one. His boat is white, right?"

Guntinsky looks out again and *damnit, the idiot was right.*

"You probably should call some back-up?" Worthy suggests.

Officer Stein nods. "Want me to call the boats, sir? We can go out or I can get some officers for you."

"No, no, no." Clarkson says. "I have a better idea." *And one that won't bring more of Riga's finest in my way.* He looks to Guntinsky. "Let's just wait for the boat to dock and question him then. If we play it right, he'll probably let us search the ship. He shouldn't have anything to hide."

Worthy glares at Clarkson suspiciously. *Why exactly does James Clarkson want to search this boat,* he wonders. He looks to

Guntinsky, expecting him to protest but to his surprise, Guntinsky agrees.

"Sounds good. Let's just make sure that we don't alarm him. He hasn't done anything wrong. We don't have any grounds to detain him or his property, so do not accuse him. We don't need him to become defensive."

Clarkson takes Stein's binoculars and peers out at the ship. "Alright, coach. Good speech but let's get off this pier. If we can see them, they can see us."

"Devin! Dr. Bauer!" Samantha's shouting startles the doctor and he jumps up from the table so fast that he spills his tea. He hurries and moves the scroll before it's ruined.

Standing behind the wheel, Devin looks over to the doctor and the mess he's made. Grinning, he locks the wheel, slows the throttle and goes to help him clean-up.

"Devinnnn!" Samantha yells again. "Dr. Bauer! Come up here! NOW!"

Devin wipes the liquid up fast and sets the scroll back on the table. "It'll be fine." He assures the doctor. "Come on. Something's wrong."

The two of them exit the wheel room and join a frantic Samantha at the end of the pier.

"I was cleaning up," she tells them, "pouring out the juice, when I noticed four people standing at the end of the pier. It's those two detectives, uhh...Clarkson and Worthy, from back home. Look."

She passes Devin the binoculars and there they are, James Clarkson and Max Worthy. They're standing beside two men that he doesn't recognize —probably locals. "Yeah that's them."

He says, handing her back the binoculars. *But how did they get here, though? What is the fuck is The Elite, really?* "They must be looking for the scroll. Natalie said something was up with Mom and Dad's murder. Clarkson and Worthy work for The Elite."

He takes the binoculars from Samantha again, wanting to get a better look at the two men with them. If Devin's correct and Clarkson and Worthy are both working with The Elite then those could be the men that killed Mom and Dad.

"Duck!" He shouts and drops to the deck before Samantha can even register the words. "Duck Sam!" He shouts again and yanks her pants leg so hard she practically falls.

Samantha drops to the deck. "What?" She asks. "What did you see?"

"They were looking this way." He explains. "One of them might've seen us. Doc, check and see what they're doing."

Attempting to be discreet, Dr. Bauer half- squats, takes the binoculars from Devin's outstretched hand, and scans the shore. A young man is looking at the ship from the shore. He turns and says something to the other three.

"Stay down." Bauer says. "I'll be right back." He runs off to the wheel room, slows the ship to a crawl and is back peeing out the binoculars. He watches the three men on the pier head back to the walkway. "Okay. The coast is clear. You can stand up now."

There is a heaviness with them as they rise to their feet. Neither of them know what to do now. Clarkson and Worthy are sure to be waiting for them to set foot on the docks and if they are working with The Elite then going to jail is the least of their problems.

Devin states the obvious. "We can't be here when this ship docks. If they notice us, we'll be killed or arrested. There's no

telling what they'll do to you, Doc, but harboring fugitives is not a slap on the wrist type of crime. Once they find out that you know what this thing is you'll wind up a prisoner or worse."

"I have a life raft. I could stop, let you two out and then head in on my own." Dr. Bauer suggests. "I haven't done anything wrong and they can't possibly know that we have met."

Samantha disagrees. With the way that events have been unfolding she isn't willing to place any information out of The Elite's grasp. "We can't say for sure what they know. They knew to come here."

"Yeah. She's right, Doc. Not to mention, someone would see us rowing away in a lifeboat. No one can know we were here. It's the only way to keep you safe."

"Well." The doctor racks his brain for a solution to this present problem. The easiest thing for him to do is to just turn them both in and wash his hands of the whole matter. The knowledge hidden within this scroll has been submerged for so long who is to say that—"

"I have an idea." He blurts. "Have either of you ever been diving?"

Devin likes the doctor's plan. "Okay, Doc, you and Sam go get the equipment ready. I'll be down in a second."

Dr. Bauer and Samantha both head down to the cabin while Devin goes back to the wheel room. The scroll is lying open on the table. He moves pass it and takes down a large map of the Gulf of Riga and, after removing the waterproof covering, he discards the map and moves to the table. Very carefully, he slides the fragile document inside the thick plastic.

"Okay." He says, picking up Dr. Bauer's tea cup. He pours

the few remaining dregs on the edge of the now waterproofed scroll to check it. The beads roll of the plastic and onto the table. Smiling, he reaches for the satchel.

Better to be sure, he thinks.

"Here, Doc." Devin says, handing the satchel to Dr. Bauer. "Hide this somewhere."

Samantha looks on in disbelief. "Have you lost your mind? You know they'll try to search the ship. If they find that here, they'll—"

"Sam," Devin cuts in, "just trust me on this, okay. Doc, you just hide it good."

Samantha reluctantly agrees. "You better know what you're doing."

Dr. Bauer looks at them both and sighs. "Okay then." He says. "Let's get you two off of this boat. Come on." He leads them to the front of the deck and then hands Devin his car keys and a slip of paper. "Here's my address, too. Just plug it into the GPS."

Devin looks over to Samantha. "You ready, Sam?"

"Ready as I can be." She says.

The sky opens up and thick raindrops smack the ship. Dr. Bauer looks up at a sky that is growing darker by the second. *A storm is upon us,* he thinks, certain that this is an omen. The three of them are standing on the precipice of a new age. He only hopes that they don't go over the cliff like so many before them. The docks are only ten minutes away now. He needs to hide the scroll and get rid of any evidence that Devin and Samantha were here.

He heads for the cabin as quickly as he can, dodging raindrops along the way.

"Stein!" Guntinsky barks, diverting the officer's attention from Dr. Bauer's ship. "You and the two detectives come with me. When that boat docks, you three question Mr. Bauer while I go to search the ship."

"Yes sir." She says, glancing back at the ship. He could have sworn that he saw a man and woman staring his way.

"No sir." Clarkson retorts. "I'll help you search the boat. You saw what happened at the gas station. If those two are onboard, you'll need the backup."

"Hey." Worthy chimes in. "If that's the case then I should come too. Three of us have more of a chance than taking them down than two." He looks the two overweight men over. "Especially you two."

"Uhh..." Guntinsky stalls. He doesn't need these two idiots on his heels right now.

A thunderous boom echoes above them and thick raindrops smack the ground. *Could this get any worse*, Guntinsky thinks. "No, you stay with Stein." He says. "That way one of you is in on the questioning. And Stein's too inexperienced to go at it alone. Clarkson, you come with me."

The rain picks up. "Come on." Guntinsky says. "Let's get out of this rain."

CHAPTER FORTY-SIX

The four officers take refuge under a bait-and-tackle shop's canopy.

Standing beneath the billowing tarp they watch Dr. Bauer's ship being guided into the dock. The rain is coming down in sheets now. Dr. Bauer emerges from the wheel room and starts to secure the moorings. They wait until he is finished before making their approach.

"Let's go." Guntinsky says. "Before he exits the—"

A deafening boom resounds through the docks. Balls of fire fly though the sky like shooting stars as a raging inferno blossoms out from a large fishing boat. Chaos and confusion consume the boatyard. The officers look around at the mayhem. Worthy moves to help.

"Wait!" Clarkson tells them, stepping back out of the way of the scurrying dockworkers. "Don't lose sight of Bauer. That explosion wasn't an accident." He looks to Worthy. "It was too coincidental to be a coincidence. The kid's here somewhere."

Guntinsky suppresses his smile.

If the kid's here, the scroll is too.

CHAPTER
FORTY-SEVEN

With their heads bobbing above the water, Devin and Samantha watch the four officers huddle together beneath the canopy of a bait and tackle shop. They must be waiting for *My Little Secret* to dock, Devin thinks, and with the rain pouring down like it is, the group won't be moving from beneath that canopy until it does. Thankfully Kurt and Sophia's wetsuits were still onboard the ship. Unfortunately, the bait and tackle shop where the officers are waiting is right in front of the entrance to the parking lot—the parking lot where Dr. Bauer's car is parked.

"So what do we do?" Samantha asks. "Just wade here until they leave."

"Can't." Devin replies. Doc gave us his keys. If they think that he's helping us, it'd look real suspicious if he just all of a sudden lost his keys. Exactly when we'd need a ride. We need a distraction."

"Like what? It's not like we can just make a unicorn appear in the sky."

Squinting through the splashing water, Devin scans the docks for anything that they might be able to use to get out of here. There's nothing around here but boats, boats, and more boats. *What the hell am I supposed to do with that,* he thinks. An old fishing boat catches his eye and he gets an idea.

"Be right back, Sam. You just stay here, okay."

Before she can protest Devin has disappeared beneath the water. Samantha looks around, waiting and wondering what in the hell Devin could be up to now. She sees him emerge behind a moored fishing boat close to the docks. He climbs aboard the ship and creeps stealthily towards the engine room. He disappears inside and that's it. Five minutes later, he comes sprinting from the room and leaps off the edge of the ship.

"What did he do?" She wonders aloud.

Before long, he pops up beside her, grinning. "Okay." He says. "We have our distraction."

Samantha eyes him suspiciously. There is something in that cocky tone that puts her on edge. "Devin, what the hell did you do?"

His grin spreads. "Me? What makes you think *I* did anything?"

Her eyes tighten. "Devin, it's raining and I'm treading water in a cold bay with the police waiting to arrest or kill me. Tell me what the hell you did."

"Okay. Well, you remember how there would always be extra fuel in those old fishing boats Dad would take us out in? You know, emergency fuel; fuel for the generators?"

She nods. "Yeah. So?"

A thundering explosion rips through the docks. Giant balls of fire shoot from the fishing boat like cannon balls as the ship burst into flames. The burning shrapnel tears through the sails of neighboring ships and spreads the ravenous fire throughout the harbor.

Chaos ensues as owners and dockworkers scramble towards their vessels hoping to somehow save them from the growing conflagration. Men with fire extinguishers race down the boardwalk, pushing their way through crowds of frightened and fleeing masses. Another engine explodes, shooting a tower of fire into the sky.

Samantha glares at a grinning Devin. "*This* is our distraction?! What did you *do?*"

He shrugs. "Hey, if it's good enough for Caesar it's good enough for us. Come on. While everyone's caught in the madness."

"Wait. Look. Those detectives. They're moving."

CHAPTER
FORTY-EIGHT

D r. Bauer has a decision to make.
He can either head down to the sleeping quarters to retrieve the scroll or he can leave it hidden and pray that his ship does not get consumed by the fire. Whatever he is going to do he needs to do it quick. Those four officers are coming his way now.

Too late.

"Dr. Bauer!" Inspector Guntinsky calls from the pier. "Excuse me, sir! Are you Doctor Oliver Bauer? Kurt Bauer's father?"

The doctor looks over to the four men standing on the pier—the same men that he saw from the ship. He can't imagine that they have been waiting this long in the pouring rain just to ask him about his son. They must be after the scroll.

He nods to the Inspector's question. "Yes, I am. May I ask who's inquiring?"

Guntinsky flashes his badge. "Ivan Guntinsky, Inspector. This is Officer Stein here and these two are Detectives Worthy and Clarkson. They're from the Dominican Republic."

"And this is in regards to my son's murder, I presume."

"Yeah." Clarkson cuts in. "We think the two that killed your son may be here now, looking for you. They are probably responsible for this fire."

That's news to Worthy. He hadn't been informed that

Devin and Samantha were even here, let alone committing acts of arson. "Dr. Bauer, maybe you'd like to come with us so we can talk? This isn't the safest place to be right now."

A charred piece of wood smacks the ground by Worthy's feet. Dr. Bauer glances back over his shoulder trying to think of a way that he can get the scroll without these officers knowing. The fire is spreading too fast now. Leaving it behind is no longer an option.

"Do you need to grab something?" Clarkson asks, noticing the doctor's glance. "If you have anything valuable onboard you should get it before it's too late. They might not be able to contain this thing." He ducks as a piece of debris whips through the air. "You might wanna hurry up too."

"I'll help you." Guntinsky says. He starts climbing aboard before the doctor can give his okay.

"*We'll* help you." Clarkson retorts. He starts to follow Guntinsky onto the ship when another explosion rattles the docks. He shoves Guntinsky in the back. "Let's go. Quick!"

Detective Worthy and Officer Stein wait on the pier while Clarkson and Guntinsky follow Dr. Bauer's down into the ship's cabin. A pair of divers scurries down the boardwalk.

That's odd, Worthy thinks. *They're heading away from the water but still in their wetsuits and goggles. Guess they were diving when the fire erupted. At least they were smart enough to take their flippers off.*

He glances at their feet and takes notice of their curiously dark complexions. *And the man—are those dreadlocks?*

"Hey!" He calls out. "You two! Stop right there!"

488

Dr. Bauer sends Clarkson and Guntinsky into the anteroom to gather some personal belongings while he heads to the bathroom. Closing the door behind him, he opens the small accordion closet and pushes aside a mountain of cleaning products. There is a hidden compartment behind the mass. He opens it, digs inside and retrieves the satchel.

But now what, he thinks. There is no way that he can hide the container on his person without them noticing and there is nothing that he can conceal with. *I'll have to leave it.*

He starts to unscrew the canister when James Clarkson steps through the door. "And what's that?" He asks, unholstering his pistol. He moves towards the doctor as he speaks. "They were here weren't they? You can tell me. The kid and the girl. They were here."

Dr. Bauer backs up toward the shower, clutching the satchel tightly against his chest. "I-I don't know what you're talking about, Detective. I-I just—"

Clarkson doesn't have time for this. If he doesn't bring this scroll back home not only will he go to prison for the rest of his life but all of his assets—his car, his home, and his entire retirement savings—will be confiscated. He could really care less about his things—he's seen and done enough to live the rest of his days in poverty and still die without regrets—but it's his wife. She's always been his Achilles heel. What will she do without a home or money to pay her bills? She's too sick to work and without any income her live-in male nurse—her *boyfriend,* she says—won't be able to stay on. That alone might kill her.

"You asked for this." Clarkson says, flipping the gun around in his hand. He smacks Dr. Bauer with the handle of his pistol, knocking him unconscious. Shaking his head, he bends over to pick up the satchel and spots Guntinsky's hazy reflection in the shower's glass.

"What happened here?" Guntinsky asks, unholstering his pistol. "What's that you're holding there?"

Clarkson turns to face him—the satchel in one hand and his gun in the other—and discreetly shifts his finger to the trigger. "Don't play dumb. You know what this is. I saw how bad you wanted to get on this ship. This is why you're here, isn't it? You're after it too?"

Guntinsky points the barrel of the pistol at Clarkson's chest. "Just put your gun down, hand me that thing and everybody goes home happy."

"Happy?" Clarkson asks. "How would I be happy, Gunts? It looks like you're going to shoot me and take this thing." He glances down at the satchel. "Whatever the hell it is. Now what about that will make *me* happy?"

"That thing is a matter of national security, okay? This is bigger than you and the guy that you're after. I was told by the Prime Minister himself that I had to retrieve that thing at all costs. If that cost is your life then that is what will happen."

The Prime Minister, Clarkson thinks, raising his hands above his head. "Look, Gunts, I don't know what they told you but I definitely don't want to die. Not today."

Clarkson bends over, places his gun on the floor carefully and then sets the satchel next to it— never taking his eyes off the Inspector. He rises back up and uses his foot to slide the satchel over to Guntinsky. As soon as Guntinsky bends down to get it Clarkson rushes in, ramming him through the door. The gun drops from his hand as he's slammed backwards into the wall. He grabs Clarkson by the back of the neck, throws a hard knee into his gut, and shoves him aside. His pistol is laying a few feet away. Guntinsky moves to get it and Clarkson rushes in again, tackling him to the ground. The two men wrestle, scrambling and clawing their way to the gun. Out of breath and tired, Clarkson throws all he has into a right hook that smashes into the Inspector's ribs. Guntinsky rolls away, clutching his side, and Clarkson grabs the gun. The Inspector's eyes grow wide and he lunges for Clarkson, hoping to knock the weapon from his hand. A single shot echoes in the cabin.

Detective Clarkson rises to his feet, grabs the satchel off the floor and glares at Guntinsky. "Sorry man." He says, shaking his head. He's done some bad things in his day but he's never shot a fellow officer—not until now. "Nothing personal, it's just...I have my orders just like you have yours. I need this way out." He sighs. "I've been doing this shit for too long, Gunts."

He turns towards the stairs, already formulating his cover story. He doesn't see Inspector Guntinsky grimacing as he reaches for his ankle holster or the grin on his face as he draws the small .38 revolver on Clarkson. With his hand shaking and vision blurry, the Inspector pulls the taut trigger and the report rings through the cabin. The bullet misses wide and Clarkson spins around, raising his pistol. Guntinsky lets off two more shots and the bullets punch through Clarkson's chest and he falls on the stairs, dead.

Inspector Guntinsky releases his grip on the gun and it drops to the floor with a dull thud. His eyes close and his mind drifts. *I've finally made a difference,* he thinks. *I've stopped the terrorists and saved my countrymen. I'm a hero.*

The faint sound of approaching steps fills his ears. *Stein, you idiot.* Hurry up and get here.

- -

An ominous sound rings out from Dr. Bauer's ship.

491

Worthy's head snaps toward it. *Gunfire!* One shot. Then another. And a double tap.

He disregards the divers and looks to Stein. "You heard that? Come on!"

The two of them climb aboard the ship and sprint down into the ship's cabin. Clarkson and Guntinsky are laid out in pools of their own blood.

"Go, Stein!" Worthy shouts. "Go and call an ambulance! Two officers have been shot! Hurry the fuck up!"

Stein stands there, staring at the Inspector.

"What the fuck are you waiting for?!" Worthy screams. "Go and call a fucking ambulance!"

Stein snaps back and nods his head. "Okay." He says. "An ambulance." He races back up the stairs and Worthy goes to check Clarkson's pulse. There isn't one. Shaking his head, he crosses the room and checks on Dr. Bauer. He's alive but unconscious. He goes to Guntinsky next but with the amount of blood on the floor he pretty much knows what to expect. He checks his pulse anyway. It's there but it's weak.

Thank God, he thinks. *Hurry up, Stein.*

He looks around the room. *What the hell happened here?* Guntinsky's gun is on the floor beside a black satchel. The bathroom door has been torn off its hinges and Dr. Bauer's face looks like it's been hit with a hammer.

"What the hell went on down here?"

Worthy looks to the satchel. He knows that he shouldn't disturb a crime scene but *fuck that,* he thinks. *Clarkson's dead and I need to know what the fuck is going on.* Hopefully whatever is inside of this satchel can shed some light on all of this. He grabs the container, unscrews the lid and dumps the contents into the sink.

"What the hell?"He blurts. "A map of the Gulf of Riga." He's more confused than ever.

He leans against the sink, pulls a pack of cigarettes from his pocket and lights up. *Stein needs to hurry the fuck up,* he thinks, taking a puff.

"What the hell am I involved in?"

CHAPTER FORTY-NINE

D r. Bauer's cab strikes a pothole, splashing squalid water onto the back window as it coasts to a stop in front of his building.

The incessant downpour has worn itself down to a light drizzle and as he exits the cab he makes sure to step over the giant puddle outside his door.

"Wait here." He tells the driver. "I won't be long."

John—the building's doorman—spots the doctor approaching and pulls the front door open. Safe and dry beneath an umbrella he greets Dr. Bauer with a pleasant smile. "Glad to see that you're okay, Ollie. I heard what happened down at the pier. The fire went for about an hour, right? Your boat didn't get caught in it, did it?"

"Nothing too serious. A few scorches and burns. Lucky for me, the fire spread in the opposite direction. And it didn't last an hour, either." He shakes his head. "Who told you that—Mila?"

John smiles. Dr. Bauer's right; he did hear that from Mila, the building's receptionist. "And what about those two officers—did they really get shot on your boat?"

"Unfortunately they did but being that I was unconscious at the time I cannot tell you anything about what occurred unless you would like me to lie."

John chuckles. "Well then, that is enough gossip for me. I'll update Mila later. Good evening, Ollie. Glad that you're home

safe."

    Dr. Bauer offers a parting smile and enters the building. He tosses Mila the Receptionist a wave on his way to the elevator and she waves back-- too busy talking on the telephone to stop and question him like he knows she wants to. The elevator takes him to the third floor and he's standing outside his apartment door digging his keys out of his pocket in a matter of minutes. He unlocks the door, opens the door, and flips on the lights. His meticulously kept apartment greets him as he enters.

    Since losing his wife to breast cancer Dr. Bauer has sought to maintain a certain amount of order in his life. Not only was his wife the glue that held their family together, Sophia was the sweetest and most caring woman that he had ever known— often overlooking her own needs for the care of others. According to her doctors if she would have been more attentive to her body the cancer could have been caught early enough to treat it. Dr. Bauer mulled over this fact so many times in the immediate years following her death that it forever changed his life. What would result is a systematic structuring of his life in which everything has its proper place and nothing is neglected. It is this system that raises the alarm as he strolls though his apartment.

    Someone has been here, he thinks, scanning the living room. The stack of papers on his desk has been disturbed (the corners no longer line up), his couch cushions have been turned (the pattern on the stitching no longer matches), and his entertainment system is sitting too far away from the wall.

    And they were looking for something.

    But the doctor is lying to himself now and he knows it. *Someone. Something.* He has no doubt who the *someone* was or what the *something* is. For over thirty years Dr. Oliver Bauer has been piecing together this puzzle, drawing nearer and nearer to The Elite and their nefarious ways.

But I have never been this close. They were actually in my home. It is too late to turn back now. I have already given Devin and Saman—

Devin and Samantha! Urgency strikes him and he races to his bedroom, his bathroom, the guestroom.

Did they—

He cuts the thought short. Worrying will not help him. All he can do now is keep going.

Inside the guestroom closet the doctor rummages through an old box of books until, "Yes!" He exclaims. He retrieves the heavy volume from the box and caries it with him to the front door. He stops and looks back at his home one last time. As long as The Elite are after him he knows that staying here is no longer an option.

Someone could be watching me now. The thought rattles his brain like a head-on collision. *It's not safe to be here.*

There is no more time for sentimental moments. Closing the door behind him, Dr. Oliver Bauer leaves this life behind once and for all wondering if there is anywhere left that is still safe.

From atop the tower of Gaizinkalns there can be seen a Latvia far removed from cultural disputes, international fugitives, political ploys and recent fires. At over a thousand feet in the air even the biggest disasters seem trivial. Viewed from the tower, Latvia is an untouched countryside dominated with forests of mighty oak and immortal pine; a serene sheet of lush green plains where bear, deer, and moose all roam free.

Outside the city of Riga a narrow road cuts its way through this majestic countryside. Cradling a massive book in his lap, Dr.

Bauer sits in the back of a yellow taxicab reflecting on the last time he traveled down this road.

It seems a lifetime ago, he muses, as the yellow cab comes to a stop before a large gate. Yet here he is, reaching out and entering the pass code into the keypad.

The iron gate swings open and the cab journeys forward. Dr. Bauer looks up to at the sky. The moon's glow is temporarily blocked by an unceasing wall of trees bordering the road and the sudden darkness is a fitting metaphor for the recent changes in his life. For years Dr. Bauer has sought out knowledge and order, working to bring light to the mysteries that fill his mind and now—with Devin, Samantha—he finds himself once again plagued into the depths of the unknown.

The wall of trees comes to an end and the light of the moon shines on the colossal cul-de-sac they are now approaching. Like a slumbering giant, a monolithic mansion sits quietly guarding the entrance of this vast demesne.

"You can let me out here." He tells the driver. The car parks beneath a giant oak tree and Dr. Bauer opens the door. He can hear the animals scurrying to safety as he exits the cab and strolls up the driveway. There is a large cluster of trees to his right. He grins, remembering himself as a child climbing that mighty oak and then, years later, watching his own son swing from its sturdy branches.

But trees have always been held in high esteem, he muses, thinking of how his mother's ancestors once venerated the oak. *And they were not alone. The Egyptians, Jews, and Masons all hold the acacia in highest esteem, and the Druids, their very name means 'men of the oak trees.'*

An image of the scroll comes to mind. In the bottom right corner there is a tree—an *alchemical* tree. *Al-khemi,* he thinks.

Could it be an oak tree? The Father God of the Mysteries was often worshipped in the form of an oak.

He continues on down the driveway, his mind alive with the implications.

The Egyptian god-king Asar was slain by his twin brother Set and his seventy-two co-conspirators and then thrown into the Nile. Asar's body washed ashore and became entangled in the trunk of a tree. The king of Byblos sent a party out looking for wood and they cut down the tree. Asar's body then became a pillar of the palace.

The tamasarik, the acacia, the oak—they are all evergreens. Because they never lose their foliage, evergreens are a fitting symbol of immortality. Asar is the god of resurrection, having died and then reborn as Khenti-Amenta, Lord of the Underworld.

Dr. Bauer ascends the small flight of stairs leading to the veranda and takes out his keys. Glancing to his right he notices the garage door is up and a black BMW sits inside it. He considers entering through the side door but decides against it. He's avoided this house for too long. If he is going to be of use to anyone he must first cross this threshold and face whatever awaits.

For months Dr. Bauer would step through this door, hesitant to face his dying wife. Now, standing in the foyer of the two-story mansion, he feels that same uncomfortable churning in the pit of his stomach. He heads left, down a long hallway decorated with pictures of old family vacations. Sophia is smiling in every one, nothing like the ailing woman that left him. Each picture is but another memory and with every memory comes a searing jolt of pain, pain born of the helplessness he felt watching his wife wither before his eyes.

But I can do something now, he thinks and like a man running a gauntlet he continues on.

Stepping inside his office Dr. Bauer expects to find Devin and Samantha resting comfortably in his plush armchairs, maybe nursing drinks but to his dismay the lights are still off, the chairs are empty and his glassware appears untouched.

Maybe they're upstairs, in the bedrooms. He turns back towards the door. *Or they could have—*

"Hey Doc!" Devin says, startling the doctor as he steps out of the shadows. Dr. Bauer jumps back at Devin's sudden appearance. He turns his head and Samantha emerges next.

"We left the garage door up so you'd know we were here." She tells him. The shelves of books lining the right wall catch her eye and she moves to inspect him. "You have a nice size collection here."

Nodding, Dr. Bauer flips on the lights and looks around his office. He is somewhat amazed at the amount of disorder he used to live with and yet somehow the lack of organization feels cozy. The arrangement of the two armchairs in front of his desk, the different photographs covering the walls, his book collection and large television; this was once his favorite room in the house and during Sophia's last days it became a shameful hideaway.

He looks to the stack of books on his desk. *Kurt was in here*, he thinks, knowing well that his son would bring dates to their family mansion and it seems Devin found his stuff—now dressed in a pair of his son's old jeans and a sweater he vaguely remembers buying. Samantha has also changed into a pair of jeans and a shirt. *Sophia's clothes*, he thinks, making his way to the wet bar beside his desk. "Well, I think I need a drink." He says. "What about you two? I make a mean gin and tonic."

Devin and Samantha decline the offer. Samantha continues to scan the doctor's book while Devin goes to take a seat.

"Yeah, Doc, we thought you'd come and check on your car. We were in the garage, waiting for you. You know, after changing clothes. When you walked to the front door, we just figured you'd come here."

Sipping his gin, Dr. Bauer takes a seat behind his desk, sets the book down in front of him, and grins to his guests. "You two have very quiet feet."

Samantha smiles. "Yeah. My father practically made us ninjas."

"So what took you so long, anyway Doc? We've been here for hours."

Dr. Bauer throws back the drink and relays all that has happened—how Henry Hughes's boat exploded causing a massive fire, how he was cornered by those four policemen before he could recover the scroll, and how Clarkson knocked him unconscious with his gun.

"Really?" Samantha asks. "He hit you with his gun?"

"Yes, and when I awoke he was dead and the scroll was missing. That means they have it now. If those policemen were actually The Elite's pawns then they have won. The scroll is in their possession."

Dr. Bauer's eyes reflect the dismay he feels. If The Elite have the text then they don't have much time left. The world as they know it will shortly cease to exist. With such power in their hands nothing will be able to stop them.

Devin only grins. "Hey, Doc. Calm down, okay. They don't have the scroll."

"Wha—how can you be sure of that? I never saw it again after—"

Devin raises his shirt and there it is, encased in plastic and

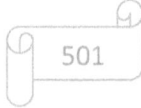

stuck in his waistline. "The canister was empty." He explains, pulling the scroll out and handing it to the doctor. "It was a decoy, you know. To buy some time. I couldn't tell you in case you didn't act it right out. As long as you thought you had it then they'd think you had it and me and Sam could slip away without being chased."

Dr. Bauer nods. It has been a very long day. He's exhausted. "I understand."

The scroll now lays open on his desk, though it may as well be 93 million miles away. The cryptic symbols shroud its meaning like dark clouds covering the Sun. He's not sure what he is supposed to do. Rising from the desk he goes to the wet bar and makes another drink. Standing before the scroll again, he takes a sip.

"The Mysteries were in possession of divine revelation." He says, waving them over. "They are said to have knew the secret of God and the destiny of man. Jesus Christ, Prophet Muhammad, Buddha, Pythagoras, Plato—they were all initiated into the Mysteries. The founders of these ancient mystery systems brought themselves together—many millennia ago—to assist humanity in reaching that destiny. They compiled many writings, books, and arcana in this effort but with the decline of virtue it is said that they began to hide their teachings in symbols, so as to protect them from the profane. Understand, symbolism is the language of the Creator, for how else does the Creator communicate his wisdom to us if not through Creation? All of Nature is but a grand symbol. Knowing this, the ancients understood that those ready and worthy would unlock their hidden secrets while the profane would simply accept the exoteric meaning as the end all, thereby preventing themselves from wielding such power."

Devin surveys the scroll, hoping to see in it something that

his mother told him or something that he might have seen in one of his father's books but nothing strikes him. They are all drawings to him.

Guess I'm not worthy, he muses.

Samantha moves in for a closer look and one of the symbols catches her eye. "Doctor, I remember you telling us that the snake is not a sign of evil like most believe. So, does that mean anything to you?" She points to an ideogram of a snake coiled tightly around an egg. "Have you seen it before?"

Dr. Bauer nods. "Yes, I've seen it before. It is rather well-known actually. It is the Orphic Egg—a symbol of the cult of Orpheus. Orpheus—like Jesus,

Prometheus and many other dying-savior gods— sacrificed himself for the benefit of mankind."

Devin shakes his head in exasperation. *Here we go with this again.* "But what does it mean, Doc? What does this stuff *mean?*"

"I'm sorry, son." He says, seeing Devin's apparent frustration. "But I cannot say for certain what it means or why it is there. There is too much left unknown."

Samantha has an idea. "Well, if you know what the snake represents and you know what the egg represents, can't you just put them together?"

He shakes his head. "It is not that simple, dear. Symbols can have many meanings individually and when combined with other symbols their connotations further multiply."

"Look Doc, we have to try something, okay? You're the one who said that we needed to come here, remember? You can help us out, right?"

Dr. Bauer avoids Devin's gaze and looks to a picture on the wall. It is a photograph of him, Kurt, and Sophia out on the boat;

the family that he's lost.

    How can I help you when I could not help my own family?

    He looks to Devin and Samantha and sighs. Whether they realize it or not the two of them are now in the middle of the oldest war in the history of mankind.

    Can I honestly offer them anything more than my minute understanding? "I don't know." He replies. "All I can do is share my knowledge with you, son. You're the one that will have to use it."

    Devin nods. "Okay then, Doc. Start sharing."

CHAPTER FIFTY

Dr. Bauer grins. "Well son, Esoterica teaches us that in the allegorical Garden of Eden tale the Tree of Knowledge of Good and Evil represents the spinal fire—the life force—called Kundalini by the Hindus and Ra-Buto by the Egyptians.

Bear in mind here that both the Goddess Kundalini and the Goddess Buto are depicted as serpents. Since, according to the tale, it was the serpent that spurred Eve to eat of the tree and thereby give man the use of that divine energy, the serpent is seen as a symbol of the Universal Savior which frees man from the bonds of ignorance by spurring us towards knowledge of Self. This is the mystery behind the so-called Devil's name: Lucifer. Lucifer is a combination of two Latin words: *lüci*, meaning light and *-fer*, 'that which carries.' Lucifer simply means that which carries light or the light bearer. The light referred to here is divine knowledge."

He stops and takes in the faces of his two pupils. They look on awaiting more.

"And as far as the egg goes," he continues, "there are many different eggs recognized by the ancients. One is the Universal Egg, a symbol for the black womb of space—the mother goddess—where the primordial God-force first existed."

"Like that picture you drew on the boat?" Samantha asks, thinking of the first of the three images.

He nods. "Yes, dear. And there is also the Auric Egg. The Hebrew Kabbalah teaches that man is enveloped in a bubble of iridescence that houses all of our latent powers. This is the Auric Egg. The Auric Egg stays with man through all of his births, deaths, and rebirths on the Wheel of Life. It is a microcosm of the Cosmic Egg which houses the potentialities of every entity—every particle, element, and principle that will ever manifest throughout all the cycles of birth, growth and decay are within this Cosmic Egg. The ancient Egyptians, from whom the Hebrew people received their teachings, spoke of this Cosmic Egg as being laid by the Great Cackler or Cosmic Goose. There is also the 'egg conceived at the hour of the great one of the Dual Force' that the Egyptians spoke of. This is the mundane or golden egg—the first manifestation of light."

Dr. Bauer combs his fingers through his soft grey kinks and stares down at the perplexing piece of papyrus before him. *It has to be the serpents*, he thinks—still unsure as to what the Cult of Orpheus has to do with the Book of Tehuti—*but every mystery system revered the serpentine life-force.*

Samantha noticed his furrowed brow. She knows what that means and so does Devin. There is something going on in Dr. Bauer's mind that he's not sharing.

"Okay Doc, so what does that mean? The egg? The snake? Can you shed some more light on it for me, Doc?"

Light. "That's it, son. Light!" The doctor is overtaken with excitement. "The Cult of Orpheus; the Book of Tehuti. It's light!"

Devin doesn't get it. He turns to Samantha and she shrugs, just as clueless as he is.

"Doc, what's up? You figure something out?"

Dr. Bauer smiles at them. "Yes. Well, I have just gotten a step closer, I believe. The ancient Egyptian word for light is 'khab.'

Those three symbols I showed you on the boat, remember, they are a representation of the Egyptian K-A-P—Khab *Am Pekht*—or light in extension. The light enters into man who then extends it throughout all of creation. The serpents represent this light. The Book of Tehuti is the way that we learn to extend this light; to become perfect conduits for the Divine Light."

The rose and cross to the right of the alchemical tree catch Dr. Bauer's eye. "That cross is alluding to the Rosicrucians. They are a mystical order supposedly founded by a man named Christian Rosencrantz—a name that is itself a symbol. Regardless, the name Rosicrucian simply means 'those of the rosy cross.' This order was involved in the same work as the followers of Tehuti—the regeneration of man. Modern Freemasonry has close ties to the Rosicrucian order. In fact, Freemasonry has a degree in its Ancient and Accepted Rite—the twenty-fifth degree if I'm not mistaken— called the Knight of The Brazen Serpent. This degree is based on the biblical tale in the Book of Numbers, chapter twenty-one, verses six through nine. Here, Moses was instructed by Yahweh to place a bronze serpent upon a pole so that when the people of Israel looked upon it they would be healed from their snake bites. You see?"

No, they don't see and the quizzical looks that they share show it. Even with the basic things that Mrs. King taught them it is proving difficult for them to follow Dr. Bauer's train of thought. Devin looks at him and shakes his head. "See *what* exactly, Doc? You lost me."

"The story about Moses is alluding to the three symbols— Khab Am Pekht. If we say that the serpent, or Lucifer—the light bearer—is the light of God then what Moses did was take it in and raise, or *extend*, the light so that it could be used to heal the people of Israel. In the New Testament Book of Acts, chapter seven, verse twenty-two, it says that Moses was learned in all the ways of the Egyptians. This story is all about the purpose of the Book which, I believe, is to give man the ability to use his powers. We must raise the serpentine life-force inside us."

He takes the large volume from the corner of his desk—the massive book that he brought her form his apartment—sets it in the middle of his desk and flips it open. "There is so much that you two need to know," he says, flipping through the pages, "if you plan on fighting The Elite."

"Whoa, Doc!" Devin exclaims, gesturing for the doctor to stop right there. "What do you mean, 'fight The Elite?' All I want to do is get my Mom's book back and find the guys who killed her and my Dad."

Dr. Bauer continues to flip through the book. "Well, son," he says, not bothering to look up, "if they killed to have it then they are not just going to give it to you willingly. You'll have to take it. And let's say you do take it—then what? It is far too priceless to destroy and too powerful to give to anyone else. All you can do is hold on to it and as long as you have it, The Elite will keep coming for you. Why do you think your mother chose to keep it hidden?"

Devin hadn't thought that far ahead. All he wants to do is retrieve what was stolen and punish his parents' murderers. "What about The Brotherhood?" He asks. "Couldn't I just give it to them?"

Dr. Bauer finally looks up from his book. He's sporting a smug grin that wrinkles the space around his eyes. "You'd have to find them first." He says. "And in order to do that you have to learn to decode their puzzles. As I said before, there is a lot that you need to know."

He flips a few pages and finally finds what he's been looking

for—the beginning of their lessons. He looks up at the pair and taps the open book. "Samantha, dear, would you read this for me?"

"Yeah, sure." She says. She moves to the doctor's side and points at the selection he tapped. "This here?"

He nods.

"Okay." She says and begins to read. "Since the beginning of time immemorial there have existed those select men to whom divine secrets were revealed. Eventually, these men banded together to form philosophic religious schools they would use to impart this divine wisdom to the masses. Every ancient nation had its own mystical elect and, while some worked inside the temples others founded secluded schools and cults of their own, they all shared the same goal: the perfection of man. For the leaders of such schools there exist only two types of men. The first type, those of mature minds, possesses the ability to solve their own destiny. The second type, those of immature minds, must be led like sheep and taught in language they can understand. In order to make the great truths of the universe comprehendible, these ancient leaders learned to communicate their teachings in the language of Mother Nature herself— the language of symbolism. With the decline of virtue many of these teachings became perverted, distorted or lost. As the keys to unlocking the mysteries were lost and, at times, destroyed, man, in his ignorance, began to worship the symbols and accept the allegorical as historical. Throughout all of this there were a select few remaining who sought to preserve the secret doctrines from destruction for they held firm to their goal of uplifting humanity."

"That's good, dear." Dr. Bauer stops her. "The Elite are descendants of these early wise men," he looks to Samantha and smirks, "*and women.* They feel themselves uniquely qualified to guide mankind. They are working towards the establishment of a totalitarian one-world government that they will rule with their so-called *divine* wisdom."

He shakes his head at the thought of it. In an Elite-ruled world the majority of humanity would only exist to serve. It's a frightening thought. All of the personal liberties that we cherish would go up in the smoke of burned books and dissenting opinions.

As if reading his mind, Samantha asks the very question he would hate to have answered. "And what about the rest of us then?"

Devin answers for him. "We'll all be slaves, right? If not literally on chains then we'll be forced to do whatever job they think is best for us. Like that book *1984* by Orwell."

Dr. Bauer nods. "He's right, dear. The Elite see us as cattle, beasts of burden, unable to figure out what is best for ourselves and our communities. Anyone that does not agree with them will be ostracized and murdered—just as it was during the birth of Christianity." He flips a few pages ahead in the book and points to a paragraph. "Here, Samantha dear. Let's continue here."

With a nod Samantha begins reading the passage. "Jesus' death splintered Judaism. By the year 50 CE, when the writing of the Gospels is said to have begin, there were various sects claiming to understand the true message of Jesus. One of these sects, the Gnostic Christians, believed that Jesus was sent to reveal the spiritual path to heaven. They understood the key to salvation to be a process of searching inward for Truth and then going outward with Love. For this they were labeled 'heretics' and persecuted by the Church."

"You can stop there." Dr. Bauer cuts in. "The term Gnostic is derived from the Greek *'gnosis'* and means knowledge or wisdom; Heretic from the Greek *hairetikós*, meaning 'able to choose.' In 325 CE the Roman Emperor Constantine convened the Council of

Nicea to unify Christianity under one theology, thereby eliminating the right of one to choose. Groups like the Gnostics, those that held to this right, were then labeled heretics and sentenced to the punishment of death. The Gnostics claimed to understand the secret knowledge of early Christianity. They kept their teachings hidden from the unworthy and taught them only to a small group of specially initiated persons. Any of this sound familiar?"

Devin nods. "They were one of those groups like The Elite? That's why they were persecuted—because the Church learned their plans?"

"I don't think so, son. By this time in history the mystery schools had spread all over the ancient world and their teachings had been assimilated by every nation in some form. Some saw these doctrines as tools for gaining power while others simply wanted to aid their fellow man. Since Church and State were not separate, to control a person's beliefs meant control over their life. Sects like the Gnostics threatened the Church's power. This inspired the Crusades, bent on eliminating them and their teachings. You see, the Gnostics were not like The Elite at all. They were actually The Elite's greatest threat and what you must become: one that knows the truth and unselfishly shares it with mankind. As long as the world believes that it must find its salvation in a building, a deity, or another man, The Elite will always be able to accomplish its goal."

Devin and Samantha share another glance. First they have to fight The Elite and now they have to find the truth and share it with the world.

"You know what, Doc, what we need to do is find the Fountain of Youth and then you can do all this stuff. I mean, seriously Doc, if you know everything about this stuff then you must know this *truth* you keep talking about."

Dr, Bauer smiles. "I'm flattered son but it is not my calling to fight, simply to aid the chosen it seems."

Devin's stomach growls. "Well, Doc, it seems like my calling is to eat. Anything in the kitchen?"

"I'm sure Kurt kept something there. The kitchen's downstairs. Help yourself."

"Alright, Doc." Devin says and pats the doctor on the shoulder. "I'll see you in the morning. After I eat, I'm out. Been a long day."

He heads out the door, stops in the hall, and turns around. "You coming, Sam?"

She smirks. "Yeah, don't touch that stove until I get there. This house is too beautiful to go up in flames."

"Whatever." He retorts. "Just hurry up." Dr. Bauer and Samantha share a laugh and Devin disappears down the hall. The Doctor closes his book and looks to her. "So you think this house is beautiful, dear? Sophia would have loved to hear that. She helped redesign this place." He takes a picture frame from his desk and hands it to her. It's a picture of him, a boyish Kurt, and his wife. "I think she would have liked you."

Samantha studies the late Mrs. Bauer's photo. She can only imagine how beautiful she and the doctor's children would have been. Not wanting to cry she sets the photo back on the table and changes the subject. "Who is in that other one?"

"Oh." He says, picking up the photograph. "That's me on vacation in Egypt. Those two men were working at a dig site that I visited." He passes her the photo. "You might recognize the man on my right."

"He does look familiar but I can't place him." She studies the image a little longer before giving it back. "Nope, can't recall him."

"That is Devin's grandfather." He tells her. "John St. Claire. It was his dig I was visiting. He was looking for a buried library, I believe."

"Really?" She picks the picture back up and looks at it again. "Mom had shown me some of his pictures before but I don't Devin ever met him. Who's that other guy with him?"

"He was the funding the dig. He funded a lot of Robert's work. Very wealthy; very powerful. You could feel it in his presence."

"Yeah." She nods. "I was raised by men like that."

"Yes, well, him and Robert seemed to be very good friends."

"Really? Do you remember his name? Maybe Devin knows him."

"Oh, yes dear. I'll never forget it. It's Gustuv Barchulé."